Falling
for YOU

OTHER BOOKS AND AUDIO BOOKS

BY KRISTA LYNNE JENSEN

Of Grace and Chocolate

The Orchard

KRISTA LYNNE JENSEN

Falling for YOU

a novel

Covenant Communications, Inc.

Cover image *Couple Holding Hands Outdoors in Snow* © OJO Images Photography, courtesy of Veer.com.

Cover design copyright © 2014 by Covenant Communications, Inc.

Published by Covenant Communications, Inc.
American Fork, Utah

Printed in the United States of America
First Printing: February 2014

20 19 18 17 16 15 14   10 9 8 7 6 5 4 3 2 1

ISBN 978-1-60861-240-6

For Chelsea Lynne, Maren Lily, Braeden Errol, and Jacob Michael. You inspired three amazing kids. Love you, my gumballs.

Acknowledgments

I WANT TO THANK MY family, my friends, and the writing community for supporting my dreams. At age thirty-eight, I discovered what I wanted to be when I grew up. Thanks for being patient with me while I figured it out, and thank you for saying, "Yes! Now, go, go, go!"

Thank you to my Cody writing group, as ever—Carla Parsons and Norma Rudolph—I love you. To my friend Abel Keogh, thank you for your honest feedback and for loving this romance about a widower and second chances. Thank you to my readers, Kimberly VanderHorst, Becca Sorensen, Shelli Larson, and Chelsea Bare; your feedback was priceless. And free. So thanks for that too.

To the Bear Lake Monsters, you are my super-friends. Keep writing.

Thank you again to Covenant Communications, Inc. Thank you for taking my stories and making them glow. Sam, I'll try to keep making you smile. Big.

Thank you to my kids. I think that I can't love you more, and then I do.

Thank you, Brandon, for bringing me home. It feels really good. Let's go get our China girl.

Chapter 1

ON HER YOUNGER SISTER'S WEDDING day, Elizabeth Embry sat in the waiting room of a Mormon temple, surrounded.

High walls and ceilings and carpets of varying shades of white contrasted occasionally with large serene paintings. The quiet, opulent setting oddly reminded Elizabeth of a library, a hospital, a wedding, and a funeral all at once. It was a bit . . . holy.

She reached over to the end table next to her and picked up a Church magazine. A title drew her attention, and she began to read.

Abruptly, she looked up. Her father, Keith, stared at her with an eyebrow raised and an amused reproach in his smile. His girlfriend, Sheryl, leaned her head on him, her eyes closed, relaxed. Elizabeth shifted her gaze to her youngest sister, Amanda Stewart, who had *both* eyebrows raised and a hopeful grin playing at her mouth. Elizabeth pursed her lips and shut the magazine, dropping it back on the table as Amanda's husband, Greg, chuckled quietly. He and Amanda were both recent converts to this religion.

She didn't need to encourage another "discussion," so she stood. "I'm going outside for a little while." She walked through the foyer, where a man dressed in white from head to toe smiled at her with a nod. Only in this building could someone pull that outfit off. She turned and headed out the sliding glass door.

The sounds of outside greeted her ears, though these were only the soft sounds of a few cars in the parking lot, a breeze through the trees, an occasional bird, and water splashing somewhere. She lifted her face to the sun and breathed, walking along one of the paths meandering around the grounds.

Elizabeth's other sister, Alisen, and her fiancé, Derick Whitney, were being married somewhere in that building. Without her and the rest of their family. But they were supporting the marriage anyway—even Aunt Rachel, who had still not forgiven herself for interfering with Alisen's love life. No one had been offended when Alisen had gently let them know they, her family, wouldn't be able to witness the wedding itself. Alisen had explained that the marriage rooms were very sacred, and only members of the Church who were keeping their promises to God were allowed to enter. The family had conceded. After all, it had taken years for Alisen and Derick to find each other again through misunderstandings and manipulation. The family hadn't exactly been supportive of Alisen's new faith and her love for Derick, but they'd been shown how wrong they were. Amanda and Greg had followed after Alisen into the LDS faith and would raise their coming baby in the religion. Elizabeth and her father had realized they either had to accept this religion as part of their family's lives or risk alienation.

Elizabeth looked up at the spires shining in the sun. She had no problem accepting that Alisen had made this choice. But she felt foreign to this religion—any religion, for that matter. Though she respected these clean, good people, even if they sometimes seemed a little naïve, she just couldn't see herself among them. She didn't belong.

"Elizabeth."

She pulled out of her thoughts and looked to the front of the temple. Her father was waving to her. He softly called, "They're coming out."

She smoothed the moss-green silk gown she'd helped Alisen pick out, looked down at her nosegay of stephanotis and blue hydrangea blossoms, and made her way back to the front of the strange and beautiful building, where a photographer was setting up.

* * *

Elizabeth had been asked to turn her phone off soon after entering the temple. Now, on her way home at the end of a long day, sitting in the back of her father's car, she checked the two messages she found waiting for her.

She listened to the first one with a pounding heart and gazed out the window as the trees flew past. She would have to answer that one later. She listened to the next message with interest and again gazed out the window.

She narrowed her eyes. "Hmm."

Her father glanced in the rearview mirror. "What's that, Elizabeth?"

"Business."

"Something good?"

"Possibly." She looked at her phone, her mind turning possibilities over and over. Her father turned his attention back to the road and Sheryl. He picked up Sheryl's hand and kissed it. Leaning her chin on her hand, Elizabeth gazed back out the window. Sheryl Camden had changed her father in so many ways. Good ways. Elizabeth sighed quietly and closed her eyes.

Willingly, her thoughts turned to the voice of the first message. She'd thought a lot about *him* recently. She guessed Alisen was to blame, and her father, with this new "being in love in the twilight of his years" thing. She couldn't keep her mind from returning to that night in the markets of Tokyo. It was a buyer's trip for Saks, and she'd been there before, but this time she had extended her stay to meet with the reps from Riyadh, Dubai, and Bahrain. One evening, she'd been led to a place, a restaurant tucked away in a crowded corner, and he had cooked for her and smiled, and she'd kept her guard up. But he had somehow found his way through her brazen, detached exterior. And for a short time, a few weeks, she had felt like someone she would like to always be. With him, she saw her true self. Like a dream. Even so, when it had come time to go home, he had asked her to stay. She could've. Part of her had wanted to. But she'd listened to the other part. She'd come home.

That was nearly two years ago. And he'd stayed there in the back of her mind for those two years. They would get in touch every now and then, a funny text or a light phone call, but it had been awhile. She'd seen a few other men, nothing serious, nothing that had stayed. But there he was, his voice on her phone.

Liz, please call me. It hadn't sounded urgent, just, well, *him.*

She fingered the phone, then decided. She pressed a few buttons. "Hello, Nancy, it's Elizabeth. Yes, I just got your message. I'm very flattered . . . I don't know what to say." She laughed quietly at the reply. "How about I say I will think about it for a couple of days and get back to you. Thanks, Nancy. I really am amazed. Just give me a little time. I'll talk to you soon, then. Good-bye."

She caught her father's look in the mirror. "Later," she mouthed.

He nodded, and she rested her chin once more on her hand and watched the world darken around her, unable to still her thoughts.

It was late when they finally pulled up to her father's condo. She lifted her dress off the hook in the backseat and carried her own bags in.

"I'm taking Sheryl home."

"Whatever."

"Hey."

She looked at her father, then muttered, "Sorry . . . tired."

He nodded.

"I'll be in bed when you get home." She covered a yawn with her dress.

"All right. See you in the morning."

"Thanks, Dad."

He nodded again and got back in the car.

"Good night, Elizabeth," Sheryl called sleepily from the car.

"Good night." She waved the dress and let herself into the house.

She flipped on the entry light and looked around. The cathedral ceilings made the room feel extra large, or maybe she just felt small tonight. The furniture was simply arranged in front of the fireplace on the right wall, and the back windows overlooking the golf course were black, only reflecting the room and her own image. She took a deep breath and headed for her bedroom.

She hung up the dress in her closet, set down her bag, and sat on the bed. Her heart began to thud a little too uncomfortably, and she took another breath. Gripping her phone, she pressed the callback button.

"Hello?"

"Hello, Paul."

"Liz. How are you?"

His smile quickly surfaced in her mind. She breathed as she spoke, trying to hide the rapid movement she felt from her heart to her throat. "I'm good. I'm sorry I couldn't return your call earlier. I've been on the road."

"Where to this time?"

"Actually, not too far. My sister's wedding."

There was a pause. "Well, that's great."

"Yes, it is." She tried not to overdo the enthusiasm as she smiled. "It was lovely."

"Good, Liz. Man, it's great to hear your voice."

She looked at the clock when a possible time difference occurred to her. "Are you still in Tokyo?"

He laughed quietly. "No. I'm in Maine. I opened a restaurant here awhile back."

"Oh." She hadn't expected that. "It's still late though. I'm sorry." He didn't say anything. "Should I call back in the morning?"

"No, no, of course not."

"So, Maine?"

"Yes. An old friend offered me a chance at his place, and I couldn't turn it down. I missed the homeland. And the restaurant is doing really well . . ."

He sounded as if there was more. She waited, gently biting her manicured thumbnail, then encouraged him with an, "And . . . ?"

He took a deep breath, and she pictured him scratching his hair back and forth as he raised his eyebrows. "And, I'm getting married, Liz."

She blinked and felt heat rising up her neck, then her face. She didn't breathe as her mind flipped too fast to land on something to say.

"I wanted to tell you . . . before you heard it from somebody else."

She nodded, somehow finding her voice. "Anyone I know?"

"No, no. She's a schoolteacher here in Maine. She's . . . she's really great, Liz." His voice was gentle, not boasting.

Elizabeth swallowed, hoping to get control of the water accumulating in her lower eyelids. It didn't help. "I hope she is."

They were silent for a few stretched moments. Finally, he spoke.

"Liz . . . I—" He cleared his throat. "Take care of yourself, okay?"

She nodded. She was good at that. "Paul?" A lump lodged in her throat. "Yes?"

She felt the hot, unwelcome sting of a tear escape down her cheek. "I hope everything works out . . . with the restaurant and . . . everything."

"Thanks, Liz." He paused. "Liz?"

"Hmm?" Couldn't she just go now?

He hesitated, then whispered low, "You're more than you think you are."

Her hand came to her stomach as if she'd been hit, and she tried to swallow. He had said those words to her before, in a much different situation. She was forced to let them sink in once more.

Finally, she whispered back, "Good-bye, Paul."

She ended the call and dropped the phone. She sat there holding her stomach, holding back the tears, steadying her breathing.

It didn't matter. It had been so long; why should it matter? She'd had a chance at . . . at what? She didn't even know. It had been too good. He had been too good and . . .

And it didn't matter now.

She slowly got up and changed into her nightgown, skimming past her shimmering red kimono robe, noting to herself that she could never wear it again, hating herself for being that sentimental.

She climbed into bed, set her alarm, pulled the light covers up, and closed her eyes. An hour later, the silent sobs came when she was too tired to fight them any longer.

And she knew her cries weren't just for him.

Chapter 2

SHE RAN HARD, CIRCLING THE entire course and the surrounding neighborhoods. Running helped clear her head so she could think about what she wanted to do, what she needed to do. She stopped at the top of a hill, where the road ended in a circle of empty lots overlooking Kalispell, Montana. She turned slowly, breathing hard and taking in the valley. She had no ties here, no roots. The condo had been her father's home for less than a year, a base between travels and her tiny apartment in New York. She turned south, looking as far as she could see, feeling a sense of urgency to make the next move. It was time. Taking another deep breath, she pushed away the hated emotion dragging under the surface and took off again, heading for the house.

After a long, hot shower, she emerged from her room. Her father sat on the sofa, reading the paper, but looked over his reading glasses as she walked past on her way to the kitchen. "Good morning."

"Good morning, Dad." She needed fuel. As she banged around in the kitchen, she felt a pang of hurt but breathed it away. She turned on the blender as her father entered the kitchen. After she sat down with her smoothie and a straw, he sat across from her, looking expectant.

She drank down half the glass and then pulled out her phone. She pressed some buttons, listened for a second, and handed it to her dad.

He listened and raised an eyebrow, watching Elizabeth pull on her straw, then hung up the phone and set it down.

He lightly tapped the table. "How do you feel about that?"

She pursed her lips. She meant to be careful, but a smile played at her mouth. "I think . . . it's good."

He nodded. "I thought so."

"What do *you* think?"

"What I think doesn't matter."

She protested with a look.

He held up a hand. "*But* I have heard you mention here and there the desire for a change, to stay put somewhere. And Nancy is so well known, such a valuable reputation. It would be a positive connection."

He was right. Not only had Nancy Colette been a mentor and friend, but she'd also been a stepping stone for Elizabeth to early success in the fashion business. "It's only a short flight away. I just think with things the way they are here . . ." She hesitated to continue and reveal too much.

He read her anyway. "With Alisen married and Amanda and the baby . . ."

She looked out the window.

"Elizabeth, you're your own person, and we're your family. We'll be here when you need us and even when you don't."

She turned her head abruptly and stared at him.

"What?" He looked offended.

She leaned forward, narrowing her eyes. "You just want me to move out so you can ask Sheryl to move in."

He stared at her, then laughed.

She half smiled. "You know, you better ask Alisen's permission before you do any of that."

He rubbed his forehead as he chuckled. "I know. I already did."

"What did she say?"

"She said, 'Dad, how can we bring your grandchildren here if their grandpa isn't married to their grandma?'"

Elizabeth's eyes grew wide. "She said *that*?"

"Yes. She's not pulling any punches, that one."

She looked at her dad with mock sympathy. But then her look softened. "She's happy."

He smiled and nodded slowly in agreement. "I think she loved our wedding gift."

Elizabeth made a huffy sound. "She should. Ten days in the tropics, nowhere near soil-testing equipment or shovels." She shook her head and allowed a full smile to cross her face. She envisioned a honeymoon in her new brother-in-law's occupation, going about from one third-world country to the next, teaching people how to teach other people how to farm. She shuddered. It seemed to work for him though. She looked out the window again. "I always thought Puerto Vallarta would be a perfect honeymoon."

This time, her dad stared gently.

"Did I say that out loud?" She rolled her eyes at him and stretched. She reached across to pick up her phone and stood. "Well, if you'll excuse me, I have a phone call to make." She strode out of the kitchen, not allowing him any more comments.

* * *

The wind had picked up on the tarmac, and another plane had just come in. Elizabeth held her phone close, covering her other ear, her purse swinging above her carry-on as she climbed the propjet's stairs. "What was that?" She could barely hear Nancy on the line. "Just a second, let me get on the plane."

She barely glanced at the flight attendant greeting the passengers as they came on board. The noise inside the plane was minimal compared to outside. She found her seat in business class and set the phone down, deftly stowing her carry-on and grabbing a blanket before she picked up her phone and continued.

"I'm sorry, Nancy. What were you saying?"

"I called to let you know disaster has struck."

"What? How?" Did this affect Nancy's offer? Elizabeth hoped not.

"I may have mentioned a few times how this house needs a remodel?"

Elizabeth breathed out. Nancy had moved into a grand, lovely, but out-of-date Victorian and had given Elizabeth a phone tour several months ago. "You may have mentioned a few needed changes, yes." She recalled Nancy's mentioning the plumbing, the tile, the plaster walls, the tiny closets, the carpets over the original wood floors, the 1970s updates, rewiring the electricity—the list went on.

"Well . . ." Nancy sighed, exasperated. "Hank decided, before I told him you were coming, of course, to get a little start on a few projects."

"Oh?"

"Elizabeth, I no longer have a guest bathroom, and he's knocked out walls in the spare bedrooms. He gutted the kitchen, and I only have a small hotplate, which is fine with me, you know, but not when we have *company*." She went on. "And he has window replacement scheduled for the whole week. You *know* how many windows this place has, Elizabeth. I'm afraid I would have to issue you a hard hat just to sleep here."

Elizabeth chuckled. "I can just get a hotel room."

"Exactly. I know of a wonderful bed-and-breakfast my friends just rave about. I hope you don't mind, but I already booked you for two weeks. It's *so* much more personal than a hotel, and the location is gorgeous and close to everything. It's my treat."

"Oh, Nancy, you don't have to—"

"I insist. I'm the reason you're having to stay elsewhere, and this is a business deal."

Elizabeth knew her friend well enough not to bother arguing further. "All right. Thank you."

"I'll see you at the airport, then. Have a good flight."

"Thanks. Bye."

A bed and breakfast? Elizabeth didn't care for *more personal*. Give her cold, unassuming, shiny brass hotels any day. An image came to her mind of a small cabin on the edge of the forest, a deer in the yard, and birds at a feeder stuck on a post. Old lace doilies.

She grimaced and spread the blanket over her knees as the plane filled up around her. The engine revved, then the plane took off, and Elizabeth watched the world become a topographical map below.

She would just think of the bed and breakfast as her own getaway. Wasn't that what she was doing? Getting away?

Her mind retraced the last few weeks. The wedding reception at the orchard had been beautiful, elegant, and simple at the same time. Derick and Alisen left for their honeymoon, and Elizabeth left for a buyer's trip to Mexico, followed by another in Seattle. She'd also spent two weeks in New York, coordinating the spring lines. It had been enough moving around and steady work to keep her focused during the day and too tired to think at night. Still, her rare excitement about what this new opportunity would mean had begun to settle in.

Not that it really was all that exciting. It was just . . . it was what she had wanted to do since she was a little girl. Owning . . . co-owning a women's boutique in an alluring location people visited from all over the world. And Nancy, the woman who had taught her practically everything she knew of the fashion world that hadn't come naturally, had offered it to her.

Only, this location wasn't a place she had ever considered alluring. Or exotic. Or remotely intriguing. And despite this, it felt right. Here she was, going to check it out, a two-week trial, and if it clicked, she would find her own apartment, sign papers, and begin.

She closed her eyes and soon fell asleep.

* * *

Saying the Jackson Hole Airport was smaller than the usual international airports she frequented, some of them practically cities, would have been a serious understatement. Where was the parking garage? The elevated gates with the ramps connecting directly to the planes? The rush to make connecting flights a mile away amid throngs of travelers? Elizabeth easily made her way to baggage and found Nancy immediately. No one else was holding a white piece of cardboard reading *Elizabeth Embry* in pink lipstick.

Tall and not as slender as she used to be, Nancy still carried herself with grace and confidence, and her natural beauty always showed in her smiling features. Her straight blonde hair was cut short and had started to go silver, but she didn't seem to mind at all. She shouldn't. It looked great with her black turtleneck, silver jewelry, and quilted, hot-pink jacket. Elizabeth glanced again at the sign. Nancy was also kind of a nut.

Elizabeth grabbed her luggage off the conveyor and smiled wryly at the woman grinning at her, teeth gleaming.

"Hello, darling," Nancy said as she gave Elizabeth a hug and light peck on the cheek. "Good flight?"

She nodded. "I slept." Elizabeth smelled the perfume that always announced and enrobed Nancy Colette. Nancy pulled away and took Elizabeth's arm, dropping the sign in a wastebasket as they walked to the glass doors exiting the airport.

"Are you hungry? We can stop for a bite."

"I don't know. That little package of crackers on the plane was filling."

Nancy smiled at her sarcasm, then really looked at her. Elizabeth flipped her hair back with a flick of her head and stood up straight, an automatic movement when she felt she was being appraised. She smiled thinly back.

"Are you *glad* you're here?" Nancy asked.

Elizabeth sighed and answered truthfully. "Yes. I am . . . curious."

Nancy nodded. "Good. Me too."

They left the lights of the airport behind them. "I think you'll love the place you're staying. I went to check it out when I made the reservations. I hope you don't mind, but I'm going to sleep on a cot in your room and sit in the soaker tub and flirt with the hunk-a-hunk who runs the place. Mm-mmm, he sure was nice."

Elizabeth raised an eyebrow and shook her head. "I won't be out in the woods somewhere, will I?"

Nancy laughed. "Well, yes. No. Well, almost. But woods are everywhere here, darling. There's no avoiding them. You were raised in Montana. Don't you live in the woods?"

Elizabeth laughed. "Not by choice. There are woods, but I haven't *gone into them* much lately. I just mean, I hope I'll be close to town."

"You will be."

Looking out at the darkness, the only lights Elizabeth could see now were coming from a large, rocky Frank Lloyd Wright meets Frederick Remington–looking building on the right, situated on an outcropping over the highway. "What is that?"

"The National Museum of Wildlife Art. I'll take you there. A lot of stuffed animals, but it's quite breathtaking."

Elizabeth watched as they passed, then faced the front again. "I thought we were going somewhere. It looks like we're going nowhere." A faint scattering of lights ahead of them rose up high into the dark, mountain-shaped horizon.

Nancy chuckled. She glanced over Elizabeth's Hermes scarf thrown around her shoulders and her black slacks and leather heels. "No country in the country girl?"

"This girl's been *out* of the country so much that if there was any here to begin with, it's long gone."

"Well, this place will put it *right* back."

Elizabeth looked dubious.

"And," Nancy tilted her head at her, "from what you've told me, I don't think that would be a bad thing." She winked at Elizabeth and turned back to the road. Gesturing grandly to her left, she announced, "That back there was the elk feeding station."

Elizabeth smiled and shook her head. What had she gotten herself into?

Then, as if in answer to her question, they pulled into the town of Jackson, Wyoming. She looked at the large arch built entirely from antlers and could only reply with a "Hmm."

"Here we are."

Nancy pulled up to the front of a restaurant lit warmly from inside. Elizabeth's stomach rumbled.

"Goodness," Nancy said, bringing her hand up to her chest. "I think we made it just in time."

* * *

Nancy grabbed the carry-on out of the trunk, and Elizabeth heaved her suitcase. All these years of traveling and she still overpacked every time. Nancy shut the trunk, and Elizabeth surveyed the property. It *was* gorgeous. Not as rustic as she had fearfully imagined. She noted the well-placed spotlights shining upward, illuminating trees and shrubs already burnished red and gold in the cooler weather, and the mixture of texture and color on the broad building.

Stacked stone pillars and warm pine logs framed tall, angular windows and a large front porch. Black rocking chairs and Bentwood tables and chairs were scattered along the porch, and lit black iron lanterns hung from the entryway. Through the glass, she could see a few mounted antlers and old oil paintings on the wall behind a long polished bar. Someone stood behind it, head down, reading something, she assumed.

She turned to Nancy, who was smiling at her.

"Welcome to Wyoming," Nancy said. She started up the paved path from the parking area to the front porch.

Elizabeth heard wind through tall trees and smelled pine and chimney smoke. She had a fleeting feeling of being twelve again. The sound of an opening door turned her attention to the entry and a man walking toward them.

"Hello," he said. "Elizabeth Embry?"

"Um, yes."

The man took the carry-on from Nancy, then approached Elizabeth with a smile. Was this the hunk-a-hunk Nancy had mentioned? She guessed he was Nancy's age, if not older. He was a nice-looking tall man, silver hair, most of it still there, strong jaw, and kind eyes behind frameless glasses.

"Welcome to the Lantern, Miss Embry. I'm Jeff Brennan."

She took his offered hand and nodded.

His light eyes were penetrating. Elizabeth started as she realized he was waiting for her suitcase. She let him take it from her.

He turned and nodded at Nancy. "Ms. Colette, good to see you again. Just follow me, ladies."

Nancy linked her arm through Elizabeth's and spoke quietly. "I'm eager for you to get settled in and comfortable. I can tell you're still wary, but it's nothing a good night's rest won't cure. I know from experience." She looked up at the sky. "So many stars. I know they'll work their magic."

Elizabeth rolled her eyes but looked up at the sky. She caught her breath at the array and heard Nancy laugh softly.

Nancy leaned in close. "I'll make a believer out of you yet."

Yeah. That's what Elizabeth needed. Magic stars. Still, for a brief moment, looking at them, Elizabeth felt a compulsion to look deeper, farther, before Nancy pulled her along.

They walked up the steps, and Jeff held the door, expertly maneuvering the luggage out of the way as Nancy let Elizabeth in first. As Elizabeth stepped over the threshold, she surveyed the interior furnishings and layout.

Warm wood greeted her everywhere, from the plank floors to the central staircase just beyond the long desk. The large common room to her left contained leather furniture and a few antique tables. An old upright grand piano sat tucked back in a corner. Prints of scenic oil paintings set in dark frames punctuated the walls, portraying the Grand Teton Mountains and surrounding areas. A wood fire crackled in the large stone fireplace.

Three large lanterns hung overhead, and the area might have been dark, but the stucco walls were painted white, and the room glowed softly. A gray-haired couple sat at a table playing a card game. The woman slapped a card down and satisfactorily exclaimed, "Ha!" The man, who Elizabeth assumed was her husband, smiled, and they started over again.

Cozy rugs and vases of fall leaves and berries had been well placed throughout the room. Impressed, Elizabeth gave the décor a name: *refined rustic*.

She turned her attention to the front desk, where Jeff Brennan was leaning over the bar, talking to someone on the other side.

She turned to Nancy. "Is something wrong?"

Nancy smiled at her. "I just asked them to make sure you had a key to the outhouse."

"What?" Elizabeth felt a twist in her stomach.

Jeff Brennan chuckled. The second man stood with a small package of business cards and held them out to Nancy over the bar.

Nancy winked at him. "Thank you, Ryan. I'll set these at my counter."

The man smiled at her in thanks. It was a handsome smile, genuine. Elizabeth pursed her lips a little sheepishly and narrowed her eyes at her friend. "Not nice," she said.

Nancy laughed and gestured to Ryan, who looked at Elizabeth for the first time.

"Elizabeth, this is Jeff's son, Ryan Brennan. Ryan, Elizabeth Embry."

Ryan stuck his hand out over the bar, leaning forward with a smaller smile. "Welcome, Miss Embry. Please know we are fully plumbed, and your suite has its own bath."

This was definitely Nancy's hunk-a-hunk. Elizabeth took his hand and felt a flush. She wasn't easily embarrassed, but she usually wasn't so gullible either. "Of course it does." He shook her hand warmly and let go to come around the bar. Elizabeth turned to Nancy. "A suite?"

Nancy just shrugged. "I know you like your space, and you'll be here for a while. You needed a *home*."

"That really isn't necessary. I would be fine with a standard room."

"Too bad," Ryan said. "All the other rooms are filled. I'm afraid you'll have to make do." He looked over at Jeff, who headed down a hallway leading behind the stairs. "Thanks, Dad."

Jeff raised his hand and turned to the ladies. "We'll see you later. Have a good night and sleep well."

Elizabeth gave a silent, short laugh. She felt as though she had just entered some sort of extended family vacation. *Good night, Uncle Jeff. Have a good sleep.* She shook her head. What had Nancy said? *More personal.*

"Can I get those for you?" Ryan was watching her, and she noticed for the first time his intelligent gray eyes, his eyebrows pulled slightly over them. His mouth was set, she thought, in a tense smile. His eyes, though, were kind, and he had a strong jaw. Like his father.

She blinked, tired. She stepped aside, and he took the bags and led the way up the polished wood staircase. Nancy followed.

He spoke as they climbed the stairs. "Your room has a view of the Tetons, so be sure you take a look in the morning. We've had a cow moose and her baby coming through the property the last couple of weeks, mostly in the mornings or the evenings. I guess he's not much of a baby anymore, but I have to warn you not to approach either of them. Mothers are very protective . . ."

As he spoke, she noticed the way his chestnut-brown hair fell in short waves every which way, and she could see a touch of gray at his sideburns when he turned his head. She watched his jaw move as he spoke and his neck muscle from behind his ear to where it met his shoulder. She shook her head again. "I'm sorry, what?" She realized he had just asked her a question.

He was taking a key out and had turned left at the top of the stairs, then turned left again, making for the last door on the right. Her room would be in the northwest corner of the inn. She peered down over the railing at the foyer and the tall front windows reflecting everything back.

"I asked where you were visiting us from. I didn't mean to pry." He gave her a forced smile as he put the key in the lock.

She hadn't meant to ignore him. But neither was she comfortable giving out personal information.

"She's from Kalispell," Nancy answered. "But I'm not sure how many moose she's seen."

"I've seen plenty of moose, Nancy," Elizabeth murmured.

Ryan's brow lifted in mild surprise. "Well, you should feel right at home, then."

"Sure. Right at home," she answered, sounding more sarcastic than she'd intended. She really needed some sleep.

He paused but then pushed through his welcome pitch. "If you would like to give us a schedule of your week, whether you have business or free time, we can work up an itinerary of things to do during your stay." He opened up the door and stood back with that careful smile.

"Thank you, but I don't—"

"That would be wonderful, Ryan. Thank you." Elizabeth looked at Nancy, who threw out her hands. "What? I want you to get to know the area, and a lot of the area is fun. We won't be working *all* of the time. At least, *I* won't." She crossed her arms in front of her and turned to Ryan with her eyebrows raised.

Ryan's careful smile widened, and the wrinkles at his eyes deepened.

Nancy leaned toward him. "I'll give you a loose schedule on my way out." She winked again.

Elizabeth rolled her eyes at her friend. When she looked back, Ryan gestured into the room. She entered, and they followed.

He set the bags on a table and went to turn the light on in the bathroom. The room was mostly white: the furniture, the trim, and the large four-poster bed piled high with a down comforter and pillows. A large white lantern hung high from the exposed beams in the ceiling. Another old painting of the local peaks hung above the bed. Here and there, touches of red, soft green, and brown added color, and the warm wood floor and large hooked rug anchored it all. Again, she was struck by the decorator's classic taste. She stepped to the dresser and fingered a basket filled with chocolates, lotion, a crossword puzzle book, a bottle of water, and a tin of mints.

Of all the traveling she had done, of all the exotic locations and luxurious places she had stayed, this was surprisingly just as appealing as some of those. She felt herself relax and began to picture burrowing into the lofty bed. Stifling a yawn, she turned and found Ryan watching her. Maybe . . . *just maybe* . . . she would like this.

Chapter 3

"Breakfast is between six thirty and nine in the morning." Ryan looked at her again, noticing the strain in her brown eyes. But she seemed to like the room. "If that's too early, I could set something aside and have it waiting when you come down."

She nodded. "Do you make green smoothies?"

Nancy raised her eyebrows.

Ryan responded without blinking. "If you'll give me a time you'll be down, I'll have one ready for you." They had the occasional request from guests and did what they could to oblige. He held out the key, and she took it. "Anything else?"

"Yes. Where can I run? Are there trails nearby or an athletic club?"

"How far do you want to go?"

"Five to ten miles."

"Well, we have plenty of trails around here, but there have been some bear sightings, even this close to town, in the last couple of weeks."

"Bears?"

"They're coming down looking for more food before they hibernate. It's been a slim season for their usual fare, so they're coming closer in. I think you'd be fine, though, if you stayed on the road you came in on. That's about five miles to town. If you would prefer to be inside, the athletic club isn't far." He paused. "If you're open, I'll be guiding small group hikes all week. Some of the trails are more difficult. It's a great workout."

She folded her arms. "What about the bears?"

"They tend to stay away from groups of us. We make a lot of noise."

Ryan sensed she was reading him to see if he knew what he was talking about. He narrowed his eyes, guessing that maybe she'd learned to doubt men in general. She was beautiful enough, and he had a few ideas as to how that had happened. It was the interesting thing about running a place like this. He learned to read people. Sometimes he even got to see if he was right.

Finally, she looked toward the window. "I'll be down for breakfast at eight." She turned back to him. "Will that work for you?"

He couldn't help feeling like this was some sort of a challenge to his suggestion of holding breakfast for her so she could sleep in. He fought a grin. "That would be just fine." He turned to Nancy. "You're going to give me that schedule?" She nodded. He nodded to them both. "Good night, then."

"Oh, here." Elizabeth rummaged in her purse for a tip.

He put his hand up. "That's not necessary."

"You're sure?"

He thought he saw the corner of Elizabeth's mouth come up. *Man, she's beautiful.* "Save the tip for housekeeping." He turned and shut the door. *Beautiful and cold.*

* * *

Elizabeth could tell Nancy expected her to say something about their host. So she didn't say anything.

But Nancy did. "What did I tell you?"

Elizabeth had already turned to her luggage and was starting to remove items. "It's a lovely place, Nancy. Beautiful. And *certainly* different from a hotel." To avoid sounding ungrateful, she added, "Thank you."

She took her toiletry bag and crossed over to the bathroom, feeling Nancy's eyes boring into her. The bathroom was larger than it looked through the doorway, and a deep soaker tub lined with votives along the wall called to her. She selfishly felt the need to get rid of Nancy. She touched the plush white robe hanging on a hook.

"And? Forgive me, darling, but you were a bit short with our handsome host." Nancy wasn't going to let it go.

"I tried to tip him," she answered.

Nancy laughed bluntly.

She came out of the bathroom and surrendered. "Okay. He is really very good-looking if you like that sturdy, windblown, sensitive type. But, Nancy," she looked at the hopeful expression on her friend's face, "I am not looking for a relationship right now." She winced at the words. So cliché. "I'm not even looking for a *date* right now. Let alone flannel or moose or . . ." She shook her head. "Besides," she turned to open a drawer and dropped in some sweaters, "he may be married for all we know . . . He could have a family."

"Oh, but I do know."

Elizabeth stopped. Of course Nancy knew. Nancy would have asked. She turned and put her hands out in front of her to gently push Nancy toward the door. Nancy tried a couple of times to speak, but Elizabeth shushed her. She reached the door and opened it.

"Tomorrow I need to rent a car. I can't have you coming out here to pick me up for every little thing. What time are we going to the shop?" Elizabeth gave Nancy a warning look that said, "Stick to the subject."

"I'll pick you up at nine." Nancy said resignedly.

Elizabeth softened. "Nancy, I just . . . I just can't. Okay?"

Nancy smiled tenderly. "All right. I'll let whatever happens happen." She sighed.

Elizabeth figured that was the best she could do. "Thank you. Thank you for everything."

"I'll see you in the morning, darling. Sleep well."

"Good night."

Nancy turned and headed down the hallway. Elizabeth turned to the room, about to close the door behind her but then thought better of it. Instead, she listened in the doorway. She could hear Nancy greet Ryan again, their voices floating up softly from below. They exchanged a little small talk about the weather tomorrow and the fall colors coming on. Nancy dictated an approximate schedule, and Elizabeth noticed she left Wednesdays totally free. She pursed her lips but told herself to relax. This was a *getaway*. She shut the door as she heard Nancy thanking Ryan and saying her good-byes. Leaning against the door, she closed her eyes. Then she went to start the bath water.

* * *

Ryan gave Nancy a wave and sighed when the door finally closed. He could tell as they were talking that she'd wanted to say something more, but to his relief, she hadn't. When she had come in the day before, she hadn't been too subtle about her friend who needed a room for two weeks. Fortunately, he'd had a cancellation and was happy to offer the room to her.

Then Nancy had asked him if he was married, if there were kids in the picture, and what had brought him to Jackson, and she'd told him her friend was single and gorgeous, and could use some . . . what was it? Male companionship. He looked up toward the room. What would the *cool* Elizabeth Embry think of that? He chuckled and shook his head.

He knew Nancy was well known in the community, almost a celebrity of sorts, but he hadn't met her until yesterday. She had the reputation of being very friendly and having impeccable taste, good business sense, and an eccentric sense of humor. The fact that she liked his place and wanted his business cards for her counter was a good thing. Still, he would rather she left him out of any male-companionship ideas she had for her friend, even if the friend was gorgeous. Which she was. Gorgeous and superior. His brow furrowed.

The phone rang. "Hello, you've reached the Lantern. How can I help you?"

"Hi, Dad."

"Hey, pumpkin. What's up?"

"Ew, Dad, don't call me that."

"Okay, turnip." No way was he giving that up, ever.

"Ugh. Okay, Lily is still up, and I can't get her to go to bed."

"Did she have a drink?"

"Yes."

"Did she brush her teeth?"

"Yes."

"Did you read her a story?"

"Yes."

"Did she say her prayers?"

"Um. Oops, forgot that one. Okay, thanks."

"Sure. I'll finish up here and be home soon."

"Okay. Bye." Her voice rose. "Come here, Lily. We forgot—" She hung up.

He sighed again and turned to the computer. He had another hour before close. He pulled the paper toward him with the work schedule Nancy had dictated, but before he got to that, he had to look up one thing.

Surprised by the number of options that came up, he picked one recipe and read. Grimacing, he clicked another one. Slightly better. Spinach and berries in a blender? He shrugged his shoulders and hit print. Easy enough. He would have to run to the store before 8:00 a.m. though. He didn't think they had any ground flaxseed in the pantry. He didn't think the grocery store would have any either, but he aimed to please.

He looked over at the couple in the great room. Mr. Frank stood and placed a hand on his wife's shoulder. She looked up at him with a smile that made Ryan feel like he was invading a special moment. He lowered his head but watched again as the gentleman pulled his wife's chair out for her and gave her his arm as she stood. It had been years since Ryan had shared a look like that with anyone. Flashes of memories came and left, leaving him hollow. Mrs. Frank gathered her cards, and they walked to the counter, where he got up to meet them at the end.

She handed him the deck of cards. "Thank you, Ryan."

He smiled at her. "No problem, Mrs. Frank. Same time tomorrow?"

She laughed softly and nodded.

"Good night." He nodded at Mr. Frank, who returned it, and Ryan watched them walk together down the hallway next to the stairs to their first-floor room. He stared after them for a minute, sobered.

He sat back down at the computer and pulled up the sample itineraries he had compiled for guests and looked at Elizabeth Embry's workweek. He heard a door open in the back and soft footsteps padding on the wood floor. He looked up. "Hey, Mom."

"Hi, my Ryan." She walked over to him and pulled him over for a kiss on the cheek. She reached up and ruffled his hair. "You need a haircut." He ignored her, and she sat down on a stool. "Everybody in?"

"Still waiting for the Holidays."

His mom snickered. "Well, they're just around the corner." She opened up into a grin.

Ryan shook his head and rubbed his hand over half his face. "Cute," he said. "Cute." He smiled as his mom looked up at him, eyes sparkling. The Holiday family was supposed to check in tonight before ten. He looked at the clock: 9:47. Ryan yawned and stretched.

"I can take over for you if you'd like to get home."

"Oh, that's all right. I need to do this itinerary for Miss Embry anyway."

"Ooh, your dad said she was stunning."

He looked at the computer screen, copying and pasting. "Mm-hmm."

"What's she like?" She was whispering now.

He looked at her. "*I don't know*," he whispered back. "But this," he moved the paper toward her, "is what she wants for breakfast."

She looked over the recipe. "Hmm. Easy enough."

He smiled.

"I hear you need to grind up the flaxseed, or it just passes right through you, and it wastes the nutrients."

He gave his mom a quizzical look and drew the paper back. She reached up and passed his hand through his hair again as he leaned away. "Cut it out, Mom." Sometimes she made him feel like he was fifteen.

That was Chloe's age.

But he was thirty-seven. He looked at his mom again. He sighed and leaned his head toward her. She immediately rubbed his hair with both hands and kissed his cheek again.

"I love you, my Ryan."

"Love you too, Mom."

"Sleep tight." She padded away down the hall.

He hoped the Holidays would get here soon so he could go tuck his kids in.

"Well, they're just around the corner," he murmured with a crooked smile. Chuckling, he turned once again to the computer and pasted in a difficult hike for Elizabeth Green Smoothie for next Wednesday. He thought a minute, clucked his tongue quietly a few times, then scheduled a massage for her and Nancy at Hot Rocks afterward. The schedule was optional, of course.

As the itinerary printed out, he saw lights coming down the road. He smiled again. The Holidays had arrived.

* * *

"Chloe?" He half whispered, half called as he came in the dark house. He could faintly hear the television on. Turning down the hall, he opened a bedroom door and peeked in. He walked quietly to the pink bed and leaned over. He kissed the soft, pink cheek and reached over to turn off the small lamp. The princess night-light glowed.

Lily was so small, dependent, and once again, he was moved to question his efforts. Was he doing enough? Was he doing this right? He sighed.

"Good night, pook," he whispered. He walked back out, leaving the door open a crack.

He followed the noise and tried again. "Chloe?"

"Yeah, Dad?"

He went downstairs, following the sound of the TV. A half-eaten bowl of popcorn sat on the low table in front of the sofa, and tall cups with straws stood empty on napkins.

Sam poked his head up from the sofa. "Hey, Dad." He stretched.

"Hey, kiddo, I'm home." He turned to Chloe. "How did it go?"

"Good. Lily went to sleep after prayers. Actually, she almost fell asleep *during* her prayers." She smiled at him. "She went on and on."

"As usual," Sam added.

Ryan nodded. "Great." He came around and sat down between the two of them, glancing at the commercial on the TV. "What are we watching?"

"Some dumb movie Sam wanted to watch."

"Hey, now . . ." Ryan said.

"Chloe, you wanted to watch it too. It's not dumb, Dad. It's hilarious."

Ryan looked at Chloe, and she rolled her eyes. "Actually, it's not that bad."

"Then apologize to your brother."

She turned to the television and murmured, "Sorry the movie is only slightly less dumb than I thought it would be."

Ryan sighed and counted to three. He threw his arm around Chloe's shoulders and tickled her until her squeals sounded a little more apologetic.

The movie started again, and he let her go, grabbing the bowl of popcorn. She righted herself, and Sam giggled as Chloe tried to get her long hair back into place so she could see.

Ryan lifted a cup and looked inside. "What did you guys make?"

"Smoothies," Sam said.

Ryan chuckled. "Were they green?"

"Uh, *strawberry*, Dad," Chloe answered. She shook her head at her father as Sam took the cup and looked more closely at the color of the remains inside.

Ryan laughed again as he sat back and put one arm around his son and offered Chloe more popcorn. "You missed a spot," he said. She tried finger-combing her hair once more as they turned back to the movie.

"All *right*! This is an *awesome* movie." Ryan high-fived Sam. "*Young Frankenstein*. This is a classic."

Chloe dropped her head into her hands.

Chapter 4

Ryan's truck rumbled down the familiar road to town. He knew this stretch better than he knew the hotel. But not by much. He yawned. He hadn't slept well, though he rarely did. He glanced again at his shopping list: bananas, eggs, milk, orange juice, nondairy creamer, and ground flaxseed. He growled a sigh and shoved the list in his pocket.

He'd been up for a while, of course. He'd gotten the kids up and ready for school, making sure they were out to the bus on time, and he'd walked over to the inn to take the trash to the heavy bear-proof receptacles. He'd placed the daily newspaper at the door of each room for the tenants who had requested it and helped his mom start breakfast while his dad ran the front desk and answered phones. It had been so nice having Chloe's help during the summer. The two-and-a-half-hour breakfasts made the mornings a little crazy. Even Sam had learned his way around the kitchen and could make a mean batch of scrambled eggs. But with school going again, Ryan and his parents were back to dealing with everything themselves. He needed to hurry and get back to the inn. The Holidays alone meant five more mouths to feed.

He saw Elizabeth Embry up ahead. Looking at the time, he calculated the distance and stepped on the gas. She looked and nodded as he passed. He waved and kept going, watching her ponytail swing behind the headband covering her ears, and then wondered how fast he could fill the cart.

He parked and pulled out his shopping list as he got out of the truck and jogged to the doors. He grabbed a cart and headed to customer service. First things first.

"Excuse me, do you have *ground flaxseed?*"

The young man behind the counter blinked at him. "I'll find out."

"Thanks."

He picked up a phone and called someone to the service desk. In a moment, a woman with long, very curly hair bounced up.

"Good morning. What do you need?"

"Hi. Ground flaxseed."

"Golden flaxseed or brown?"

Ryan hesitated. "Whichever you can find."

"Hmm. Follow me."

She took him to the bulk items area, then narrowed it down to grains.

"Flax, flax, flax," she mumbled as she passed each bin.

This is ridiculous. His eyes roamed to a display of small spice jars. "Wait. Here it is." He picked up the little jar. "Huh."

"Oh, great!" she enthused. "You found it."

He turned to her. "Thanks."

"No problem. Have a nice day," she said and bounced away.

He looked at his watch again and quickly filled the cart. Hardly anybody shopped this early, so he breezed through the checkout, jogged back out to the truck, loaded the bags, and headed back.

There she was, almost back to the inn. The question was, would she want the thing before she showered or after? He banked on it being after. He passed her swinging ponytail again and parked at the side entry leading to the large kitchen. He grabbed the bags and shoved his way in the door.

"That was fast. Wow." His mom looked at the clock. "You going for a new record?"

He nodded and unloaded the bags, then hung his coat up on a hook by the door. He took a deep breath, then went to the sink to wash his hands, letting the warm water run over them a little longer than usual. He shook his head at himself. He'd rushed as if her entire stay depended on this smoothie being ready on time. Why had he let that get to him? Had he been in the people-pleasing business too long? He dried his hands and turned to his mom. "What do you need me to do?"

They kept busy with eggs and hash browns, but at ten minutes to eight, he walked to the bulletin board, where he had stuck the recipe, got out the blender, and gathered the ingredients. He measured, grabbed, and poured, then put the lid on and let her rip. His mom came over to watch.

"Hmm. It's green," she said.

He gave her a hard look. Then he removed the lid, stuck in a spoon, and tasted it. His eyebrows came up, and he nodded his head. "Hmm. You can't taste the spinach at all." He threw the spoon into the sink and set the smoothie in the large refrigerator. Well, now he knew.

* * *

Elizabeth had slept like a rock. The long soak had practically melted her, so by the time she climbed into bed, she was barely conscious of placing her head on the pillow. Still, as the alarm went off, she had to pull herself out of sleep like she was climbing out of a deep crevasse. Why had she ordered that smoothie at eight? Another forty-five minutes would have been just fine.

But she had enjoyed her run once she stopped checking behind her every few seconds for bears. Now she was hungry. The smells floating up from the kitchen had her reconsidering her order. She came down the stairs, taking in her surroundings in the daylight. The views out of each window vied for being the most picturesque.

"Good morning, Elizabeth." Ryan's father greeted her at the base of the stairs.

What was his name again? "Good morning . . . Jeff." Again, there was that feeling of being pulled into somebody's family reunion.

"Did you enjoy your run?"

"Yes, thank you."

"Are you ready for breakfast?"

"Yes."

"Follow me."

He didn't waste words. She followed him down a hall next to the staircase leading toward the back of the inn. Another hallway led to the left, and Jeff pointed. "These are the first-floor rooms. My wife, Dayle, and I live in the farthest one down. It's really nice. And the Franks are staying in this first one for two weeks, so you'll get to know them."

Elizabeth wondered why on earth she would get to know the Franks.

He went on. "Then across the way here to the right, we have the kitchen, as you can see." He leaned into the wide, doorless entry to the kitchen and called out, "Hey, lazies, we have a pretty girl out here who wants her milkshake." He turned and winked at her.

She couldn't help but smile and shake her head. Elizabeth liked Uncle Jeff. She heard a cupboard door close and some shuffling, but the older man beckoned her on.

"Now, you came here at night, so I bet you couldn't see much of the surroundings," he said.

"What I could see was beautiful."

"Well, you're in for a treat."

They were passing photographs on the walls, some black and white, some faded color, and some new. Elizabeth stopped at one. Jeff turned.

He came forward, tilting his glasses up. "Yup, that's me." He pointed a strong finger. "That's my wife, Dayle. Isn't she gorgeous? And that little one there is Ryan."

Elizabeth leaned closer. They stood in front of a long log cabin, with a sign next to them that read *The Lantern Bed & Breakfast*.

"Is this the same place?"

"Well, that was our first place, but we still have it. It's just down a ways." He motioned to the front of the inn. "When Ryan's wife died, he built this one and moved into the old one himself." He looked around. "This was a labor of love."

Elizabeth stared.

When Jeff met her gaze, he quietly answered her unspoken question. "She was killed . . . in a car crash. It's been a few years."

Her eyes moved back to the pictures. "I'm . . . sorry."

"Well, that's all right. It was a long time ago. We move on, don't we?"

Elizabeth nodded gently. *But we don't forget.* She looked to the front of the inn, seeing it differently now that she knew who built it.

Jeff was inviting her forward again. "Here on the right is the indoor dining room."

She looked down a long room completely lined with windows on the back and far walls. Tables of varying sizes stood against the windows, and a fireplace crackled in the far corner, sharing a wall with the kitchen. Old skis and poles, snowshoes, and memorabilia hung on the long wall opposite the windows. She imagined being snowed in and not caring.

Jeff lightly took her arm and turned her back to another set of paned double doors at the rear of the hallway. "Ready?" he asked as if she couldn't already see outside through the glass.

She chuckled. "Yes."

He opened one of the doors, and she stepped through onto a series of three large hardwood decks descending to the last one that extended over a river cutting through the forest in shallow cascades. The upper deck was set with tables and chairs for dining, and the second deck had several glider benches for viewing and a small wooden swing set with a slide. The smaller, lower deck was empty except for a few long benches and a young couple looking out over the water. Colorful pots of fall flowers and foliage framed each level in reds, yellows, oranges, and purples. Red Virginia Creeper wound its way along the railings and up half the inn, and the surrounding green pines and yellow aspens filled Elizabeth's artistic senses. The placement of the decks and the greenery made the inn a part of the living woods, as though the river was created for it.

"Ryan did this?"

Someone cleared his throat and said, "Yeah, but I had help."

She turned. Ryan stood with a tray holding her breakfast.

"Oh." She looked for Jeff, but he was talking to the older couple she had seen last night. She glanced back at Ryan and chose a smaller table. "Here is fine." She pulled out the chair and sat, ignoring her sudden flush.

He set the tray down. A strawberry hugged the rim of the tall glass. Next to the smoothie was a small plate with a steaming cinnamon roll on it, laced with creamy frosting.

She looked up at him questioningly, and he shrugged. "Everyone gets one. My mom just took them out of the oven."

Elizabeth had met Dayle Brennan briefly before her run. Dayle had said something about "having legs like that" and being "more like a dachshund." "Tell her thank you." She reached for the smoothie.

He lowered his head and raised his eyebrows at her. "I really hope you enjoy that." He waited.

She took a sip from the straw. "Mmm. Yes, it's very good. Thanks."

He seemed to look relieved. "Do you like your room?"

"Yes. The view is amazing . . . the sun hitting those mountains . . ."

He nodded, then turned to go back inside, but she stopped him, feeling the need to be kinder than she had been last night.

"Ryan?" She winced at the familiarity using his first name implied. She had never addressed a single hotel staff member by their first name.

He frowned. "Yes?"

She looked out at the river. "This really is incredible. You're very talented."

He looked out over the decks, then down at her with a small smile. "Thanks."

She studied him, seeing this time what she couldn't place in him before. He nodded and went back inside. She watched the door a moment, then turned to gaze into the woods as she listened to the river and finished her smoothie.

Nancy suddenly sat in the chair opposite her, a wide smile on her face. "Good morning."

Elizabeth smiled back. "Good morning. You're early."

"I know. I'm so excited; I couldn't stay away. Besides," she looked out over the view, "what a way to start a morning." Nancy reached over and took a large chunk out of the cinnamon roll. She pulled a piece off and popped it in her mouth. Her eyes rolled. "Mmm. Now *that's* the way to start a morning."

* * *

Nancy pulled the car up. "We'll park out front for now, but there is a parking space for you in the back. I could even put your name on a reserved sign if you want."

Elizabeth chuckled. Nancy knew this was not a done deal. This was a trial. Elizabeth looked at the large front windows of the shop, tucked under a covered boardwalk. White mannequins dressed in clothing with simple classic lines in vivid colors and more eclectic accessories and trims sat on display. She noticed a uniting theme of having something of the outdoors in the colors and textures. Elizabeth had no doubt that Nancy had been influenced by her surroundings. Fall leaves on clear filament hung at varying lengths from the ceiling, and the floor was piled with them. Trunks of aspen trees stood randomly behind the mannequins, the upper portions of the trees disappearing into the ceiling.

Elizabeth read the lettering across the lower half of the windows.

W I L D B E R R I E S
Nancy Colette

Perfect. She looked at her friend and nodded.

Nancy accepted her simple approval with a little squeal. "C'mon." She got out of the car.

Elizabeth followed, and as they approached the window, Nancy flourished her hand near her own name. "Of course, your name would go *here*." She reached for the door and opened it for Elizabeth. A bell jingled, but Elizabeth's gaze lingered on the display a little longer before she stepped into the boutique.

The scent and sound of the place enveloped her. Guitar music played softly, and though she acknowledged the definite smell of the fabrics she was so familiar with, she smelled vanilla with a trace of lime and . . . sandalwood?

"What is that scent?"

"Do you like it? It's part of a home and personal fragrance line we carry. I think this one is *Dream*."

"I do like it."

Quicker than Elizabeth could move, Nancy took two steps to a display and returned with a box, presenting it to Elizabeth. "Here . . . a homecoming gift." She watched Elizabeth, eyebrows raised.

Elizabeth allowed the meaning behind her friend's words to roll over in her mind. Of course, it was too soon, but Elizabeth looked around and her heart beat a little faster at the idea of staying here. She glanced outside and imagined a picturesque street leading to her own place, maybe in the trees, and as Ryan Brennan's face flashed through her mind, she blinked and gave her head a little shake.

Nancy still watched. "No decisions yet." She moved the box closer to Elizabeth. "For your little home at the inn."

Elizabeth allowed a small smile and took the glitter-dusted box. *Dream.* The box held a small canister of room spray and a glass bottle of eau de toilette. She breathed deeply. "Thank you. I really do like it."

"Well, enjoy." Nancy winked at her. She looked around. "Now, where is my hired help? I'm pretty sure I didn't leave the front door open when I closed the store yesterday."

"Here I am," a friendly voice called from the back. A young woman bustled up to them. "I was in the back going through that new shipment of winter accessories, and I heard your voice, Nancy, so I just continued. Of course they're gorgeous. I already have mine picked out. I think. I'll probably change my mind once I go back there again. Don't you do that sometimes, when you leave something for a minute, then you come back with fresh eyes?" She turned to Elizabeth and stuck her hand out. "Hi, I'm Marisol Espinosa. You must be Elizabeth."

Elizabeth took Marisol's hand, and Marisol shook it with energy. She was a pretty girl—she had bright, deep brown eyes, though her brows were a little heavy, and beautiful maple skin. But the most astonishing thing was her smile. Beguiling, with tiny pinprick dimples at the corners. Her smile held no judgment.

Elizabeth smiled back and shook her head a little. "Elizabeth Embry. It's nice to meet you, Marisol."

"Wow, you are beautiful. Nancy's told me so much about you and that you might be coming here to stay. I hope that's true. Have you decided yet?" Her hand came up to her mouth. "Oops. Probably too soon, huh? Well, take your time . . . but I hope you like it here. I love working here. Don't I, Nancy?"

Elizabeth looked at Nancy and back at Marisol, a little dazed by this flurry of energy.

Nancy had been pursing her lips, and her eyebrows came up. "Mm-hmm," was all she offered.

Marisol continued. "Nancy had to give me an allowance out of my paycheck. Otherwise, I would spend all of my money here, and my rent would go out the window . . ." She looked at the front of the store. "Or out the door." She turned to Elizabeth and gave her that stunning smile again.

Elizabeth wondered if Marisol was done talking or if she should wait a bit. She finally asked, "How long have you been here?"

"Here at the store? Or here in Jackson?"

"Either."

"Well, I grew up in Jackson. My parents moved here from California when I was ten."

Elizabeth noted a Spanish accent when Marisol said her own name and *California*. Maybe the Spanish accounted for the speed at which she spoke. Or maybe that was a California thing.

"I've been working for Nancy almost since the beginning, haven't I, Nancy? She hired me about two years ago, after my freshman year at college. I was an art major."

"Marisol is very talented. She does the window displays." Nancy gave Elizabeth a knowing look.

Elizabeth was impressed. "How much school have you had?"

"Not enough." Marisol rolled her eyes. "But Nancy sends me to seminars and shows, and I take all kinds of notes, and I'm learning so much. I am *so* lucky to be working for her." She turned to Nancy and took her hand. "She is an amazing teacher."

A corner of Elizabeth's mouth came up. "I know."

Nancy just smiled and allowed the compliment to hang in the air. She turned to Marisol. "Did you want to put that shipment out?"

"Oh, yes. I should do that. I need to finish tagging them, but then I'll add them to the floor." She turned to Elizabeth. "I just know you're going to love it here."

"Here at the store? Or here in Jackson?"

"Either." The smile flashed again, and Marisol patted Nancy's hand, then turned, her long black hair swinging around in a thick wave with occasional ringlets. She sang something to herself as she moved to the back of the store.

Elizabeth turned to Nancy. "*Wow*," she mouthed.

Nancy laughed. "She's something. I wouldn't lose her though. There's a reason she's been working for me for so long."

"That's not surprising," Elizabeth murmured softly. "Even if you tried to let her go, you couldn't get a word in edgewise."

"I *heard* that," Marisol called in an unfazed, singsong voice from the back. Nancy snickered. "Oh, this is going to be fun."

Chapter 5

THEY WALKED TO THE RENTAL car.

"Oh, this is nice," Nancy said.

Elizabeth nodded at the Mazda. "This is the same kind of car my dad drives."

"Well, now you get to follow me. I want you to see my wrecking ball of a house and meet my Hank." She paused. "Or maybe I should say I want you to see my house, and meet my wrecking ball of a husband."

Elizabeth laughed.

"After that, we'll go out to eat."

"Where are we eating?"

"Well, let's see, shall we?" Nancy took a piece of paper out of her purse and unfolded it.

"What's that?" She leaned over Nancy's shoulder.

"It's your itinerary—the one *Ryan* made up for you."

"How did you get that?" She reached for it, but Nancy snatched it away. Elizabeth didn't like the small emphasis she had put on the word *Ryan*.

"I asked for it at the desk this morning. I told him you probably wouldn't take it from him. He agreed."

"Well, you were both right. What's on there anyway?" She reached again.

"Uh-uh-uh." Nancy still held the paper out of reach. "I've made an executive decision, and *this* is all going to be a surprise."

"But I hate surprises."

"I know, darling, and we really need to work on that. Starting now." She folded the paper after one last glance, then shoved it down deep into her purse. "Let's go meet Hank."

Elizabeth followed Nancy's car and wondered at her friend. Hank was Nancy's third and, she swore, final husband. They had met three years ago at an antiques auction in Denver, bidding on the same vanity. She'd won, but he had asked her out in an attempt to romance the piece away from her. He'd gotten more than he bargained for. Hank had asked Nancy to marry him after a month and had talked her into returning to Jackson with him. After a two-week adjustment period, she'd set up the boutique and determined herself to forever be a Wyomingite.

In Elizabeth's mind, and from what Nancy had told her, there couldn't be two more different people in the whole world. But her devotion was apparent, and it seemed to be working out. Elizabeth was very interested to meet the man who had changed her world-traveling, club-hopping, Manhattan-sipping friend's heart.

She thought of the relationships she was somewhat privy to in life: her sisters', her mother and father's long ago, and now her father's with Sheryl, along with others she'd casually observed, not always knowing what the life-altering effect was, but she had a limited understanding that it *was* life-altering. Someone had to give something up or gain something or both that was *lasting . . . marked*. Was she frightened of what changes like that would bring to her? There were no guarantees. Elizabeth's mother had died suddenly, leaving her father reeling. Even Ryan, who Elizabeth was sure had expected to live a long and happy life with his young wife, had been changed. She'd seen it in his eyes.

Did she want to open herself up to that possibility? Wasn't she safer the way things already were? *Safer*. Not the most exhilarating word. She'd left Tokyo to be safer.

Without paying attention, she had pulled over and stopped behind Nancy's car. Nancy stood waiting, halfway up her walk, watching Elizabeth with her arms folded. Elizabeth unbuckled and got out of the car, walking quickly to join Nancy.

"You were pretty deep in thought there. I decided to just let you be."

"Thanks, I . . . was just working something out . . . sort of." Elizabeth turned toward the house. "Oh my . . ."

Nancy grabbed her arm. "What do you think? Is it atrocious? I know; it's an eyesore. It will be better when it comes together . . ."

"Shhhhh."

Nancy whispered, "What?" She watched her friend's expression and waited.

Elizabeth spoke softly. "You remember that movie . . . with Hayley Mills? *Pollyanna*?" Emotions swirled, uninvited.

"Yes?" She looked back at her house.

Elizabeth swallowed. "This is like that house. Not as big, but . . ." She shook her head. This was ridiculous. "I'd forgotten I loved that movie when I was little," she whispered. "My mother would play it for me when I was sick." She'd completely forgotten.

"So, you like it?"

Elizabeth nodded slowly, still looking at the turrets and the gingerbread trim, the scalloped roofing, and the endless array of windows in every direction.

Nancy handed her a tissue. "Well, I didn't expect *that* reaction, not from you, darling, but I'll take it."

Elizabeth gave a small laugh. "Surprise." She dabbed at her eyes, annoyed.

Nancy squared herself to Elizabeth and looked her in the eye. "Tell me."

Elizabeth knew that look. That look drew out the truth every time. She took a deep breath. "Paul is getting married." There. She'd said it out loud.

"Oh . . ." Nancy watched her closely, and her voice was cautious. "But I thought . . . but that was ages ago."

"I know. It was. And I let him go." Her gaze followed the turnings on the front porch framework. "It was all me, and now he's moved on." Her words rushed out now. "And I have too. I mean, not in the same way he has, obviously, but . . . still . . ." She wasn't making any sense, and she rolled her eyes. "I made my choice."

"Tell me again . . . why you chose to come home."

Elizabeth straightened her shoulders and looked away from the house. It *was* ages ago. Like a far-off dream. "My work."

"You could have worked in Tokyo, anywhere."

She knew it. "I couldn't . . . I wouldn't allow myself to . . . to settle down like that . . . He deserved someone who . . ." She folded her arms and watched the ground. "He wanted more, and I couldn't give him that. He . . . deserved more."

Nancy was quiet for a moment. A breeze disturbed the mottled leaves of two massive Hawthorne trees flanking the front path.

"Everyone deserves to be happy, Elizabeth."

"And now he will be." She nodded her head at the rising mountains beyond the town.

"I wasn't talking about Paul."

Elizabeth turned. Nancy's eyes were gentle.

Not everyone. Elizabeth shrugged against the cold.

Nancy threaded her hand around Elizabeth's arm. "Come on. It's a bit of a mess on the inside, but you'll just have to see past it."

Elizabeth knew Nancy referred to the house but laughed quietly at her affinity to the request as she let Nancy lead her toward the front door.

* * *

"Elizabeth? Elizabeth Embry?"

Elizabeth turned her head from her menu, as did Nancy and Hank. She looked up at the man who had spoken her name and paused, taking in the deep burgundy sweater, the dark blond hair, and the green eyes. The familiar turn of his mouth. Her eyes flew open in surprise.

"Travis?" She smiled. "What are *you* doing here?" Elizabeth moved to get up. Hank stood. So did Nancy.

Travis smiled back, shaking his head, and took Elizabeth's elbow, leaning in for a small kiss on the cheek. "It's so great to see you. You look great."

Elizabeth looked around the crowded restaurant, noisy with conversation. "Is Nicole here?"

Travis brought his hand up and ruffled his hair above his ear, a familiar move when he was coming up with an answer. "No, it's just me."

Nancy cleared her throat.

"Oh. Nancy, Hank, this is a friend of mine, Travis George. Travis, did you ever know Nancy Colette?"

He leaned forward and took Nancy's hand. "No, but I have heard of you. Good things. It's a pleasure to meet you."

"I hope it wasn't *all* good," Nancy teased. Travis chuckled.

The woman was a flirt. "And *this*," Elizabeth continued, "is Nancy's husband, Hank Carter."

Hank took it all in stride, shaking hands. "Travis, good to meet you."

Elizabeth looked at Travis. "What are you *doing* here?" she repeated. When was the last time she had seen Travis and Nicole?

"I could ask you the same thing." Travis looked around. "I live in Star Valley, in Auburn."

Elizabeth blinked. "You do?"

He chuckled again. "I know . . . a far cry from London."

That was it: London. She'd stayed with them in their flat. She had absolutely refused to try to make the guard at Buckingham Palace smile. It had driven Travis crazy, and Nicole had finally whispered something in the guard's ear, drawing a corner of his mouth up. It was a good memory. They were good friends. But she'd lost track.

"What are you doing in Star Valley?" She couldn't place him anywhere but in the city with Nicole.

Just then, the waitress appeared, looking a little confused as to why they were all standing.

Nancy spoke. "Why don't you join us?"

Travis smiled. "I'd love to. I'm meeting a client though."

"Client?"

The waitress excused herself, promising to return in a few minutes.

"I'm a financial consultant now. Listen, I have a ton of questions for you. Are you visiting or . . . ?"

"I'm looking into a partnership with Nancy. She owns a boutique here in town."

He shook his head with a smile. "Crazy. I'm staying at the Holiday Inn tonight. Can we get together tomorrow?"

Elizabeth nodded. "Sure." She turned to Nancy. "I could do lunch, right?"

"Of course you could," Nancy answered.

"Great. I can't believe how good it is to see you, Liz. Here's my card. Call me at eleven thirty. I'll be done with work by then." He turned to Nancy and Hank. "It was good to meet you."

"You too," Nancy said, and Hank nodded.

He nodded at Elizabeth again and headed to another part of the restaurant. Elizabeth watched him walk away.

They sat down, and Nancy said, "Well, it certainly is a small world. How do you know him, Elizabeth?"

"I worked with Nicole at Saks. She and Travis dated for a couple of years. They married before they moved to London. I was a bridesmaid . . ." She trailed off at the memory.

"Well, he seems like a nice guy."

"Yes," she agreed. "One of the good ones." She looked in the direction he'd gone.

Nancy opened her menu. "Those are rare, indeed," she murmured and winked at Hank.

* * *

Ryan and his mother looked up from the desk at the sound of the front door. Elizabeth came in on the arm of an older, weathered man wearing a tweed sports jacket, jeans, cowboy boots, and a cowboy hat. He was tall, and Elizabeth clung to his arm.

"Careful now," the man said.

"Hank, I'm fine."

"I know, I know." He led her to the desk and removed his hat, looking at Ryan with apologetic eyes shaded by thick eyebrows. He smiled. "I am dropping Miss Elizabeth off tonight."

"Is everything all right?"

"Oh, I would guess so, but I was under strict orders to deliver her to a Mr. Ryan Brennan. You wouldn't happen to be him, would you?"

Elizabeth closed her eyes and shook her head.

Ryan looked back to the man with the hat. "I'm Ryan." He looked at Elizabeth with concern. "Miss Embry?"

She raised her eyes to the ceiling and sighed. "I missed *one* step." She turned to the man. "Tell him, Hank."

Hank smiled and shook his head, then looked at Ryan. "Do you know my wife?"

Ryan glanced at Elizabeth, who rolled her eyes. "Should I?"

Ryan's mom drew in a quick breath. "Oh, you're Nancy Colette's husband. I've seen you at some of the chamber events."

He extended a hand toward her. "Hank Carter. Pleasure."

Ryan's mother reached across and shook his hand. "Dayle Brennan. Nice to meet you."

Hank turned his attention back to Elizabeth. "Nancy is fairly protective of this one and thought I should drive her home. She missed a step coming out of the restaurant, and well," his hand reached up and adjusted his hat, "Nancy thought Elizabeth might need a bit of a hand."

Elizabeth shook her head, looking up. "I had *half* a glass of wine. *With* dinner."

Hank nodded at her. "Yes, that's true, but"—Hank turned to Ryan— "apparently, it doesn't take much to, uh—" He made a tipsy gesture with his hand.

"Which is why I'm careful." She looked like a teen caught in high school. "Please, just let me go to my room."

Hank eyed the stairs, then Ryan. "I'm under strict orders," he repeated. He looked out the doors behind him to headlights waiting in the drive. He turned to Elizabeth as Ryan's mom nudged him with her elbow.

"Help her," Dayle whispered.

Ryan hesitated, and Dayle raised her eyebrows at him.

"Fine," he mumbled. He came around the bar and stood awkwardly next to Elizabeth, who was looking down now, shaking her head.

"Now, I'm sorry, Elizabeth," Hank said. "I hope you won't hold this against me. You know Nancy."

"Thank you, Hank."

He patted her arm. "'Night, darlin'."

"Good night."

Hank tipped his hat to Dayle and placed it back on his head, nodding his thanks to Ryan as he left.

As the door shut, Elizabeth glanced up at Ryan. "I really am fine."

"Okay," Ryan said quietly, "but I think Nancy is still watching, so let me take your elbow and lead you upstairs." He held out a hand.

She nodded and gave him her arm, and they walked to the stairs.

"I'm twenty-eight years old," she said. "You would think I could be spared the embarrassment of a seventeen-year-old." She went for the first step and missed. She closed her eyes and murmured something under her breath.

"You only had half a glass?" He asked it carefully.

Her defenses came up. "*Yes.*" She took a breath. "What Hank said was true. It's never taken much, and my coordination is the first to go."

Ryan looked up the stairs, calculating. He pulled her elbow to his other hand and placed his free hand on her waist. He could feel her shy away from his touch, but he wasn't going to have her fall in his inn. She smelled really good, not like other guests he'd had to help before. "Okay, let's go."

She reached for the rail, and they walked up together. His arm was firm around her, but he kept his touch light. They reached the top steps.

"Can I ask you something?" His own voice surprised him.

She laughed softly, sarcastically. "Why not?"

He paused. This wasn't even his business. He went ahead. "Why do you drink if it throws you off even this much?"

They reached the landing, and she looked at him. He braced himself for her response.

"Doesn't everybody?"

He raised his eyebrows. "What was that about high school?" Now he was really overstepping his bounds. *Shut up, Ryan.*

She conceded his point with a look but remained still, considering. He watched her brown eyes search for an answer in his shirt. Finally, she shrugged. "I actually don't . . . very often. I used to, a lot . . ."

He took just her elbow again, relieved she wasn't upset by his personal question, and they started down the hall to her room.

She continued, the sarcasm back in her lowered voice. "Apparently, I was a lot of fun at parties. Unfortunately, I didn't figure it out until later . . ." Her voice trailed off.

As they reached her door, she asked, "What about you?" She looked him over, then met his eyes. "Are you a *non*drinker?"

He held out his hand. "Key?"

She opened her purse and pulled out the key.

He took it, and as he opened the door, he said simply, "I don't drink. Couldn't ever see the point."

"Ever?"

"Not ever." He held the key out. He looked at her again as he held her door open, and he saw something different.

She was searching again, this time his eyes. She softly smiled, shaking her head a fraction, and something tugged at his chest. When she finally looked away, he blinked rapidly and took a breath he didn't know he'd been holding.

She lowered her eyes. "Thank you, Ryan." She reached to take the key from him. "It won't happen again."

He wondered if she meant forever or just while she was staying here. "Will you be all right?"

She nodded, still fingering the key. She gave another little laugh. "Sure." She looked up again, appearing on the verge of tears, but smiled. "I always am."

He cleared his throat, and she turned into her room, delicately bringing up a finger to her eye. She turned back as she closed the door. Still looking down, she said, "Good night."

"Good night."

The door shut.

What had he just seen in her flawless features? He stood there and ran a hand over his jaw. It was vulnerability. She had been so . . . guarded. That was it, then. She had let the wall down, just briefly.

He checked to make sure his was still up.

He took a step away, then heard a loud thud from the room. He quickly reached over and knocked on the door. "Elizabeth? Are you all right?"

A second passed, and he was about to rush for the extra key downstairs, but then he heard her.

"I'm good," she sheepishly called out. "Somebody . . . put a chair leg right in front of my foot."

He sighed and laughed quietly enough that she couldn't hear him. "Are you sure you're okay?"

"Yes. *Please*, go away."

He suppressed his smile. "Good night."

She sighed loudly, then muttered, "*Good night.*"

He allowed the smile then and walked away.

His mom watched him as he came down the stairs. "She all right?"

He nodded. "She isn't drunk . . . just a little loss of coordination."

She nodded. "It's more than that." She took out a clean rag and some wood polish and started spraying the counter.

"Hmm?"

His mom started wiping. "I know that look." She finished the counter, picked up the bottle, and started for the great room. "That girl is alone."

She didn't look at Ryan as he watched her move around the room. He glanced ahead at the doors, at his own reflection glancing back at him.

Finally, he said, "I'm going home, Mom."

"Okay. Good night, son." She turned to him. "I love you."

"Love you too." He turned his back on the reflection, walked through the kitchen, grabbed his jacket, and left out the side door.

Chapter 6

ELIZABETH CATALOGUED INVENTORY, A CHORE Nancy had assigned to familiarize her with the shop, the stock, and the floor. It was tedious, but Elizabeth had a knack for efficiency and floor display. The clock read nearly eleven thirty, and she was nearly done. She looked out the window at the drizzle that had begun a short while ago. The gray clouds and mists seemed to brighten the fall colors outside. Her mind wandered.

She'd had another good run this morning and had been glad she had *not* run into Ryan. After the mild humiliation last night, she'd lain in bed considering his blatant admittance that he didn't drink. Ever. The idea was foreign to her. People just did. At least in her world. In most of the world. Didn't they?

Her sister Alisen had given it up. And Amanda, for that matter. And their husbands.

So some people just didn't. No matter what the society norms were.

Ryan did, however, leave her a smoothie for breakfast. The older couple, the Franks, had said good morning to her, and Dayle had made sure she'd slept warmly enough. The temperature had dropped last night. She found herself wondering where Ryan had been. She gave her head a shake.

That was three times now. Three times she'd found herself wondering about Ryan Brennan that morning. Wondering what kind of impression she was making on him . . . doubtful that it was the one she'd intended—not that she had intended to make any on him at all. Last night . . . his eyes . . . He hadn't passed judgment. He hadn't been patronizing or suggestive. He was . . . unexpected.

She wondered if Travis's stay at the hotel had been nice and impersonal.

"Are you all right?" Nancy had been on the phone at the counter. Now she looked at Elizabeth, eyebrows raised.

"Umm, yes."

"Darling, I'm sorry about last night. I'm just a little . . . overprotective. You know that."

Elizabeth nodded. "Yes, I know. And thank you." She meant it. Mostly. It wasn't like she'd never given Nancy reason to worry. She changed the subject. "Is this the slower season?" She had wondered about the lack of customers because the books showed Nancy's boutique was a successful addition to the community.

"Yes, it really slows down in the next few weeks. The whole town sleeps. Then ski season opens up, and we are off and running again." Nancy glanced at her watch. "Isn't it time to call that friend of yours?"

Nancy was a personal day planner. Elizabeth excused herself and went to the back room. She fished out the card from her purse and entered the number.

It rang twice before he picked up. "Travis George."

"Hi, Travis. It's Elizabeth."

"Elizabeth, your timing is perfect. Meet me at the Sweetwater in twenty, okay?"

"Okay."

"See you soon."

She hung up and smiled. It would be good to talk to Travis. She went to ask Nancy where the Sweetwater was.

Exactly eighteen minutes later, she pulled up to a restaurant that had all the appearances of an old log cabin, complete with dripping rain barrel and weathered wood porch. She walked past the aged but overflowing flower boxes and through the heavy plank doors and was immediately enveloped in warmth and the smell of comfort food.

"Liz." Travis rose from a bench, and they greeted each other with a kiss on the cheek. "I can't get over how good it is to see you." He put his arm around her shoulders.

"I know, I know. It's been . . . how long? Three years?"

"Two and a half. That trip to Barbados, remember?"

Elizabeth closed her eyes. "Oh yes, how could I forget?"

He chuckled and motioned to the hostess, who grabbed two menus and said, "Follow me, please."

She seated them at a window and left them alone with the menus.

"Elizabeth, you look great. Really."

"You've said that. You look good too. I like how you've cut your hair. It used to be so shaggy." She made a face, and he laughed.

He leaned across the table. "What are you *doing* here?"

She leaned forward and tapped the top of his hand with her fingers. "I know, crazy." She pulled her hand back and opened the menu, smiling. "Who would have thought we'd both be in the same restaurant at the same time in Jackson, Wyoming? Did you tell Nicole yet?"

There was no reply. She looked up. His brow was furrowed as he studied the menu. "Not yet."

"Well, she'll get a kick out of it. We just . . . lost touch, didn't we?"

He nodded. "So, tell me, Wild One, are you going to stay here in Jackson?"

She flinched at the nickname. He didn't know he was inflicting a wound. She tried to ignore it, shrugging. "I don't know yet, but I think I might." She calmed a tremor of anticipation. "There's a lot to consider."

She could sense him studying her. The waitress returned and took their order. As she walked away, Elizabeth asked, "So, what in the world are you doing in Star Valley, Mr. Financial Consultant?" Travis had been a banker, so Elizabeth guessed the transition had been a smooth one. "Besides riding horses and milking cows?"

She was kidding, but Travis raised his eyebrows at her.

"You mean, you *are* riding horses and milking cows?"

He smiled at her bewildered expression. "Well, I only milk every once in a while, but I ride the horses quite often."

Elizabeth sat speechless. Was this the Travis who got them into the hottest nightclubs in London?

"See, I came to Star Valley to help my grandparents. They kind of raised me, so when they needed help—they're older now—I did what I could." He tapped the table with his finger. "Believe me, I tried to find help for them, but . . . this seemed to work out for the best." He looked down, then took a sip of his water.

"Wow, Travis, that is really, um, *noble* of you."

He about spit out his water, and they both laughed. "Yeah, well, that's me." He held his hand out and made a small bow above the table.

Elizabeth sobered. She finally heard it. The plural was missing. "What does Nicole think of Star Valley?"

He looked away, then down. "Elizabeth . . ." He tilted his head to the side and watched his finger tap on the table. "Nicole and I split up." He swallowed and raised his eyes to hers.

She stared, stunned. She had known only Nicole with Travis, Travis with Nicole. They'd been married only a few years, but they were the ubercouple, finishing each other's sentences, kissing without reserve in public, something which had made Elizabeth cringe. They were always laughing, playing, teasing, smoldering. If anyone was going to make it, it was Travis and Nicole. And they hadn't.

Their food came, and Travis thanked the waitress. He looked carefully at Elizabeth. "Sorry. I didn't want to shock you like that. I'm . . . still getting used to it myself."

Elizabeth blinked. "But . . . what happened? I can't picture this. How could you . . . ?"

Travis shrugged over his plate. "It's not like we didn't try."

"How hard?" She had not meant to sound angry, but she was. How could they let this happen? Of course it happened. Every day it happened. But not to them. She felt . . . she felt betrayed, and she couldn't quite get a handle on why. This had nothing to do with her.

"Liz."

She brought her eyes up to him and saw the pain there, and guilt washed through her. She was right. This had nothing to do with her. "I'm sorry, I just . . . I guess I just don't know how to react. The last time I saw you two, you were . . ."

"Lip-locked at the airport?"

She nodded, an apologetic smile on her face.

"Believe me, I understand." He took a deep breath. "I've been angry a long time."

"Travis, I understand if you don't want to talk about it, but . . . *what happened?*"

He halfheartedly picked up his fork and started moving his food around. "I'm still not sure. I've lost a lot of sleep over the question, believe me. I've sort of narrowed it down."

Elizabeth waited, unable to eat.

"She had a series of long trips for work. *You* know. I became resentful when she didn't seem to miss me." He shook his head. "We became distant, silent." His voice quieted as he spoke. "I accused her of having an affair, she admitted it, and I sought payback." He stopped, then whispered, "It was a mess."

Elizabeth couldn't breathe.

Travis moved his fork in his food again. "Then, when my grandparents called for advice, I saw an opportunity and a chance to start over . . . *with* Nicole. A new life." He shook his head slowly. "She didn't buy into it."

Elizabeth let the silence between them slip on.

She had one more question. "How long?"

He looked at her. "We've been separated four months. We're working out the details of the divorce."

So soon. It hadn't taken long at all. What a waste.

Without trying, her mind switched to an image of Ryan. He hadn't had a choice. Again, she felt the anger warming her face, but she kept it hidden.

"I'm sorry. I didn't want to bring things down like this. It really is so good to see you, Liz. Makes me feel like old times."

She nodded and took his offered hand. He gave hers a squeeze.

He tilted his head at her, narrowing his eyes. "You've changed."

She nodded again. "We grow up, don't we?"

He chuckled, a little sadly. "I don't know if you felt this way, but I remember when I was a kid, before my parents divorced, I couldn't wait to grow up."

Elizabeth nodded thoughtfully.

"Grown-ups had the money, they could stay up as late as they wanted, go wherever they wanted . . . They made the rules, you know?" He was going over her hand with his fingers now, absently. Then he covered her hand with both of his. "It would be great to be a kid again."

She ruminated over that. To be a kid again, before the bad things, before her mother died . . . "It would be great to be a kid again, for a little while."

Their eyes locked, and she suddenly felt that maybe he was holding her hand a little too long. Just as she was about to pull it away, though, he let go and sighed deeply.

His demeanor brightened. "Of course, there are good things about being an adult . . ." His voice dropped to a murmur. "I just can't think of anything right now." He smiled warily.

"I thought *I* was the cynic," she teased him, hoping to help the mood shift.

"Yes, you were, weren't you? Are you still?"

She nodded. "The cynic, without the party."

He broke into a grin. "Sounds fun."

She chuckled, and they picked up their forks to eat.

When they were finished, he held the door for her as they exited the restaurant and walked her to her car. It was still drizzling, but neither of them had an umbrella. He reached for her shoulders and squared her to him.

"Thank you, Liz. Thanks for listening to me. You don't know how glad I am to see you."

"I'm glad too. It's nice to see a familiar face. I'm . . . I'm sorry about what you're going through. If you need anything . . ."

They embraced, and he whispered in her ear, "I'd like to see you again, soon."

The whisper raised goose bumps along her arm. Or was it his words? She pulled away, nodding, searching his face for his meaning.

He just smiled. "I'll call you next time I'm up. You'll be here for two weeks, right?"

"Right." She was feeling . . . cautious. It was something she'd never had to feel around Travis.

"Soon, then." He leaned forward and kissed her cheek, then let her duck into her car. He stood there for a minute as she started the ignition, then he backed away and turned to his own vehicle.

She shook away the caution she felt. She was thinking too far into things. She'd never had walls up for Travis. He was safe. On the other hand, she was usually right about this. It helped so many times, the warning to cool things before they got started. But this was Travis, and Nicole was only four months in the past. He was still *married*. And he was one of the good ones. She swore under her breath at Nicole. At both of them. Why hadn't they fought harder?

She chastised herself.

Like I know anything about marriage. Or love.

The last part stung.

* * *

Back at the shop, the dripping rain kept time with the piano CD playing low.

Elizabeth fought restlessness. She wondered if she should find that gym Ryan had mentioned. She liked to run when she was upset, almost craved it. It cleared her head, allowed her to think things through in an unattached way, like she was a machine intent on moving her body, keeping the rhythm, sorting through the muck, and clearing it out. She drummed her fingers absently on the counter.

Nancy bustled in from the back and interrupted the rain song. "Elizabeth, we're taking a day off tomorrow."

"We are?" Tomorrow was Wednesday. The itinerary. "What are we doing?"

"We are taking you into the park. We'll visit Jenny Lake and see why everyone is so crazy about those mountains."

Elizabeth looked outside. "I didn't pack rain gear, Nancy."

"It's supposed to clear up. The weather is like that this close to the mountains. It can change on a dime."

"It could get worse," Elizabeth said, and Nancy gave her a patient look. Elizabeth had to smile. *The cynic, without the party.* "Sorry. Who is *we*?" She shifted her tone to one of interest.

"Ryan Brennan is guiding a group."

Elizabeth raised an eyebrow. "One of his hikes?"

"No, actually; this is more like a tour group. We'll be in a vehicle."

"Oh."

"But there will be some walking and a boat ride."

That didn't sound so bad. "All right. What time?"

"I'll meet you in the morning at eight."

"Is Hank coming?"

"No, darling. He pulled up flooring yesterday. Yards and yards of old carpet. Hooray! He's refinishing wood as we speak. It will take a few days. Then the tile will go in too." She sighed. "My, how I love watching that man work. Mm-mmm." She looked across the shop. "I think we'll put the new shipment of outerwear over there."

Elizabeth chuckled once and shook her head as Nancy crossed over and began to rearrange the racks. Then she thought about tomorrow. Good. Something to look forward to. She thought again about lunch, about Travis and Nicole and expectations and being a grown-up.

"Nancy?"

"Yes?"

"Why did you want me here? Why did you ask me to be a partner?" She could feel her brow furrow, and she attempted to smooth it out.

Nancy came back over, looking at her curiously for a moment. Then she took a breath and answered. "I trust you; I trust your taste, your decision-making. There is nobody else I would have asked."

Elizabeth looked down, accepting the compliment with a swallow. "But why a partner?" She looked around. "Do you really need one?"

Nancy smiled at her. "Yes, I do. Hank and I aren't spring chickens, and I want to spend more time with him. Having you here frees me up to do that. I'll admit, calling you was not a long, thought-out decision. But when inspiration strikes, I'm pretty quick to obey it." She reached over and squeezed Elizabeth's arm. "It's never steered me wrong." She winked and went back over to the racks, then moved to the back room. On her way, she called, "It might have had something to do with keeping an eye on *you* as well."

Elizabeth broke into a short laugh. She had a feeling that had more to do with the decision than Nancy was admitting. Dear, insane woman.

Taking care *of me, more like. Someone to take care of me . . .*

She knew she could take care of herself. She was just a little tired of it.

Chapter 7

ELIZABETH SAT QUIETLY IN THE car, looking out the window. She would do this as a child on road trips—just sit and watch the trees and hills and world go by, looking for anything that hinted at magic or hidden worlds, talking animals or gingerbread houses or unicorns. She wouldn't look for those things now, but the memory had been buried, and she almost enjoyed its resurfacing.

Nancy was right. The clouds had cleared, and the day was crisp and bright. Everything was still wet, of course, but the colors sizzled in the morning sunshine. Already the mountains reflected the light with brilliance, even from a distance. What had been rain in Jackson was snow up in those heights.

She yawned. She hadn't slept well, tossing and turning, waking from dreams she couldn't remember. The only thing that saved her was that in the quiet of the night, she could hear the river beyond her window, so she'd concentrated on that, finally drifting off deeply in the early hours of the morning.

She glanced at the driver's seat and folded her arms over her middle. Ryan kept his eyes on the road, answering questions from the passengers behind him and pointing out anything of interest as they drove. Elizabeth still wondered how she wound up in the front seat with him. Nancy had pulled her over to the passenger's side of the suburban, gotten in the second row of seats, and shut the door in Elizabeth's face. The remaining seats had filled quickly from the other side, and there was nothing to do but stay in the front. Nancy had just smiled innocently.

"So, Ryan, how do you like the bed and breakfast business?" Nancy leaned forward as far as her seat belt would allow, resting a forearm above Elizabeth's shoulder.

"I like it. It's interesting, mostly quiet. We meet a lot of people from all over."

"Any interesting places lately?"

He thought. "Denmark, Japan . . . Brazil, Thailand."

"You'll have to send them to my shop. I speak a little Thai."

He smiled in his rearview mirror. "I will."

"I had some Canadians come into the shop last week. Does that count? They have excellent chocolate in that country."

He chuckled and nodded.

Elizabeth imagined she could listen to his lower, mellow voice for a long time. Her face flushed at what she was thinking, and she looked down as if to check something on her sleeve.

Get ahold of yourself, Elizabeth.

"Is it hard, though, being tied down? I feel that way with the shop at times. Elizabeth will help with that, though, won't you?" She patted Elizabeth's shoulder.

Ryan looked at Elizabeth, then back to the road. "It's a lot of work, but we get a lot of free time when the work's done right. My parents have been doing this for a while, so it feels natural, I guess." He gestured to the scenery out the windows. "Plus, I get to do this on a regular basis."

Elizabeth watched the corners of his eyes crinkle just a little as he smiled at the thought of his occupation. She wondered how old he was. She guessed thirty-something but couldn't get closer than that. She was usually better at that game. He glanced in her direction again, and she looked ahead, his strong profile infuriatingly on her mind.

"This is the town of Wilson. In a little while, we'll be heading through the Rockefeller Ranch. It was private, but now it's part of the park. They have a visitors' center and quite a few hiking trails."

There were murmured replies from the backseats. The Holidays.

After a few more minutes, the car slowed. "There's a herd of elk over there."

They looked where Ryan pointed as he pulled off to the side of the road. Elk filled a large open area in front of a low line of trees, with the mountain range beyond. A soft mist rose around the animals. Several bulls were scattered among the cows; one in particular stood out from the rest, his antlers spread wide and back. The peaceful scene brought Elizabeth forward in her seat, just across the center console. She could hear cameras taking pictures and made a mental note to invest in a good one. If she was going to live here, she may as well—

The thought startled her. Was she deciding? No, just planning. *If* she was going to live here, she would need a good camera.

Ryan had been leaning toward his window, but he turned back abruptly, reaching for his water bottle, touching her arm instead and sending a mild current up the back of her neck. They both withdrew, murmuring apologies.

She gestured to his water bottle in the holder. "Go ahead."

He smiled and took it. "Thanks."

She settled back into her seat, folding her arms again, watching from a safe distance.

What is the deal? She wanted to scream or run. Why was her heart pounding, and why could she barely say one word to him? The place where he had touched her still tickled on her arm. *Ridiculous.*

She tried to focus on the field again, but she watched him take a drink.

"Elizabeth."

She jumped.

"Oh, I'm sorry," Nancy said. "I didn't mean to startle you, darling."

"That's quite all right."

"Well, I just wanted to ask you if they had elk like this in Montana."

Elizabeth stared at her, and she heard a muffled laugh from Ryan.

She answered patiently. "Yes. Yes, they do. Glacier National Park is right there."

"Oh. Oh, okay." Nancy pressed her lips together and smiled, shrugging her shoulders, eyes wide. "Aren't they lovely?"

Elizabeth couldn't hold it. She broke into a full smile at her friend. "Yes. They're beautiful. It's a beautiful setting." She looked again toward the window but instead found Ryan watching her, a crooked smile on his face. He suppressed it, though, and looked behind him.

"Ready to move on?"

There was a general agreement, and they continued on to the park.

When they got there, everyone piled out of the car and stretched. They followed Ryan to a dock and a broad, open boat with benches along the sides, meeting at the bow. A man stepped forward and shook hands with Ryan, and they turned to help everyone get in.

After releasing Ryan's warm hand, Elizabeth found Nancy saving her a seat near the back. As she sat down on the white bench, she looked over at the water. She could see round rocks of every color and striation at the bottom.

"It's so clear," she said as she reached her hand over the side to pull her fingers through the calm water. "And *really* cold." The ripples from her touch spread across the water, crisscrossing with those made from the movement of the boat. She shivered, wishing she had brought a jacket.

"Can I have everyone's attention? I'd like you all to meet our captain, Matt." Ryan made the introduction, and they went to work untying the boat and pushing it away from the dock.

The ride was smooth, and the scenery became more and more majestic. It reminded Elizabeth of home, of the lakes around Flathead, the woods. She hadn't thought about them in so long. What had she been doing?

She watched Ryan talk with Mr. and Mrs. Holiday and answer some of the kids' questions as they pointed. He laughed quietly at something, and she felt the corners of her mouth go up.

Then she felt Nancy's eyes on her. She blinked and looked out over the water, feigning new interest. "Looks like we're docking."

Ryan heard her. "We'll find the trailhead here up to Hidden Falls. For those of you who are up for it, the trail forks and continues up to Inspiration Point, which holds a fantastic view of almost the entire lake."

They docked the boat, and the two Holiday boys joined in, throwing bumpers out. Once again, Elizabeth reached for the warm strength of Ryan's hand as he helped her out of the boat.

"Thanks," she said, her voice somewhere in the back of her throat.

He nodded and turned to Nancy, who took both of his hands and winked at him, grinning. Elizabeth thought she caught him blowing a sort of exasperated breath out after Nancy turned away, but it was an amused gesture.

They began their walk, following the signs. The family moved up ahead, and Elizabeth kept pace with Nancy, following Ryan. Trees lined the wide, smooth trail. Nancy kept up an easy chatter and, every once in a while, would stop and pick up a fallen leaf or pinecone. She picked up a crimson and gold leaf and held it up to Elizabeth's chin.

"This color would look gorgeous on you. Here."

Elizabeth raised an eyebrow at her friend but took the leaf. "I'm supposed to wear this?" In a moment of rare playfulness, she held it up to her hair. Nancy giggled, and Ryan turned around.

He appraised Elizabeth as she removed the leaf and looked down, twirling it in her fingers.

"Ryan, what do you think?"

Elizabeth's head snapped up to Nancy. Then she peeked at him, sure she was as scarlet as the leaf.

He raised his eyebrows in surprise at the question and cleared his throat, then just smiled crookedly and shook his head. "C'mon ladies, let's go." He turned and continued walking. "The bridge up here is halfway to the falls."

Elizabeth threw Nancy a stern look, and Nancy's eyes widened. "What?" Nancy answered loudly.

Elizabeth just closed her eyes and took a deep breath. When she opened them, Nancy was walking on, smiling.

The bridge was made of planks and rough-hewn logs. The creek rushing under it could easily be mistaken for falls, and the sound and sight of clear water tumbling over rocks and limbs held their attention for a moment.

Nancy took the pinecone she'd been carrying and tossed it upstream, then watched it course back toward them. As it went under the bridge, she leaned over the low railing to follow it and nearly bent in half before she lost her balance.

"*Eep!*" she said, her leg slipping out from under her as Elizabeth reached to grab her waist and shoulder. Nancy dragged Elizabeth with her as Elizabeth leaned forward instead of back.

"Ah, *Nancy!*" Elizabeth cursed her friend, then suddenly felt firm arms around her waist.

"Have you got her?" Ryan asked as he stopped her from falling over. She nodded, and he began to pull.

Nancy found her footing and came up panting. She turned and leaned against the railing, with Elizabeth's hands on her shoulders. Some of the group had turned to see what the ruckus was.

"Thank you, darling, and Ryan too. Whew."

Elizabeth became very aware of Ryan's arms still locked around her waist, and she shifted. He pulled away quickly, stepping to her side and placing his hands on his hips.

"Are you all right?" he asked.

Nancy nodded, looking sheepish.

Elizabeth frowned. "Did you want to take a little ride with your pinecone friend?"

Nancy laughed and put an arm around Elizabeth, steering her forward.

Elizabeth's eyes met Ryan's. "Thanks for saving me—*us.*" *Nice, Elizabeth.*

He nodded, narrowing his eyes. "No problem." He smiled crookedly again and held his arm open, inviting them to continue across the bridge. He walked behind them the rest of the way.

It wasn't lost on Elizabeth that she could still feel the warmth where his arm had been securely wrapped around her middle.

The trees became dense as the group wound up the trail. Abruptly, the trail opened to the falls. Except for the roar of the water, Elizabeth never would have guessed the falls were there. The torrent of water cut through rock outcroppings above and blasted its way toward them, slicing the forest in two.

"What do you think?" Ryan had come up to stand beside her.

She watched the force of the water propel itself down, crashing against rock and spraying out to fall even farther. "What is it about waterfalls?" she said. "I mean, I remember traveling with my family, and every once in a while, my mother would call out, 'Look, kids, a waterfall,' and we would all stop what we were doing and look." Elizabeth still reacted that way whenever she saw one. She felt Ryan watching her, and she rolled her eyes. "Sorry, I just—"

"No," he stopped her. "I was just thinking. Maybe"—he turned to the waterfall—"maybe it's because they don't look like an accident . . . like they were shaped that way simply for us to enjoy." He shrugged.

She nodded and raised her eyebrows. "And maybe because they're so powerful but still entirely graceful."

"When have you known water *not* to be graceful?" he asked.

"That's true." She laughed and lowered her eyes.

"But I think you're right. Hmm." He turned to look at her. "There are a lot of falls to see in this area, trails all over. You should check them out."

That almost bordered on an invitation. She nodded. "I'd like that."

He dropped his head and moved away from her. He raised his voice to the group. "If any of you are interested, we could backtrack on the trail here and take the fork up to Inspiration Point. It's a steeper climb, a bit strenuous, but worth it."

Mrs. Holiday sat down on a bench, and Nancy went to join her, announcing that she and strenuous didn't mix. Elizabeth moved that direction, but Nancy shooed her away.

"Don't waste that fabulous body sitting here. Get over there. Enjoy it while you can."

Elizabeth ignored the loud compliment. "You're sure?"

"Of course I am. I'll just sit and enjoy this splendid waterfall. Go."

Elizabeth felt a little like a child as she turned around to join the others. This whole place brought out memories and feelings of the past and where she came from, reminding her of being a kid again, like Travis had said.

Thinking of Travis drew her inside herself, and she was silent for most of the climb up the trail. The others around her spoke quietly, but as the trail became steep, there was less talking and more sips from water bottles.

Travis and Nicole were no longer together. And he was here, obviously anxious to see her again. He was . . . her friend's husband, but they had always gotten along so well, often ganging up against Nicole in a very teasing way, and though he and Nicole had always been so physically . . . expressive to one another, Elizabeth had allowed herself to flirt a little, allowed the smile . . . because Travis was safe. Nothing would come of it. And Nicole had seemed to like the chance it offered her to claim her territory and remind a grinning Travis in not so many words who his woman was.

Ironic. Nicole had been so possessive, and yet she'd broken their marriage with an affair.

Elizabeth sighed and dug her shoes into the dirt. And now Travis was here, and she wasn't sure what that made her. She flushed a little at the thought of what flirting with him now might lead to.

Then she thought of Ryan, and her heart gave another surprising pound, like a single drumbeat that had her catch her breath. Her eyes came up as the trail bent, and she exclaimed softly. "Oh."

The entire valley opened up before them to reveal most of the shimmering lake, the tops of the lower forest, unknown peaks beyond. She shivered and rubbed her arms with her hands.

"Here." Ryan came up next to her and handed her the jacket he'd tied around his hips.

"Oh, I'm okay."

He raised his eyebrows and looked pointedly at her arms hugging herself.

She conceded. "Thanks." She pulled it on, naturally breathing in the aftershave scent that came with it.

"Better?"

She nodded.

He pointed behind them, up. "Look."

Next to the rise behind them, in a gap in the trees, the Tetons hovered like bright sentinels keeping watch, silent but very present.

The others took their cameras out and started snapping pictures of the views and of one another. Again, she kicked herself for not bringing a camera along. Next time.

She looked to where the trail continued up and around. "Does this keep going?"

"Yes, for miles. It takes you into a higher canyon and past a couple of mountain lakes. It's breathtaking. But we won't do that today."

Imagining herself coming back here, believing that there would be a next time, came easier. She remembered having a similar feeling when she first began to travel, that she would easily return. Of course, with work, she did return to most places, but it was just occurring to her that she might not see some of those parts of the world again. She found she didn't mind.

The way back down was a little tricky. The trail was wet and slick in some places, dry and clay hard in others. Distracted by the view, as she stepped, she stumbled and caught herself on Ryan's back. He half turned and balanced her with his arms.

"Sorry," she said, trying to dismiss the fact that she and Ryan couldn't seem to keep their hands off each other in a very accidental way. She'd never blushed so much in her life, and it was starting to irritate her.

"It's okay." He placed his hands on her arms. "All right?" His eyes were steel marbles in this light.

She nodded. "Perfect." She rolled her eyes as he turned away and brought his hand up through his hair. They started walking again, and from behind, she saw him take a deep breath and blow it out, probably annoyed. Ugh. *Ugh*.

Back in the inn's suburban, she listened to the hum of the engine and the quiet murmurs from the backseat. Everyone was both invigorated and tired. Ryan slowed the car, and they stopped to watch a moose amble through the edge of the woods. It was some distance away, but the cameras clicked. A fox jumped and ran across the field, now empty of elk. Elizabeth looked behind her to see that Nancy had fallen asleep.

As the car sped up, Elizabeth wrapped her arms around her waist, and she realized she still wore Ryan's jacket. She leaned her head against the seat and watched the scenery fly past her window. Her eyes closed, and she suppressed a smile as she listened to him hum an unfamiliar tune.

In her dream, she was falling fast and could hear voices laughing, mocking. Then Ryan caught her, and she looked up, but it wasn't Ryan, and she shied away from the chilling face, pulling back, only to lose her balance and start falling again. This time there was a ruckus below her, and again, she felt arms grabbing her, pulling, wrenching.

Elizabeth.

She woke with a start.

The voice calling her name had soothed the nightmare. Now she heard the sound of seat belts unlatching. They were back at the inn. She furrowed her brow and stretched.

A bright-eyed Nancy met Elizabeth as she slid from the vehicle. She linked her elbow through Elizabeth's arm. "Have a good snooze?"

"I'm not sure." It was the truth.

They walked around the car.

"Thank you, Ryan. That was wonderful."

He turned to Nancy. "You're welcome. There's so much more to see, but that's a good half-day trip. And that part of the park will be closing soon, so it's good to get a trip in when we can." He turned to Elizabeth. "Did you have a good time?"

She stood a little straighter and took a breath. "It was a beautiful trip. Thank you."

That seemed to be enough, and he turned to the inn, walking with the Holidays.

"Well, I'm starving," Nancy said. "Want to get some lunch?"

"Actually, I'd like to go back to my room, lie down for a bit. I think I feel a headache coming on."

"Oh, do you want to take something for it?" Nancy started rummaging around in her purse.

"No, I have some Tylenol in the room. You go ahead. Maybe Hank can use a break from wood floors."

"Okay, if you're sure. That was nice though, wasn't it?"

"The trip? Yes. It was nice to get out and see things. I wish I'd brought a camera."

Nancy's eyes sparked. "Next time."

Elizabeth smiled carefully. "Perhaps."

"Well," Nancy gave her a peck on the cheek, "I hope you have a good rest. Call me later?"

Elizabeth nodded and waited as Nancy walked to her car. She waved and turned toward the inn.

As she entered the inn, she found Ryan shaking hands with—with *Travis*. She blinked a couple of times. No, he was still there. Both men turned to her. She took in their appearance or, rather, their contrast.

Travis's blond hair smoothed back in a wave from his hairline. He was slender but strong in his overcoat, pressed slacks, and shined dress shoes. An olive-green scarf hung carelessly around his neck and down the front of his coat. He looked like he'd just stepped out of a magazine. *Esquire*.

Ryan stepped back to lean against the counter in a plaid flannel shirt with the sleeves rolled up over a navy Henley, his khaki cargo pants bunched up over hiking boots. His hair was the disarray of chestnut it was before, trimmed at the sides and back, finger combed away from his face. He'd stepped out of a different magazine. *Field and Stream.*

She was tugged out of this comparison when Travis said her name.

He stepped forward, placing his hands on her arms, and pulled her in for a kiss on the cheek. He lingered for just a second, and she pulled away.

"Travis. What are you doing here?" Her eyes flickered to Ryan, who watched patiently.

"I called, a few times." He grinned at her. He motioned with his head toward Ryan. "The Brennans are clients of mine. Some coincidence, huh?"

She dug for her phone. "You called?" She looked. "Oh, you did."

Ryan spoke up. "Cell phone reception is iffy out where we were."

She nodded. "I'm sorry I missed you."

Travis still held her arms gently but brought one hand up to lift her chin. "I'm sorry too. I know how you feel about surprises."

She pressed her lips together in a smile and looked down. He released her and stepped to her side, placing his arm around her shoulder. Had he been this touchy-feely before? She searched her memory. Of course he had—but with Nicole.

She blew out a deep, soft breath, trying to gather herself.

"How do you two know each other?" Ryan's expression was casual, light.

Elizabeth opened her mouth to answer, but Travis spoke first. "Elizabeth and I go way back. Right, Liz? We've been all over together."

What was he saying that for? She matched his jaunty tone. "Well, you and Nicole, me and myself."

She could tell by his pause that he hadn't expected Nicole's name to come into his tales of world travel, but she had to draw a line somewhere. He got the hint.

"Well," his voice softened, and she felt a twinge of guilt, "it's been a few years, but I saw her at the Rendezvous, of all places, the other night. Talk about coincidence." He bent his arm around her neck in a fake chokehold. "And I just had to see her again, right, Liz?"

This playfulness she remembered. She brought her hands up to pull out of his grip, and she gave him a half smile as he released her. She ran her hand through her hair.

Travis grinned. "We'll be about an hour. Then do you want to get something to eat, maybe catch a movie?"

"Uh," her eyes flickered again to Ryan. She wished she would stop doing that. This time, she was sure Travis had caught it because he glanced at Ryan as well.

Travis looked down and shifted his weight, his smile fading. "You know, just to catch up some more. If you don't have anything else to do . . ."

He reminded her of a puppy, really. Playful, expectant, and vulnerable. She sighed and smiled. "That would be great. It will give me time to freshen up." *And take something for this headache.*

His smile returned, his expression grateful. "Good. See you in a bit."

Both men watched her, waiting for her to leave first.

She swung her arms. "Right. See you later." She walked between the two of them to the stairs but paused, remembering Ryan's jacket. She grimaced and turned and pulled the jacket off, walking directly to Ryan. "Here. Thank you."

He took it from her and nodded. "You're welcome," he said.

She looked at both men again, raised her shoulders, and turned slowly. She could feel eyes on her as she climbed the stairs, then she heard Ryan.

"C'mon, Travis. Let's go on back, and I'll find my mom. Can I get you anything? Coffee? Danish?"

Splash of cold water? She really needed that Tylenol.

* * *

The tension and amusement Ryan had felt as Travis George declared his association with Elizabeth Embry surprised him. They had both watched Elizabeth return to her room, and they had both looked at each other pleasantly but with an undertone of measurement. And although Ryan gave as much as he got, it still surprised him the way his stomach knotted as Travis had so easily approached her, kissed her cheek.

Ryan didn't have any claim that would justify those feelings. He'd kept them dormant, emotions he hadn't felt since he and Brooke had started dating years ago. It didn't make sense. He didn't know Elizabeth at all. Still, he had almost laughed out loud when he'd seen the apparent discomfort Travis's touch had given her. It was the same reaction she'd given Ryan at the bridge.

Later, though, when she'd tripped into him, she'd pulled away quickly, but he thought he'd seen a flash of . . . well, it wasn't discomfort.

He shook his head and sighed as he brought Travis his coffee.

"Did Elizabeth enjoy the park?" Travis asked.

The question puzzled Ryan. "You can ask her yourself, but I believe she did very much."

Travis furrowed his brow. "Hmm."

"Is that a bad thing?"

"Oh, no, I was just curious. She's such a city girl. Paris, London, New York. I can't picture her out here, on a hike, in the woods . . . hiking shoes."

Ryan just nodded.

"But she seems to like it here."

"I hope so," Ryan said steadily.

Travis raised his eyebrows.

"It's my job to see that she enjoys her stay."

Travis nodded slowly.

"And hiking shoes aren't a far cry from running shoes," Ryan added.

"She runs?" Travis's eyebrows rose again.

"Every morning. Ten miles."

Ryan watched Travis look back down the hall and purse his lips. "Hmm. I didn't know she'd taken that up."

Why did Ryan feel a sense of victory? Ridiculous. It soon faded though.

"She was quite the party girl, if you know what I mean." Travis chuckled and lowered his voice. "Oh, man, the things that girl would do with the right motivation."

Ryan's jaw clenched, and his expression stopped Travis's reminiscing. Travis leaned back in his chair. He had the nerve to look sincerely contrite.

"I shouldn't have said that about her. Sorry."

Ryan shrugged. He didn't want to talk about Elizabeth with Travis. She was just a guest at the inn.

"It's been awhile since I've seen her, and my divorce is messin' with my brain. Sorry. She was always great. Always a great friend. Amazing."

Ryan wished he had something to do with his hands, but all he could do was tap his fingers on the table.

"Look, I'll shut up about that now. How's business through the slow season?"

Ryan cleared his throat and sat up. "Good. The inn's full now, but it'll taper off next week, as expected."

As they discussed the economy, Ryan couldn't help thinking Travis would be leaving with Elizabeth for the rest of the afternoon. And again, he chastised himself for having no grounds on which to feel in any way concerned about that.

Thankfully, his mom appeared with her books.

"Hello, Travis." She shook his hand warmly as he stood for her to take a seat. "How is my portfolio? No, don't tell me. I'm having a beautiful day."

Chapter 8

OKAY, HOW AM I GOING to work this? He is obviously missing Nicole or . . . someone. I'm his friend; we have a history . . . sort of. We're comfortable with each other . . . Well, now he is, and I'm . . . He is very attractive, very . . . communicative. And still married. What do I feel? I feel . . . his feelings need to be considered. He's vulnerable. Ugh. Ugh, ugh. This isn't high school anymore!

Dinner was good. It was early, and they talked mostly about Star Valley. She was surprised there was so much to share, actually. Then Travis leaned across the table and took her hand, inviting her to come see him this weekend. She talked around it, and he finally asked her to think about it. She was definitely thinking now.

She felt the weight of his arm around her shoulder, casual but . . . not. The running conversation in her head was louder than the dialogue on the movie screen. He traced his finger on her upper arm. Normally, she would have already removed his arm and made some flippant remark, and he would have sulked through the rest of the movie. She glanced at him.

He grinned from ear to ear.

He could take it. *But be nice.* She reached for his wrist and pulled it above her head and back down to his side. He deftly flipped his hand over and wove his fingers into hers, leaning his shoulder into her.

Hmm. *That didn't work like I thought it would.*

Unless she was mean, she was stuck. At least until the movie was out. She wasn't going to make a scene with forty minutes of romantic comedy left. She made one last effort.

Leaning away from his shoulder, she rested her chin on her other hand. He smoothly pulled the hand he held across him and up to his lips.

Okay, back to the handholding. She leaned back the other way and grabbed his hand, placing it firmly on the armrest between them. She heard him chuckle, and she narrowed her eyes at the screen. At least she hadn't hurt his feelings. Hmmph.

Suddenly, he breathed into her ear. "Relax."

Goose bumps made their way down to her toes, but she didn't obey him. She allowed her mind to work out scenario after scenario of what might happen, what could happen, and how to make this work. Or not. Then a question came to her mind, just appearing without invitation.

What would I do if this were Ryan Brennan?

She lingered on the question. Not the answer, just the question, because the fact that she was asking it . . . was significant. Would she consider letting someone . . . not just someone, but *him*, through her defenses? She shoved the beginnings of any possible answers away. The effort kept her preoccupied for the remainder of the show.

After the movie, Travis walked her to the passenger's side door and stopped. He held both her hands and stepped closer. She tried to put more space between them, but the car was in the way.

"Do you want to go back to your place?"

"Yes." She was firm.

"Or . . . we could go back to mine." He brought his eyes down to her level. Their noses were almost touching.

A tiny part of her growled, *Why not?* She breathed out a shallow breath. "Mine. Definitely mine."

His eyebrows rose, and a corner of his mouth came up. "Okay, we'll go to yours." He leaned down and kissed her. He'd misunderstood.

She pushed against his chest. He broke away.

"What?" he asked a little impatiently, considering how patient she was being with *him*.

"Because, Travis . . ." She thought. "Because of Nicole. She's all I can see you with. *She's* my friend too, and technically, she's still your wife." She saw confusion in his eyes and the stubborn set of his mouth. "I'm sorry. I don't mean to hurt you. I'm just . . . not sure what I want right now." Though she was getting a better idea. "You're just moving a little too fast, and I can't . . . think."

His eyebrows shot up in surprise, and he took a step back. "Wow, you *have* changed."

She ignored his implications and folded her arms, narrowing her eyes. "I never cheated on a friend, and this is all new enough to me that it feels like I am." *Was that it?* "Can you understand that, please?"

His expression softened. "You never cheated?"

She realized what her words meant to him. "No, Travis. Never."

He looked down, thinking. Then he raised his eyes. "I'm sorry about what I said. I've been saying some really stupid stuff lately."

She searched him. "It's okay. You're going through a lot right now."

He nodded, resigned. "Well, should I take you back to the inn and leave you there by yourself?" An impish grin grew as he spoke, and Elizabeth fought a smile.

"Yes. All by my lonesome."

He nodded exaggeratedly and stepped around to open the car door for her. "You sure know how to squelch a guy."

"Thank you," she said as she slid into the seat.

He got behind the wheel. "Will you still come see me this weekend?"

She scrutinized him for several seconds as he tried to look as innocent as possible.

"Please? I'll behave myself."

She caved. "I'll come on Sunday." He began to say something, but she interrupted. "Uh-uh. I'm not staying over."

His pout grew into a smile. "Okay, Sunday. I'll take you out to feed the cattle." He started the car and shifted gears. "I hope it snows."

* * *

Ryan anxiously glanced at the clock: 8:20 p.m. His dad had come to take the night shift, but he'd turned him away. His pen tapped the counter as he browsed the Internet. He found himself looking up Flathead Lake, Montana. He was just curious.

Hmm. Cherry orchards. Who would've thought? He clicked a link to Glacier National Park. That kept him interested for a few minutes.

Headlights drew his attention to the front doors. Someone got out of the car and came around to let someone else out of the passenger's side. They walked up the porch together, and when the man leaned down to the woman, she turned her head, and he got her cheek. Ryan only watched out of the corner of his eye, but he muffled a short laugh.

He knew who it was and felt a certain sense of justification as Elizabeth came through the front door, a look of concern and . . . irritation? . . . on her face. He wouldn't admit the relief he felt. Neither did he want to ask himself *why* he felt it. There was something wrong about the way Travis had spoken about Elizabeth. He ignored the voice that told him he just didn't want to believe what he'd heard.

A small smile grew on her lips as she approached the counter, and she shook her head.

"Good evening," he said.

She sighed and leaned against the bar. She looked behind her, then faced him.

"Early night?"

She pursed her lips and nodded. She threw her hair back a little and tilted her head to the side.

He smiled at the movement. Strong but graceful.

After Travis left with Elizabeth, Ryan had told himself this was the way out. He wouldn't have to worry about why he couldn't get her off his mind, why he wondered who she really was or what kind of person she had been or whether or not she was going to take the partnership and stay here. He didn't need this; he really didn't. And the more he held on to that determination, the more frustrated he became with himself.

But he still couldn't help thinking that Elizabeth didn't feel the same way about Travis George as Travis obviously felt about her. That she didn't deserve someone who talked so openly about her past. So much for a way out. He was back to worrying and wondering and keeping his walls up so as little of his emotions showed as possible. And what if the walls weren't enough? What was he supposed to do then?

Oh yeah, and by the way . . .

He didn't even know why he was considering anything. He just knew he couldn't get her off his mind. Taking that into account, he thought he was handling it pretty well.

This all raced through his mind as he stood across from her.

"Ryan?"

He looked over at the Franks, standing at the end of the counter. He smiled and moved to take the deck of cards held out for him.

"Thank you, Ryan." Mrs. Frank beamed up at him. She looked over at Elizabeth and nodded.

Elizabeth gently smiled back. There was something there in that warmth. He'd only seen it surface a few times. He wanted to know why she hid it, what she was hiding from.

The Franks pulled his attention away again.

"Good night," they both said.

"Good night." He watched them walk together down the hall.

"Well, I'm going to turn in," Elizabeth said.

He turned to her. She was looking at the computer screen with an amused expression. He reached over and closed the window on Glacier National, revealing the Flathead site. He clicked that closed too. *Subtle, Ryan.* He ignored her questioning look. "Long day?"

She smiled again. "You have no idea."

He glanced out the doors behind her. "I could guess." He smiled. "Can I get you anything before you retire?"

"A life of ease and contentment?"

He laughed. "No such thing, I'm afraid."

She nodded. "Well, good night." She started for the stairs, then turned. "Ryan?"

"Yes?" His pen tapped on the counter.

"I may sleep in. Don't worry about a smoothie."

He broke into a grin. "All right."

She smiled at his expression and climbed the stairs.

He blew out a quiet breath. After he heard her door close, Ryan called his dad. "Hey, come work the front desk. I'm going home."

The walk was long, and he hunched against the cold night air. Several times, he turned and looked back at the Lantern, only to turn himself around again, scowling. Walking was good, and he rarely drove the distance, keeping the truck at the inn. When he walked, he could sort through his muddled thoughts.

He stepped in the house and called, "Hey, kids."

He heard footsteps up the stairs.

"Hey, Dad." Sam put his arms around Ryan's middle and squeezed.

Ryan ruffled his son's hair, thinking it was time for a haircut. "Where are the others?"

Sam looked up at him. "Chloe is doing her homework on the computer, and Lily is crying in her room."

Ryan pulled back. "Why?"

Sam shrugged. "She won't tell us. We tried to make her feel better, but she yelled at us to get out."

Dayle walked in from the kitchen. "Hi, honey."

"Hey, Mom." He took off his jacket and hung it up. "What's up with Lily?"

His mom sighed. "Muffins for Mom."

"Oh." His shoulders sagged.

"I tried, but she was inconsolable." Dayle looked toward the bedroom.

"Why didn't you call me?" He could have been here. He should have been. He made his way back to Lily's room, Sam and his mom following.

"I thought I'd let her calm down and try again. We can't bother you about every little thing."

He stopped and turned. "Is this a little thing?" He wasn't sure. The tightening in his chest told him it wasn't.

Dayle looked at him, no answer in her searching expression.

He sighed. "Okay." He knocked on the door. "Lily? Can I come in? It's Daddy."

He heard a sniffle. "Mm-hmm."

He opened the door, and Sam made to follow him in. Ryan put out his hand. "I'll handle this, son. Is your homework done?"

Sam looked down and made a face. "Naw."

"Go do it, then get to bed."

Sam turned, and Dayle put an arm around his shoulders as they walked away down the hall.

Ryan entered the room. The little lamp next to her bed was on, and Lily had her face buried in her pillow.

"Lily?"

Another sniffle. He sat on the edge of her bed. When had her legs gotten so long? He brushed her hair with his fingers. "Lily, do you want to tell me about it?"

He glanced at the framed photo next to the lamp. Lily moved to sit up and snuggled into his side. She pushed the hair away from her face.

"Tomorrow at school we have Muffins for Mom day." She sniffled. "And Mrs. Straussmeyer said that if anybody's mom couldn't come, they could bring a special friend." Her face pulled down, and her eyes closed. "But I don't want to bring a special friend." She started crying again.

He rubbed her little shoulders and rocked, swallowing the rising emotion. "You wish you could bring your mom?"

She nodded and raised her wide brown eyes to him. "I miss her. I know I don't remember, but . . ." She looked at the photo by her bed. "I want my mom." She started to cry in little bursts, and it was all he could do to keep himself together.

"I know, sweetheart, I know." He reached for the frame and held it so they were both looking at it. "I bet she wishes she could go too. But how about if Grandma went with you?"

Lily shook her head.

He breathed, thinking.

"How about . . . you take this picture with you?" He could barely choke the words out. He swallowed. "Grandma could come and sit with you, and you could set this picture there with you too."

Lily didn't answer right away. Then she looked up at him sideways. "Then I could think that she was watching me?" She ran her hand under her nose and sniffled.

"Mm-hmm."

She took the frame out of his hands and looked at it for a minute. "Okay," she said quietly.

He sighed. "Do you want some ice cream?"

She smiled a little smile. "Okay."

"Go tell Grandma. I'll be right there."

She nodded, slid off the bed, and padded out of the room.

He picked up the picture and looked at it for a long time, his thoughts pained, jumbled, and incomplete.

The memory materialized out of the churning: He placed his hands on the casket, one wrapped in a bandage up his right arm. Only his mother stood behind him, her hand on his back. He bowed his head, picturing, replaying, denying, and knowing. He gave in to the waves of sorrow that took over his fragile control, and he was overcome with loss. His tears fell onto the polished mahogany, and his shuddering invited his mother to rub his back, unable to say or do anything else herself. He pressed both hands to the wood and touched his forehead to its cold surface. His head rocked back and forth, and he took a jagged breath.

"I'll never forget." He took another halting breath. "Never."

Then the door opened behind him at the other end of the room.

His mom whispered, "Honey, the kids are here."

He straightened and wiped his face with his hand. He pressed his fingers to his eyes and took a couple of sharp, deep breaths. He set his hands on either side of his hips and turned around.

His lights, his reason, his meaning for everything stood watching him, waiting. Ten-year-old Chloe held the baby, and seven-year-old Sam stood close to her, his fingers gripping her sleeve. Their little bodies suddenly seemed so fragile.

He held open his arms, and they moved forward quickly, needing no further invitation. He leaned down to better wrap himself around them, unable to kneel because of the brace up to his thigh. The baby reached over to pull his hair. Their muffled cries and words of comfort quieted further as the sound of the organ reached them from the larger room down the hall. The door opened again, and family slowly filled the room to carry or accompany the casket to the chapel.

Ryan took a shivering breath and set the picture back down on Lily's bedside table. He turned off the lamp and stood in the dark. The sound of laughter pulled him out of his seclusion, and he left the room to join his family.

* * *

It was only eight thirty in the morning when the school called him. So here Ryan sat, in the principal's office, less than an hour after he had put his kids on the bus. He looked around the room and felt a twinge of nostalgia. How much time had he spent in this same office?

He looked at the principal. "What exactly happened?"

The principal tapped some notes on his desk with the end of a pencil. "Well, after interviewing all three boys, as far as we can tell, Sam was defending his friend Caleb from a bullying situation, and the boys lost some . . . control." He sighed. "We'll bring Sam here in a minute. I'll let him give you details."

Ryan rubbed his eyes. "But he was defending though, right? Not bullying?"

"Yes." The principal leaned forward in his chair. "Listen, Sam is a good kid. The whole staff knows that. But we can't tolerate fistfights in the halls . . . for any reason. Those kids were throwing *punches*. I'm going to have to suspend Sam for the rest of the day."

Ryan's head came up. "One day?"

"The other kid's getting three." The principal suppressed a smile.

The door opened, and the secretary had her arm on Sam's shoulder, leading him into the room. Then she left, closing the door behind her. Sam looked guilty and a little frightened, and his lip was swollen. The neck of his T-shirt hung loose and stretched out.

"Hey, bud." Ryan patted the chair next to him instead of reaching for Sam and drawing him in for the hug he needed to give him. He'd do that later.

Sam sat, staring at the floor.

"Can you tell me what happened?"

Sam waited a moment, then he nodded. He took a breath and spoke quietly into his chest. "Well, Caleb, he's a friend, and he's kind of small, and the other kids pick on him." He paused.

"Mm-hmm?"

"Well . . . this morning, Caleb's mom came into the classroom to talk to the teacher about something, and she was pretty short. *Really* short. Like, that's where Caleb got it from." He sniffed and wiped his arm under his nose. "Some of the guys were laughing after she left the room." He shook his head and took another breath, deeper this time.

Ryan leaned forward, his chin on his fist. He had an idea where this was going.

"Then it was time to go to the library. So we lined up in the hall, and Austin started calling Caleb shorty and puny and stuff, and then"—Sam drew his lips together tightly, and his nostrils flared—"when he saw the teacher wasn't there yet, he started calling his *mom* names, like midget lady, and teeny, tiny woman, and he asked Caleb if she had to stand on a *stool* to tuck him into bed at night, and then . . ." Sam brought his red eyes up to his dad's. "Then he called her a puny little . . . *B-word*." He dropped his head back down and mumbled, "So I tackled him."

Ryan took a breath. "So you were *punching* him?"

Sam nodded. "He punched back."

Ryan lifted Sam's face. "Obviously." He placed his hand on Sam's head and rubbed his hair. His son lowered his chin again.

"Well, you know your punishment?" He looked at the principal, who nodded.

Sam nodded too.

"Okay. And you were defending your friend?"

Sam waited a minute, then slowly shook his head.

Ryan furrowed his brow. "You weren't?"

Sam placed his elbow on his knee and rested his chin on his fist. Still looking down, he quietly said, "I was defending his mom." His eyes came up to meet Ryan's, filling with tears. "You don't make fun of moms, Dad."

Chapter 9

THE ROAD HOME STRETCHED ON forever. Ryan went over the conversation in the principal's office again. He glanced at Sam, downing a giant hot-fudge sundae. Ryan and Sam had sat in the car while Ryan had reinforced the idea that it was not right to throw punches . . . while they'd waited for Dairy Queen to open. Then he'd let Sam order anything he'd wanted in the drive-thru. He wasn't sure it had been the right thing to do, but it felt good anyway.

He repeated in his mind the last part of that conversation. It revealed a depth of loss on Sam's part that Ryan had been unaware of. He understood that Sam would always feel loss, would always feel a level of sadness in missing his mom, but the kid was so happy, so even-tempered, and apparently, so good at hiding the emptiness he felt with her absence.

And then there had been the thing with Lily last night.

Ryan stared at the jagged line of treetops ahead of him, separating earth from sky. Was he doing the right things for his kids? How would he know until they were grown?

"Dad. *Dad*!" Sam pulled Ryan abruptly from his thoughts.

"Oh, crap." Ryan slammed on the brakes.

Elizabeth turned around, flung her arm out at the truck with a *thunk*, and disappeared off the shoulder of the road. The truck skidded to a halt.

"Stay here," Ryan shouted and was out the door in a split second. He found Elizabeth pulling herself up slowly from a headfirst position down the embankment edging into the woods. He slid down next to her and gently grabbed her arms, helping her sit up on the slope.

"I thought you said all I had to worry about on this road was bears." She groaned.

"No, I said you should be *all right* on this road." His hands shook.

"I guess you were wrong."

He started checking her limbs, gently brushing off pine needles and pieces of fallen leaves. "Where does it hurt?"

"Umm . . ."

He looked up at her and reached his hand behind her neck, gently laying her down. He brushed some leaves out of her hair and checked her pulse. "Don't move."

He ran up to the truck on Sam's side, opening the door and the glove box. He grabbed a small flashlight.

"Dad, is she okay?"

"I'm not sure . . . We'll see," he answered hurriedly. He ran back down and moved the arm she had placed over her eyes. She looked at him. He shined the light in her eyes, one at a time. "You still haven't told me where it hurts." He put the flashlight down and moved his hands along her jawline and down the sides of her neck.

"Actually, I think I'm fine. My hand hurts where I swatted your truck out of the way. Were you a doctor in your past life?"

He shook his head. "Which hand?" His were still trembling.

She waved her left hand at him. He gently picked it up and felt along the bones. She winced.

"I'm so sorry," he whispered.

* * *

Elizabeth watched him for a moment. "Hey." She slowly sat up and wrapped her free arm around her knees. He still concentrated on her hand. "I don't think it's broken. I just reached out when I heard the wheels skid on the road, and it bounced off. It was a gut reaction. It'll be sore, that's all."

"Move your fingers." He frowned in concern.

She gave them a wiggle. It would probably just bruise. "I think I'll live."

He brought his eyes up then. The look on his face surprised her. It was the look of a worried, lost little boy. She finally turned her hand over to take his. She could feel his shaking. Without thinking, she reached her other hand over to hold his hands steady. "Are *you* all right?"

Eventually, he nodded. "I'm so sorry," he quietly repeated. He tightened his jaw and shook his head.

"I'm *okay*." She removed her hands from his and brought them up. She wiggled her fingers again. "See?" He ran his hand over his mouth and nodded.

"Look, if it makes you feel better, I'll threaten to sue you. My father's a lawyer; I'm sure he'd be all over this."

She saw the flicker of amusement in his eyes, but it faded again.

"I can't believe how close I came to—if anything had happened to you, I—" He growled in self-loathing and blew out a shaky breath.

She looked up at him with realization and looked in the direction of the inn.

Ryan's wife died. In a car crash.

"I'm okay." She pushed up and stood quickly. "See? Whoa . . ." The ground tilted beneath her, but Ryan caught her.

"Easy."

She froze in his arms. She blinked and swallowed, his nose close to her cheek, a messy lock of her hair between them.

"Just breathe." He was in control now.

* * *

In that moment, he knew his wall had taken a hit. His heart beat clumsily, and he was stuck. Holding her again.

Breathe. *Yeah, easy to say.*

Hesitantly, she turned her face a fraction, her hair brushing against his face.

She quietly cleared her throat. "I'm all right," she whispered.

He nodded and stepped back half a step, still supporting her in his arms. She looked down at the ground around her, and he took the opportunity to breathe deeply and attempt to clear his head.

He looked up the embankment. Where had *that* come from? He'd nearly lost it. How could he have allowed his fears to grip him like that after all this time? His heart had pounded in his ears, but he was better now. Somewhat.

"Is this how you treat *all* of your guests?" she asked softly.

He looked at her, and the corner of her mouth came up. Her natural beauty dazed him, even after she'd been run off the side of the road. Even with moss on her cheek. He swallowed.

"What did you hit me for anyway?" She was provoking him. He needed that.

He gave her a small, apologetic smile. "I guess I don't like the way you skip breakfast." She muffled a laugh, and he relaxed further. "I was . . . thinking, not paying attention to the road. If it hadn't been for—"

"Dad?" The truck door opened and shut. Sam stood at the top of the embankment. "Is she okay?"

Ryan stepped back again, still holding Elizabeth's arms. He steadied her carefully as she watched the boy come toward them. She wobbled just a little, and Ryan put his arm around her waist, taking her elbow to lead her up to the truck. She didn't pull away this time.

She was probably too stunned.

"I think so," Ryan answered. They stopped walking as Sam reached them. "I was just telling her if it hadn't been for *you*, she wouldn't have gotten off so easy."

He could still hear the shake in his voice. Elizabeth glanced at Ryan, then turned back to Sam.

"Elizabeth, this is my son, Samuel. Sam, this is Elizabeth Embry. She's a guest at the inn."

Elizabeth hesitated. "Hi, Sam." She blinked and swallowed. "Wow, you look just like your father."

Sam grinned. "Everybody says that." He hesitated, then said, "I'm sorry we swiped you off the road. I didn't think Dad would get that close, but he just kept going, so I yelled, 'Dad, Dad!' And then *he* yelled, 'Oh, cr—'"

"*Hey* now." Ryan cut him off.

Elizabeth smiled, taking a breath like she'd been holding it. "Well, I'm glad you yelled." She looked a little closer. "Did he run *you* over too?"

Sam was suddenly shy but still smiled. "No, I got in a fight today at school." He kicked the ground with his toes.

Elizabeth looked up at Ryan. He sighed and nodded. "We were just coming home from the principal's office."

She turned back to Sam. "Did you win?"

Sam jerked his head up to her, and the smile widened. He nodded.

Ryan cleared his throat, and Elizabeth grimaced at Sam, but Sam giggled.

"C'mon. Let's get you to the truck." Ryan still held her as they walked up the slope, and Sam jumped into the backseat. Elizabeth let Ryan help her in, and he looked at her again. "Are you sure you're all right?"

"I think so." He watched her consider the question. Then her face relaxed, and she smiled like she had the other night. It took him a moment to draw away.

They drove back to the inn, Sam chatting with Elizabeth the rest of the way. Ryan listened to her laugh quietly with his son—and felt his wall crumbling. He caught her watching him a couple of times, and when their eyes met, his smile came too quickly. Unusual.

As they pulled up to the inn, Sam asked, "Hey, Dad, when the girls get home after school, can I tell them about everything?"

Ryan looked in the rearview mirror and gave Elizabeth a sideways glance. She had looked down, and he couldn't read her expression.

"Well," he said carefully, "you'll have to ask Elizabeth's permission for some of that." He parked the car.

Sam leaned over between the two front seats. "Can I?"

Elizabeth turned to him briefly, then looked out the front window. "Well, who are 'the girls'?" she asked.

Ryan thought he saw color rising in her face.

"Chloe and Lily, my sisters," Sam answered matter-of-factly.

Her eyebrows rose, and she gave Sam a sideways glance. "Sure, you can tell them." She swallowed.

"Yesss!"

"Hey, bud?"

"Yeah, Dad?"

"Run on home and get cleaned up. I've got to help Elizabeth inside."

"Okay, Dad. Bye, Elizabeth."

"Bye, Sam. It was nice to meet you."

As Sam climbed out of the backseat, Ryan said, "Hey, bud, don't forget you're grounded. No TV, no gaming."

Sam slowed only slightly. "I know." He shut the door and took off running down the road to his own house.

Ryan watched him, then his eyes rested on Elizabeth's profile as she looked down, her lips pursed. He tapped his finger on the steering wheel. The concern he felt about her thoughts surprised and frustrated him because he knew what was coming. She opened her mouth to speak, pushing a loose lock of hair behind her ear.

"So, you have . . . three . . . children?" She was trying to sound nonchalant.

"Yes." He was careful.

"And . . . Sam is the oldest?"

"No. Chloe is fifteen. Lily is six."

She nodded slowly and looked down again. "Pretty names. Jeff told me about . . . your wife . . . How long ago . . . ?"

That was the look he'd seen on her face back there. She knew. He swallowed. "Five years."

She looked up at him, mild surprise on her face. Then she looked past him. "Well, I guess if the youngest is six . . . So she was only a year when . . . ?"

He nodded.

"Can I ask how it happened?"

He looked out the windshield and tapped his finger on the steering wheel again. He took a breath and let it go. "We were coming home, the two of us. The roads were icy . . . an oncoming car hit a patch and swerved, then hit dry, and the car tipped up, rolled end over end . . . We hit ice . . . I couldn't —" He sucked in more air. "The car collided with her side . . ." It had been awhile since anyone had asked.

She was quiet for a moment. "I'm sorry."

He nodded.

"And . . . you're doing this alone . . . I mean, there hasn't been . . . anyone . . . ?"

He shook his head.

She moved the hair off her face again. "I'm sorry; I'm asking personal questions here."

"That's all right." It was, but he was on guard. He waited for the inevitable.

"It's so hard, to lose them like that . . ." she said so quietly he could barely hear her, and she trailed off. She looked around as if waking from sleep. "I, uh, really need to shower, and I'm supposed to be at the shop. I mean, Nancy will understand." She looked toward the inn. "I slept in . . . I missed breakfast . . ."

Ryan looked out the windshield. "I'll have something sent up to your room."

"Oh, you don't have to do that."

He looked at her and forced a smile. "It's the least I can do. What with you dropping the lawsuit and all." He raised his eyebrows.

She breathed out a nervous laugh, then sobered. "Thank you."

He met her eyes and nodded. "Do you need help inside?" He knew the answer.

"Oh, no thanks. Really, I'm fine. You go be with Sam." She smiled as she opened her door and stepped out. "I'll see you."

He nodded. "Yup."

She closed the door and walked to the front door of the inn. He watched her hand come up to her forehead.

He started the truck and backed out, then turned up the road.

What was I thinking? What is this pull? She's not even my type. Who knows what kind of girl she is? He tried to think what his type was. His heart lurched when he remembered. He swallowed the knot in his throat.

She wasn't a member of the Church. *She is a daughter of God.*

She wasn't motherly. *She hadn't been thinking of herself on the embankment.* Images of her easy conversation with Sam came to mind. He brushed them away. Sam was that way with everyone.

She was . . . she was a snob. *You have your own walls too.*

He didn't even know if she'd ever been married before or . . .

"She was quite the party girl, if you know what I mean."

He shook his head. He didn't know *anything* about her, and he shouldn't be letting himself even consider . . .

No.

He pulled up to the front of his house. His kids had *him*. He looked at the log cabin. Wasn't that enough? Hadn't he had enough love with one person to last a brief lifetime? His chest felt suddenly heavy. He breathed hard. No, it hadn't been enough. But it was what he'd been given.

He got out of the truck and shut the door.

Strong walls.

He checked the mail and walked into the house. Maybe bills would remind him of reality. Sam came out of the hallway in a new shirt, and his hair was combed.

"Hey, Dad."

"Hey." Ryan thumbed through the letters and junk mail.

"Elizabeth is really nice."

"Mm-hmm."

"And *really* pretty."

Ryan looked at his son. He gave him a smile and nodded a little.

"Is it weird that . . . I'm kind of glad we ran her over?"

Ryan's eyebrows came up, and he swallowed. "You know she's just a guest."

Sam grinned sheepishly. "Yeah, I know."

"Okay."

"She was just"—Sam looked in the direction of the inn—"really nice."

* * *

Ryan walked without being aware of his movements, his footsteps matching the erratic beat of his heart. He was shaken and disturbed and disoriented. The narrow trail through the underbrush led him to a quiet place where he could sit and think as his hands ran along the smooth beams and he looked vacantly at the water and woods.

He looked down at his hands in his lap. He stared for several minutes, then took a tortured breath. As he breathed out, the pain in his chest deepened . . . and then he couldn't breathe. After several seconds, he took another aching breath and felt the burning in his eyes, the tears coming. His fingers pressed against his closed lids, but his shoulders jerked up and down. Giving up, he let the emotion take over.

After several minutes, he wiped his sleeve across his face and blinked, trying to regain his focus, to see the woods. Something about the woods always brought him peace. He took a deep breath of the autumn air and rested his head back.

How can I . . . ? He couldn't finish the question. He tried again. He closed his eyes, a rogue tear escaping. *How in the world am I supposed to . . . ?* He dropped his head as it whirled with questions and phrases of conviction and images of long ago and now . . . the faces of his kids and the woman he had loved them with . . . the woman he'd never stopped loving. He looked up. "Why?" It was not a bitter question; it was searching.

After a few minutes, he shook his head. "Not that it matters now any—"

She needs you.

He stopped all thought.

She needs you.

He tried to deny it. He thought about his kids' needs. He already had enough needs to attend to. He shook his head again. *It's enough. I can do this alone. I am doing this alone.*

He looked again at the woods, focusing on the gurgle of the low river around the rocks, the slight brush of overhanging branches and grass as they played with the passing water beneath them. He was filled with a sudden calm, a familiar warmth shimmering over his skin, over his hands. The knot in his chest loosened. He sat motionless, some awareness inside of him wanting the feeling to stay.

You are not alone. And you need her.

He swallowed, and the feeling drifted away as gently as the aspen leaves on the water. "Brooke," he whispered.

Chapter 10

ELIZABETH'S HEAD ACHED, AND SHE didn't know if the knot in her stomach was hunger or anxiety. She gave a small wave and a weak smile to Jeff at the front desk and went straight up to her room. She shook her head at herself, knowing how she must have looked to Ryan. She opened her door and immediately felt a sense of quiet.

She found a couple of Tylenol in her purse, filled a glass with water, and drank it down, remembering there had been a time when she really *would* have called her father, throwing a fit about liability and compensation. She set down the glass and looked in the mirror. A short laugh escaped her. A smudge of dirt highlighted one cheek, and a small leaf stuck out from her disheveled ponytail.

Rapidly, her look changed from amusement to confusion. Who was she? What did this person in the mirror *want*? Was she too *afraid* to have it? Was that what it boiled down to?

She rolled her eyes as they became wet. Wasn't this supposed to be a *getaway*? What—a getaway from everything safe and known and valued in her life?

She looked in the mirror again.

You're more than you think you are.

She shook her head. *I'm not enough.* She felt a warmth around her waist, where he had held her. She shook her head again. *Three kids.* She closed her eyes, and a tear rolled down her face. *A wife he loved.*

Impossible.

She looked down at her hands and remembered. *I calmed him.* She knew she had. She had seen it . . . his shaking hands weren't from nerves. He'd been reliving a portion of the past, and her only thought had been to help him out of that. *And it had worked.*

You're more than you think you are.

She shook her head. This is crazy. Why was she thinking this way?

No.

She turned to start the water, making it extra hot.

She sighed, remembering his hands.

Her thoughts turned unexpectedly to Travis. He was so much more like her. If he weren't still married . . . It would be so much easier if . . .

* * *

Elizabeth went to answer the soft knock at the door, basically dressed, her hair still wet but brushed. She looked in the peephole before opening the door.

After a brief hesitation, she opened it.

"I heard you had a rough morning." Dayle stood there smiling sympathetically, holding a tray of food.

Elizabeth's eyes were drawn first to a small bouquet of white flowers in a perfectly round glass vase. Twigs of leaves and small red berries were interspersed here and there, hanging down over the glass. "Oh," was all she could think to say.

She stepped aside, and Dayle walked past, setting the tray on a small table near the french doors. "I know you like those smoothies, but I figured after this morning, you might want something more . . . substantial." Dayle sniffed the air. "Something smells wonderful in here."

"Oh, it's a fragrance from Nancy's shop."

"Well, it smells really good."

Elizabeth eyed the food. She could see french toast, sliced strawberries, blueberries, a fluffy little pile of scrambled eggs, a dish of hash browns, and a glass of orange juice next to a mug of what looked like hot cocoa. There were also little cups of syrup, cream, and ketchup. "*That* smells wonderful." She turned to Dayle. "Thank you. Really."

Dayle smiled up at her. "Sure, honey. It's the least I could do after one of our owners runs you off the side of the road."

Elizabeth paused, unsure how to talk to room service staff who called her "honey." "Um, will you sit down?"

Dayle looked a little surprised but gladly pulled out a chair. "Thank you." She lowered herself with a sigh.

Elizabeth joined Dayle at the table and picked up a fork, placing a napkin in her lap. She tried to remember the last time she'd had a real breakfast as she put a forkful of french toast in her mouth. *Mmm . . . too long.*

Dayle looked out at the view, but her gaze moved to the flowers.

Elizabeth swallowed her bite. "They're beautiful. Thank you."

"Oh, they're not from me, honey."

Hesitantly, Elizabeth reached for the small card tucked underneath the vase, and Dayle rose from her chair as if to get a better look out the windows.

"Are you enjoying your room?"

Elizabeth opened the envelope and drew out the card. "Yes. It's lovely, thank you." She looked up. "I actually wouldn't mind just spending the day in here."

Dayle nodded, smiling back. "Good." She looked around. "I think that's what Ryan had in mind when he designed this room. It's the honeymoon suite."

Elizabeth paused. A *honeymoon* suite. Of course. It was perfect. She swallowed, suddenly more aware of the romance of the room. He'd thought of everything. She dropped her gaze. "He must have . . . loved her very much." The thought was pasted around the room, in every hint of embracing the start of a life together.

Dayle dropped her hand from the curtain she'd been fingering. She leaned her head to the side and nodded. "When she was snatched away like that, it left him reeling. I'm not sure he knew how to live without her. But those three kids . . . well, they saved him."

Elizabeth looked away, wondering for an instant if Dayle could read her thoughts, her fears.

Then Dayle took a deep breath. "Well, I hope you enjoy your breakfast. And I hope your day goes a *whole* lot better." Elizabeth made a move to get up. Dayle put out a hand and smiled. "I'll let myself out."

Elizabeth watched her. Did these things *always* happen at a bed and breakfast? "Thank you, Dayle."

"Sure, honey." She closed the door.

Elizabeth stared after her, unnerved by what this place was doing to her. She still held the card, unread. On the front was a tiny watercolor image of the inn, the lantern glowing brightly above the entry. She opened the card.

I'm so sorry. About everything.
I would have told you.

I know I would have.
Ryan

Her heart seemed to pitch. A man of few words. He knew she'd been caught off guard, that finding out he had kids—*three* of them—had been alarming, that there was something to this . . . acquaintance? Friendship? She blew out a tremulous breath.

She wasn't out of this yet. She still didn't see how it could possibly . . . She still had her fears, and they weren't small. But he'd said there hadn't been anyone else, and if he was feeling *something* for *her*, well . . . didn't that say something? So somehow, she wasn't out. And she was scared to death.

She went to the bedside table and opened the drawer. She pulled out the phone book and found the number, then stared at the phone for a full three minutes. Finally, she entered the number.

"Hello." At the sound of his voice, her heartbeat took off.

"Hello . . . Ryan?" Her voice was quiet. *Ugh. Be strong.*

There was a pause. "Yes?" He was quieter too.

"It's Elizabeth . . . Embry." She swallowed. "You know, from the side of the road? You, uh, checked my eyes with a flashlight." She squeezed her eyes shut.

"Um, yes." He laughed softly. "I remember."

She breathed. "Well, I wanted to thank you . . . for the flowers."

He was quiet.

"And the card. Thank you."

"You're welcome."

She could sense his need to know more, but she didn't know how to say it. Her mind raced. "So, I'll see you?"

He spoke again. "Will you?" He sounded as uncertain as she felt.

She smiled though, knowing what he meant, feeling the heat rise in her cheeks. "There seems to be no avoiding it."

* * *

Nancy threw down her pen and took off her bifocals. "That's it. Are you sure he didn't hit you on the head?"

Elizabeth furrowed her brow and gingerly felt around her head. "No, I don't *think* so . . . Wait . . . Where am I? Who are you?"

They were back in the office going over books, inventory lists, and the favorite clothiers Nancy ordered from. Elizabeth had brought up Ryan to Nancy only to explain her lateness. Otherwise, she was avoiding that subject at all costs.

"Well, you're fidgeting, and you never fidget. And I asked you the same question twice, and you're staring off into the far reaches of the universe."

Elizabeth tried to look as innocent as possible. "I'm . . . just thinking about what we're going to do tonight." She widened her eyes. "What part of Jackson are you going to show me next?"

Nancy narrowed her eyes at her. "Well, I'll tell you so you can concentrate. We're taking you to the museum tonight, then dinner." She reached for her glasses and put them back on but peered over the lenses at Elizabeth. "All right?"

Elizabeth smiled. "That sounds great."

Nancy pulled some catalogs up from a file. "That reminds me," she said, still looking down. "When we break for lunch, I need to take you shopping."

"What for?"

"Darling, do you *ever* need a reason to go shopping?"

Elizabeth grinned. "I meant, why during lunch?"

Nancy looked up. "Because Ryan said to be sure you had some good shoes." She smiled and didn't say more.

"Why would—what?" As much as she wanted to know what Nancy meant, she didn't want to encourage further discussion about Ryan.

Nancy looked down and started humming to herself. Elizabeth narrowed *her* eyes. She really needed to get a look at that itinerary.

She heard the bell ring.

"You get it, dear," Nancy said. "I'm going to reorganize this mess so we can get on to other things."

Elizabeth got up and walked toward the front of the store. "Hello. May I help you?"

The woman turned and smiled. She held the hand of a little boy, and the way her jacket fell open around her, Elizabeth could see she was expecting.

"Oh, thank you. I'm actually looking for something for my mother for her birthday."

Elizabeth looked around. "Well, we have plenty to choose from. We have new winter accessories over here, and don't forget to look at our fragrance collection. If you have any questions, feel free to ask."

She could feel a little pair of eyes on her and looked down at the small boy peeking around his mother's legs. She raised her eyebrows, and he disappeared. She breathed a laugh and walked behind the counter, where she picked up some of the boutique's tags to run lengths of fine jute cord through the punched holes. It was busy work, and her mind went back to where it had been since she'd read Ryan's card that morning.

Her eyes strayed to the woman and her little boy. His shyness was starting to wear off, and he was beginning to play hide-and-seek in the clothes.

"Levi, stop that." His mother kept her voice soft, and the boy giggled. She showed him something Elizabeth couldn't see. "Do you think Grandma would like this one?"

The boy came out of the clothes. He nodded his head, and his mother showed him something else.

"Or this one?"

He tilted his head, his finger going to his mouth. He shrugged.

"Well, which one is your favorite?"

The boy looked, then pointed. "That one."

"I think it's my favorite too."

He looked proud of himself. She continued around the room, and he followed her, touching things here and there, a pearl button, a fuzzy scarf, a shiny boot. Elizabeth smiled. He reminded her of the television shows she'd watched as a child as he explored the textures, humming a little song. She hadn't thought of those shows in a long time.

Finally, the woman came to the counter and set a scarf, hat, and gloves down, along with an enameled pin with a robin on it.

"Oh, these are beautiful." Elizabeth held up the scarf with a small paisley print swirling in plum, chestnut, and red tones. She folded it neatly and scanned the tag. "Does your mother have the same coloring as you?" she asked the woman, glancing at her brown wavy hair loosely pulled back.

She smiled. "Yes."

"Perfect." Elizabeth peeked over to the boy. "You picked out a pretty one." He disappeared behind his mother's legs again, but Elizabeth caught his smile. She scanned the other items and wrapped them in tissue.

The woman paid, and Elizabeth looked at her again. She hesitated. Then she asked, "I'm sorry, but do I know you?"

The woman looked at Elizabeth, searching. "Hmm. I don't think so. Did you go to school here?"

Elizabeth shook her head. "Montana, then New York. I've only been here a few days, but . . . you just look familiar."

The woman stuck out her hand and smiled. "I'm Nora Dalton."

Elizabeth reached across and took her hand. "Elizabeth Embry."

The woman smiled broadly. "It's nice to meet you." She reached around and placed her hand on the little boy's head, running her fingers through his hair. "This is Levi. He's not as shy as he looks." He grinned a toothy grin up at his mother. "What brings you to Jackson?"

"My friend owns this shop. She's asked me to be her partner."

"So you're staying?"

Elizabeth looked past the woman, out the door at the sunlight and the vivid red trees lining the walks. She began to nod her head. "I think so." As she said it, she couldn't help smiling, and she felt a little silly that the smile was so big. She rolled her eyes. "Not completely sure yet, but . . . I'm enjoying it so far." *In an emotional, havoc-wreaking sort of way.*

Nora laughed pleasantly. "Well, good. We love it here."

"How long have you been here?"

She shrugged. "My whole life. I went away to college, I guess." Her eyes gleamed, and Levi started to tug on her hand. "But it's a special place . . . and to be able to come back here, well . . . I feel very blessed."

Elizabeth nodded. She could understand that already.

"Do you know many people here?"

"No, not many. Nancy . . ."

"Nancy Colette? Oh, she's a crack-up."

"You know her?"

"Just from coming in here. She's great though."

"She's one of my best friends, so at least I have her here."

Nora looked at her for a second as if deciding something. She set the bag down, choosing to let go of that instead of Levi, who was pulling harder at her hand, and removed a card from the purse over her shoulder. She grabbed a pen from the counter and wrote her first name and a phone number and handed it to Elizabeth. "We're having a get-together with some friends at our house on Saturday night. It would be a great chance for you to meet some really fun people. Call me if you're interested because I would love to have you. Okay?" She smiled.

Elizabeth's eyebrows came up as she looked at the card. "Thank you. I'm flattered."

Levi gave a particularly strong yank on Nora's arm.

"Levi. *Stop.*" Nora shook her head at Elizabeth. "Do you have children?"

Elizabeth chuckled and shook her head.

"Well . . . it's a lot of *fun*, let me tell you." The word *fun* came out jerkily because of another tug. "Mar–*ried?*"

"No." Elizabeth muffled a laugh.

Nora gave up and looked down at Levi. "Okay, let's go." She turned back to Elizabeth. "It was so nice to meet you, Elizabeth. I know where to find you." She opened the door and ushered Levi out, scolding him again for pulling on her arm. "If people saw me yanking on your arm, they would think I was a mean mommy. What do you think they think when they see you yanking on my arm?"

"That I want to go home." The door closed with a jingle.

Elizabeth smiled, shaking her head. She looked down at the card and flipped it over. *Dalton Woodworks & Log Homes, David Dalton.*

"Hmm."

She walked to the back of the store and into the office.

"Who was that? You were chatty."

"Nora Dalton." She handed Nancy the card, and she looked at it, then handed it back. "She said she's talked to you a few times here in the store."

"What does she look like?"

"About five foot four, reddish-brown hair, pretty . . . She's expecting."

Nancy's eyes showed recognition. "Did she have a darling little boy with her that you just wanted to smoosh?"

Elizabeth gave her a quizzical look. "Well, I don't know about the smooshing part, but, yes, that was her."

"Oh, she is so nice. Did you make a friend?"

Elizabeth hadn't thought about kindergarten in a long time, but this was twice in one day. "I don't know, but she said she knew where to find me if she wanted to go out and play on the swings."

The back door opened, and they both turned their heads. Marisol came whistling into the doorway of the office. Her hair was piled up on top of her head today, and once again, Elizabeth was dazzled by her unaffected good looks. "Hello, ladies. I am here to relieve you for lunch and shopping. Did you know it was snowing? Just a little; I don't think it will stay, but when do we get to start playing the Christmas songs, Nancy? When it snows, for some reason, I want to hear Christmas music. Can you believe it is already October? We should put out something Halloween-ish in the displays. Hmm." Her gaze drifted off. Then she came back with her dazzling smile. "Well, have fun at lunch." She swung away to the front of the store, humming "Jingle Bells," and the bell rang as another customer came in.

Nancy turned to Elizabeth, smiling mysteriously. "Shoe-shopping time."

Elizabeth returned to the inn that evening holding several sporting goods bags.

Ryan worked steadily at the computer as she came in. She stopped only briefly, wondering if she should say something but decided not to disturb him and started up the stairs.

"Eight a.m."

She turned. Ryan looked up at her.

"Eight a.m.?" she asked.

He nodded. "No run."

She looked back steadily and ignored the little race of her heart. "No run."

He turned back to his computer, a small grin playing at his mouth.

Her turn. "Green smoothie?"

He turned back to her. The grin had spread. "Green smoothie."

Chapter 11

ELIZABETH LACED UP HER NEW hiking shoes. She had opted for the running style, thinking she could use them on her own runs in the woods. Yesterday, the guy at the store had promised they would hold up to this weather.

Did Ryan's wife like to hike? She held her stomach as a small knot twisted at the thought that had seemed to come out of nowhere. She shook her head, looking outside as she tied her laces. So what if she had? She probably liked a lot of things. Elizabeth shook her head once more and cleared the unsolicited thoughts from her mind.

Marisol had been right. It hadn't snowed much, just a scattering of tiny flakes that melted before they hit the still-warm ground. Elizabeth stood, smoothed her hands along the olive trail pants she'd chosen, and gave the zipper on her navy sweatshirt a tug. She'd layered, just as suggested, even her socks to avoid blisters.

It hadn't been far into the sales pitch when Elizabeth had figured out she would be hiking today with one of Ryan's groups. She had argued with Nancy that it was a Friday and she could work.

"Work shmirk. You're here trying us on for size, and I don't run a sweat shop."

Elizabeth didn't know anything more than the time they were meeting at the front desk. She stepped to the french doors of her room and opened them so she could step onto the small balcony. The air had turned crisp overnight. The sun wasn't quite up yet, and the sky was gray. She shivered, even in her jacket, but knew she would warm up quickly on the hike. She looked down to the river and drew in a breath.

A large moose walked along the river's edge, followed by another smaller, leggy moose. They would take a few steps, then pause to pull at aspen leaves or nibble around the muddy bank.

An excitement stirred her. Elizabeth went back inside, grabbed her key, hat, and gloves, and left her room. She jogged down the stairs and turned down the hall, only to collide with a figure and bounce back half a step. Her hand came up to her mouth as she caught the startled look on Ryan's face.

* * *

"Oh. Sorry," she whispered.

Ryan hadn't even seen her coming. She was smiling, her eyebrows up. Was she flushed?

"Are you all right?" he asked. Man, she smelled good.

She grabbed his arm, which was a surprise in itself, then pulled past him. "C'mon." She led him to the back doors, carefully opened them, and pulled him through. She brought her finger up to her lips and looked down to the river.

He watched. Her. She released his arm and took slow steps to the second deck, where she sat down on a bench. She looked behind her and caught him watching. Her expression sobered and warmed, then she dropped her eyes.

He found the moose, walked over, and she looked up with a smile again. He smiled back, sat down, and watched with her for a few quiet minutes. The moose slowly meandered away into the woods, and Ryan turned to Elizabeth.

She looked a little sheepish. "It's been awhile." She sighed. "What is it about this place that makes me feel like a kid again?"

"You grew up in Montana, right?"

A look of chagrin flitted across her eyes, but she nodded. "Yes, but I've forgotten some things. Like the woods."

"How is that possible?" He tried to imagine forgetting something like the view in front of him.

She looked away, and he didn't press. "Let's get some breakfast."

She followed him, and he pulled the door open for her.

She paused in the hall, and he said, "Kitchen." And they made their way down the hall and to the left.

* * *

Dayle stirred batter next to a large griddle already sizzling with bacon. Jeff came out of the walk-in refrigerator, arms loaded with various ingredients. A big slab of bacon sat on a tray on the butcher-block island, and he dumped everything next to it, then pulled out another cutting board. He grabbed some peppers and tomatoes and took them over to the big stainless-steel sink.

Ryan came around the island, grabbing some tongs to start turning bacon. He reached for a large cookie sheet, lined it with paper towels, and set it on the counter next to the bacon. Without hesitation, he turned to the island and deftly started slicing mushrooms out of a blue foam container.

"Thanks, son. Here." Jeff placed the clean vegetables next to him on the butcher block and started to grate the cheese from the pile of ingredients. They continued in this manner as Dayle ladled pancake batter onto the greased griddle. Ryan was halfway into chopping onions when Elizabeth let out a small sneeze.

"Bless you." Ryan looked at her with a smile as Jeff stopped mid egg-break and Dayle whirled around with her spatula.

"Where did *you* come from?" Jeff's surprised expression mirrored Dayle's, and Ryan laughed.

"She came in with me. You didn't know she was in here?"

"Well, you came in so quietly," Dayle said. She smiled at Elizabeth. "Good morning."

"I didn't mean to disturb you." She looked at Jeff as Dayle turned back to flipping. "I came down early to see the moose. I saw them from my room."

"They were out there, huh? I'm glad you got to see them." Jeff continued to crack eggs, and Ryan scraped the onions into a bowl with the mushrooms and peppers, then started on the tomatoes.

"This is amazing. I've been mesmerized watching you." Elizabeth laughed to herself. "It's like a dance."

Jeff finished the eggs and went to throw the shells away and wash his hands. "We've been doing this a *long* time. Isn't that right, sugar?"

Dayle nodded and put her hand on her hip, thinking. "Has it been thirty-five years?" She looked at Ryan. "Yes. Ryan was two when we started. Oh, that was a tough beginning. Doing this with a toddler running around. Mm-mm." She turned away again and started piling pancakes on a platter.

Elizabeth glanced at Ryan. Thirty-seven.

She could hear people coming down and milling around now. Ryan finished the tomatoes as Jeff started beating the eggs with the biggest whisk she had ever seen. She spied the block of cheese. "Would you like me to finish grating the cheese for you?"

Ryan looked up at her. "That would be great, actually. I need to go see who's ready to eat."

She went to the sink to wash her hands, and Ryan joined her. Standing close, she wasn't sure why, but as she rinsed and dried, then he followed, they were both grinning, and she laughed softly, shaking her head. She turned to the cheese and started grating, and he headed out the doorway, both of them with stupid grins on their faces.

Jeff opened a large cupboard and brought out two large frying pans. After setting them on the gas burners, he leaned over and gave Dayle a kiss, which she happily returned. Elizabeth brushed away the momentary feeling of embarrassment. This was *their* kitchen.

Jeff came over and gently mixed the vegetables Ryan had chopped. He divided them between the two frying pans, and as he returned for the bowl of eggs, Ryan came back.

"Four full plates, three omelet only, four pancakes and bacon only. Six OJs, and the Franks would like their bran muffins. And they'll need more decaf out there in a minute."

As he gave these orders, Dayle pulled out plates and set them on the one counter yet to be used in groupings of four, three, and four and handed two smaller plates to Ryan. She reached up for juice glasses. Jeff put the lids on the frying pans, turning down the heat on the omelets, and the two of them started filling plates with pancakes and bacon.

Ryan set the dishes down and pulled out a colander of strawberries, and with a new knife, sliced them nearly to the tops, then fanned them out. He did more than a dozen of these as Elizabeth finished up the cheese. He went to a glass-fronted cooler and pulled out two large, wrapped brown muffins. As they warmed in the microwave, he placed a strawberry on each plate. He grabbed a tray and started loading it with filled plates, adding more strawberries as needed.

As he left the kitchen, Jeff came over and took the plate of grated cheese. "Thank you, Elizabeth."

"Oh, sure. You couldn't have done it without me."

He winked at her and turned to the omelets.

She went to the sink and rinsed her hands once more. After she dried them, she turned around to find Ryan leaning back against the end of the butcher block with his arms folded. He looked a little smug.

"What?" she asked.

"Green smoothie?"

She looked around the room, breathing in the smells. She shook her head. "No way." She smiled back at him.

* * *

In a closet under the staircase, outdoor gear hung from hooks and lay piled on low shelves. From behind Ryan, Elizabeth saw snowshoes, skis and poles, boots, climbing harnesses and ropes, helmets, several pairs of snow boots and bibs, some backpacks of different sizes, and a tricycle. He closed the door of the safe. Grabbing a few items, he turned around, walked past her, and headed out of the kitchen toward the front room. She followed.

He deposited his cache on one of the big chairs in front of the tall windows and turned to hand Elizabeth a small day pack. She paused, then took it from him, hefting the weight. Peeking inside, she saw a small first-aid kit, a few survival items, two water bottles, some energy bars, and a flashlight.

She looked at Ryan. "Thank you."

He nodded and held out two ski poles. At least, they looked like ski poles.

"What are these for?"

"Hiking. It's a great cardio workout, and it's easier on the knees."

She raised an eyebrow at him, and he smiled. "Trust me."

She took them and held one in each hand. As she looked back up, he was strapping on a holster with a handgun in the pocket.

"What's *that* for?"

He turned, pulling a jacket over the gun. "Bears," he answered simply. She swallowed but blinked and nodded.

"So is this." He pointed to a medium-sized canister hanging on his belt loop. "You never know."

The small knot in her stomach tightened again. Ryan reached over and put his hand on her arm. "Hey, it'll be okay. Trust me."

She took a deep breath and nodded. He looked at her curiously.

"Is . . . anybody else coming with us?" she asked.

"The Holidays were going to come, but with the colder weather, they decided to drive into the park."

"Oh." She bit her lip. Part of her was glad; part was wary. Generally, she didn't like guns. Or bears. Or being alone with a man she barely knew and had growing feelings for. She shook her head in frustration at herself and searched his gentle, concerned eyes. "Okay."

He watched her for another moment, swung his backpack on, and placed his hands on either side of his mouth.

"Can I have everyone's attention?" he called in a booming voice.

Elizabeth looked around quickly as people down in the dining area stopped shuffling around—the Franks, who were playing cards in the room with them, looked over, and his parents poked their heads out of the kitchen. Elizabeth's head came up as two doors above opened, and the tenants peeked over the railing. What was he doing?

"I am taking Miss Embry on a hike up Two Ponies Trail. I am taking proper defenses against bears, and I have a walkie-talkie with a ten-mile range. My father, Jeff, has the other one. We should return within four hours. If we are not back before then, send someone out to look for us. Thank you. That is all."

She could only stare at the long, polished counter across the entry. She heard amused murmurs and some wishes of "Good luck" and "Have a good time" and "Don't get eaten." She slowly turned to look at Ryan.

He was watching her, a half smile on his face. "Feel better?"

Her eyebrows came up, and she said a little shakily, "Oh, yes. Thank you."

He took her poles and backpack from her, turned her around, and slipped the pack up her arms. She shrugged it onto her shoulders, clipped the front, and turned back to him. He gave her the poles, grabbed his from the side of the chair, and opened the front door, holding it for her. "We'll be okay," he said.

Elizabeth shivered in the cool air and pulled her hat and gloves from her pockets. She remembered his hand carefully going over hers on the side of the road. She pulled her hat on. "Let's go," she said.

* * *

She walked past him and out the door. The gray of the early morning had lightened to a pale blue sky. He joined her, and they descended the porch stairs, the smell of damp earth and pine filling her nostrils.

"How do you use these things?" She tried a few strides, naturally falling into a rhythm with the hiking poles.

"Like that." He took the lead around the side of the inn and paused at a small trailhead. "We'll have to cross the river, but there are some good rocks at a wider part a little farther down. This is our trail here, but it leads up to one of the forest trails about a mile on."

She nodded.

They followed the river south for a while. He pointed ahead and up toward the road. "That's my place up there."

She peered at the back of the house, a wide log cabin. A high deck ran the entire width. She could see an eating area with a grill and some Adirondack furniture. The cabin had been built on a slope, and a daylight basement lay tucked underneath the upper deck. A small lawn stretched down to meet the woods. At the edge of the yard, a large old pine tree supported the weight of a rustic tree house, complete with a ladder and swing hanging from one of the old limbs.

"We built that over there last spring."

She looked where he pointed. A trail left the lawn and wound its way toward the river. Then, through the trees, she could see a small gazebo built in a clearing just above the water.

"Oh, how pretty," she said, rising up on her toes for a better view.

"Chloe wanted that. I think she was getting too big for the tree house. She sits out there, does her homework . . . She calls it her thinking spot."

Elizabeth dropped back down. "It's nice. The whole place." It was a family place, she thought. The little knot hiccupped.

They moved on and were cutting over to the riverbank now. He began placing his feet carefully but surely on the large rocks staggered across this shallow portion of the water, using his poles to balance. She followed, choosing the same rocks he had. He checked behind him on occasion, and soon, she made a little jump off the final rock, and they were across.

They went on, and Ryan picked up the pace. The trail was narrow but smooth and was edged with fallen logs and upturned roots, the remaining flowers of late summer, and the mottled red leaves of the berry bushes. Elizabeth could see the sky through the silhouettes of the tall pines and the flash of quivering aspen leaves, like coins glinting in the sun. The sound of the river became distant, but her senses sharpened to the chatter of small animals. She breathed deeply, filling her lungs with the forest air.

She was sure that if she were alone out here, she would be afraid. There was power here, in the height of the trees, the sound of the wind, the rush of the water, the strength of the rocks, the age of the forest. Here, a person could easily feel small and powerless. She shuddered. She didn't want to think that way.

She took a few quick steps closer to Ryan. She *wasn't* alone out here. And she trusted Ryan.

As if reading her thoughts, he slowed and turned. "Are you all right?" he asked.

She nodded. "It's beautiful . . . and . . . timeless."

He looked at her steadily. "Mm-hmm."

"But . . . it's powerful too."

Ryan nodded. "Deceptively." He was giving her that look again. Like he was trying to figure her out.

She blinked and looked away.

"The main trail is just up here. We'll head north for a while. The climb is gradual but steady."

"Okay."

"Elizabeth."

She turned her gaze to him. He was studying her again, making her heart stammer. She couldn't seem to settle her nerves. He took a step toward her, and she steadied herself.

He lowered his voice. "If you don't feel comfortable, we can go back."

She blinked. "Oh." She bit her lip. "No, please. I'm fine."

He raised his eyebrows, looking doubtful.

"Really. I . . . I like this. I've forgotten the feel of the woods. It's good that you're with me." She straightened up, gripping her poles. "This is good for me."

He narrowed his eyes at her, but the look was gentle.

Gray flannel, she thought. *His eyes are like gray flannel.*

A corner of his mouth came up. Now she did feel like he could read her mind.

Chapter 12

THEY WERE UP HIGHER NOW, and Ryan could again hear water nearby. Elizabeth had removed her gloves, and he had stowed his jacket in his pack. They had spoken very little, and though he was fine with the quiet, he fought the urge to ask her questions, to find out everything he could about her, to figure out this pull he had toward her and then maybe understand what the heck he was supposed to do about it.

He knew only a handful of things about Elizabeth Embry. And he had about a million *guesses* about her. She'd been hurt. She seemed to be rediscovering a forgotten love of this natural beauty and her childhood. She was either ashamed or very protective of her past, whatever kind of past that was. He hadn't seen much of the woman Travis had described, though Elizabeth had hinted at it that night on the stairs. And she was searching, at a crossroads, wondering. She was afraid.

That girl is alone.

She'd been so guarded. Walls. He knew those. They were what kept him from asking her questions. But here she was, even after she'd learned he was a package deal. Her defenses had lowered to a degree. He wasn't sure about his. He wasn't sure about much. He was just . . . trying.

He saw the place and veered off the main trail, pushing through the overgrowth. This new trail was barely visible.

"Ryan?"

"Yes?"

"Where are we going?"

"I want to show you something . . . just a little farther up." He turned as she slowed. "It's just something I found one day out here." She was stopped, looking at the main trail.

He leaned on his walking poles. "It has to do with what we talked about the other day at the park."

She furrowed her brow, still not moving.

"You'll like it. I promise."

She pulled in a breath and blew it out. "Okay. Show me."

She was trusting him, and he counted it a small victory. He could hear the water as they neared the spot. The small bluff came into view, overgrown with bracken. He took a few steps around the bend, then stepped aside.

He heard her pause, and he smiled to himself.

Ryan looked up twenty feet, where the water rushed softly over the rocky ledge.

"Of course, it's bigger in the spring, but . . ." He shrugged.

"It's lovely," she breathed. She stepped around him and leaned to touch a bare hand to the falling water.

He held her other arm, and she looked back at him. "Just in case." He gave her a patronizing look.

She grinned and continued holding her hand under the freezing water, feeling the force of it pressing down. She ran her fingers over tall grasses bending in clumps as the water flowed over them. Finally, she pulled away and wiped her hand on her pants.

He still held her arm. "Hand cold?" It had reddened in the icy water.

She looked up at him, nodding. "Thanks for showing me."

He reached into his pack and brought out a small towel and a hand warmer. "How is it feeling since the truck incident?"

"Good. It's fine."

"Yeah, sure."

She smiled and dried her hand, and he carefully helped her put the hand warmer in her glove. He felt her gaze while he worked. He didn't mind.

They watched the water a few minutes more, then he turned back the way they'd come.

"C'mon. We're not done."

She picked up her poles and followed him.

About thirty minutes later, they came to a clearing against a rocky portion of the rise.

"Ryan? Can we stop here for a minute?"

Her eyes were bright, and her cheeks pink. He nodded, and she pulled off her backpack and one glove and took out a water bottle. She drank half of it, then looked around her. A large boulder rose out of the ground near the trail. She walked over, set her poles down, and climbed the rock, standing tall, looking at the descent behind them.

He took off his backpack and headed over. She smiled down at him. He took out some water and stepped up onto the rock. Tapping her shoulder with his water bottle, he gestured upward, and she looked.

"Is that a golden eagle?"

"Yup."

They watched it fly in a couple of circles and move higher. Elizabeth turned north to follow it and caught her breath. He could see them too. The craggy peaks rose up one after the other. A fresh layer of snow lay in the clefts, and the midmorning sun reflected brilliantly. They seemed to loom just beyond the treetops, but he knew they were much farther away.

"They make you feel so small," she barely whispered. Then she laughed. "I was feeling pretty tall on this big rock." She shook her head at herself.

She sat down cross-legged, and Ryan looked down and sighed. He sat and stretched his legs out in front of him. He took a drink.

"You've always lived here?"

He hesitated and swallowed his gulp of water. He shook his head. "No."

She looked at him. "You went away for school?"

He nodded. "Yes. Flight school." He stared ahead but could feel her surprise. "I wanted to fly, so . . . I became a pilot." He looked at her.

"Just like that, huh?"

He chuckled. "Yeah. Just like that."

"So what did you do with that?"

"I flew planes."

Now she chuckled. "What kind of planes?"

His only hesitation in sharing this with her was that he knew where it would lead. But he continued. There was a part of him that wanted her to know. "I flew for United Airlines."

"You mean, big passenger airplanes?"

He set down his water bottle. "Yup. All over."

She took that in. "Were you . . . were you flying on 9/11?"

"Flying and praying. Of course, we were grounded for a time after that."

"I . . . I don't even need to ask. That must have been . . ."

"Mm-hmm."

She thought for a minute. "Is that why you stopped . . . ? Flying, I mean?"

"Nope."

"Nope?"

"Actually, I was anxious to get back in the air." He looked at her. "I wanted to show them we weren't beaten, you know?"

She nodded. She was really searching him now. She leaned back against her hands on the rock, her shoulder brushing his. "Then why did you stop flying?"

There it was, the question he knew would come and the answer he had to give her. "That's a tough question to answer . . . and an easy one too, I guess."

She waited. A breeze blew a few stray strands of her hair out from under her hat. He kept himself from reaching out and brushing them back.

"We were living in Salt Lake. When Brooke died . . . I, uh . . . couldn't justify leaving the kids. I just couldn't. I gave it up to be with them." He looked around, his brow furrowed. "It was my mom's suggestion to come here. To come home, run the inn, take over when they retire." He looked at her. "It just made sense."

She watched him with an unreadable expression. "Your wife . . . was she from here?"

He shook his head. He thought he sensed a masked look of relief. Maybe he understood it. "We were always so busy. We didn't visit as often as we should have." He looked away.

"What did she do?"

He looked at her again, wary of the way she bit her lip and watched the sky. He kept his answer simple. "She was at home with the kids, mostly. But she was a dancer and taught ballet lessons for a long time."

Elizabeth only nodded, pressing her lips together, and he watched one of her knees bounce. She took a deep breath and leaned forward, wrapping her arms around her knees. The posture made her look younger. Finally, she turned her face toward him again and played with a shoelace.

"Was it a good move, then? Coming here?"

He nodded. "Good for the kids."

"And you?"

"And me," he conceded.

"You miss flying though?"

He nodded, looking up. "I'd miss my kids more."

They sat there a little longer, and he got the impression she was waiting for more but wasn't going to push it.

"Sam is a great kid. Very likeable," she finally said.

"Yes, he is. They're all pretty great." He turned to meet her gaze and saw a trace of . . . worry.

She brushed her forehead with her hand.

It was his turn. This was the opening. She'd asked him questions, and he'd answered. And now he wasn't sure where to start.

"So tell me about—"

But she had stiffened, grabbing his jacket and pulling in a breath, whispering jaggedly, "Ryan . . ." Her gaze was fused to the trail they had climbed.

He looked in that direction, his stomach lurching, and then he shifted slowly, placing his body between hers and the bear's. His heart pounded in his ears, but he could still hear the grunt, the low growl. The grizzly was fifteen, twenty yards away, and it had seen them, smelled them. Ryan quickly analyzed the bear's rising silver ridge between muscular shoulders and its narrow eyes set in its broad skull above a long snout and bared teeth.

He barely moved his mouth. "Slowly, get behind the rock. Look down." He could feel her indecision and fear. He carefully reached for the bear spray, feeling the panic rising, but it was for *her*. He fought to keep his breathing steady. She was frozen. "Elle, please." Slowly, he felt her move, scooting away from him, still clutching his jacket, but then she let go, and her hand moved across his back.

She didn't get far when the bear lifted up on its hind legs and let out a territorial roar. Ryan felt his heart drop, and Elizabeth's hand gripped his shirt through his jacket, but he pulled the canister up and cocked the trigger as the bear dropped down with a ripple of muscle and weight and rushed him. Ryan aimed a jet of spray, and it hit the bear in the face and shoulder. It was enough to slow him, to surprise him. Ryan reached for the gun and removed the safety as the bear pawed at its face, groaning, grunting, still fighting the discomfort but coming forward. Seven yards. Five yards.

Ryan pushed up, standing tall, and fired in the air. The explosion ricocheted off the surrounding rock and echoed off into the woods. The bear jerked at the sound and turned. Ryan fired again. The bear lumbered off to the west, moaning as it disappeared into the trees and around the curve of the foothill.

They stayed motionless for what seemed like forever. Then Ryan whirled around to Elizabeth, shoving the gun back into the holster. She was crouched on her knees, her mouth still open, her hand still extended where his back had been, grasping for it still. He reached for her hand, breathless himself. "Elizabeth, breathe."

Her eyes focused on his, and suddenly, in one move, she was in his arms, huddled as he leaned against the rock. He pulled his arms around her, and they stayed like that long enough to breathe again, Ryan rocking her gently as he kept his eyes searching around them. He could breathe, but his heart hammered.

Finally, he whispered, "We have to go. I have to get you back." She tightened her grip on his shirt, shaking her head. He removed her hat and ran his hand over her hair, brushing it out of her face. "Elizabeth, we need to get out of here. He may come back."

That seemed to click. Ryan slid off the rock, and Elizabeth moved with him, still holding his jacket. He loosened her grip and placed both of her hands in one of his, then bent down to pick up their packs and the can of bear spray, which he had dropped when the bear had lunged at him. He helped her with her pack, then put his on, but she kept ahold of him the whole time. He picked up the poles and cinched them into the laces of his pack, smoothed her hair once more, and replaced her hat. He took another look around and started back down the trail. She wrapped her hands tightly around one of his as he pulled out his walkie-talkie. The contact made his pulse continue to stutter.

He cleared his throat. "Lantern? This is Flyer. You there?"

"Hey, Flyer, this is Lantern. How goes it?"

"We're, uh, headed back. We, uh, just had a run-in with a grizzly." Ryan attempted a deep breath.

There was a pause. "Are you lyin'?"

He chuckled weakly. "No. Not lyin'. We're pretty shaken, but we're all right. I'm bringing Elizabeth back to her—" He felt her shaking her head fervently against his shoulder, and he looked down. "What is it?" he whispered.

"I want to stay with you." Her voice was hoarse.

He swallowed. "Hey, Dad?"

"Yeah?"

"We're about six miles out, and Elizabeth is pretty shaken up. I'm taking her to my place until the shock wears off."

"That's fine, son. Take care of her. Do you need anything?"

"I need you to report that bear." He gave him the location on the trail and the direction the bear headed. "I used the bear spray and fired a couple shots in the air."

"Right. Son?"

"Yeah."

"I'm glad you're all right. Be careful coming back. Make a lot of noise."

"All right. Thanks, Dad. Over."

He took a deep breath. *Okay, a lot of noise.* He paused and looked around. He reached around to his pack, which was difficult because Elizabeth was still holding his hand tightly, and pulled out a water bottle. He opened it and held it in front of her mouth. "Drink." She obeyed. That was good.

He put the lid back on and moved just off the trail so they were walking through shrubs, snapping twigs, and making more noise. But Elizabeth remained silent.

"Elizabeth, we're going to have to talk, all right?" He felt her nod. "I'm going to ask you some questions, okay?"

"Okay." Her voice was small, but he went ahead.

He looked around, feeling a little paranoid, remembering the size of that bear on his hind legs. This wasn't how he'd pictured getting his answers. "Tell me about your family. Your parents—start with them."

She adjusted her grip on his hand. "Umm. My dad's name is . . . Keith. Keith and Anne. They bought a house on a lake in Montana before I was born, and, um, we still have the lake house. My sister and her husband live there now . . . They just got married. My dad lives in Kalispell."

She jerked around at a sound behind her. He looked, but it was nothing. He rubbed her arm.

She turned back, taking a breath. "My other sister lives nearby with her husband. But the lake house is in a valley, so it isn't in the woods like this. Though we do have a few trees on the property." She laughed softly. "My mom's cherry orchard." He squeezed her hand. A laugh was good. "Flathead is close to Glacier." She looked up at him. "Have you been there?" He shook his head. "Well," she looked back down, "we would go there a lot when I was little. We would camp."

He seemed to have asked the right question and guessed her adrenaline was helping the flow of words out of her mouth. She watched their feet moving together, and she kept up with his stride.

"It was fun growing up there. I mean, we had the water fun with the boats, and we'd take walks along the river. My mom made it fun. My dad, he would take us to fancy restaurants and show us off everywhere. I've told you he's a lawyer. Everyone would say how much I was like him, and that was great, but . . . I wanted to be like my mom. She was . . . She was . . ."

He noticed she kept referring to her mother in the past tense. "What happened to your mother?"

She spoke quietly. "She died. I was nearly seventeen. She fell off a ladder . . . broke her neck. It was so strange to have her there one minute and then the next minute . . . just gone. But you . . ." She drew her eyes up to his and slowed to a stop. "You know that."

He swallowed, meeting her gaze, then made himself nod. He couldn't breathe.

After a moment, she blinked, and they began walking again, watching their feet. It wasn't difficult for him to wrap his arm around her. She didn't even falter in her step as she took hold of his other hand.

"My dad, well, he sort of . . . changed. Well, of course he did, but nothing was ever the same after that."

He listened closely. "How did he change?"

She told him about how they stopped doing anything together, about her father's estrangement from her younger sister Alisen, how he'd buy Elizabeth anything she wanted but, really, all she wanted was for her mother to come back so they could be a family again.

"I became angry though. I knew even if I got everything I asked for from Dad, I still wouldn't have what I really wanted. So I just took what I could and flaunted what I had. I, uh, partied on the weekends, and I made people feel bad who didn't look like me or didn't have what I had." She winced. "I was the worst kind of spoiled brat."

He smiled to himself but kept her going. "But you left, right?"

She turned her face up. "I went to school. I knew even when I was little I wanted to work in fashion. Nancy was one of my teachers and encouraged me to go into buying . . . Who doesn't like to shop, right? So I was hired by Saks Fifth Avenue, a dream job, and I was eventually able to leave, go all over, choose clothes and accessories, entire lines for this major department store. It was sort of glamorous: the travel, the clubbing, the shows, and meeting all kinds of people all over the world. I wasn't stuck at home anymore, having to face the reality of a lost dream." She took a deep breath. "All of the important stuff centered around my job, my travels, my social life. I kind of just put my family away . . . just like my dad did." She shook her head. "Then I—I met other people . . ." Her voice faded.

He waited. "What other people?"

"Bad people," she whispered. Her lips clamped shut, and she shuddered. A shadow drew over her features, raising the hairs along his arm, and her grip tightened again around his hand. "It's nothing. I just made some stupid mistakes." She quieted, and he pulled her closer as he felt her withdraw. She had shared more than he'd expected from his simple question. And her answers had affected him more than he was prepared for.

He looked behind him. Now that his adrenaline had slowed and his thoughts were filled with other things, he was pretty sure they wouldn't see the bear again. He looked ahead and knew they didn't have much farther to go.

"Let's stop for a minute."

"Okay." She slowly pulled her hands away. Her arms wrapped around her own waist as he dug out two energy bars and offered one to her. She took it. "Thanks."

"We don't have much farther, but you need to eat something."

She nodded and opened her bar, taking a bite.

He thought about what she'd told him. Her father had been left with three children. Ryan was pretty sure he'd made better choices than her father had, but still, he worried about his kids' happiness, how his choices would determine their futures.

Elizabeth looked small, slouching in on herself, looking around at the forest. He pulled a new water bottle out and moved closer, offering her the drink. She took it and drank, closing her eyes. But a tear slid down to her jaw as she tipped her head up. He moved to wipe it away, and she shied a little at the touch.

She finished her drink and handed the bottle back to him, whispering her thanks as he finished the bottle. He put it away, and they started walking again.

"Can I ask you something?" He had another question.

"Maybe."

"You don't have to answer." She approached his side again, and he hesitantly opened his arm to her. She stepped in. Holding her felt . . . quieting now. He furrowed his brow. "I just wanted to know . . . if your dad ever . . . moved on?"

She slowed her pace and thought before she answered.

Finally, she exhaled. "My dad . . . *Now* it's easier to see, but *then* . . . He was miserable, really. He loved my mother so much. She was *everything*. We couldn't see how much he was suffering because he had this mask—*cool* and unemotional."

With a start, Ryan recognized the word he'd used to describe Elizabeth.

"Then, and it's only been a few months, he met a woman, Sheryl, and the difference . . . It was Dr. Jeckyl and Mr. Hyde. We *love* Sheryl." She seemed to blush at her expression of emotion. She shook her head and shrugged. Ryan watched the smile creep into the corners of her lips. "She makes him . . . who he really is. And it's good. So it's true; he's moved on, but," she added carefully, "he hasn't forgotten."

Chapter 13

HE OPENED THE DOOR FOR her, and she stepped in, pulling off her hat and looking around, curious and nervous. Ryan left the poles leaning against the house outside and threw both packs into a closet. He stepped around Elizabeth and picked up a sweatshirt off the floor, walked into the front room, and removed some books from a sofa in front of a wide river-rock fireplace stretching up to a peaked ceiling.

She reached down and pulled off her shoes, which were killing her feet, and sighed with fatigue. She watched Ryan pick up a pair of pink cowboy boots and socks and a stuffed bear, which he looked at and held up, shaking it with a small growl.

"Ha, ha." She smiled at his attempt to lighten the mood.

He took his load into another room and came back without the gun. "C'mon." He held out his hand and led her around to sit in front of the fireplace. She almost refused, almost excused herself because the panic had subsided and foolishness was beginning to wag its finger at her. But her body followed his lead, and she sank into the sofa as he'd beckoned. He crouched down, taking a few logs from the iron cradle next to the hearth, and began to build a fire as she continued to look around.

She knew this had been his parents' first bed and breakfast, but she couldn't quite get a feel for how it would have worked that way. Solid carved doors led to other rooms, and wide planked floors had mellowed with age. A hallway disappeared around a corner behind them, and toward the back of the house, a large dining room with french doors led to the deck outside. The place had been made over into a home.

She gazed through the front windows and pulled the band holding her ponytail out so she could brush her fingers through her hair. The log walls were chinked with white and were unadorned. The split-log mantel above the fire held several framed photographs, though, and an elk carved from a hard wood. In the corner stood an old, ornate grandfather clock, its pendulum swinging in rhythm to a soft *tick . . . tick . . . tick.*

She rubbed her hands on the soft cushions, leaving finger trails in the faux suede upholstery. Ryan sat next to the fire on a large round ottoman, shifting the logs into a better position. He replaced the poker in the tool stand, pushed the ottoman up to the sofa, and picked up the blanket he'd been sitting on. He handed it to her, then sat down with her on the sofa. His weight pulled her toward him, and she allowed herself to lean against his shoulder. She threw the blanket out over her legs and offered him a portion of it. He took it and tossed it over his legs, stretching them straight out in front of him. He kicked off his shoes as he leaned back, letting them fall to the floor, then closed his eyes and sighed.

"Did you call your parents?"

He nodded. "Mom brought some soup over for lunch and left it on the stove."

"I thought I smelled something good."

He opened his eyes a little and looked at her. "You smell good."

Her brows came together. "That's fear."

He leaned closer to her hair. "Smells good."

Goose bumps again. She shook her head, fighting the small smile at the corner of her mouth, and looked into the fire. She was too tired to accept this as reality. Instead, she started to replay their hike and recalled the spiraling dread she'd experienced when Ryan was trapped against that rock . . . when he'd urged her away, but she couldn't leave him. She'd never experienced anything like that before.

The heat reached her toes and crept slowly up to her eyelids. The last thing she was aware of was the soft sound of his breathing, deep and steady against the tick of the clock.

* * *

She woke to the sound of the door opening.

"Daddy?"

"Dad?"

She froze, and she may have ducked. She looked over at Ryan, who had just opened his eyes to look at her. His eyebrows came up. She thought he ducked a little too.

Quick footsteps.

"Hey, kids." That was a whispering adult, and it wasn't either of them. They looked perplexed at one another.

The voice continued. "Hey, you need to be quiet, okay? Your dad and his friend went for a long hike today, and they're resting by the fire."

Elizabeth's mouth came to an *O* as she realized it was Dayle's voice. She felt Ryan's hand reach under the blanket to find hers. It was warm and masculine and surprisingly welcome. Her heart pounded in her throat. They watched each other, waiting for what would be said next.

"What friend?" Sam asked.

Elizabeth could tell by the tone of his voice he was probably up on his toes, looking over to see for himself.

"Daddy has a friend? Is it Dave?"

That must be Lily, Elizabeth thought.

Ryan smiled, amused, she could tell. Her heart raced, and she wished it would stop. He moved his thumb along the backs of her fingers. He wasn't helping.

"No, it's his friend Elizabeth. Shhhhh."

"*Elizabeth*?" Sam asked and received another shush. She could hear Dayle leading the kids into what Elizabeth guessed was the kitchen, with a promise of cookies.

She breathed out a sigh of relief when they were out of the room. She looked around. She had completely curled up next to Ryan, and his arm was around her shoulders. When had that happened?

"Did you have a good sleep?" he whispered. She lifted her head as he brought his arm from around her and stretched.

She pushed her legs out to the floor and ran her fingers through her hair. "Apparently," she whispered back. "I don't remember anything after you smelling me."

He muffled a laugh. "How do you feel?"

She thought about it. She was cold now along the place his body had been next to hers. "I feel . . . like it was all a dream . . . but"—she shivered, and a bit of dread returned—"*not*. You?"

He leaned his head back on the cushion and nodded, looking at the embers of the fire. He spoke softly, introspectively. "Do you remember when you were a kid and you had a nightmare . . . the really scary kind, where you wake up and you're breathing hard and already crying because it was so real?" He swallowed, and she watched his Adam's apple move up and down.

"Yeah." She remembered.

"Then your mom or dad comes in and switches the light on, and even though the dream was so real and so scary, you have to accept that you'll be okay." He lowered his voice further. "And you know you can go on because your dad is standing there with the light on, and he's saying your name and telling you it will be all right."

She listened quietly, taking in his words, their meaning. His voice was soft, but she felt it wrap firmly around her heart, invited or not. She was unable to breathe.

He turned to her, meeting her gaze. "Elizabeth . . . when we woke up, it was like . . . somebody had—"

"Daddy!"

The spell was broken, and Elizabeth pulled away from him, barely aware until then that they had been so close.

Ryan threw off the blanket, and she scooted back to make space for the little person who had come hopping into the room.

As Lily came running around, Ryan broke into a smile so big Elizabeth drew in breath.

"Daddy!" The little girl threw herself into his arms, and he gasped and laughed.

"Lily, sheesh. What are they feeding you at school?"

She laughed, a tinkling sound. "Lunch, Dad." She knelt on his lap and played with his chin. "You feel rough."

His hand came up to rub his jaw. "Do I?"

She nodded her pointed chin. "Mm-hmm. You need to shave."

"I will in the morning."

"No. Right now."

"Right now? *Right now?*" He began tickling her ribs. "How about I shave *you?*"

Lily squealed, and Elizabeth watched, transfixed by this side of him and this little girl with soft chestnut hair swinging above her shoulders. She had big brown eyes and a few freckles across her nose, and Elizabeth could see the same shape in her mouth as Ryan's.

Lily caught her watching and dropped her chin, smiling shyly.

"Can you say hi to Elizabeth?" Ryan asked.

Lily turned more to face her, keeping her chin down. Her hand came up to scratch her shoulder. "Hi, Elizabeth."

"Hi, Lily."

Lily smiled. "Did you go on a hike with my dad?"

"Yes."

Lily's hand moved to scratch her nose. "Why?"

"Umm, because he asked me."

Lily giggled roughly. "I thought you were Dave."

Elizabeth smiled. "I get that a lot."

The little girl giggled again.

"Lily, guess what," Ryan said.

"What?"

"We saw a *bear*."

Her eyes got bigger. "Really?" She looked behind Ryan. "Sam, guess what. Dad and Elizabeth saw a *bear*."

"Really?" Sam walked in, eating a cookie. "Was it scary?"

Ryan nodded. "*Very*."

Elizabeth laughed weakly.

"Did you get to use the bear spray?"

Ryan nodded.

Sam grinned. "Cool." He turned to Elizabeth. "You're having a rough week, aren't you?"

Elizabeth smiled at his observation. "Yes, I guess I am." Her eyes met Ryan's. "Or your father is."

Ryan smiled, and Lily leaned forward to whisper something in his ear. He looked at her and nodded, and she hopped down and ran off.

"She wants to show you something."

Sam sat down on the ottoman. "So, Elizabeth, how long are you staying here?"

The question made her smile. She took a breath, gathering her scattered nerves. "At your house or in Jackson?"

"Both."

"Well, I don't know how much longer I'll be at your *house*, but I'll be in Jackson until next Saturday, and then I'll decide if I'm coming back"— she felt Ryan watching her—"to stay." She looked at Ryan, sure she could read his mind.

Sam nodded and turned to the dying fire. "Hey, Dad, can I put another log on?"

"Sure. Be careful."

Sam got to work, and Lily came skipping back into the room, holding a Barbie doll, the doll's blonde hair swinging back and forth. She slowed and approached Elizabeth, holding it out to her.

Elizabeth took it and asked, "Is this your doll?" Lily nodded, her hand coming up to rub her eye. "What's her name?"

"Elizabeth."

Elizabeth raised her eyebrows. "Really?"

Lily nodded again. "'Cause she looks like you."

Elizabeth looked down at the doll and smiled, hiding a laugh. "Well, thank you. That's very nice, Lily."

Elizabeth looked at Ryan out of the corner of her eye and saw his mouth drawn together, hiding his amusement. Lily held her hand out for the doll, then skipped away.

"Somebody needs to put some clothes on that doll," Elizabeth said under her breath.

Ryan laughed.

"You two hungry?" It was Dayle, coming in with a tray.

Elizabeth moved her hand to her stomach.

"I'm starving," Ryan answered.

Dayle set the tray on the ottoman and arranged the two bowls of stew and some thick slices of bread with butter. Two mugs of what looked like hot cider steamed there as well. Elizabeth shook her head at the way this woman kept turning up with food for her at just the right moments. A wave of self-consciousness washed over her as she realized Dayle would have seen her nestled next to her son on the sofa. Ryan must have had the same thought.

As Dayle straightened with a smile, Ryan asked her quietly, "When did you get here, Mom?"

Dayle reached down and took his hand, patting and rubbing it. "About an hour ago. I knew the kids would be coming home soon, and . . . I just had to see for myself that you were all right. Oh, honey, a grizzly?" She sat down on the arm of the couch. "What happened? Wait, eat first. Elizabeth? Eat, honey."

They obeyed. Then Elizabeth excused herself to use the bathroom, and Dayle led her down the hall.

"It's the second door." She put her hand on Elizabeth's arm. "I know it may not seem like it with these unpleasant things happening, but . . ." she looked back to the front room, "it's good that you came." She looked into Elizabeth's eyes and patted her arm, then left.

Elizabeth stood there a moment, repeating Dayle's words in her head: *It's good that you came.*

When she returned, Ryan was finishing telling Dayle about their ordeal, and his voice was solemn. "I don't know if she'll want to go hiking again."

Would she ever want to go hiking again? Part of her said it would be pointless, as she would be checking for bears coming out of every curve, out from behind every tree, turning with every snapping twig or waving branch. But she remembered the beauty, the feeling of power around her, following Ryan, the waterfall, standing with him under the intimidating mountains, talking with him, his arm around her.

She entered the room. "Yes, I would."

He turned to look at her. Dayle smiled and nodded her head.

Elizabeth gave Ryan a small smile and said with a challenge in her voice, "I'd need a good guide though."

Dayle turned her smile to Ryan. "There you go." She got up to clear the dishes, and the clock hummed, clicked, then chimed the half hour. "Just a reminder," she spoke as she turned to walk away. "You have another child coming home soon. And she won't be so easily distracted by cookies." She turned the corner and disappeared.

Ryan looked at the old clock in the corner. He got up from the sofa and walked to Elizabeth with a shrewd look. "How do you feel about interrogations?" He crossed his arms.

Chloe. She looked over at Sam and Lily in front of the revived fire, talking to each other about whatever. She looked out the back doors, where she could just make out the roof of the gazebo by the river, noting again how things had changed between Ryan and her since this morning . . . no, since she had arrived at this place in the middle of breathtaking nowhere. Her feelings, in any direction, had intensified. A very few had been clarified. She was dazed.

She sighed. "It's been a long day."

He nodded. "Then can I walk you back to the inn? Or would you rather we drove?" The challenge was in *his* voice now.

She smiled back. He nodded and called over his shoulder, "Mom, I'm walking Elizabeth back to the inn."

Lily got up. "You're *leaving*?" She bounced over and grabbed Elizabeth's arm. "Will you come back again?"

Elizabeth returned her smile. "Maybe."

"Okay."

"Bye, Elizabeth," Sam said. "I hope you decide to stay here. In Jackson." He grinned at her.

"Bye, Sam." She surprised herself as she reached out to feel Lily's soft hair. "It was nice to meet you."

Lily nodded up at her and looked shy again as she turned to walk more slowly back to the fire. Elizabeth felt Ryan watching her. When she didn't return his look, he walked to the closet and pulled out a jacket. She pulled her shoes back on.

"Are you warm enough?"

She nodded, and he opened the door.

"Bye, kids."

"Bye, Dad."

"Bye, Daddy."

They walked out into the afternoon sunshine. Elizabeth lifted her face to it, closed her eyes, and breathed. That felt real. She turned to Ryan and shook her head. "Wow."

He looked down and turned in the direction of the inn. As she moved to follow, he extended his hand for her to take. Against every sensible instinct in her body, she reached for it.

* * *

They walked in silence for a time, and Ryan was trying to figure out *if* or *how* or *when* to tell Elizabeth something important. He couldn't shake the feeling that if this thing with Elizabeth was going anywhere, he should probably mention his faith. He may have been out of the dating game for a while, but he knew that dating a Mormon was different from a lot of dating scenes out there. And he definitely wanted to date this woman. He stuck his free hand in his pocket.

What had happened to his wall? It lay in rubble. For five years, it had been strong. There had been *nothing* like this. How was he supposed to feel about that? Was he relieved, or did he feel weak? Neither. But he didn't quite know what to do *next*. This wasn't just about him. He rolled his eyes. He knew there was a next step. He just wasn't sure how to take it, and he wrestled with the argument of whether or not he had plenty of time.

"Ryan? Has anything like that ever happened to you before?"

He looked at her blankly. *Oh.* "Umm, no. Never like that with a grizzly. I've seen bears way up on mountainsides, black bears closer, but they run away." He sighed. "Never like that."

"When . . . when you were trying to get me to move away . . . you . . ." She paused, blushing.

"What?"

"Nothing." She pulled him to a stop. "Thank you. I haven't said that yet." She took a small step closer to him. "Thank you."

Her eyes were lighter than he'd originally thought, like chocolate milk, deepening around the edges. He stepped closer.

"Sure. You're welcome for putting you in mortal danger—again." He looked down at their hands, how they came together, his skin against hers.

She spoke softly. "What were you going to tell me about the nightmare?"

His eyes stayed down, but he started to nod. "I was going to tell you"— he lifted his gaze, and his heart continued to thud—"that when we woke up, it was like someone had switched a light on and was telling me it would be all right . . . and I'd be able to go on."

He watched her reaction. Her breathing deepened. But he thought he saw that flash of . . . Darn it, what was it? Doubt. It was doubt. A little wrinkle between her eyebrows. And he was sorry he'd told her.

"Ryan, I . . ." She shook her head, looking down at their hands, and whispered so softly he could barely hear her. "Do you smell that?"

He didn't understand.

She whispered again. "Fear."

He softened his expression. He nodded slightly, his hand coming up to smooth her cheek, and she looked up. He swallowed. "Elle."

Light came to her eyes, even as the wrinkle between her brows deepened. "Yes?"

"Can I call you that?"

"Yes."

He leaned closer, pulling her slowly, and her eyes closed. He swallowed hard.

A loud rumble shook the ground, and a flurry of leaves kicked up as the school bus passed.

They both closed their eyes tightly, then looked at the back of the bus.

"Oh no," Ryan said. "I'm in trouble."

"Why?"

He still looked back down the road. "That was Chloe's bus."

Understanding filled her voice. "Oh," she said cautiously. "She might have seen . . ."

"Oh, she saw." He looked at her with a half smile filled with guilt. "She's one of the last stops on her route. There are only four or five kids left on that bus."

"Ohhh."

He stepped back, still holding her hand. "C'mon," he said with a wary smile. "I'll take you the rest of the way." He looked back the way they had come and sobered. "I think there's a storm coming."

Chapter 14

RYAN HUNG UP HIS JACKET and stepped farther into the house. He moved cautiously through the dining room and into the kitchen, where his mom sat reading a magazine at the counter.

She looked up. "So . . ."

He raised his eyebrows. "Is Chloe—"

"You were kissing her?"

He moaned and put his hand to his forehead. "No, I wasn't. I didn't kiss Elizabeth."

"Oh. Then—"

"I *almost* kissed her."

Dayle pursed her lips. "Son, don't you think it's a little soon to be . . ."

He threw his hands out. "I haven't kissed her yet. Sure it's too soon. I don't know, Mom. I'm a little out of practice." He put his elbows on the counter and put his head in his hands. "It's been a long day."

"It's not even four yet."

He brought his face up and scowled.

"And your daughter is waiting for you."

"In her room?"

Dayle nodded to the window and went back to her magazine. He looked out the window, then turned to the dining room.

"Ryan?"

"Yes?" He hadn't turned around.

"Be careful, sweetie. She remembers her mother."

He took a deep breath, trying to push down the anger suddenly rising inside him. "So do *I*."

He felt his mother's hand on his arm. Her gentle voice floated up to him. "My Ryan, I know you do. I meant . . . the others were little. They're more open to . . . change."

His shoulders relaxed a little, and he exhaled. "Sorry."

She pulled him down to kiss his cheek. "No need." She went back to her stool.

He turned. "Mom?"

"Hmm?"

"Am I doing the right thing?"

She blinked at him. A gentle smile came to her face. "What are you doing, sweetheart?"

He paused and felt like he had to catch his breath. "I think I'm . . ." He couldn't say the words. He shook his head and turned to go out the back doors.

What was he supposed to say to Chloe? How was he supposed to make this right? He'd gauge his reaction by hers. He'd known this would be tricky. He just hadn't thought it would get this tricky this soon. Man, what was he thinking? His hand came over his jaw. So she thought they were kissing. Well, that was understandable, and at least he could refute that, but that really wasn't the point. The point was, Chloe had no idea who Elizabeth was, and she'd thought he'd been kissing her, and her friends might have seen too.

He slowed and closed his eyes.

Help me.

He could see her looking out over the river as he approached. He stepped up to the gazebo and paused, putting his hands in his pockets. She was sitting on the bench lining the interior of the structure. Her red hair hung straight and thick over her shoulder, and he could see she'd been crying. It filled him with remorse.

"Hey, pook."

"Don't call me that."

He took a breath. "Your grandma told me what you thought you saw—"

She whirled at him. Her gray eyes, so much lighter than his, pierced him through. "What I *thought* I saw?" She turned back to the river. "So, what, I was imagining things? Everyone on the bus was *imagining things*?"

"Chloe, I didn't . . . I wasn't . . . I wasn't kissing her." There, he'd said it.

"Really?" She didn't sound convinced.

"Really. I . . . I almost did, but then . . ." Why did he feel like he was the kid and she was the parent? "But I know that doesn't matter," he said, though he *felt* it mattered. It seemed to matter a lot. He sat down next to her, and she scooted away.

"How was I supposed to answer, Dad, when Dillon asked me who the *hottie* was or when Stacy said she didn't know my dad was seeing anybody?" She started an angry laugh. "Or how am I supposed to feel when I hear *Ty Freeman* say to Hayden Graham, 'Well, *she* may be cold, but her dad's girlfriend—'" She couldn't finish.

He sat there with his head down, feeling a mixture of pain for his daughter, anger at those kids—he'd never liked Ty Freeman—and defensiveness because he was just . . . he was just *trying*.

Chloe sniffled, and he carefully reached his hand to her shoulder. She didn't move but started to cry harder. He pulled her to his side, and she crumpled into him.

"I really hate you right now."

"I know," he said. He held her at his side until her crying eased.

"So," she threw a hand out and sniffled again, "who *is* she?"

He took a deep breath. "Her name is Elizabeth Embry. She's . . . staying at the inn." He let that much sink in.

"Well, that's new." She brought her head up sharply. "*Isn't* it?"

"*Yes*," he nearly growled but tried to remind himself his daughter hadn't done anything wrong. He waited for the next question, not sure what she needed or would want to hear.

"How long have you been seeing her?"

He decided to be vague. "Not long."

He watched her brow furrow as she thought. She sniffled and brought her hand up to her nose. He wished he'd thought to bring tissues with him.

She sighed. "Is she a member of the Church?"

Hmm. This would be a tough one. "No."

She looked at him incredulously and made a dismissive sound. "Great, Dad. You sure know how to pick 'em."

His defensive feelings crouched, and his voice rose. "You know what, Chloe? I *don't* know how to pick 'em. How the *heck* am I supposed to know how to pick 'em after your mother? Huh? Elizabeth . . . she just, we just . . . *happened*. She came to the inn, she didn't want breakfast, she fell up the stairs, I hit her with my truck, then she *did* want breakfast, and we went on a hike and almost got *eaten by a bear. I wasn't . . . looking for this*."

Chloe stared at him. "You hit her with your truck?"

"*Yes*." He tried to catch his breath.

"And the bear . . . ?"

"It's a long story."

They both stared out at the river.

"Chloe, I'm really sorry. I wanted to tell you about her in a very normal way. I told you, I haven't been seeing her long. I just . . . don't know what I'm doing." He dropped his head.

After a minute, Chloe said, "If she's staying at the inn, then . . . where does she live?"

A reasonable question. "She may be moving here. She's from Montana."

"And she's not a member. Does she know *you* are?"

He shook his head. "Not yet."

She raised her eyebrows at him. "Maybe I'm wrong, but . . . isn't that kind of important?"

He sighed again. Yup, this was very different from his other kids. "I told you, this is very new."

"And you were kissing her?"

"I wasn't *kissing* her."

"Yeah, well, I'll have to remember that one."

He jerked his head around. She smiled a little. Even with the sudden lurch of his stomach, he couldn't help but smile back.

She took a deep breath. "So, you haven't seen anyone . . . ever. Well, there was that one time when Dave—"

"Let's not talk about that, shall we?"

She snorted.

He took that as a good sign.

She sobered again. "You haven't seen anyone. I'm just wondering . . . why now?"

He shrugged. "I told you. I don't know. But the more I'm with her . . ." He remembered Elizabeth's words. "The more I feel like who I was before . . . who I really am."

She looked at him, considering. "But aren't you yourself with us?"

He nodded. "Yes, with you and your brother and sister. Always. But"— would she understand?—"I'm your *father*. Outside of you guys, I've just . . . had to try really hard not to feel sad."

Chloe looked out over the river, considering. "Or alone," she added.

She understood better than he'd thought.

* * *

"Now, this is the good stuff." Nancy closed her eyes and smiled.

Elizabeth moved her chin to the towel, looking straight ahead. The warm stones were soothing, but she couldn't completely relax. Nancy, on the other hand, was enjoying her massage.

"Elizabeth, next time I beg for chocolate, just drop me off here, all right?"
Elizabeth laughed feebly.

"What's wrong, darling? You said you had fun on your hike. Are you sore?"

"Mm, a little."

"Well, this should help, then."

Elizabeth nodded.

Somebody switched a light on, and I knew I could go on. The implications of his words were . . . tremendous. They had immediately drawn her in—and terrified her. To hear him . . . She swallowed. But she wasn't a light. He couldn't give her that much credit. She was . . . damaged goods. He didn't know. She swallowed again. What kind of woman had his wife been? A ballet dancer? A doting mother? A shining light whose brightness withstood so much time?

The implications of what had happened with the school bus hadn't really hit her until after she was back in her room, alone. Not a great way for Chloe to be introduced to a potential . . . *somebody* . . . after thinking of her dad with *nobody* for years. Elizabeth's anger with Ryan rose when she thought about it. Why hadn't he seen someone, light or no light, so his kids weren't shocked by the idea?

 · She checked herself. That wasn't fair. Sam and Lily had been easy. But what about that? What kind of conclusions would they jump to if they were to see even just a little bit more of her around? What was she ready for? Her stomach tightened. What did they deserve?

Ugh. Ryan wasn't safe. He should've had caution tape all around him. Quiet, unassuming, gentle Ryan was a danger zone.

She chuckled at that, realizing she wasn't even thinking about the truck or the bear. She felt eyes on her and looked over to see Nancy watching her with a confused expression. She ignored it and turned back to her towel.

She sighed. She imagined his hand on her cheek, the way he'd looked at her like she was the only one who might . . . She shook her head. How could *she* fall in love with . . . ?

Oh. Oh no. Am I?

She thought some more.

"What are you smiling about?"

I am. I'm in love with Ryan Brennan. He has three kids, and he lives in a log cabin in the woods, and he still loves his wife who died five years ago, and he somehow thinks I am . . . good enough.

She face planted into her towel and groaned.

"I'm going to have to talk to Ryan. Those hikes are too strenuous."
Elizabeth nodded into her towel.

* * *

Pulling bags of new clothes out of the trunk of a car was a reassuring feeling for Elizabeth. She knew shopping, had control over it. Trying on a pair of pants, she knew two things: they fit, or they didn't. A pair of shoes? They either made the outfit or not. There were items that looked great and items that were comfortable. If you could find something possessing both qualities . . . well, that was perfection. Her number-one rule: if she wasn't sure, she didn't buy. Her number-two rule: looks beat out comfort.

Neither rule did the churning inside of her any good. Ryan wasn't a scarf, and the argument for looks versus comfort had her head spinning in circles. Not to mention the idea that if a pair of jeans fit her, she could say she fit the pair of jeans.

She sighed and closed the trunk with her elbow.

Even if Ryan fit her . . . she couldn't say she fit him. She wouldn't.

"Elizabeth?"

She almost dropped her bags.

"I'm sorry. I saw you with your hands full and thought you could use some help."

She breathed. "Oh, Jeff. I . . . I've got it, thank you."

He raised his brow, looking at the bags of all sizes hanging from her hands, wrists, and elbows. "How about I just take these here?" He reached for the handles of the bags she had squeezed between her arms and one that was cutting off the circulation in her little finger. "Have some fun shopping?"

"Yes. Therapy." The word was out before she could help it, and Jeff eyed her, amused.

"Your stay hasn't been relaxing?"

She caught the play in his voice and smiled. "I have a lot on my mind. With the new job and everything."

"Mm-hmm."

He was probably reading into that. "There's just a lot to think about, you know—New York City . . . Jackson Hole. I mean, the differences between them . . ." She chuckled. "The list could go on and on."

He paused and looked over his shoulder. "Why, Miss Embry, are you being *snooty?*"

She drew in a breath. "Oh, no. No, not at all. It's just that I've worked in that environment, you know, for so long, and so many other big trade centers of the world. It's *so* different. It's what I've known, my element. What if I do stay here, and then, what if it doesn't work? What if I . . . don't fit?" *Blah.* Why was she still talking? Jeff had stopped and was studying her. She grew fidgety under his gaze and bit her lip.

"Well, in my experience, I think a lot of that depends on how much you want to make it work."

She shifted the weight of the bags in her hands and looked down. "In my experience, what you want doesn't always matter. And where you've been is such a huge part of you, there's no way to shake it." A quiver had come to her voice, and she inhaled the clean air surrounding her, then blew away the threatening emotion. She peeked up at Jeff. His eyes were soft, compassionate.

Great. Now she was a basket case on the outside as well. She rolled her eyes and straightened her shoulders. "I'm making too much out of this." She began to walk again toward the doors of the inn.

"Elizabeth."

She paused.

"I have a guess that in your heart, you have plenty of room to add on." He reached past her and opened the door. "And I'm willing to bet the views would be spectacular. Maybe *because* of where you've already been."

* * *

Her room door stood ajar, and she approached carefully. "Hello?"

"Oh, housekeeping. Sorry, I'm just about done." The young woman bustled over to the pile of sheets in the corner and loaded them into a basket on the side of her cart. She was flushed with work.

"That's all right." Elizabeth dropped the shopping bags on the freshly made bed and sat, leaning against the bed post. "Just pretend I'm not here."

The girl paused slightly, eyeing her, then flipped her long braid over her shoulder and emptied the garbage. She moved to the bathroom.

Elizabeth sighed and got up, reaching for a bag. She pulled out some lacey underthings and held up a satin babydoll she'd bought in a girl-power moment. As she moved to the dresser, she caught the girl staring at her in the bathroom doorway, concern clearly on her face. As soon as the girl saw Elizabeth looking at her, she hurried, gathering the cleaning cart and pushing it out the door.

Elizabeth held out a tip for the girl, and she took it, shoving it in her pocket.

"Thank you," Elizabeth called as the door shut firmly. She took two steps and flopped back down on the bed in the midst of the bags. She had never thanked hotel housekeeping as far as she could remember. Grabbing a pillow, she pulled it over her head, Jeff's words running through her mind.

Her phone rang. "Hello?"

"Elizabeth?"

She smiled cautiously. "Ryan."

"Yes. How are you feeling?"

That was a loaded question. She gave him the short answer. "Okay." *My heart is pounding, Jeff thinks it could have spectacular views, and I think I love you, and that scares me to death.* "I really need to get a copy of that itinerary. Nancy wields way too much authority with that thing."

He chuckled. "Well, only one more week, so . . ."

That hung in the air between them.

"How did it go . . . with Chloe?"

He paused. "She's pretty mad at me. Sounds like the kids on the bus didn't help either. Did you know you're a hottie?"

She closed her eyes, grimacing, imagining the things that might have been said.

"But I think it'll be all right . . . Might take some time, but she'll forgive me. I'll be doing some serious making up for it though. We're going to see some teen musical thing tonight at the high school."

Elizabeth laughed quietly.

"She's . . . curious . . . about you."

"I'll bet."

"Elizabeth, I'm sorry I've put you in this awkward situation. I didn't mean to . . . I had no idea . . . I just can't seem to . . ."

She put him put out of his misery. "Finish a sentence?"

He exhaled. "Yes." He laughed, but it faded. "Elizabeth . . . I haven't done this in a while."

"You're doing just fine."

They were both quiet, though her heartbeat was annoyingly loud.

He broke the silence. "Would you have dinner with me tomorrow night?"

She couldn't smile big enough. Darn it.

Chapter 15

MARISOL HAD CREATED HALLOWEEN DECORATIONS, and Elizabeth stood in the window display helping her install them. She was currently holding a gauzy ghost up as Marisol arranged its body to peek out from behind one of the tree trunks. They had fixed feathered and jeweled masks on the mannequins, and battery-operated jack-o-lanterns lined a path through the piles of leaves on the ground. Each mannequin held a trick-or-treat basket filled with scarves, hats, and other colorful accessories, and a strobe light flashed intermittently, like lightning. It was good. Elizabeth had wanted to say how good she thought it was . . . but Marisol was talking.

"We were headed over to Lander, and we were going to try this new restaurant, which, I know, *Lander*, but we heard it was good, so why not? And we have to stop because there is this herd of elk right in the road, and they spook, like, really easily, so we're just stuck there, and my friend Ashley tells this story about a woman and her daughter down in Star Valley who were right by a herd of elk in their car, and they stopped to take a picture, you know, from inside the car, and somehow the herd got spooked and trampled *right over* their car and practically smashed the car flat . . . You know those elk are big, like horses, some of them, so she is telling us this story as we are *in* this herd of elk—"

She stopped and quickly drew in her breath. Elizabeth looked down to see what was wrong. Marisol stared out the window.

"Oh my gosh, there he is."

"Who?" Elizabeth looked in the same direction and saw a cowboy walking from across the street. He carried a large rectangular portfolio Elizabeth could only guess contained artwork. "Do you know him?"

"Yes." It was a squeak. "He goes to my church."

They watched him reach the boardwalk just beyond their window and continue on, his boots clomping on the wood.

"He's probably taking some artwork to the gallery next door." Marisol sighed and leaned her head against the tree trunk.

"Is he an artist?"

"Yes. He paints. He works his family's ranch, but he paints. He's really good. I think so anyway."

"Well, let's go see him. I'd like to see his painting."

"Oh no. No, no, no."

"Why not? He knows you, right?"

"Oh, I think so. Maybe."

"But you've seen his paintings."

"Yes. I go next door every once in a while to check them out."

"So let's go." Elizabeth felt up for an adventure. Things seemed to be going that way lately, even if it was just next door at the art gallery.

"No. I don't think he would like that."

"Why not? Artists love to have their work admired."

Marisol sighed. "Because he is so shy. He is so shy he hardly ever speaks. I've only heard him talk a few times. I . . . never know what to say to him. I don't want to make him uncomfortable."

Elizabeth watched Marisol look off the way the cowboy had gone. She couldn't imagine Marisol *ever* not knowing what to say. "You like him."

Marisol looked down and nodded her head. "Yes, I do. I like his strawberry-blond hair and his farmer's tan, his mustache, how it comes down the sides and meets his goatee. I like his turquoise-blue eyes and his lanky body and how he wears a cowboy hat everywhere and nods it up and down at people because he's afraid to say hi. And sometimes when he is looking down with his hat on and someone calls his name, he looks up from under his hat, and he smiles." She sighed.

"Hmm." Elizabeth stuck a tack with fishing line attached to a ghost's head into the ceiling above her and took Marisol's hand. "C'mon."

"Where are we going?" Marisol asked as Elizabeth pulled her out of the window and headed for the front door.

"I want to see some art." She'd never had trouble meeting men; it was afterward that she was a disaster. She passed Nancy at the counter. "We'll be right back."

Nancy looked over her glasses at her and mumbled something about not knowing what she'd do without them.

As they entered the gallery, Elizabeth looked around, still holding Marisol's hand. She drew Marisol up so she was standing next to her instead of cowering behind her and whispered, "Now, where are his paintings?"

Marisol pointed down an aisle, and they walked that way. Fortunately, the cowboy was just beyond that, showing his paintings to the man behind the counter. Elizabeth browsed.

Marisol stopped in front of a grouping of the artist's paintings. Elizabeth read the name plates. *James McAllister*. The bold brushstrokes surprised her, as well as the use of vivid color. From the way Marisol had described the artist, Elizabeth had expected something more . . . sedate. But here were landscapes and horses wild with movement and life. One of the landscapes in particular caught her eye, striking her with its simplicity.

"Are you finding everything you need, miss?" the man behind the counter asked. "Oh, hello, Marisol. How are you?"

Elizabeth looked and so did James.

"I'm just fine, thank you," Marisol answered feebly.

James removed his hat, watching them.

"This is Elizabeth Embry," Marisol said, clearing her throat. "She'll be at the shop now too. Elizabeth, this is Andrew Reynolds, the owner. And, uh . . ."

"This is James McAllister," Andrew said. James nodded and put his hat back on. "Those are his paintings there. Come take a look at these new pieces he just brought in."

Elizabeth approached the counter, and Marisol followed. James stepped aside.

Andrew positioned a painting so they could see it better. "Nancy said you would be coming, Miss Embry. How are you liking Jackson?"

"I'm warming up to it."

He nodded. "Just you wait until winter comes. That's the test. It's beautiful though. You make it through your first winter, you'll be here for life."

"I'll do my best."

He smiled back at her.

She turned her attention to the paintings. "These are amazing, Mr. McAllister. The play of light and shadow . . . It seems as though the leaves are moving. And this one—look at the water, Marisol. You could dip your hand in it." She turned to James. "You're very talented."

He shifted his weight, nodded his head, and looked down, a small smile there. Marisol hadn't been exaggerating.

"Marisol says she knows you from church."

Marisol's head came up with a snap. She looked at James, whose hat had come up as well. "Oh, I, uh . . . well, I've seen you there, of course. Right?"

James shifted his weight again. He nodded with his small smile. "Sister Espinosa, right?"

This time Elizabeth's head came up with a snap. *Sister* Espinosa? Marisol wasn't a nun. That could only mean . . .

Marisol smiled brilliantly at him. "Right. Marisol." She stuck her hand out, and he took it, but he took it like a man takes a woman's hand to help her out of a car. He nodded his head. "Marisol. The sea and sun, right?"

She laughed. "Yes. You served a Spanish-speaking mission?"

"Mm-hmm. Mexico City." He dropped her hand.

Elizabeth watched them intently, recognizing their vocabulary when six months ago she wouldn't have had any idea what they were talking about.

Marisol began speaking Spanish faster than Elizabeth thought possible. She watched, amazed, as James interjected fluently, and they laughed every so often. He looked down a lot but would bring his smiling eyes up from under his hat to glance at Marisol.

Elizabeth smiled at Andrew, who shook his head, laughing under his breath. He turned back to some other work, and she wandered back to the painting that had caught her eye.

The painting showed a deep woods. A trail cut through the trees and brush alive with color and light. Then it bent and disappeared into the darker forest, still beautiful, almost lit from within, but unexplored from the viewer's point of view. She looked at the title. *The Trail Less Traveled.* She recognized the nod to Robert Frost's famous poem.

Her phone rang.

She reached for it and walked to the front of the store.

"Hello?"

"Elizabeth?"

"Yes, Dad. How are you?"

"I'm good. How are things going? You sign anything yet?"

"I told you I wouldn't until I go over it with you. I think Nancy's lawyer may be faxing you some papers to look at soon."

"You've decided, then?"

"I'm getting closer." She had to keep her head on straight and make this decision based on business. This was a business deal that would affect her entire future.

"Well, I'm not surprised. If I know Nancy, she's charming you with everything she's got."

If only he knew.

"Are you getting to know the area?"

"A little. There isn't much to the town, but Nancy has kept me . . . very entertained. I think she's afraid I'll figure out how nonmetropolitan this place is. But . . ."

He waited. "Yes?"

"I think that's what I like about it. Part of me thinks I might be ready for this."

"You've been going and going for a long time."

She'd thought about that. She remembered feeling restless if she was home too long. She'd lost that in the last couple of years. She'd lost her appetite for it.

"Has Nancy introduced you around?"

"You could say that," she muttered.

"Hmm?"

"Yes. I've met a lot of people. She has me staying at this bed and breakfast . . . It's like summer camp."

"Uh-oh."

She ran a finger along the frame of a moose painting. "No, it's beautiful. I've done some hiking, made some friends." She smiled. "Oh," she remembered, "I ran into Travis George at a restaurant the other night."

"Who?"

"My friends Travis and Nicole. They were in London for a while. I worked with Nicole those first few years at Saks."

"Oh, right. You went to Barbados with them."

"You remember that?"

"I tried to keep tabs on you every once in a while. It wasn't easy."

She sighed. "Well, they're divorcing now."

"I'm sorry to hear that."

"Yeah, it's . . ." She remembered Travis's kiss. "Strange."

"He's a banker, right?" he asked pointedly.

"Dad." It was a warning. She did not want to get into that right now.

He chuckled. "Okay. Well, I need to go. Call me if you need anything."

"I will. Thanks, Dad."

"Bye, pumpkin."

Okay, that gag was getting old.

"Good-bye, Father."

She heard his laugh as she hung up, followed by Marisol's giggle from the back of the gallery. She sighed deeply.

* * *

The rest of the day flew by until a bouquet of flowers arrived with her name on it. Nancy fussed, and Marisol questioned, and, of course, Elizabeth tried not to give any of her feelings away, but when she read the card, she remembered. She was supposed to see Travis tomorrow in Star Valley.

Nancy was a little confused when Elizabeth told her the flowers were from Travis. Nancy let Marisol wander away before she dug deeper.

"Travis? Your friend from London? I thought they would have been from . . ."

Ryan. Elizabeth looked at the lilies and spider mums. They were from Travis, all right. How many similar arrangements had she seen before? Ryan wouldn't send these. Ryan sent roses and daisies and berries.

"I thought you said he was married?"

Elizabeth explained things to Nancy.

"Oh my." Nancy sighed.

"Oh my," Elizabeth agreed.

Nancy paused. "Well, what are your feelings? After all, he's one of the good ones, right?"

Elizabeth hadn't told Nancy anything about the hike with Ryan or their date tonight. Even she wasn't sure what bearing Ryan had on her relationship with Travis. She wasn't sure about anything.

She decided to stick with what she'd told Travis after the movie. "I don't think I can start something with someone who was married, who *is still* married, to one of my girlfriends." Although, she hadn't spoken to Nicole in a very long time. And she'd stolen a boyfriend or two in high school. And she'd flirted shamelessly with her sister's boyfriend. Yeah, she was a real angel. "Travis still loves Nicole."

"You're sure that's it?" Nancy's look was probing, and Elizabeth turned away.

"Yes. Of course. It would be foolish to get involved."

"With anyone?"

Elizabeth turned her head sharply, her defenses rising. She lowered her voice. "What does that mean?"

Nancy saw right through her. She reached for Elizabeth's hands and pulled her closer. She shook her head and whispered, "You deserve to be loved."

The hard lump in Elizabeth's throat burned. "No, I don't."

"What happened wasn't your fault."

Elizabeth tried to swallow. "How was it not my fault?"

"Your choices that night did not justify what that . . . that *monster* did. You can't keep doing this to yourself. You'll—"

Elizabeth pulled away and wiped the moisture from her eyes, trying not to disturb her makeup. "Enough." She sniffed and reached over the counter for a tissue, eyeing the front door and then the back. She cleaned up and shook her head. "Enough."

Nancy thought about that, then nodded. "What a shame," she said, looking at the flowers, wishing, Elizabeth was certain, that they'd been from Ryan. "There's so much loneliness in the world."

Elizabeth eyed Nancy and steadied herself. Were Travis and Ryan so different from each other after all? Both had lost someone they loved, both were trying to move on. She took a breath, feeling heavy with confusion. "I'll still go see Travis tomorrow. I'm still his friend. How do you get to Star Valley from here?"

Nancy paused and then seemed to accept Elizabeth's stand. She fluttered away. "I'll call Hank. He gives the best directions."

Elizabeth moved behind the counter and tried to ignore the flowers. *What a shame*, she repeated to herself. It would be easier, wouldn't it? With Travis? If the divorce were final? He might have a flashing light or two but no caution tape—

She jumped as the phone rang, and muttered under her breath. She straightened and picked up the phone.

"Wildberries. Elizabeth speaking. How may I help you?"

"Elizabeth. This is Nora Dalton. Remember me?"

"Yes, Nora." It was a relief to hear a voice so unrelated to the confusion she felt around her. "How are you?"

"Oh, I'm good, thanks. How are you? Are you getting to know Jackson?"

"Um, little by little."

"Is that good?"

Elizabeth bobbed her head uncertainly. "Yes."

"Oh, good. I'm just calling about my invitation. Are you free?"

"Oh . . ." Elizabeth closed her eyes. "Actually . . . I have a date tonight." Elizabeth looked toward the back of the shop, making sure there would be no big whoop of joy from Nancy. "I'm sorry. It was . . . unexpected."

"Oh . . . oh *no*." Nora caught herself. "I mean, that's great, but I'm disappointed. Next time I'll be more persistent."

Elizabeth smiled. "Thank you, Nora. Have fun tonight."

"Well, you too."

Nora really did sound disappointed.

Nancy came out on the floor as Elizabeth hung up. "Anyone important?"

"Nora Dalton."

Nancy looked at her for a second. "Oh, right, right, right."

"She, uh, invited me out tonight."

"Oh, good! That will be good for you." Nancy rubbed Elizabeth's back as she passed. "Hank has been after me about paint colors, and he will love to hear he can have me all to himself tonight."

Elizabeth blinked. "Okay." Was that a lie? She couldn't bring herself to mention her date with Ryan. Nancy would explode and then want to discuss it in depth. She'd had enough therapy for the day. For a lifetime.

"You're sure you'll be all right, darling?"

No. "Yes." An image of Ryan passed through her mind. She breathed. "Yes."

* * *

She put on lipstick and smoothed out the edges with her finger. Her heart fluttered a bit as she checked out her front and back in the mirror. She didn't know quite what to do with her hands, so she shook them at her sides, then gripped them together when she saw how silly that looked. What was she doing? At least she'd look good making a fool of herself.

The cocoa wrap sweater matched her eyes, and she'd layered it over a deep gold camisole and dark, slim jeans. Her only jewelry was a pair of thin gold hoop earrings. She'd piled her hair up like Marisol's, and she looked down at the warm brown cowboy boots she'd just purchased. When in Rome . . .

She sprayed her perfume and grabbed her wool jacket off the chair and her purse, then looked around and left her sanctuary.

She hurried a little down the stairs, then paused near the bottom. Ryan had just turned toward her, standing next to the counter, one hand tapping the surface. He wasn't smiling. He wasn't frowning either.

The first thing she noticed was his hair. It had been tamed. The ruddy brown waves had been smoothed up and back, curling on the ends. It showed off the cut of his sideburns and his jawline, which looked just shaven.

He wore a pair of silver-tipped cowboy boots and a charcoal V-neck sweater, a silk blend from what she could see, over well-cut jeans.

She finished walking down the stairs, slowly, and remembered to unclench her fists.

A slow smile spread across his face. She smiled back.

"You look . . . incredible," he said.

"The same thought crossed my mind about you."

He reached for her coat, and after some awkward maneuvering that proved how nervous both of them were, he helped her put it on, grabbed his own, and turned to lead her outside.

"Ahem."

"Crap," he said, and she looked at him. He grimaced, then slowly turned.

She looked behind her and saw Jeff and Dayle standing expectantly where she and Ryan had been just a moment ago.

She muffled a laugh. They both stood with their arms crossed, and Dayle was even tapping her toe.

"Just where do you think you're going, young man?"

"Aw, Mom." He barely moved his lips. "Please, no."

Elizabeth bit her lip, smiling at this grown man confronting his mother like an obstinate teenager. She knew some of this was show, but there was an underlying current of reality as well.

"Have her home before midnight," Jeff said in such a firm tone Elizabeth gulped.

"And no wild parties," Dayle continued. Elizabeth caught a wink from Jeff, and she covered a smile.

"You have your cell phone. Call if you need anything."

"And wear your seat belts."

"And mind your manners."

"Put on your jacket; it's freezing out there."

"Remember who you are." They were talking over one another.

"The shortest distance between two people is a smile."

"A bird in the hand is worth two in the bush." Dayle giggled.

Ryan deftly steered Elizabeth out the door and shut it as Jeff called out, "Don't take any wooden nick—"

As they stepped down from the porch, Ryan looked up at the sky. "I apologize with my whole being."

She shook her head, aware that much of her anxiety had faded with the display. Carefully, she linked her arm through his. "Your parents are amazing."

He looked at her. "Yeah. Amazingly *what* though?" He smiled crookedly and sighed, looking back up at the sky. "I wish it was clear."

She looked up at the dark sky.

"Those clouds are full of snow," he said.

She wondered how he knew.

They drove out of town, into the woods, and up through a winding road. She'd lost her bearings completely. "Where are we going?"

He looked at her and smiled, then turned back to the road. "Be patient."

She watched the outline of dark trees go by. Sure enough, snow started to drift down in front of the headlights.

She raised an eyebrow and looked at him.

He tapped his temple. "Snow."

She smiled and shook her head.

A few more minutes passed, and she began to fidget. She couldn't stand it. "Where are you taking me?"

"You really don't like surprises, do you?" he teased.

She let out a low laugh of frustration. "No."

"Okay, I'll tell you, but only because you look incredibly beautiful."

"That's a good reason."

He smiled, looking ahead, and she watched his profile. *He makes this seem so easy. This isn't easy. He has to realize this isn't easy. Right?*

"I'm taking you to Seven Pines. It's a lodge. It's nice." He glanced at her and reached for her hand. "You'll like it."

"Oh yeah?"

His brow furrowed in concern. "I *hope* you will."

She allowed a laugh, recognizing the warmth his hand brought to hers and settling back into her seat. Almost comfortable.

Soon the road flattened out, and an angular log building rose from out of the trees, lit with white Christmas lights around the roofline, windows, and walks.

Ryan parked the car and looked at her. "Seven Pines," he said, announcing their destination.

"Why seven?"

"Well," he began confidently, pointing his finger out toward the forest of dark trees, counting silently, and then blowing out his breath. "I have no idea. I count way more than seven."

She smiled, and he got out, walking around to open her door. As she stepped out, he produced an umbrella over her head. She took it with a grateful smile, and they walked to the front doors.

"This is gorgeous. Not as great as the inn, but . . ."

He squeezed her hand at the compliment and opened the door for her. They walked inside to warmth and glowing lights. A young woman took their jackets and the umbrella, hanging them up in a small alcove lined with hooks.

Did he ever bring his wife here? Elizabeth winced at herself for thinking the inane question. *Stop it. Not tonight.*

"Name?" the hostess asked when she returned.

"Brennan."

She checked a list on the podium in front of her. "Ah. Right this way."

She led them toward the vast dining area, softly lit by half a dozen enormous antler chandeliers. A massive round fireplace stood in the center of the room, and placed in concentric circles around the fireplace were semicircular, high-backed leather booths facing the heat. Tables dotted the outer edges of the room, with views out the windows, black now in the night except for flickers of falling snow. The large number of patrons surprised her. Her gaze drifted to the source of soft music: an older man sat playing a large grand piano.

"Hmm," she said.

"What?"

"I'm just surprised." She gestured to the man at the piano. "A Beethoven sonata."

"Yeah, well, I'll put in a request for 'Tumbling Tumbleweeds' after we're seated."

She laughed but kept her eyes on the piano as they walked, letting Ryan lead her along.

They reached one of the booths facing the crackling fireplace. He guided her in and sat down beside her. With the huge fireplace in their view, it almost felt like they were alone. The hostess left them.

"This is unexpected," Elizabeth said.

"I'd like to think that's a good thing."

She nodded her head, feeling him watching her closely. "I think . . . it might be."

He leaned over, and she turned her face partly to him so he nearly spoke against her cheek.

"I think I should let you know," he said quietly, "that Chloe made me promise I wouldn't kiss you tonight."

Her pulse quickened as she felt his breath on her skin, his scent mixing with the burning wood.

"But you need to understand," he said slowly, "that I really . . . really . . . want to."

He straightened back up, smoothly opened his menu, and pretended to read as she tried to regain her composure.

She watched him, and that slow smile spread across his face. He glanced out the corner of his eyes, and she exhaled softly through pursed lips. The idea flickered that his restraint could be her undoing.

She swallowed. "Okay, then." She opened her menu, blinking her eyes.

The waiter had brought a wine list. Ryan ordered a ginger ale and politely handed her the list. She glanced and then ordered the same. Ryan didn't comment, but when the drinks were served, he made a small toast.

"To stairs."

She grinned. "To stairs."

Over dinner, he asked her more questions about her childhood, happy memories she hadn't dug up in years. He asked about her mother, simple questions that weren't difficult to answer. She described her sisters, the lake house, her first car, the rock on the river where her mother told them stories. She started to shy away when she thought he might ask an uncomfortable question, when the subject came dangerously close to leading where she didn't want to go, but he never asked those questions, and she soon found herself completely relaxed.

They talked about growing up near the mountains and what the lodge had been like when he was a kid. He mentioned a sister but avoided talking about her much, joking that she was mostly a pain in the rear.

He told her stories of pranks he would play on his teachers and the punishments he would defy in high school.

"Didn't they get angry?" she asked with a laugh.

"Yes, but what could they do?" He shrugged. "I was a straight-A student, valedictorian." He chuckled. "Well, there was one teacher . . . She actually kicked me out of her class."

"Really? For the day or . . . out?"

"*Out*, out." He shook his head, smiling. "Mrs. Gravenstein. We called her Mrs. Greenshoes because she wore these awful bright-green vinyl shoes with fake green flowers on the toes with leaves and stamens and everything."

Elizabeth was already holding her stomach in anticipation as he continued.

"And one day, she was wearing them, and I just couldn't take it anymore and started doing the fake sneeze, you know, during her lesson." He demonstrated, covering his mouth. "*Greenshoes . . . Greenshoes!*" He shook his head. "*So* obnoxious."

Elizabeth put her hand over her mouth. "And . . . she kicked you . . . *out?*"

"Yup." He shook his head again. "I deserved it. It wasn't very nice." He sipped his ginger ale.

She raised her eyebrows. "No, it wasn't. What class was it?"

He grinned. "Spanish. I had to take French." He made a face. "The funny thing is, I don't remember any French, but my Spanish is pretty good." He grinned and nodded, seemingly proud of himself. "Hola, cómo estás? Muy bien, gracias. Dónde está el baño? Mis zapatos son verdes."

She choked on her drink.

He chuckled. Then his brow furrowed suddenly. "I should have been nicer." He picked up his fork and pushed around some broccoli remains. "Maybe she just really loved those shoes."

Elizabeth smiled openly. She didn't understand it, and part of her was frightened, but the last three hours had been the happiest she could remember. She leaned toward him, brushing his ear with her fingers. He tilted his head to her and closed his eyes, an automatic reaction to the touch. She lowered her voice. "I really . . . really . . . want to kiss you too."

He turned, taking in her smile, and she let him. He leaned toward her, watching her mouth. Her heart missed a beat, but he stopped and turned his head, lifting up his drink. "Aahh, Chloe," he growled.

Elizabeth laughed again, and he chuckled into his glass.

Chapter 16

THEY DROVE DOWN THE MOUNTAIN, and Ryan squeezed her hand in his. "I'm curious," he said. "What does Nancy think of this?"

Elizabeth eyed their interwoven fingers. "Nancy doesn't know."

She watched him raise his eyebrows. "How did you manage that?"

"I sort of . . . fibbed."

He laughed outright. "Fibbed?"

She nodded her head. "I'm not sure I'm ready for Mount Nancy to erupt yet."

"Well, when—*if*—you break the news, make sure she isn't near any swiftly moving water, okay?"

She laughed just as her phone rang.

"Travis," she said, looking at the caller ID.

"Travis George?" he asked in a low voice.

"Mm-hmm. I better take it."

She looked at Ryan as she answered, noting the set of his jaw and his furrowed brow.

"Hello?"

"Liz."

"Hello, Travis. How are you?"

"Great . . . excited about tomorrow. When will you be here?"

"Umm, about ten thirty."

"How about this snow, huh? Let me give you directions to the house."

"Just a minute." She found a notepad and a pen in her purse.

"Did you get the flowers?"

"Yes, I did. Thank you." She glanced at Ryan, who was concentrating very hard on the road. "Okay, directions?"

She wrote them down.

"Be careful driving in this. It shouldn't be too bad. It's only October."

"I will."

"I can't wait to see you, Liz."

"Travis—"

"We'll have a good time, I promise."

She had to trust him. "Okay. I'll see you tomorrow." She wanted to get off the phone.

"Drive safe."

She hung up and threw the phone in her purse.

Ryan was quiet, patient.

She took a breath. "That was Travis."

"So I heard." A smile played at the corner of his mouth. He waited.

"I'm going to see him tomorrow."

He looked up at the snow coming down. "In Star Valley?"

"Yes. We planned it last week. He wanted me to see his place, and I . . . need to talk to him."

"So you've been friends long?"

"Almost five years. He and a friend are just going through a divorce. I'd lost track though. I had no idea he was here."

He was quiet, then calmly offered, "I could drive you. The roads are going to be questionable."

She noted the way he covered any concern he might have aside from the weather. *Yes, drive me . . . No, beg me to stay here with you. We'll be snowed in at the Lantern and forget about everything else.* She swallowed. "I better go alone. He's going through a tough time, and I need to somehow . . . be a friend."

He nodded.

"I'm not staying long."

He reached over and took her hand again. "It's all right. Anyway, this is new. Who am I to stand in the way of old friends?"

She peeked at him, and he looked at her out of the corner of his eye.

"Anyway, I have a bunch of meetings tomorrow," he continued. "I will worry about you on the roads though."

She squeezed his hand.

"Among other things," he muttered.

She suppressed a smile, and he lifted his hand to lightly touch her cheek. She closed her eyes. He turned his fingers to caress her cheek, and she closed her eyes. *Why am I letting him do this?* He took her hand again.

"Thank you," she said. "This has been one of the best nights of my life."

"Really?" He sounded incredulous.

She nodded. "Mm-hmm."

He furrowed his brow but held his smile. "We need to get you out more."

She didn't care about the *out*. She found herself considering the *we*.

The snow thinned and had nearly stopped by the time they got home.

Still, he offered to drive her to Star Valley one more time. She hesitated but stuck to her decision to go alone. She didn't think showing up with Ryan would lift Travis's spirits.

He walked her to the base of the stairs and stopped.

"This far, huh?" she asked.

He nodded. "Yup."

He caressed her hand. The soreness was already fading. "Thank you. I had a really good time . . . much easier than I thought it would be." He smiled, and his soft eyes shone.

She shook her head.

"What?" he asked.

"You're too . . . perfect."

He let out a sharp laugh. "No, no, I'm not."

She frowned at his hands. "But you're not going to kiss me, are you?" This was a turnaround for her. There was no need to put him in his place or squelch his intentions. She peeked up at him.

"No," he repeated softly. "No, I'm not . . . tonight."

She smiled a little, and he turned her to the stairs.

"Call me for anything tomorrow . . . Leave a message if I can't answer. I just want to make sure you make it there. Okay?"

She nodded.

"I'll see you when you get back." He looked up at her as she climbed a few steps backward.

She held his hand out, then let go. "Good night. Thank you, Ryan."

"Good night, Elle. Don't dream about bears."

She shivered pleasantly and turned up the stairs, barely noticing when she made it to her door, undressed, brushed her teeth, and fell into bed.

* * *

The snow was really coming down now, and she glanced at the map as she watched the road through the windshield wipers. It was pretty much a straight shot south from Jackson, but she wanted to make the turnoff. Hank had warned her it was easy to miss if she didn't watch.

She spotted it up ahead as the highway curved to the left, a spur on the right, the sign barely visible in the snow. She turned on her blinker and gripped the steering wheel tighter, not because of the road conditions but because she was closer to having to face whatever Travis had planned. Although she hoped he'd gotten the message the last time they were together, she knew his interpretation was still up in the air. The gloves might have to come off.

The snow seemed to intensify as she entered the broad valley. She pulled up behind what she could only guess was a very top-heavy truck full of hay. It reminded her of Atlas holding the world on his shoulders, only it was teetering a bit. She chuckled.

She saw her next turn come up and followed a road back into a small canyon between two tall mountains rising up out of the valley. She admitted the trees were beautiful, white and draped with thick snow. A creek ran along on the left, and she came to a sign. *George*. No frills. She made the turn and crossed a wooden bridge that led her past the main house, a white clapboard farmhouse with a dark-green metal snow roof. She continued on to a single-story square house with the same green roof. The drive had been shoveled already, and she parked.

The front door flew open, and Travis came bounding out, giving her no time to collect herself before he pulled her out of the car and swung her around in a big bear hug.

He pulled away, breathless from the cold, and smiled. "You made it. What do you think?" He threw his arm wide.

She looked around, breathing the cold air. "It's pretty. Beautiful . . . winter wonderland." She looked Travis over. "That's a new look for you."

He was wearing jeans bunched up over heavy work boots, which were unlaced like he'd just thrown them on, and a plaid flannel shirt open and hanging over a long thermal shirt.

He grinned. "We're working today."

"We are?" She raised an eyebrow warily.

"Well, I am. You just have to sit there and look good. C'mon."

He put his arm around her waist and led her inside. He let her go just inside the door and reached around to shut it, pushing a second time to make sure it latched. She took a couple more steps in, looking around.

Light-blue shag carpet led to a brick semicircle floor underneath a black wood stove, logs glowing behind the grated door. Wood paneling covered the walls, and a couple of old sofas and a rocking chair surrounded the stove. A stereo system sat neatly on an old sideboard against the right wall, and a hallway led back to bedrooms and bath, she assumed.

An old refrigerator hummed from the kitchenette. Ruffled curtains framed the large windows, and a clock shaped like a cat hung on the wall, its tail swinging the seconds away.

"What do you think?" he asked for the second time since she arrived.

She nodded her head. "It's very . . ."

"I know . . . Grandma decorated. But," he shrugged, "I grew up here. And I've been able to live in a few really cool places, so it evens out."

She couldn't suppress a smile at his cheerful outlook. "I was going to say it's very *homey*."

He half smiled, running his hand through his hair. "That's a good word."

Then he was looking her over. "Do you need something to drink or eat?" He gestured to the hallway. "The bathroom is back there, first door on the right. Hold down the handle to flush." He made an apologetic face.

"Thanks," she said as she made her way back. Maybe this wouldn't be so bad. He was his old self. Maybe she'd been worried about nothing.

When she came out of the bathroom, he was rummaging through a coat closet near the front door, tossing out an item here and there.

"Lose something?" she asked.

He stood and turned, holding a boot. "No. Found everything." He gathered the items littering the floor in front of the closet and shut the door behind him with his foot. "Here." He handed her the pile of things.

"What are these?"

"Well, I'm assuming you didn't bring warmer clothes than what you have on."

She looked down. "Um, no."

"Well," he moved to the front window and pointed, "we're going to be out there for a couple of hours, so . . ." He pointed to the things in her hands. "Bundle up."

She looked out the window, then at her pile. "What will we be doing out there?"

He smiled at her as though she was crazy for not knowing. "Feeding cattle. Remember?"

She stared. "I kind of thought you were kidding about that."

He laughed at her and grabbed her shoulders, turned her around, and steered her back to the bathroom. "Bundle up," he said again and swatted her behind.

* * *

Forty minutes later, she was dressed in old sky-blue ski bibs, a pair of purple snow mittens, a multicolor scarf, a pink-and-green-striped knit hat with a big poofy pom-pom on the top, and moon boots. Her own wool jacket topped off the ensemble. And she was grateful because she was sitting on a bale of hay on the back of a large flat sleigh in the middle of a huge, snowy pasture, being pulled along by two very burly looking horses as Travis and his grandpa threw forkfuls of hay out to very big cows following closely along. She held a pitchfork in her hands but had only kicked some of the hay off the sleigh with her boots after deciding she and pitchforks didn't get along.

"How many cows do you have?" she inquired above the sound of the wind, the bells on the horses, the crunch of the snow under their weight, and the mooing cows.

"Cattle," Travis corrected her. "About eighty head."

"Hmm." She turned her attention back to the view. The snow had lightened enough for her to see the base of the mountains surrounding the George property. And even though there was noise, it was muffled against the snow, and the sleigh runners made a soft whooshing sound as the horses pulled slowly forward. She tried to imagine Nicole here, and she just couldn't do it.

It really was pretty, like a Christmas card. A snowy, blustery, wintry Christmas card you sent in December, *not* October. The cows didn't seem to mind. Or cattle.

She sighed, but Travis caught it.

"Having fun?" He smiled challengingly at her.

"Yes, actually, I am." And it was true. It wasn't the *best* time, but it was something new, and she was warm enough, though her toes were starting to protest.

"Good." He breathed heavily from the work. "We're almost done. We've made good time. We'll eat at the big house as soon as we finish."

"Sounds great." She wondered what Ryan was doing. She'd called and left a message that she'd made it there. She looked around again. He would probably love this. Maybe she should have let him come.

After a large, warm lunch, Travis took her hand, gathered up her things, and led her back outside. They tromped to his place and went inside to hang things up to dry and become a sort of rumpled version of their former selves. With the warmth around her and the food inside her, she was suddenly exhausted.

She tugged again at the plastic zipper on her bibs, but it stuck. She pulled again, then tried to pry the fabric out of the teeth.

She stomped her foot. "Ugh."

Travis chuckled and came over. "Here."

She threw her hands down to her sides and brushed her hair out of her face.

Travis tried. "Hmm."

She was suddenly aware of the close proximity of his face to hers, and she leaned away a little.

"Just a second. I almost have it."

She steadied herself, holding her breath.

The zipper gave way. "There." He smiled at her and stepped away.

She breathed and scolded herself. "Thanks, Trav." She peeled out of the bibs while he set their boots near the stove. "What time is it?"

"About one."

"I should be heading back soon," she said as she hung up the bibs on a hook to dry.

He was putting more wood in the stove, so she went to sit on the couch and leaned back. It felt good to sit against something warm.

"Liz."

"Hmm?"

He paused and smiled crookedly. "Your hair's a little frazzled."

"Is it?" She ran her fingers through it and could feel the job the pink pom had done with her hair.

"Here." He sat next to her and smoothed some of the strays.

"Thanks."

His eyes met hers, and her alarm went off, but not in time.

He moved in, his lips touching hers, pulling softly. Then urgently, he was everywhere and kissing her mouth so solidly she didn't have time to think, and her response was almost automatic: the easier option.

He paused for just a moment to breathe. "Liz."

That put her in the right direction. "Travis . . ." She shoved him away. "No." He pressed back, kissing her again. She didn't want to hurt him, but she bit down hard on his lip.

He yelped. "Oww."

She jumped up, standing in front of him. He grinned and reached for her hips, but she jumped back, almost landing on the brick. She held her finger in front of him. "No, Travis."

He looked up at her, the grin still there. "But . . . why?"

"Because . . . because you're just . . . lonely."

He cocked his head and grinned again. "So are you." He said it so matter-of-factly it threw her.

He stood up slowly, taking the two steps he needed to close the distance between them. He wasn't malicious. If he had been, this might have been easier for her. She held her hands up between them.

He placed his hands gently on her arms. "Don't you see? We're both here in this totally obscure part of the world at the same time. We need each other, Liz. The timing is perfect."

He leaned in, slowly this time.

It gave her time to think.

"What about Nicole?" she blurted out.

That stopped him. His look hardened. "What about her?"

"You still love her. I can see it. You're not over her."

"No. I'm not."

She blinked.

"But she's over me."

"You don't know that."

"Yes, I do."

"But I saw . . . the way you were together. She was—"

"She's *with someone*." He dropped his hands.

Elizabeth's mouth hung open. "Oh," she said softly. "Oh, Travis, I'm sorry. I didn't know." She instinctively brought her hand up to his arm, and he leaned into her, dropping his forehead to her shoulder.

He kept his hands to himself, so she brought her arms around his shoulders and patted him a couple of times. "I'm sorry," she repeated.

He stayed there for a minute, then his hands slid around her ribs to her back.

She rolled her eyes. *I'm an idiot.* And now she was trapped between him and the hot stove.

He kissed her gently along her neck, and she blew out a quick breath. If she shoved him, she'd probably end up on the stove behind her. "Travis," she said as steadily as she could. No response. Unbelievable. How could Nicole have stood this for as long as she did? She didn't mean that. She tapped him on the shoulder, hard. "*Travis.*"

"Sorry," he murmured. Then he moved her around so she wasn't next to the stove anymore and came up to whisper in her ear. "C'mon, Wild One. I know you're in there."

Anger reared up inside her. She'd had enough. She shoved hard.

A little too hard. Travis fell back on the stove, putting his hands down on the hot surface. "Ah!" he yelled and jumped up. He looked at her, frustration in his eyes. "What? What is wrong?" he yelled.

She stood her ground, breathing hard. "Travis, I don't want to *do* this," she said firmly. "I don't *feel* that way about—"

He jerked his head toward her, shouting, "You didn't feel that way about a *lot* of guys!"

She drew in her breath sharply. Reaching back, she slapped him hard across his cheek, then, after realizing what she'd done, brought both hands up to her open mouth. Tears stung her eyes at the sight of his shocked expression, and she did the only thing a girl could do in this situation. She bolted for the bathroom and locked the door.

"Liz. *Elizabeth*."

Her chest heaved, and she tried to keep her breathing quiet as his painful words ran over and over through her head. She shoved herself into the corner next to the shower and slid down, feeling hurt and humiliation course through her.

He was right. No wonder he expected . . . That's what she was. Her sobs evened out, and sadness engulfed her.

"Elizabeth." He spoke through the door. "I'm . . . I'm sorry. I shouldn't have said that."

She pressed farther against the wall.

"Liz, please. I promise I won't touch you."

She no longer cared what he did. She had come here because . . . "I came here to be your *friend*," she whispered.

He slid down against the door.

"Sorry," he mumbled again.

A few minutes later, she heard him get up. The front door opened and closed. Had he left? She wanted her purse, her phone. She wanted to call Ryan, to hear his voice. She was immediately filled with self-loathing. She stayed put, and the sadness intensified. She closed her eyes. *I deserve this.* The front door opened, and she watched the crack under the door.

Footsteps.

"Liz." He spoke softly.

She wouldn't answer.

He sighed deeply.

She closed her eyes again as she heard him walk away.

Chapter 17

ELIZABETH.

The voice in her sleep soothed.

She opened her eyes and blinked. She blinked again. Her eyes weren't working. She rubbed them, then looked at her hands, trying to find them.

Realization came. She'd fallen asleep, and now it was dark.

She sat up, trying to work out this disorientation, suppressing her panic. She'd been in the bathroom. Now she lay on a cushion.

Her eyes adjusted, and she blinked again, looking around. The glow of the wood stove came into focus. She lay on a couch in the front room at Travis's house. Except for the sound of sizzling wood in the stove, it was quiet. She breathed.

Cautiously, she pulled off the thick quilt and stood. She tiptoed to the kitchen and squinted at the cat clock on the wall. Seven o'clock. In the morning?

Her hand flew to her head. Ryan would be worried. Nancy would be worried. She looked around the room, trying to locate her purse. The front doorknob jiggled, and she flew back to the couch in two leaps. Throwing the quilt back over her, she closed her eyes as the door opened and somebody stepped through, stomping feet and huffing. The movement stopped.

"Elizabeth." It was Travis. "Liz. You're not fooling anyone. I saw you land on the couch."

She grimaced. She pulled the covers over her head and heard foil scrape on the table. He flipped a light switch.

"I brought you some dinner."

Dinner? Not breakfast? She pulled a corner of the quilt down and peeked out with one eye, watching his legs walk around in front of her. He crouched down slowly, and she ducked into her blankets.

"Liz." His voice was pleading. "I'm sorry. Please talk to me. I won't *try* anything."

She hesitated.

"Look." He opened the palms of his hands to her. They were wrapped in gauze.

She sat up slowly, folding down the quilt with her arms. "Is that . . . from . . . ?"

"My stupidity, yes," he finished. He looked down.

She allowed him that. She looked down at the quilt. "How did I get out here?"

"That lock hasn't worked in twenty years."

She looked toward the bathroom. "Oh."

"I just thought you might be more comfortable out here."

"Thank you." She was still a bit disoriented. "So, it isn't morning?"

He paused, then smiled a little. "No. It's the same day it was . . . earlier." He looked down again.

She looked around. "Where's my purse?"

He brought his head up. "Umm." He stood and walked over to the stereo, then returned. "Here." He held it out.

She took it from him and hugged it to her chest. "I should go."

He rubbed the side of his head with his fingertips. "Well . . . here's the thing . . ."

She narrowed her eyes.

He saw it and took a breath, pausing. "Well, maybe you should see for yourself, then." He got up and turned to the window, pulling back a ruffled curtain.

She pushed up off the couch and stood. She straightened her shirt, and keeping her distance from Travis, she stepped to the window.

"Ohhh no." She exhaled, and her breath made a foggy spot on the glass. She leaned forward and pressed her forehead to the cold window.

The porch light had no trouble reflecting off the white, making it easy to see. Almost three feet of snow covered everything. She looked at her car and could see where someone had tried to dig around it and the drive, but the snow was still falling. Big fat flakes, fast and hard.

She looked at Travis, then down at his hands.

"I tried. I really did. My grandma just changed the bandages." He shook his head and looked truly sorry. "It's just falling too fast. Even for the snow blower."

Elizabeth looked out the window again. She sighed. "Okay." She turned away from the window. "I have to call some people." Pulling out her phone, she asked, "Do you have a hairbrush?"

"A . . . hairbrush?"

She knew how she sounded, but she was serious. "Yes." She could think more clearly when her hair didn't look like a pile of hay.

"I think I can find one, yes. Probably even a toothbrush."

"Great. While you're at it, bring me a nine iron, 'cause I'm sleeping with it tonight."

Amusement crossed his face, and she narrowed her eyes.

He sobered.

She turned and walked back to the couch as he went to find what she'd asked for.

"Hello?"

"Hello, Nancy, it's me."

"Oh, hello, darling, having a good time?"

"I'm stuck here until tomorrow." Her voice was a little more monotone than she'd intended.

"What?"

"You heard me. Three feet of snow. Don't you have it there?"

"No, just a few inches. Oh, I'm sorry. Is everything . . . *going all right?*" She whispered the last part.

"Peachy. I'll talk to you later, okay? I just wanted to let you know I won't be in tomorrow until I can get out of this snow."

"All right, as long as you're safe. They're pretty good at getting the snow plows out nice and early."

Elizabeth finished the call and dialed the next number. She took a deep breath as Travis came back into the room. He handed her a hairbrush and toothbrush.

"Where's the nine iron?" she asked, looking up at him, eyes still narrowed.

"I don't golf."

"Maybe you should take it up."

His mouth twitched.

She took another breath and accepted the offering, and he backed away to sit on the other couch, keeping his distance.

She pressed call.

"Elizabeth?"

She couldn't help the warmth that washed through her. "Yes. Hi."

"Are you all right? I've called. You didn't try to drive home, did you?"

He *was* perfect.

"No. It's just too much."

"I know. I've been keeping an eye on it. I almost went out there to get you when you didn't return my call."

"You did?"

"Yes. Is that too protective?"

She smiled. "No. We were outside for a long time, feeding cows—I mean, cattle."

Travis and Ryan chuckled at the same time.

"Then I fell asleep, and it started doing this. Three feet. Travis tried to dig me out, but . . ." She sighed again. "I'm sorry."

"It's not your fault. I'd rather you stay put than go out on those roads."

She hesitated. "You don't know what you're saying."

"Oh?" He was quiet. "Does Mr. George need to be told where to put his financial advice?"

She muffled a laugh and glanced at Travis, who skulked. But she didn't want to get into it. "He's . . . behaving himself." *Because Mr. All Hands is now Mr. All Thumbs.*

"Hmm. Do you want me to come get you?"

Yes. "Please just talk to me for a little while. What did you do today? How were your meetings?" She felt Travis's eyes on her, but she didn't care. Let him stew. He'd hurt her. He'd been a jerk.

"I, uh, took the kids to church."

Ouch. Tipping the perfection scales.

Her voice came up a little higher. "Oh." She cleared her throat. "How was that?"

"Nice." Did he sound amused? "Maybe you could come sometime."

She gulped. "Nancy said there were only a few inches of snow there." Travis flinched, and she guessed right. He had assumed she was talking to Nancy.

"Yeah, the storm passed to the south, obviously. It should ease up late tonight. You'll be able to leave later in the morning."

"I'll do that."

"But you'll still have to be careful."

"I'll do that too."

There was a sound in the background . . . someone calling.

"Lily says hi, and she hopes you'll be safe."

Her heart fluttered. "Oh. Tell her . . . thanks."

He paused. "She asks about you."

"She does?" She tried not to sound worried. "What does she ask?"

"Oh, when are you coming back over . . . What is your favorite color . . . Whether or not you like broccoli. That kind of thing."

He spoke casually, but she felt the words a little deeper than that.

He let her take it in. Then he said quietly, "Actually, I'm wondering the same things."

She felt the smile coming.

"Well, not about the broccoli. I got that answer last night. Yes on broccoli. I wasn't all that surprised either. I mean, you'd probably throw it in a blender with a mango or something."

The smile came. Was it really only last night? She sighed. "I had a great time."

"So did I." He paused. "I've got to go. Chloe's got me hosting game night. I figure if I'm good, she'll let me off early."

She felt a flash of nerves but still said, "You'd better go play, then."

"I'll see you tomorrow."

"Yes."

"You can call me anytime."

"I know."

"Elizabeth, are you sure you'll be okay?"

She looked again at Travis, whose head was down. She almost felt sorry, but it passed. "Yes, I'm sure."

There was a smile in his voice. "I'll see you tomorrow."

She hung up and sighed.

Travis cleared his throat, looking uncomfortable.

She gathered the brushes and her purse and pointed at him as she stood and walked to the bathroom. "If I so much as hear that doorknob *jiggle*, you are going to have more than your *hands* to worry about."

He nodded solemnly, and she went to take a shower.

*   *   *

She came out of the bathroom feeling better. She heard the microwave ding, and as she rounded the corner, Travis placed a plate of food on the table.

"Here you go." He said it without looking up. He gingerly opened the fridge and asked, "What do you want to drink?"

She took a deep breath. She still felt hurt crawling around inside, doing whatever damage it could, and a fresh gnawing of self-doubt too, but her conversation with Ryan and the shower had calmed her. She was thinking more rationally.

"Water?" she asked.

He got her a glass and filled it with ice and water and set it down by her plate. Then he turned to leave.

"Where are you going?" She was feeling a pang of pity.

He turned around. "I am going to *try* to shower." He gestured with his hands to emphasize how difficult that might be. "I'd threaten you with something so you'll stay out, but you don't seem to have that problem." He turned and walked away.

She stared at her meal and then muttered under her breath and picked up her fork.

When Travis was done, she was doing the dishes and wiping the kitchen down.

She turned to find him wearing a pair of flannel sleep pants, watching her.

"I need help with this." He held the bandages out.

She tossed the dishrag in the sink and wiped her hands on her jeans, walking to the table. She sat down, and he took the seat across from her, letting the bandages roll toward her. His hands were turned down, and she reached for them, turning them over.

She gasped. The large blisters were torn and weeping, covering his palms and finger pads. His hands had a slight tremor.

"Oh, Travis," she whispered.

She looked up at him and then to the front window, picturing the attempted shoveling around her car and the drive.

She took the antibiotic cream and a swab and applied the ointment as gently as she could. He winced a few times but held still. She wrapped the gauze carefully and taped it, then wiped away the tears on her face and shook her head.

"That shouldn't have happened," she said.

"I know. None of it should have," he answered quietly. "But I . . ." He searched for words. "It's my fault. I'm sorry." He tipped his head to the side, quiet for a moment. "Why didn't you tell me?"

"Tell you what?"

"That you were seeing somebody."

Her mouth hung partially open. She took a breath to say something but wasn't sure what to say. She tried. "Because . . . I guess I really didn't know I was . . . until that happened. It's new."

"Hmph. Figures." He shook his head and closed his eyes.

She pursed her lips and tapped the table.

"Who is he?"

Here's where it would be tricky. Travis and Ryan did business together. Her gaze drifted out the kitchen window. She didn't have to tell him, but part of her thought it would be best he knew, especially if she would be accepting the partnership. He watched her, and she looked down.

"Ryan Brennan," he guessed.

Her head snapped up. "How did you . . . ?"

He shrugged. "I don't know . . . I guess I tried to ignore the way he watched you . . . the way you watched back. He got to see you, what, every day?" He went to put his face in his hands and stopped himself before he hit the bandages. He folded his arms on the table. "I'm not blaming you, but . . . I wish you would have told me."

She looked at him. "Would that have made any difference?"

"Yeah." He nodded.

"Why?" She couldn't see how, remembering how determined he'd been.

He looked down. "Because you don't cheat."

They were both thoughtful for several minutes.

Later, she lay stretched out on the couch, and he was on the floor. They watched a small TV Travis had pulled out of a closet. The reception was awful, but the sound was good on an old episode of *M.A.S.H.* They chuckled occasionally but were mostly silent.

"You know what I told Nancy about you, Travis?" Elizabeth asked during a commercial.

"Hmm."

"I told her you were one of the good ones."

He looked over at her. "Yeah, I guess I really proved that today, huh?"

She smiled, tired. "I meant it. I'd always thought that."

"And now?"

She narrowed her eyes at him. "Prove me right."

He looked at her. He clenched his jaw and nodded his head slowly, then looked back at the TV. "Brennan has kids, doesn't he?"

"Mm-hmm. Three." She didn't mean for it to come out so hoarse. She swallowed.

He nodded. "I guess I could see you doing that."

She made a sound of disbelief.

He turned to look at her. "What?"

"Isn't that a little contrary to what you said about me earlier?"

He sighed and shook his head. "I wish you would forget I said that."

"It was the truth," she whispered.

"Yeah, but," he turned back to the TV, "that was a long time ago."

She watched him staring at the TV screen until he faced her again.

"What made you change?"

She pressed her lips together and shook her head. "I don't want to talk about it." He nodded and turned back to the black-and-white fuzz. She swallowed hard. "Things just had to change."

He nodded again, and she knew he wasn't really paying attention to the TV.

"I'm sorry she left you, Travis." She watched his chest rising up and down.

He answered. "I'm sorry you're not my second chance."

The commercial ended. They continued to watch until the snow finally stopped falling, and then they fell asleep.

Chapter 18

IT TOOK THREE HOURS PLUS a half-hour break to get the drive and her car cleared enough to reach the main road. Elizabeth had insisted on being shown how to use the snow blower so Travis didn't have to further injure his hands. He'd made some calls, but everyone was digging themselves out. He did get some promises for help for his grandparents while his hands healed though.

When she could get the car out, she took Travis to the doctor, threatening him with a crowbar she found by the snow blower in the barn. She took him to get the antibiotics he needed and drove him back home. He, in turn, insisted on feeding her.

It was nearly four thirty when she was on the road, headed home. Her muscles were stiff, and she was emotionally drained, but home sounded good.

Home. She smiled crookedly. She wasn't even thinking of Kalispell . . . or the lake house. The knots in her stomach tightened. She might make it before six.

Or six thirty. Traffic had stopped where someone had hit a deer, and then traffic was slow-going after Alpine. It gave her a lot of time to think.

C'mon, Wild One. I know you're in there.
He's too perfect.
I took the kids to church.
You didn't feel that way about a lot of guys.
Lily asks about you.
Chloe is curious.
I'm not sure he knew how to live without her.
She was a dancer.
The view would be spectacular . . . because of where you've been.
Too perfect.

Relentless thoughts she tried to shove away.

When she saw the city-limit sign, she breathed a sigh of relief. She shook her head at the three inches of snow on the sides of the wet but clear roads.

The Lantern was a beacon on the long road, just at the curve south to Ryan's cabin. She pulled into a parking space and leaned her head against the steering wheel, clearing her thoughts.

It worked, somewhat, and she pulled herself out of the car and hurried inside. She checked in with Dayle at the front desk, who greeted her with a hug Elizabeth should have cringed at, and went right upstairs. She'd barely collapsed on the bed when the phone rang.

She reached. "Hello?"

"You made it."

She sighed. "Yes."

"Can I see you?"

"When?" she answered too eagerly.

"Now."

"Where are you?"

"Downstairs."

"Give me a few minutes, and I'll be right down."

"Good."

She took a quick shower, dressed in fresh clothes, and pulled her hair back into a ponytail. She peeked over the railing as she left her room, and he stood there, waiting. He turned and looked up, breaking into a boyish smile. She breathed out a derisive laugh at how helpless such a simple gesture made her feel. This was insane. She came down the stairs, and he stepped forward to meet her.

"Hi." He carefully took her hands in his, as if to make sure it was all right to do so.

She couldn't help it. Her smile broadened, and she squeezed them back. "Hi."

He brought his hand up to the side of her face. They looked at each other for a minute, her mind racing with empty ideas of how she could escape. Empty because she didn't want to.

"Are you tired?" he asked.

"No." She shook her head.

"But you want to relax?"

"Please."

Ryan looked over at the great room. "I was wondering . . . if you'd like to play a game." He looked at her expectantly.

She glanced over where he had and saw the Franks sitting at the table, smiling and waiting. Four places had been dealt. When she looked questioningly back at Ryan, he had a pleading expression on his face.

"Um, all right."

He grinned and pulled her toward the table. The older man stood.

"Wayne, Celia, this is Elizabeth. Elizabeth, Wayne and Celia Frank."

Wayne put his hand forward, and Elizabeth took it. "Pleasure to meet you, Elizabeth." He motioned for her to have a seat, so she took the one next to Celia.

Celia leaned toward her as Ryan and Wayne sat down. "Bet you didn't think you'd be doing *this* tonight." She winked at her with an amused smile.

Elizabeth smiled back. "No, I can't say that I did." She glanced at Ryan, who was watching her. "What are we playing?"

"Gin rummy," Wayne said.

Elizabeth picked up her cards. "I think I remember that one. Run of three, set of three?"

Wayne nodded. "And the Joker's *wild.*"

The way he said it made her chuckle. She shook her head. "I don't think I've played this since summer camp."

"You went to camp?" Ryan asked her.

She nodded, sorting through her cards. "Music camp. Two weeks every summer."

"Oh, what do you play?" Celia asked.

Elizabeth hesitated, glancing at Ryan, who watched her intently. She cleared her throat as the game began. "The piano. I played the piano. But I haven't played for a very long time." She saw Ryan look over at the piano in the corner. He started to say something, but she cut him off. "No."

"But . . ."

She looked at him, eyebrows raised, and gently but firmly said, "No."

He placed his chin in his hand as she drew, then discarded. She detected a small pout. It wasn't unpleasant.

"So," she changed the subject, "where are you two from?"

Wayne answered as he discarded. "Buffalo."

She nodded. "New York."

"No, Wyoming."

She laughed, surprised. "Where is that?" It was her turn again.

"Just east of the Big Horns. This side of Sheridan."

She nodded, knowing she had probably learned that in school at some point. "So you're just here for a holiday?"

"We've been coming here every year since we've been married," Wayne said.

"We came here for our honeymoon, right, Ryan?" Celia drew a card and organized her hand.

Elizabeth did some calculating and looked at Ryan, who concentrated on his cards.

"Mm-hmm," was all he offered.

"Well, how long have you been married?" She was curious now.

Wayne and Celia looked at one another and smiled so tenderly Elizabeth looked down.

"Four years tomorrow," Wayne said.

Elizabeth brought her head up and looked at the two of them as Wayne reached over and held Celia's hand. Celia turned and saw Elizabeth's face. She nodded her head. "It's true. You don't need to look so shocked, dear. We know quite a few people who have been married far longer than that."

Ryan chuckled, and Wayne joined him. Wayne reached over and kissed Celia's cheek, and she beamed. Elizabeth smiled and shook her head.

"It's your turn, Liz." Wayne got the game moving again.

An hour later, Elizabeth satisfactorily discarded her last card. A groan went around the table. "I win," she said.

"Again." Ryan looked at her, shaking his head.

She raised an eyebrow at him and nodded, grinning.

He suddenly leaned toward her, a look of intensity in his eyes. He wrapped his strong hand around hers and said in a low voice, almost a growl but much more inviting, "I'll bet you lose this next round."

She leaned toward him, eyes narrowing. "I'll take that bet." She'd won three games in a row.

Ryan kept up his intensity, a smile playing at the corners of his mouth. "If you lose, you have to play the piano for us."

She wavered and bit her lip, thinking quickly. "If I win, I get to ask you to do anything I want."

Wayne and Celia laughed quietly.

Ryan blinked and swallowed. "You're on."

Wayne slapped his hand on the table, and Ryan jumped. "Well, all right, then." Wayne licked his thumb and started dealing the cards as Elizabeth laughed silently.

The pleasant banter and small talk that had filled the previous games were gone. There were still smiles, grunts, sighs, and secretive looks, but the game was on, and there was a bet to win.

Elizabeth's knee started to bounce up and down, and Ryan looked at his cards like he would set them on fire if he could. They all drew, discarded, shuffled, laid down.

"Ha!" Everyone looked. Celia sat with her arms folded on the table, a smug smile on her face, her last card lying upside down on the discard pile, where she had tossed it.

Elizabeth felt Ryan's eyes on her, triumphant. She felt the color drain from her face and a soft hand on her arm.

"Sorry, dear. I just couldn't help it."

Elizabeth smiled and shook her head, looking over at this little lady with gray hair curling up in a roll at the ends, probably the same way she'd worn it since she was in school.

"I would really like to hear you play something though."

How could she refuse that voice? She drew in a deep breath. "Okay."

Ryan scooted his chair back and pulled hers out for her.

How gentlemanly.

She stood, and he held his hand out toward the piano. She took a couple of steps around the table and stopped. "I don't want to wake anybody up."

"It's only eight fifteen," Ryan said.

She looked at him. It felt a lot later than that. He smiled encouragingly and mouthed the word *please.*

Ugh. She walked over to the piano and pulled out the bench. She sat down, and the others gathered around her. She fingered the wood and lifted the cover gently. Her fingers touched the ivory, moving softly between the black keys. They started to tremble a little, and she took another breath. She looked up at Ryan. "What should I play?"

"Whatever you want." He reached his hand to her chin and held it for a moment. She could tell he would let her off the hook if she really wanted.

She turned back to square herself to the keys. "Okay." She shook her head. "But I haven't played in a really long time." She inhaled and blew out a shaky breath, lifting her wrists above her fingers. She *really* didn't need this. She began to play.

"Für Elise"—her mother's favorite.

She played timidly at first, her fingers remembering, trying to keep up with the music she saw in her mind. But as the recognition set in, clicked in sync, she felt the music begin to move through her, connecting her to the instrument. The emotion of the notes and the rhythm flowed with the pressure of her fingers as they moved up and down the keys. She no longer had to concentrate so much, and she closed her eyes, absently leaning her head to the side. Her breathing swelled with the music as the tempo picked up and leapt around, then calmed down as the composition simplified, quieted, then ended as she crossed her hands up the scale to hit the last hovering note.

She discreetly brought a finger up to wipe the tear away. Then she heard applause. She turned on the bench and was surprised to see several more people in the room, a few on the staircase leaning over the railing, and Jeff back at the front desk. He stuck his fingers in his mouth and whistled. She breathed out a smile but turned back around, her head down over the piano, fingering the keys again. She felt a hand on her back and looked up at Ryan, who smiled appreciatively. She smiled back and shook her head, sensing the other people milling back out of the room, going back to whatever they'd been doing before she had interrupted their lives.

"Oh, that was beautiful, dear. Did you play professionally?"

She looked up at Celia. "No, no. I just . . . played." She shrugged her shoulders.

"Well, thank you. I'm glad you lost." Celia gave her a twinkling smile, then looked at Wayne. "Well, dear, should we turn in?"

He nodded. "You bet." He nodded at Elizabeth. "Thanks, Liz. That was something."

"Thank you." Elizabeth pushed the bench back and stood up next to Ryan, who easily placed his arm around her waist, sending chills through her.

They said good night to Wayne and Celia. She watched them walk away, arm in arm, occasionally looking at one another, sharing that tender smile. She felt a pull sideways.

"C'mon." Ryan steered her to the front doors, nodding at his dad as they passed. Jeff nodded and winked.

He led her to the far end of the porch, toward the swing, but he didn't sit down. They leaned together against the end railing, and he looked up at the sky, beyond the porch roofline.

"Wow," she said as she looked at the myriad stars sprayed across the sky.

"Mm-hmm."

She faced him, and he was watching her. She looked down.

"How long has it been since you played?"

"About ten years."

"Since your mother died."

She nodded.

"Why?"

She breathed in the fresh night air, shivering. Ryan grabbed a blanket off the swing and threw it around her shoulders.

"Thanks."

He folded his arms and leaned next to her on the railing.

The blanket was heavy and warmed up with her body heat. "I played for my mom. She loved to listen, and it would be just us, where her focus was on me, and I knew I was doing something she loved. When she was gone . . . there just didn't seem to be a point. It was . . . painful to play and not have her listening."

He was quiet for a minute. Then he asked, "How did you feel tonight? When you were playing?"

She looked at the stars. "It felt good. Wonderful. I forgot how it feels, the music. I wished . . . she was there listening. It was almost like . . ." She stopped, a lump forming in her throat.

Ryan took her hand and caressed it. "What would you think"—he looked at her hand—"if I said I thought your mom was there listening?"

She felt the stinging in her eyes and nose. She looked at him like he was crazy but at the same time felt he was right, that she had felt her too. She wanted to agree, to nod her head and embrace it as truth, but it was too painful to believe, too frightening to embrace if it turned out to be wrong. She had too much to think about. She was better off not believing.

He sensed the contradiction. "It's okay. It's just an idea. If she could have heard you, though," he proceeded with caution, "she would have been pleased . . . happy. I know it."

She allowed that. She leaned her head on his shoulder.

"You *are* tired."

She nodded and shrugged. "It's been a *long* couple of days."

"Did you want to talk about it?"

She shook her head. "Not now."

"Okay."

She felt the question rise and hated it. The more she suppressed asking, the harder the question pushed. He'd been so pleased. She had to know. "Did she play?"

"Who?"

She breathed and said the name. "*Brooke.* Did she play the piano?"

His fingers paused along her hand. She didn't dare move as she waited, not breathing. She tried to tell herself it didn't matter. But it did matter. She didn't understand why it mattered so much.

"No, Elle. She didn't." His fingers moved along hers again.

She breathed, a touch of foolishness warming her face. She changed the subject. "The Franks are nice. I would have never guessed they hadn't been together their whole lives."

He chuckled softly. "I know. It's quite a story, actually."

She looked at him expectantly.

He brought her hand up to the side of his face, then turned and brushed his lips against it, watching her. She felt her knees go weak as her heart raced. He smiled and placed their hands back down on the railing.

"They met on an airplane, both returning from Florida. They had both hated it."

"Really?"

"Yup. Too hot. Too humid. They got to talking and found out they had grown up about twenty miles from each other and their fathers had done business together."

"You're kidding. What kind of business?"

"Her father ran a bootlegging operation."

Elizabeth laughed. "What did his father do?"

"He was a cop."

"Really?"

Ryan laughed and nodded.

"Oh no."

Ryan continued the story. "But they each grew up, left home, and he went to war without ever meeting her. They can remember the same events, though—parades, dances, Fourth of July picnics—so they both had to have been there at the same time. They each got married, lived in different parts of the country, had families. Life happened, and then they met on the plane, both widowed . . . I think Celia a couple of times."

Elizabeth furrowed her brow.

"So they discovered they both had children living in Buffalo, and they had both recently moved there to be closer to their grandkids." He smiled at Elizabeth. "And they got along so well that a week after they got home, they announced to their families that they were getting married." He looked back up at the stars. "Their families were thrilled."

Elizabeth blinked, wondering at the way life worked. "Happily ever after."

Ryan dropped his eyes. After a minute, he said, "A year later, Celia started showing signs of Alzheimer's. I remember . . . she would get confused about where she was . . . just barely noticeable, but it happened often enough during their stay . . ."

Elizabeth couldn't take her eyes off him. She'd wanted to hear something good . . . a happy ending. She waited.

He turned to her and drew her up, his arms around her blanket, his hands clasped behind her back. Their breath had begun to make puffs in the chilled air. "He can't let her wander off, but I think he likes being close to her, protecting her. He feels needed. They play card games to exercise her mind. Sometimes she gets frustrated." He looked to the windows. "Tonight was a good night."

Elizabeth watched his profile, felt his strength around her. "She's lucky to have him, then."

"Yes. That's what *she* says. She said she never wanted to find love again, didn't consider it, but," he looked at her again, "she feels like Wayne was sent to her so she wouldn't have to be alone. Even if she would only be able to know him for a little while."

They looked at each other, and everything stilled. "You should play the piano more," he softly said.

She tried to breathe. "You should . . ." But she couldn't think of anything more she would have him do.

Then she thought of one thing. One terrifying thing.

She lifted her chin, watching his mouth, and he drew closer, hesitating, his eyes tracing her features. "Elle, we need to take this slowly," he whispered.

She nodded, her heart pounding like a jackhammer.

He whispered again, his nose brushing hers. "Are you . . . staying?"

She nodded again. His hand gently cradled the back of her neck. He tilted his head nearer as her eyes closed.

"Wait." Her eyes flew open, and she swallowed. "What about Chloe?" she whispered.

The corner of his mouth turned up. "She'll get over it."

He pressed his lips to hers. Her fear mixed with something . . . Desire? Need? Joy? Any of those. All three of those.

At her sound of pleasure, she felt him smile, and he took the opportunity to show her that five years or ten gone by, Ryan Brennan knew how to kiss a girl.

Chapter 19

ELIZABETH WALKED IN THE BACK door of the shop and was hanging her coat on a hook when she heard a sudden yelp from the office.

She jumped back as Nancy came flying out and threw her arms around her in an embrace, rocking Elizabeth back and forth like a tall ship as she spoke. "Oh, I'm so glad you made it back safe and sound. I was worried sick. You'll have to tell me all about it." She pulled away and gave her a stern look. "Elizabeth Mariah Embry, why didn't you call when you got home?"

She had flashbacks of being twelve. "Oh, I'm sorry, I—"

"Why didn't you answer your cell phone last night?"

"I didn't have it with me. I'm sorry."

"And you didn't check your messages?"

"I didn't. I just went right to sleep. I was exhausted." It was the truth. Ryan had walked her to the base of the stairs, said good night, and once again, she'd kind of floated upstairs and couldn't remember much after that. She started to smile at the memory, but Nancy pulled her out of it.

"And this *morning*?"

"Really, Nancy, what is wrong? What did I miss?"

Nancy broke into a wide grin. "I found a place."

"What?"

"I found a place . . . for *you*. Of course, I'd put the word out, darling, and a friend of mine called me last night. Oh, it's gorgeous, but it will go fast, and she'll only hold it for a couple of days. I wanted to take you there last night, but I guess this morning would be just as good. You can see it in the daylight."

"But, Nancy, I haven't decided yet."

"Oh, I know, but if you wait to start looking on the day you decide, well, you'll run out of time to look for a place, now won't you? Besides,"

Nancy stood and walked past Elizabeth to get her coat and purse, "you know you're staying."

Elizabeth shook her head. "*I* know I know, but how did *you* know I know?"

Nancy faced her and leaned close. "Darling, everywhere we've been, everything we've seen and done together, I have *never* seen more glimpses of *you* than since you have been *here*." She reached for Elizabeth's coat and tossed it to her. "You're staying. I'll have the lawyer bring over the papers. They're all ready for you." She took a few steps to the front of the store. "Marisol, I'm taking Elizabeth to look at the apartment. We shouldn't be gone too long."

"Have fun."

Elizabeth looked in the direction of Marisol's voice but was jerked backward by Nancy, already halfway out the door.

They drove to a section of town she hadn't seen yet. The townhomes Nancy pulled up to were nice, clean, new. They got out of the car, and Nancy smiled. "What do you think?"

Elizabeth nodded.

"Let's see the inside."

Nancy led her up to the front door and rang the doorbell. A woman Nancy's age opened the door, greeted them, and led them around the apartment. It was narrow, with two levels, very clean, and quite beautiful.

It was just what Elizabeth should have wanted, but she was very aware of her lack of enthusiasm. Still, she needed a place, it was close to work, and it suited her needs. They shook hands and decided Elizabeth would move in at the first of the month.

Nancy was ecstatic. "Oh, I feel we should celebrate." They were headed back to the shop.

"It's ten in the morning."

Nancy ignored her. "*Oh*, I know." She parked in front of a bakery. "I'll be right back."

Elizabeth waited in the car and watched Nancy return carrying a white box. She got in and placed the box on Elizabeth's lap. "Ta-dah."

"What did you get?"

"Sweets for the sweet. Which, in this case, means you, me, and Marisol."

Elizabeth peeked inside. The aroma of freshly baked cinnamon bread wafted through the car. "Oh, yum." She closed her eyes and took a deep breath. "Nancy?"

"Yes?"

"Is it all right if I bow out of our plans Thursday night?" She peeked at Nancy.

"What? We were going to see that cowboy poetry thing."

"I know, I know . . . but something has come up."

"Elizabeth, what could possibly come up?"

Elizabeth braced herself. "I . . . sort of . . . have a date."

"You what? How . . . who?" Her eyes grew large. "Oh. *Oh* . . ."

Elizabeth saw the exact moment Nancy figured it out.

"*Ryan*! Oh, I *knew* it." She turned to Elizabeth, who already had her hand up to shield herself for what was coming. "It's *Ryan*, isn't it?" Nancy didn't even wait for an answer. "It was the hike, wasn't it? I *knew* you were acting funny. Oh, he is so handsome. And kind—you can see it in his eyes. You see? It was written in the stars. You coming here, meeting him. And *I had a part in it.* I tried to tell you, didn't I? But you wouldn't listen; you just kept shushing me, but I knew. And his *family*—oh." She stopped her exclamations of joy and grabbed Elizabeth's hand. "Oh my, that's big, isn't it?"

Elizabeth had to try really hard to keep from laughing because Nancy was giving Marisol a run for her money. She nodded. "Yes, which is why I need to cancel our plans. I'm . . . having dinner with his family." She sighed.

"Oh my." Nancy patted Elizabeth's hand. "Well, I won't say anything more about it. You go ahead and don't even think about Hank and me."

"Thank you."

"You must be a nervous wreck."

"Nancy."

"Sorry, darling." She started the car and backed out. "Now *I'm* a nervous wreck."

Later, as Elizabeth handed Frank a lovely bouquet, she tried to explain to him that it was *her* fault Nancy had backed into a floral delivery truck.

* * *

"Hello. Wildberries. This is Elizabeth; how may I help you?" She twirled one of Ryan's business cards from the counter display in her fingers.

"Hi, Elizabeth, it's Nora Dalton. You sick of me yet?"

Elizabeth set the card down. "No, of course not." She felt a twinge of guilt about bowing out of her last invitation. "You told me you would be persistent."

Nora laughed. "That's why I called. I've found myself with some free time tomorrow and thought of you. Want to do lunch?"

"That would be great. I have the day off. What time?"

"Want to meet at the sushi place? Do you do sushi?"

"I love sushi."

"Good. I'm craving it like crazy."

"I thought pregnant women couldn't eat raw fish."

"I get the steamed stuff. I need it like a window needs a wall." Elizabeth laughed.

"Okay, meet me at noon at Nikai."

Elizabeth wrote the name of the restaurant down. "See you then."

* * *

Ryan stayed home with the kids that night because Sam had a fever and Chloe needed his help with a school report. Nancy had a chamber meeting, which she insisted Elizabeth not attend or endure until she absolutely had to.

So Elizabeth had picked up takeout on the way home, eaten in her room, and was now browsing the bookshelves in the front room at the inn. Her fingers ran over the titles above and below her. A lower shelf seemed to be committed to religious subjects, and that strange little knot in her stomach tightened as she straightened up and steered clear. She finally settled on an interesting-looking novel and lounged on the sofa in front of the fireplace.

At ten o'clock, she felt a hand on her shoulder. Ryan slid down to sit beside her as she set her book aside.

"Hi," he said as he wrapped his arms around her.

"Hi." She ignored her usual instinct to pull away. "How are you?"

"Good. I escaped."

She chuckled and leaned into him as he smoothed her hair. He reached over and picked up her book, looking at the title.

"This is a good one."

"How does it end?"

He frowned. "It's a surprise."

She grinned.

He handed the book to her. "Go ahead. I don't mind."

"Are you sure?"

"Yup." He reinforced it by settling farther back into the couch and placing the book in her hands.

She read, curled up next to him, as he watched the fire.

Every so often, she was struck by a feeling of true contentment.

And the gnawing feeling that she didn't deserve it.

* * *

She found herself in the kitchen the following morning sprinkling cinnamon sugar over a long, buttered rectangle of soft dough.

"Don't be shy, honey; we like our cinnamon rolls strong."

Elizabeth shook the can of cinnamon harder.

"That's it. Now we roll the dough like this and pinch the seam closed."

Elizabeth copied Dayle's movements and peeked over at Ryan, who was expertly cutting fresh pineapples. He caught her eye and winked. She smiled back.

Jeff had been at the stove frying sausages, potatoes, peppers, and onions, but he moved to the island and grabbed a bag of powdered sugar. He pulled at both sides to open it and was immediately assaulted by an explosion of fine white powder.

Stunned silence settled along with the sugar, then a rising chorus of snickering filled the kitchen.

"Sweetheart," Dayle said as she wiped a tear from the corner of her eye, "when will you ever learn?"

Elizabeth shook even harder as Jeff used his fingers to wipe his frosted glasses like windshield wipers.

After the rush of the breakfast crowd, Ryan found a folder of sheet music. He and Elizabeth sat at the piano, and she played. When she finished the first song, he handed her another song.

"Play this one."

She looked. "How Great Thou Art."

"Mm-hmm. I like it."

She couldn't refuse. She played, glimpsing the words now and then, smiling when she heard Ryan hum a little. It was a powerful melody.

"Now this one." He was like a kid trying out a new toy.

"Root Beer Rag?"

He nodded, his eyebrows raised.

She grinned and played the song she remembered learning as a child. She challenged herself to play as fast as she could, and when she finished with a pounce, they both broke out laughing. He grabbed her up, and she kissed his cheek.

"That sounded great."

They both turned to see Jeff, now cleaned up, standing with his hands on his hips.

"Oh," Elizabeth said, still laughing softly. "Thank you."

He lowered his chin and looked at both of them. "I meant the laughter." He turned and walked away, whistling "How Great Thou Art."

Elizabeth snorted a chuckle as she spotted a patch of powdered sugar on the back of his neck. Ryan laughed at her snort.

They looked at each other a moment, and just before Elizabeth was going to turn away, he kissed her softly.

"Thank you," he whispered.

She shook her head slightly. Then she pulled away, looking at the clock. "I almost forgot. I have to go."

"Go?"

"To lunch. A woman I met at the shop invited me."

He furrowed his brow, and she grinned at his expression.

"I'm sorry, I forgot to tell you. I forget a lot of things when I'm with you."

"Is that good?" He was teasing her.

"Mostly." She looked down. "But it's a little confusing when I'm without you again." A corner of her mouth came up, but her eyes remained down.

He lifted her chin, and she looked at him. "Then hurry back," he said.

A smile stole across her face.

* * *

Elizabeth entered the restaurant and immediately found Nora waving from a table.

"Elizabeth!"

She went to join Nora, looking at the array of dishes and pots on the table. Nora held chopsticks grasping sticky rice.

"I went ahead and ordered for us. I hope you don't mind."

Elizabeth smiled. "No, that's fine." She looked again. "Hungry?"

"You have no idea. My mouth has been watering for this since yesterday. It's so weird."

Elizabeth sat down.

Nora pointed with her chopsticks. "We've got dumplings and spring rolls and California rolls, of course . . . edamame and grilled asparagus, some tempura, oh, and this spicy diablo roll, which I might really regret later, but I just can't help myself, and a few other things." She looked up. "I hope that's all right?"

"Of course." Elizabeth helped herself to the small buffet. "Is this the entire menu?"

Nora smiled and chewed her sticky rice.

"So," Elizabeth asked after they'd eaten most of the food, "when is your baby due?"

"January 10."

"Huh, that's a week after my sister's baby is due."

"Really? What's your sister's name?"

"Amanda."

"Boy or girl?"

"Boy."

"Is this her first?"

"Yes. The first for all of us. What about you? Is your son going to have a sister or brother?"

Her eyes lit up. "Sister. Finally."

Elizabeth looked at her. "Finally?"

"This is number four. I have three boys."

Elizabeth dropped her chopsticks. "You have *four* children?"

"Three, and this one." She patted her middle then held her fingers up. "Jacob, Jared, and Levi." She looked down and then raised her eyes to meet Elizabeth's. "And, believe it or not, this little one is Elizabeth."

Elizabeth's mouth dropped open, though she attempted to close it. "You're kidding."

"Nope, not kidding. Elizabeth Catherine Dalton. We picked it out a long time ago, didn't we?" She looked down and patted her belly again. "I will say, though," she looked up, "that when you introduced yourself at the shop, I liked the name even better." She smiled unabashedly.

Elizabeth smiled back but shook her head. "Thank you." Elizabeth watched for a moment as Nora resumed eating. "What's it like?"

Nora swallowed and lifted her glass. "What?"

Elizabeth looked busy with her food and, though she didn't mean to, lowered her voice. "Being a mother."

Nora tipped her head to the side. "It's the best. It's the most difficult thing . . . It's incredible and exhausting and more than I ever imagined it would be."

Elizabeth stopped and stared. "More what?"

Nora looked at her thoughtfully. A wicked grin stole across her face. "More *everything*." She popped a California roll covered with pickled ginger in her mouth and chewed. "It's like," she swallowed, "being pulled and shoved and beaten over the head by love. Of course, I have all boys so . . ." Nora shrugged, still grinning.

Elizabeth smiled, shook her head again, and picked up her chopsticks.

"Do you go to church, Elizabeth?"

Elizabeth looked up, pausing midbite. She quickly placed the food in her mouth and chewed before answering. "Umm, no. It, uh, never was the thing to do at home, so I don't, no." She picked up more food. "But," she raised an eyebrow, "my sisters do now. Both of them. They like it." She felt awkward with this subject.

Nora was unfased. "Oh, what church do they go to?"

She could answer that. "It's called the LDS Church. They're Mormons?"

Nora looked at her steadily and finished chewing. Her eyebrows came up high. "Really?"

Elizabeth nodded. "Yeah, they're pretty committed to it."

"Huh." A half smile played on her lips.

"What?" Elizabeth took a bite.

"Well, it's just interesting."

Elizabeth swallowed. "Why?"

"Because that's the church I go to." Nora smiled matter-of-factly at her.

Elizabeth looked at her warily. But Nora seemed to be content with a subject change.

"Have you decided to stay in Jackson?"

Elizabeth sighed heavily and smiled. "Yes."

A brilliant smile spread across Nora's face, and Elizabeth couldn't help but feel bewildered that this piece of news would make her so pleased.

Later, when Elizabeth got back to the inn, Ryan met her at the door.

"Hey, you look happy. Did you have a good time?"

She nodded. "I did, actually. But I ate too much."

He took her hands. "Do you want to go for a walk before the kids get home?"

Such an unusual sentence to her ears. "That sounds great. No bears though, right?"

He chuckled and then shivered. "No. Just a walk. We'll go west, toward town."

As they were coming back, Ryan squeezed her hand. "I was wondering if you would go to a movie with Lily and me tonight."

"I would love that."

He smiled.

"What about the other kids?"

"Well, Sam is still getting over his flu, and Mom offered to stay with him."

"I hope he's better soon."

"He will be." He chuckled. "I can hardly keep him down now. He just needs a little more rest. I may send him to school tomorrow."

Elizabeth grinned.

"What?" he asked.

"You're Super Dad."

He smiled self-consciously and shook his head.

"Does Chloe . . . not want to come?" she asked carefully.

He stopped. "She's coming around. You shouldn't worry about that."

"Mm-hmm." *Right.*

"She has her church youth activity tonight."

"Oh."

"So it's a good night to take you and Lily to a movie. Right?" He ducked his head and looked up at her with soft eyes.

She smiled again. "Yes."

They continued walking. Elizabeth sighed.

"You all right?" he asked, pulling her to him and wrapping his arm around her shoulders.

"Yes. This has been the best day off I've ever had."

He laughed. "We *really* need to get you out more."

Chapter 20

IT WAS THE WORST DAY back to work she'd ever had.

They opened the shop to a musty smell and located a leak in the roof. The melted snow had made its way down to a few boxes, and they had to sort through a shipment of sweaters, skirts, and bathrobes that had already begun to mildew.

Elizabeth eyed the bathrobes, a reminder of several things. She'd given her red silk robe away to Goodwill and hadn't replaced it yet. She would be leaving the inn at the end of the week, where the fluffy white robe she'd been using hung on its hook in her room at the inn. And she was having dinner tonight with Ryan and his kids. This last thing didn't have anything to do with the bathrobes, but it persistently ran through her mind all day.

Then the phone rang.

"Hey, Liz."

"Travis? How are your hands?"

He hesitated too long. "They're fine."

"Are you sure?"

"Yes, but I've, uh, been trying to do too much, and the doctor's kind of mad at me."

"Travis."

"I know. I'll be good. But it kind of leads me to why I called." He paused, and she waited. "My grandparents have decided to sell."

"The ranch?"

"Yes. I guess with this storm and the muck left after it melted and me unable to help . . . they're pretty discouraged. They just can't keep it up anymore. They asked me what I thought, and after I told them what this place is probably worth, what it would mean to them financially to sell, well . . . they perked right up."

She blew out a laugh. "I guess that's okay, then, right?"

"Yeah. It might take awhile to find a buyer, but Grandma is already looking at a winter home in Yuma."

She chuckled. Then she sobered. "But what are *you* going to do?"

He was slower to answer. "Well, it was hard at first, because, I don't know, I guess I got used to the idea of being here. The ranch has always been here, and I just figured it always would be. I was starting to picture . . . I don't know. Looking back, I think I was kind of losing it."

"You think?" she interjected too readily.

He chuckled. "Yeah." He sighed. "I called a friend in Denver to see if he had anything for me or knew of any openings. I'll go see him as soon as these hands are healed enough to carry luggage."

"Denver? Travis, that's great."

"Yeah, I think Denver is more my speed anyway."

They were quiet for a minute.

"Liz, I wanted to thank you."

"For what?"

"Oh, for making me see things a little more . . . clearly."

She paused. "Yeah, you cleared up a few things for me too."

He chuckled again, picking up a slightly sarcastic drawl. "Glad to be of help, ma'am." He breathed out. "I'll come see you before I go, if that's all right."

"Of course it is."

They grew quiet again.

"Can I ask you something?" She took his silence as a yes. "If you could go back, would you do it again?"

There was a pause. "With Nicole?"

"Mm-hmm."

He sighed. "That's a tough question to answer, Liz."

She nodded. "You don't think you would?"

"I would. Of course I would. But thinking that way . . . It leads to thinking I could have done something differently, and it's just too late for that."

She let that settle in. "Travis?"

"Yeah?"

"You're still one of the good ones."

He sighed. "I'll be sure to let you know where to find me if it doesn't work out with Brennan."

She smiled, but it was sad. "Thanks." She took a deep breath. "Take care."

"You too."

He hung up.

Would things work out with Brennan? What did "work out" mean exactly? She had fallen—well, stumbled, staggered . . . lurched—into this relationship without any escape route, no exit plan. Nothing was guaranteed, right? Travis and Nicole proved that.

And the kids were a huge part of this thing. She was only just beginning to see how Ryan's life was divided into three parts: Chloe, Sam, and Lily. She was just . . . an appendage. Not that he made her feel like that. He never had. At the movie the night before, he'd been both date and dad. But Lily had brightened up the evening like a bouncy ball of sunshine. How could she compete with that? No, she *shouldn't* compete with that. What little intuition she had about all of this told her she couldn't. And what did that make her? What was her role? What did she know about any of this?

How could she possibly play any sort of role in his children's lives?

There were things about her Ryan didn't even know. What would he think about her role with his kids if he knew?

She shivered, and her mind turned and twisted that way for a good portion of the day.

An hour before closing, she received a phone call. She was in the office looking for some invoices and heard her cell phone. She checked to see if it was Ryan calling to cancel after all. It wasn't.

"Hello?"

"Elizabeth?"

"Yes."

"This is Nicole."

Elizabeth suppressed the hostility she suddenly felt for this woman who had been a friend, a coworker, a confidante, a conspirator.

"Hello, Nicole."

"I just got off the phone with Travis."

Elizabeth had no comment.

"He says you've been *helping* him work things out." Her implication was too clear.

Elizabeth narrowed her eyes.

"Not that I can say I'm surprised. You always made it obvious you had a *thing* for my husband."

Her jaw clenched. "You know that's ridiculous. What do you need, Nicole?"

"I was just curious as to what he's told you."

"Why? Why should that matter?" Elizabeth didn't want to have this conversation.

Nicole ignored her question. "Stay away from him, Liz."

This was about *jealousy*? She snapped. "Listen, Nicole, *not* that it's your business anymore, but Travis has been *hurt*; he's confused, and he is trying to figure things out. I don't intend to get involved here, but I *will* be his friend. He desperately needs someone he can trust, and if I can help in that area, then that's what I'm going to do. You pretty much blew that out of the water for him." She took a breath. "How could you have done that to him? I don't understand it. You two were . . . you were . . ." *Crap.* The tears were coming.

Nicole was silent on the other end. Then she asked, "So . . . *you're* someone he can trust?" The question was laced with sarcasm.

Elizabeth took a deep breath. "Grow up, Nicole. Get your divorce and get out of his life, so he can find his own." She squeezed her eyes shut against the headache coming on. What right did Nicole possibly have to claim Travis? She didn't . . . deserve it . . .

Nicole had quieted at Elizabeth's outburst. "I think it was a mistake to call you."

Mistake? "Well, it wouldn't be the first for you, would it? You chose this. Let him go."

Silence again. Every muscle in Elizabeth's body strained in defense.

"Elizabeth." Nicole's voice was softer. "I didn't mean to—"

"Yeah, well, that's the thing about love though, right? We don't mean to do a lot of things. But some things are worth fighting for." She caught her breath at her own words. She attempted to regain her composure. "Tell me something. Would *you* do it all over again? With Travis?" She had to know. Somehow, it mattered. Seconds ticked by.

Finally, Nicole answered in a whisper. "Yes."

The answer stung, but she swallowed the hurt. "Good-bye, Nicole." She was tired.

Nicole paused. "I'm sorry, Liz." Her gentle tone twisted Elizabeth's stomach.

"Tell that to Travis."

Elizabeth hung up, hands shaking, and turned to leave the office. Nancy stood in the doorway looking concerned, worried. Elizabeth took a step and stopped, then Nancy held her arms out. Elizabeth stepped into them, and the silent tears came.

"Shhhhh. Shhhhhh."

"I can't do this. I can't . . ."

"Shhh . . . You can. You can, darling . . . It's *worth* it."

* * *

Marisol walked past them to her car, speaking Spanish a thousand miles an hour into her phone. She waved to them, flashing her dimples.

Elizabeth waved back and turned to Nancy, who had grabbed her sleeve with more force than expected. Although Elizabeth had recovered from the phone call, she could still see the worry behind Nancy's eyes.

"All right, good luck, darling, and remember it's early in the relationship, so no pressure, right?"

"Right." She disagreed entirely.

"Right. Oh my, I'm so nervous." Nancy shook her grip on Elizabeth's arm. "Oh, sorry." She breathed, letting go. "Will you call me?"

"Maybe . . . in the morning."

Nancy pressed her lips into a straight line but accepted the answer. "Oh, all right." She leaned over and kissed Elizabeth on the cheek and forced a smile. "Just be your fabulous self."

"Yeah." Elizabeth knew *fabulous* wasn't the right word. More like . . . *unqualified.*

They separated and got into their cars, and Elizabeth headed for the grocery store. She parked and walked through the automatic doors.

What do you bring to a dinner with a man who doesn't drink and is raising three kids? She headed for the bakery aisle and stood there. Her eyes roamed over the fresh flowers in the cooler, then the produce section beyond that. Her mind was blank.

Am I this clueless? She shook her head in disbelief.

* * *

"Dad, you have to tell this woman where you stand or . . ."

"Or what?" He agreed, and he was listening, but he was curious. Chloe was blushing madly, and he had to stop himself from grabbing her bouncing knee as it shook the sofa they shared.

"Or . . ." She chewed her bottom lip painfully. Her voice lowered to an urgent whisper, and she glared straight ahead. "Or she's going to try to *seduce* you."

He stifled a laugh with his hand over his mouth.

"Dad!" She glanced down the hall and dropped her face in her hands, muffling her plea. "I'm serious. This is so stupid."

Ryan gained control, for the most part, and reached to move her hair back behind her ear. "Chloe, do you really think that? That this is stupid?"

She turned her head to face him, cheeks still blazing, but her eyes were searching for answers.

He took a deep breath, smiling. "You're going to have to trust me with this one. Elizabeth is a good person, trying to do the right thing just like the rest of us."

She began to argue, but he held up a finger.

"I understand your concern. And you're going to have to trust me."

With a sound of defeat, Chloe covered her face with her hands and leaned into his side. "Don't say I didn't warn you."

He chuckled quietly and thought out loud. "Would seduction be so bad?"

"Ew, Dad!" She pulled up and shoved him hard.

"What? *You* brought it up."

Chloe stood and marched away down the hall as Ryan tried to stop laughing. He really did try.

* * *

Elizabeth rang the doorbell and bounced a little on the balls of her feet. She stopped herself. The door opened, and a sense of relief flooded her as Ryan stood there smiling gently. A voice in her head scolded her for being so completely dependent on that smile. He stepped aside, and she came in.

Ryan looked at her arms, and his smile widened. She held out the bag, and he took it, looking at its contents.

"Flowers, a loaf of french bread, ice cream, ginger ale"—he paused and flashed her a smile—"and a pineapple?"

"Yes," she said nervously. "I didn't know what to bring so . . ." He helped her with her jacket. "Isn't the pineapple some sort of peace offering . . . or symbol of incredible insecurity or something like that?"

He chuckled and stepped toward her, the bag on one arm. "Something like that," he said. "You'll be fine." He pulled her in, and she remembered how to breathe as his nose brushed along hers.

"Elizabeth!" In bounced Lily. Ryan halted, and Elizabeth's hand came up to her mouth. They both looked at Lily, who grabbed Elizabeth's arm and started pulling her deeper into the house.

Elizabeth looked back at Ryan, who was hanging up her jacket, smiling to himself. She could have used that kiss. Noises came from the kitchen, and Lily led her to it.

"We're making chicken . . . chicken . . ." Lily's finger went to her cheek, and she wrinkled her nose. She turned behind her. "What is it again?"

Sam stood at the stove, stirring a pot. "Alfredo." He smiled at Elizabeth. "Hi, Elizabeth."

She smiled back, grateful for his ease with her. "Hi, Sam."

"Oh yeah, chicken *alfredo*." Lily turned to Elizabeth again. "What does *alfredo* mean?"

Elizabeth muffled a laugh at Lily's expression. Her lips had pushed way out in an *O* when she'd said, "al-fre-*do*." "I *think* it was the name of the chicken."

Sam laughed.

Lily giggled. "Alfredo the chicken."

She felt Ryan come into the room.

"Daddy, we're having Alfredo the chicken for dinner."

"I heard." He set the bag down and put away the ice cream, then pulled out the rest of the items and set them on the counter.

Elizabeth smiled at him weakly, and he brought his hand up to her arm for encouragement, laughing under his breath. "You okay?"

"Dad, are we eating back here or in the dining room?"

"Oh, I think we'll just eat back here tonight."

Elizabeth looked to a dining nook across the kitchen, where the question had come from. A tall, slender young woman with long, shiny copper hair down her back stood at a cupboard, taking plates out to set around the table. She glanced quickly at Elizabeth, then picked up the plates and took them to the table.

"Chloe?" Ryan came around Elizabeth.

Chloe turned and stepped toward him, biting her cheek.

"Chloe, this is Elizabeth."

Her eyes came slowly over to meet Elizabeth's. "Hi." She pressed her lips together in a reluctant smile.

Elizabeth noted her light eyes, curious but guarded, and her classic features. An image of a young woman in a housekeeping uniform tossing a long braid over her shoulder flashed in Elizabeth's mind.

Elizabeth inhaled quickly. "You work at the inn."

The girl's fair complexion deepened to a rosier shade as her expression tightened, and she nodded.

"Chloe? Have you met Elizabeth?"

Chloe glanced at her father. "No. She came in as I finished cleaning her room the other day."

"You didn't say anything," Elizabeth said. "If I had known, I would have . . ." She would have what? Tipped her more?

"It's all right. You were busy."

Satin lingerie and lacey underwear . . . Elizabeth saw it, saw the challenge in Chloe's eyes. The girl was hesitant, but there was warning in those pale gray eyes. Something about those eyes . . .

Elizabeth blinked. "You look like your grandfather."

Chloe looked down, biting her cheek again. "I know."

Elizabeth thought quickly. "That's a *good* thing. You have beautiful eyes." *I didn't buy the lingerie for your father. Not entirely.* How could she tell a fifteen-year-old her father had been a complete gentleman?

Chloe brought her eyes back up under long lashes, her expression more curious now than accusing. "Thanks." She looked at her dad, who patted her back. She rolled her eyes, then continued setting the table.

Ryan looked at Elizabeth and raised his eyebrows. Elizabeth took a deep breath and let it out quietly.

"Elizabeth brought us a pineapple," he announced.

"Hooray!" Lily shouted.

Elizabeth couldn't help but release an uneasy laugh, and Ryan joined her. "C'mon, let's put your flowers in water. Sam, how does that pasta look?"

* * *

"When does basketball start?" Ryan passed Lily more bread. "Just one more piece."

Lily looked disappointed as Sam answered. "Monday. I think I need new shoes."

"Okay. We'll get you some this weekend. Chloe, more chicken?"

"No thanks. Dad, did you remember I have rehearsals on Saturday?"

"Oh, that's right. What time again?"

"Nine to noon, then two to four."

"Lily too?"

"Just in the afternoon."

"At the studio?"

"No, at the auditorium.

"Already?"

"Mm-hmm. Miss Devries wanted to start earlier this year."

Elizabeth cautiously took the opening. "What are you rehearsing?"

Chloe looked at her. "*The Nutcracker.*"

Elizabeth swallowed. "Ballet?"

She nodded and looked down at her food.

"You and Lily dance?" Of course they did.

Chloe nodded again. "My dad didn't tell you?"

"No, not yet." She glanced at Ryan, and he winked at her.

Chloe muttered under her breath. "He hasn't told you a lot of things."

Ryan cleared his throat loudly, looking at Chloe. "Chloe has been dancing since she was four. Two years ago, they had her play Clara." He looked at Elizabeth and smiled. "She was good."

"Dad." Chloe kept her eyes down.

"What part are you dancing this year?" Elizabeth asked.

Chloe pushed a little food around with her fork. She shook her head. "Sugarplum Fairy."

Elizabeth's eyes widened. "That's a big part too, isn't it?"

Chloe shrugged.

"I'm a snowdrop," Lily offered proudly. She turned to her dad. "Dad, can Elizabeth come see *The Nutcracker*?"

"I don't know . . . We'll have to see." His eyes met Elizabeth's.

She gave him a small smile. *Taking things slowly.* Her eyes moved to Chloe, who was watching her. She was being analyzed. Chloe dropped her gaze back down.

"Dad, Clay wanted to know if I could spend the night tomorrow." Sam dished himself up some more pasta. "Can I?"

"You're grounded, remember?"

Sam's shoulders dropped. "Oh, *man*. All weekend?"

"Mm-hmm."

"Awww."

Ryan suppressed a smile, and Elizabeth looked sympathetically at Sam. He was obviously over his flu.

"You can come watch me practice my ballet," Lily offered her brother.

"Thanks, Lily, but that's *not* what I want to do."

Lily shrugged. "I bet Elizabeth would want to come watch me practice."

"Oh," Elizabeth took a breath. "I'll be gone that day, Lily. I'm sorry."

"Where are you going?"

"Back to Montana and then to New York for a little while."

"Why don't you live here?"

"Well, I'm going to. But I have to get all of my things if I'm going to move into my new apartment."

Ryan turned to her. "You found an apartment?"

She'd forgotten to mention it. She smiled, conscious of four pairs of eyes watching her intently. "Yes, um, Nancy showed me one across town, and I took it. I can move in on the first."

Ryan reached under the table and squeezed her hand. She could see mild delight in his eyes, over the apartment, she guessed, and she couldn't look away for a moment. When she did, she caught Chloe watching Ryan this time.

"So . . . will you be here for Halloween?" Lily asked excitedly, kneeling up on her chair.

Elizabeth swallowed. "I'm not sure I'll be back by then, Lily."

"Awwww." Lily lowered herself back down.

Commitment. This thing with Ryan . . . this would mean commitment to an entire family.

She felt Ryan let go of her hand with one last squeeze, and he scooted his chair back. "Well, let's get these dishes cleaned up."

Sam and Lily groaned. Chloe stood and started collecting plates.

Elizabeth stood too. "I'll help." She followed Chloe into the kitchen with the bowls of food.

Chloe turned to take the dishes from her. "It's all right; you don't have to help."

"I want to."

Chloe turned slowly to the sink and turned on the water. Sam and Lily came in with a few more dishes, and Sam opened the dishwasher. Elizabeth found a dishcloth, ran it through the soapy water, and went to wipe off the table and counters, concentrating on the hard surfaces. Ryan put leftover food away, and Lily did some pirouettes in the middle of the kitchen.

Sam closed the dishwasher door and hit the start button. "Can we build a fire?"

Ryan said yes, and Lily shouted, "Hooray!"

Ryan and Sam headed for the fireplace, then outside for more wood.

Elizabeth's eyes were drawn to a hutch as they walked through the dining room. She took a closer look, needing some recovery time from the tension at the dinner table. The black distressed hutch matched the long dining table and chairs. She looked through the glass at several pieces of

Roseville pottery and a complete set of ivory china, perforated with a lattice pattern around the edges. Cut crystal water goblets sat on the second shelf, along with teacups and saucers from the set below. A framed scripture in needlework leaned against a small easel. Stitched birds and vines with berries surrounded the colorful verse.

She swallowed as her eyes fell on the family portrait. The children were smaller, grinning. Ryan looked much the same, his hair shorter. There was something there, though, in his open smile. He was carefree. Unsuspecting. She made herself look at the woman holding the baby, Lily, on her lap, the kids gathered around her. Ryan's wife, Brooke. Wide brown eyes and soft dark hair . . . Elizabeth was looking at a grown-up version of Lily. The children touched Brooke with easy adoration, and her smile was confident, self-assured. She was the centerpiece of the pose. Elizabeth didn't have to imagine why. This woman would be the center of any gathering.

She pulled her gaze away. Folding her arms over her middle, she raised her eyes. On the top shelf, she saw a series of figures, all white porcelain.

The first one was a woman kneeling as if in prayer, her hair pulled back in a bun, a little old-fashioned but graceful in its simplicity. Three figures made up the next grouping: a man and a woman crouched, their arms outstretched to the small child walking between them as if one had just let the child go and the other was waiting to catch her as she took her first steps. A smaller piece showed two girls, one a toddler, the older one kneeling, kissing her on the cheek. The final figure was different: a Christ figure, enrobed, holding His arms open and looking gently down as if He was going to embrace something or was waiting for something to come to him. Her sister Alisen had been given a similar one as a wedding gift.

"Those were my mom's."

Elizabeth looked around quickly. Chloe stood a few steps away.

"Those two were *her* mother's. Grandma Louisa." She nodded to the first two. "My dad got her that one when Lily was born." She pointed to the two little girls, sisters. "There's another of a dancer in my room."

"Oh. I . . . hadn't seen them before." She turned to look at the hutch again. "Are these her things too?"

Chloe stepped forward. "Yes. We use them for special dinners . . . holidays and stuff."

"That's nice to be able to use her things. My dad, he . . ." She stopped, not sure if she should continue, not sure of anything.

"He what?"

She took another breath. "He put all my mother's things away when she died."

There was a pause.

"When did your mother die?"

Elizabeth glanced sideways at her. "I was a little older than you are."

"You had her longer." Chloe looked down.

"Yes." Elizabeth hesitated. "I have younger sisters though. They were ten and thirteen." She fingered the satin wood, not allowing herself to look back at the portrait. "It's a painful thing at any age." She had expected to have her mother forever. She was sure Chloe had too.

Chloe lifted her head and said quietly, "At least we'll get to see them again."

Elizabeth turned at the words to find Chloe gazing up at the statue of Christ. Chloe looked back at Elizabeth and blinked, then turned away as if embarrassed, biting her lip.

Elizabeth looked up at the statue again as Chloe walked into the other room. Her gaze went back to the first statue of the woman kneeling in prayer. She eyed the scripture. *Choose you this day whom ye will serve, but as for me and my house, we will serve the Lord. Joshua 24:15.*

Elizabeth swallowed. *Those were my mother's.*

She backed away and turned to the living room, arms still wrapped around her middle.

Ryan set up a game with Sam as Lily did a little dance in front of the fire. Chloe had found a spot next to her dad. Ryan gave her knee a little shake. Chloe looked up at him, and he coaxed a reluctant smile to her face.

Elizabeth watched this domestic scene and struggled to place herself in it. Ryan looked over.

"Come sit down." He patted the other space next to him. "Please." He held out his hand to her, and she felt herself walk over to him. "We're playing Sorry." He shook his head and muttered, "Sorry."

She forced a smile as she sat. She took a deep breath, but her stomach stayed in a knot.

"Okay," Sam said. "Lily, what color do you want? I'm blue."

They played the game, but Elizabeth's mind kept wandering to what Chloe had said.

At least we'll get to see them again. She knew it wasn't a new concept, a hope of an afterlife and our loved ones going to heaven. It was something a young child believed about their grandma. But Chloe hadn't said it dreamily, and she wasn't a child. She had said it like she believed it. She had said it as fact. And she had retreated when Elizabeth had shown no sign of recognizing it as such.

"Elizabeth, it's *your turn.*" Lily's face brightened, her eyes big and round. Like her mother's.

"I'm sorry."

Lily giggled. Elizabeth cleared her throat and took her turn, trying to ignore Ryan, who seemed to be watching her closely.

While watching Lily take her turn, Elizabeth was reminded of something else: Ryan had asked Lily to give a blessing on the food before dinner. It was a surprise to hear this six-year-old give a simple but sincere prayer, seemingly unrehearsed and quite lengthy. Elizabeth hadn't felt quite at ease during the prayer and had stolen glances at the family, bowing their heads, closing their eyes, patiently waiting for the prayer to end. She had seen Sam smile when Lily mentioned four of her friends by name, and Elizabeth had been a little startled to hear her own name and how they were happy she could be there. It had left her feeling flushed. And, ironically, out of place.

"Elizabeth." It was Ryan. "Are you all right?" He spoke quietly.

She raised her eyebrows and nodded. "My turn again?"

"Mm-hmm."

After his look of concern, she made a renewed effort to pay attention to the game. She noticed Ryan relax, and she wished she could too.

* * *

"Time for bed."

"Awww."

"You heard me. Get ready for bed. Brush your teeth." Ryan stood up and took the ice cream dishes to the kitchen, and Chloe followed him.

Lily hopped over to Elizabeth, who was sitting on the sofa. "Good night, Elizabeth. I hope you had a fun time."

"Thank you, Lily. I did. Thank you for dancing for me."

"Good night, Elizabeth." Sam stood up. "Next time we'll have a ping-pong tournament downstairs. We have darts too."

"Sounds great." She smiled at him.

He held his hand out to his little sister. "C'mon, Lily."

Lily looked at Elizabeth, then reached up and smoothed her hand along Elizabeth's hair. "You have pretty hair."

Elizabeth didn't recognize the feeling that came with Lily's touch. It wasn't a bad feeling, though it included some alarm. "So do you."

Lily smiled and hopped down the hall with Sam.

Elizabeth looked at the fire, holding herself as if she were cold.

Ryan returned to the room, followed by Chloe, who stopped.

"Well, good night." Chloe folded her arms and bit her cheek.

Ryan turned, and Elizabeth stood.

"It was nice to meet you, Chloe."

Chloe shifted her weight. "You too."

"Good night, pumpkin."

Elizabeth glanced at Ryan.

"Dad." Chloe rolled her eyes.

Ryan just grinned at her. "Have a good sleep."

Chloe raised her eyebrows at him pointedly. Elizabeth noted a silent exchange between the two of them, then Chloe turned and walked down the hall. "Lily, get into bed. I'm tucking you in tonight."

A squeal sounded from Lily's room.

Ryan waited a moment, watching after her. Then he turned to Elizabeth, took both of her hands, and pulled her to him. He brought a hand up to her chin and kissed her.

Her heart raced, but she knew that was fear, not his touch. She kissed him harder to make it go away. It helped a little. As he wrapped his arms around her, she pushed the dull panic that lurked in the corners of her mind as far down as possible.

He eased away too soon. "I've been wanting to do that all night," he whispered.

She nodded in complete agreement. That would have been easier. Far easier.

He took her hand again and led her to the sofa. She numbly followed and sat down next to him, and he looked at her, searching her face. She had no idea what he would find there. The sound of doors opening and closing and water running and more doors sounded from the hall.

"This was harder than you thought it would be, wasn't it?"

She nodded and shrugged. The difficulty level had surpassed even her expectations. She looked toward the hall. "Your kids are . . . amazing."

"Chloe's still mad at me. I'm afraid some of that is transferring to you."

"No. She's amazing too. She's very . . . mature for her age, isn't she?"

He nodded and looked down. "She always has been, even when she was tiny. We called her our little lady." He got a faraway look in his eyes.

Elizabeth pressed her lips together. He seemed to realize what he'd said and cleared his throat.

"How have you done this?" she asked.

He looked up, mild surprise in his expression. Then his brows came down, and he looked at the fire. "What?"

"How," she inhaled, "have you known what to do? How did you . . . ?" She looked over at the hutch. "How do you think I could possibly . . . ?" Her hand came up to her mouth. She looked at him as his caring eyes moved away from the fire and met hers. His mouth was set in a patient smile, but there was worry there too. The man in the portrait was a different Ryan.

"Elizabeth," he watched her eyebrows come together. "Elle."

She felt herself relax a fraction as he used his name for her.

He must have noticed and hid a smile. More gently, he said, "Elle, I didn't plan . . . on losing Brooke." He swallowed, and she watched the fire reflect in his eyes. "I didn't plan on raising three kids on my own. And I didn't plan on feeling this way about anyone ever again. As a matter of fact, I planned *not* to fall in love ever again." He brought her hand up and laid his cheek against it, his eyes never leaving hers. "Look what good *that* did me."

Oh no. It happened to him too.

"I *didn't* know what to do." He brought her hands to his chest. "But . . . I've had help. I've had my parents, my family, my friends. I don't know what I would have done without them." He brushed her cheek with his fingers. "I've prayed a lot."

She shook her head. "Does that help?"

He nodded gently, still brushing her cheek. "I've prayed about how to answer their thousands of questions. I've prayed about how to care for them when they've been sick and how to punish them when they've made the wrong choices. When they've come to me crying about their little problems . . . and not so little . . ."

She listened, but she didn't understand. "But what good does it do? How are you helped?"

He softly shrugged. "Sometimes I wonder if my prayers are heard, but then I find myself on the other side of the problem, and I know they have been. Other times, it's been stronger than that." He watched her as curiosity and doubt filled her at the same time. "I've prayed about you."

She blinked. "You're praying to God about me?"

"Elle, I don't know if you've noticed, but . . ." He swallowed. "You're kind of a big deal."

She dropped her gaze. "And . . ." she was almost afraid to ask, "what does God tell you about me?"

"He tells me"—he lifted her chin and placed both hands on her arms so she was square with him—"that you are more than you think you are."

She couldn't move. Then her breathing quickened as he looked into her eyes, into her soul. She was confused and afraid and wanted to believe all at the same time. But the idea of a God who answered prayers, let alone a God who knew anything about *her* was brand-new. She didn't want Ryan's God to know about her. She shook her head, then looked over at the hutch, at the kneeling woman and the portrait. "I can't . . . I can't do this." A tear dropped onto his hand.

"Elizabeth . . . I'm sorry. You don't have to do anything." She could hear the worry in his voice. "I was only answering your question . . . with the truth." He whispered, "We don't have to talk about it anymore."

She shook her head again. "I'm sorry." She couldn't look at him. To look at him would be to see the hurt she was causing him, and that would be unbearable. "I just . . . I just need some time . . . to . . ." To what? To become Super Church Lady Insta-Mom?

"Elle," he pulled her to his side and wrapped his arms around her.

She closed her eyes, willing the fear to go away, but panic and doubt circled like vultures now. An image of his angelic wife passed through her mind. "I can't be who you want me to be," she whispered.

He stroked her hair, and it reminded her of Lily's gesture.

His voice was full of compassion. "We don't need to rush this. I don't want you to be anything but *you*."

An image of three children passed through her mind.

But I can't be who you need *me to be.*

Chapter 21

IN HER DREAM, SHE SAT on the rock on Swan River, back home, sunning herself.

"Elizabeth?"

She looked down and smiled at Lily. "Yes, honey?"

"Tell me *Cinderella*."

"Again?" Hadn't she told it a hundred times? Lily's smile filled her very soul with joy. "All right. One more time."

"Can you tell it without the scary parts?" asked a voice to her right.

Elizabeth looked. Chloe sat there, her legs gracefully crossed in front of her.

"I don't think *Cinderella* has any scary parts."

"Chloe is scared of everything." Sam jumped down from the rock and landed on the ground noiselessly.

"I am not. I just don't like the scary parts. They're pointless."

"Well," Elizabeth tried to think, "I don't think there are any scary parts in *Cinderella*." Maybe she was wrong.

They heard a rustle in the bushes behind them and turned around to look.

Suddenly, the hair rose along Elizabeth's arms and neck as a bear came through the leaves. It stopped and growled low. They all froze. A grizzly.

"Be still," she whispered. She slowly reached for Sam and pulled him back onto the rock. "The rock is safe."

But before Elizabeth could grab her, Lily jumped out of her arms and onto the ground. "I want to see the bear!" She hopped and did a twirl.

"*Lily!*" Elizabeth wanted to scream, but no sound came out as the bear grunted in displeasure and the growl deepened, the mass of rolling muscle building until the bear rose up and towered over the little girl, who abruptly froze in terror, feet away from this monster she had thought was a toy.

The bear raised its arm back in readiness to strike Lily's tiny frame. Time slowed, but Elizabeth couldn't move. She had no gun, no repellent. The horror ripped from Elizabeth's throat in a scream as Chloe whispered, "I thought you said there weren't any scary parts."

Elizabeth blinked in slow motion, and in that instant, Lily looked over her shoulder, eyes filled with tears and confusion. But she wasn't Lily anymore. She was Elizabeth's little sister, Alisen, six years old. Her unmistakable dark curls and vivid blue eyes pled to her for rescue, wrenching Elizabeth's heart in two. The bear changed too. The new image turned Elizabeth's blood cold, and hopelessness rushed through her. The bear had become a man . . . a breathtakingly handsome, well-dressed man with an enticing, wicked smile, and as little Alisen turned back to face him, he laughed as his raised hand came down with full force.

* * *

Elizabeth heard the wretched cry and sat up, breathing heavily, and then she sobbed, clutching her chest. She kept her eyes open, and the tears rolled down her face as she searched the dark for the man and pushed herself back to the headboard, huddled in the night.

Nobody came to turn the light on. Nobody called her name. Nobody told her it would be all right and that she could go on.

She stayed there in the dark until her breathing slowed enough for her to reach for a pillow and hold it to her chest, to cry quietly until morning came.

* * *

She'd missed her run. She'd missed breakfast. She held her phone and dialed.

"Hello?"

"Hi, it's me."

There was a short pause. "Elizabeth?"

"Mm-hmm."

"Are . . . are you all right?"

She felt the emotions well up. "I don't know. Are you . . . busy right now?"

"No. Elizabeth, what's happened?"

Elizabeth took a deep breath and blew it out slowly. "I, uh, needed to talk to someone. I needed to talk to *you*." She looked out her window at the mountains. "I just . . . need to hear your voice, and I need you to tell me everything will be all right."

"Elizabeth . . . everything will be all right. I know it."

Elizabeth paced the floor a couple of times. She sighed and quietly asked, "Alisen"—tears resurfaced as she clung to the pillow—"how do you know?"

* * *

Ryan stood at the front desk, glancing up every couple of minutes, tapping a pen on the polished counter top. He ran his hand over his mouth and leaned on his elbows. He picked up the phone again. Then set it down. He'd left two messages already. He looked at the clock. Fifteen more minutes, then he was going up there. He bent down and riffled through some boxes under the counter, intent on refilling the brochure rack and display of local business cards. He heard the click of her door upstairs and brought his head up quickly, only to whack it against the edge of the counter.

He cursed under his breath and sucked in air between his teeth as his hand came up to the pain. He blinked away the sting from his eyes.

"Are you all right?"

He whirled around as she made the last step to him. He paused, then stepped to her and carefully put his arms around her. She seemed to melt into him, but she didn't return his embrace.

"Yes, I'm fine."

He pulled back enough to see her face, her eyes tight and drawn down. "How are you? Are you—"

She brought her eyes to his, and he saw it there. The wall. His feelings must have shown on his face because she immediately looked away. He loosened his grip, but she stayed where she was.

He swallowed. "Are you all right? I was worried . . . after last night." He watched her as she looked around. Nobody was in this part of the inn now, everyone away at some activity or getting ready to leave, their stay nearly over. The faint hum of the laundry drummed from the back room.

She shook her head. "No, Ryan, I'm not all right. I, uh, I need some time. There are . . . some things I need to figure out." The crease between her eyebrows stood out. She reached a finger up to trace the edge of his lower lip.

He kissed it. "I can help. We can figure it out together. Elle, we can take this slowly."

She closed her eyes and said, "I love it when you call me that. Nobody's ever called me that." She shook her head again. "No, we can't take this slowly. It's too big and too important . . . I need to think. I need to . . . find some answers . . . before we get any further. I'm already . . ." She sighed. "There are just too many . . . hearts at stake."

His head throbbed where he'd hit it, but he was barely aware of that pain. "Let me help you."

She brought her eyes up to his again. "This is something I have to figure out on my own." She said it like she was trying to convince herself as well as him. "There are things you don't know . . ." Her gaze dropped again, and she whispered, "Things I don't want you to know."

It was all slipping from him, like a zipper fall during a climb, the belays ripping from the rock in rapid succession. And it had been a long ascent. He looked around and pulled her behind the counter. He whispered back, "What things? Do you think I would throw you aside? Do you think I would *judge* you?"

Her eyes came up too quickly. She looked away, biting her lip. "I'm . . . not good enough," she murmured.

He knew it wasn't true. But the way she'd said it . . . *she* knew it.

He took a frustrated breath. "If it was just me . . . just you and me, and we met here, exactly the way we did . . ."

She was already shaking her head. As her eyes filled with tears, she mouthed, "That's not fair."

He knew it wasn't. He wiped the tear away from her cheek. "What can I do?"

She looked off, raising her shoulders, then letting them fall with her breath. "I'll be at the shop today. Nancy wants me to sign the papers for the partnership . . ." She trailed off. "I'm leaving first thing in the morning."

"You're signing the papers, right?" She didn't answer. "You still have your apartment, right?" She nodded. He tightened his arms around her. She had her apartment on the first. That was in nine days. What would she be thinking about for nine days? What would she be considering? "What can I do?" he repeated. "Tell me."

She didn't look at him, but she leaned forward, pressing herself into him, threading her arms around his waist, filling him with confusion, conflicting emotions. She whispered into his neck, "You can try that praying thing."

He felt the knot in his chest loosen a little. His hand came up to smooth her hair. "All right," he whispered. He kissed her temple. "I can do that." He held her and rocked her. "Will you do something for me?"

She hesitated. "What?"

He pulled her away just enough to place his hands on either side of her face and look into her eyes, to get past the barrier she'd put back up. "Will you please consider that maybe . . . all of this happened . . . *all* of it . . . because maybe you *are* good enough?"

Her forehead wrinkled in doubt, but he gazed into her eyes until he was sure he was welcome again.

She finally parted her lips. "I'll try," she whispered.

He kissed her gently, acceptingly, hopefully.

* * *

Elizabeth hesitated. She mentally reviewed the list of pros and cons she'd made last night. She felt Nancy's eyes on her, questioning and concerned. The notary waited with her stamp. Marisol stood near the office door, hands clasped together. Elizabeth had gone over the papers with her father and had been surprised at how much of the business Nancy was turning over to her.

"Elizabeth."

She looked at Nancy.

"You don't have to decide now."

Elizabeth had given Nancy a vague report on dinner. Nancy had tried to be reassuring, but the night had been too long, the doubt too convincing.

But the boutique was another matter.

"Elizabeth, you have to stay."

She looked at Marisol. "I do?"

Marisol threw out her hands, exasperated. "Of *course* you do. You're one of us now. You've made your mark. And Nancy has already ordered your name for the window." She gestured toward the front of the store.

Elizabeth looked at Nancy, who watched her carefully and shrugged her shoulders. "You belong here, darling," she whispered, emotional. "*And you know it.*"

Elizabeth gripped the pen. *This is business. It's good business.* She closed her eyes and saw him, his hurt, his confusion, his family. The pen dropped from her hand, and she turned away.

"I . . . There are still things to consider. I . . ." She shook her head and pressed her hand against the ache in her head.

She felt a hand on her arm and turned to Nancy, straightening up and grabbing a breath. "It's not the deal."

"I know."

"It's not the business."

"I know."

Elizabeth nodded as if nodding would keep her from falling apart.

Nancy drew her in for a hug, and surprising Elizabeth, Marisol joined them.

"Take all the time you need," Nancy said. "But please, don't say no. I have plans."

Elizabeth drew back and laughed. She shook her head, knowing that plans could be elusive.

I didn't plan on falling in love again. Ryan's words.

The phone rang. Nancy reached over and answered it. "Hello. Wildberries. Nancy Colette." She grabbed a tissue and dabbed at her nose. "Oh. Certainly. Here she is."

After a deep breath, Elizabeth took the phone, but it wasn't who she thought it would be.

"Hello, Elizabeth? It's Nora."

Elizabeth smiled weakly. "Yes, Nora, hello."

"A friend just called, and she's getting a few of us together for lunch today, and I wondered if you would like to join us. You'd mentioned today was your last day here for a couple of weeks, right? Nothing fancy, but we like to get together and talk our heads off for an hour or so every once in a while. Obviously, I know you're working, but would you be interested?"

She hesitated. She wasn't really up for meeting new people at the moment. She looked over at Nancy, who watched her closely. "I would love to, Nora, thanks." She pursed her lips. She was tired, and her head still ached, but she needed a distraction to clear her head, and Elizabeth had a feeling Nancy would want to discuss Ryan in depth.

She got the time and the place and hung up the phone.

"Would it be all right if I stepped out for lunch today?"

Nancy's brows drew together. "Are you sure?"

"I need a breather."

Nancy nodded slowly. "You go out. Clear your head."

It sounded easy.

"Let's get back to work, girls." Nancy tried to look bright. "Accessories wait for no one."

* * *

Elizabeth sat on a stool at the front counter, looking out the window. Marisol put together a sale rack.

"How are things with James?" Elizabeth had debated asking but thought it the best way to head off any subject Marisol might want to bring up concerning Elizabeth's earlier display of insanity.

Marisol blushed and shook her head, smiling. "I owe you something big, something amazing. It's . . . better than I ever imagined." She smiled to herself over the clothes. "He's taking me to see a movie tonight, so I thought I would invite him to dinner too. I'm cooking for him."

Elizabeth nodded in approval.

"You know, when he speaks Spanish, he doesn't hesitate at all . . . It's like that's how we were meant to get to know each other." Marisol shook her head. "I know that sounds crazy, right? But what if it were true? What if"—she stopped what she was doing and looked off—"What if he was so shy he would have never spoken to me, but he was sent to Mexico for two years so he could come back here and talk to *me* and get to know me because we were supposed to . . ." She grimaced. "I mean, I *know* we just met, so . . . Oh, and I'm sure there were other, better reasons he was sent to Mexico, you know, for the people there . . . but . . ." She gave Elizabeth a sheepish smile and shrugged. "I'm getting a little ahead of myself, huh?"

Elizabeth was watching her thoughtfully.

Marisol loudly drew a breath at a sudden thought. Her eyes opened wide, and she wondered, "What if he is the reason my parents moved here from California?"

Elizabeth broke into a short laugh, amused and a little shaken by Marisol's simple deductions.

Marisol grinned at her, laughing too. "Well," she beamed, "you never know how you'll come across the person you're meant to be with."

Elizabeth sobered a little at that. "Do you think that? That we're *meant* to be with someone specific?"

Marisol shrugged, still smiling. "I don't know. But doesn't it feel like that when we find them?"

Elizabeth remained thoughtful for a moment.

"And then it's like there isn't anything anybody can do." Marisol was loveable but naïve. Her eyes grew wide again. "You should come to church with me."

Elizabeth blinked. "What? *Why?*"

"Because there are lots of people our age there . . ."

Elizabeth balked at the idea of her and Marisol being put in the same age group.

"And because it's fun, and you can learn good things."

Elizabeth shook her head at Marisol's simplistic way of looking at things. "Mmm, thanks, but I don't think so."

"Well, you should think about it." Marisol shrugged again, like she had just asked her to switch phone companies, which, Elizabeth thought wryly, would probably be only *slightly* less difficult.

Marisol turned back to the clothes rack, humming a song and occasionally gazing out the window.

Elizabeth's thoughts would not calm down, and she was grateful when it was time to go to lunch.

Chapter 22

"Elizabeth, this is Rochelle, Carla, Jamie, and Kim. Everyone, this is Elizabeth Embry. She's moving here from Montana and is in need of good friends." Nora gestured to a chair and took one herself. Elizabeth wondered again, as Nora smiled at her, how she seemed like an old friend instead of a new one.

Pleased sounds went around the table as Elizabeth sat down. She smiled back at open expressions and hoped they would talk so much amongst themselves that she wouldn't have to say much.

"Elizabeth, what brings you to Jackson?"

"So are you here by yourself or . . . ?"

"How long have you known Nancy Colette?"

"What part of Montana again?"

"Could you get me a discount?"

"Now, do you work out or . . . ?"

"Do they have that sweater at the boutique?"

The questions continued, but Elizabeth surprisingly was not as bothered as she'd thought she would be. In fact, it was good to not have to think too much. These questions were easy.

When their curiosity seemed to be somewhat satisfied, they turned the conversation to one another.

"Did you guys hear we might be getting a new bishopric?"

"Yes . . . Do you have any ideas?"

"Well, I don't like to speculate."

"I bet it's Brother Williams. He is such a good man."

"Or Brother Faulkner."

"Ooh, he'd be good."

"Hey, we finally got a fourth Sunday teacher."

"Oh, good; who'd you get?"

"That first name we submitted."

"Hooray."

"Who made that salad at the luncheon last week—the one with the cranberries? Does anyone have that recipe?"

"Oh, that was Sister Anderson. She makes the best salads."

"You know, we should collect the recipes from those luncheons and make a book for the end of the year or something."

"Yeah, I've thought of that . . . but who wants to do it?"

"I would."

"Really?"

"Oh yeah. I love that stuff."

"Okay, I'm making you Jackson Second Ward recipe collector."

"Woo-hoo."

"Does anyone know if Sister Orozco is out of the hospital yet?"

Elizabeth ate and listened and shook her head to herself. *Are these people everywhere?* Really, she wanted to know because she was beginning to think it was *her.*

Of course Nora had friends from her church. So of course Elizabeth sat surrounded.

She decided to ask questions. "Are there a lot of members of your church here in Jackson?" she asked casually as she raised a forkful of food.

"Oh, the usual amount," one of the women answered.

"If you don't count Utah or Idaho." Laughter went around the table.

"We have two wards and a young adult branch," Nora answered. "We're all in Second Ward, except Carla. She moved over to First Ward a couple of months ago. I have family across town in First."

Elizabeth nodded as if she understood what any of that meant.

Lunch continued fairly pleasantly though, and Elizabeth felt some ease for the first time that day. They were finishing up when Jamie turned to Elizabeth.

"So, Elizabeth, I was going to ask you where you've been staying while you've been here."

"Oh, at a bed and breakfast."

"Mmm? Which one?"

"The Lantern."

Jamie raised her eyebrows. "Oh," she exclaimed and looked at Nora.

Nora set her fork down and leaned forward. "I assumed you'd been staying with Nancy."

"Well, that was the original plan, but her husband started a remodel on the house just before I arrived."

"Well, then." Nora chuckled. "You've met my parents."

"I have?" Elizabeth wondered how. The Franks? No.

Nora's eyebrows rose, and she nodded. "Yes. That's First Ward. Jeff and Dayle Brennan."

Elizabeth stopped midforkful. She set the food back down, trying to look mildly surprised instead of completely knocked off-kilter. "Really? Jeff and Dayle are your . . . parents?"

"Mm-hmm. And my brother, he's there too. Ryan?" She felt Nora study her reaction very closely.

Elizabeth nodded slowly. "Yes. Wow. Small world." She looked again at Nora, this time easily seeing the resemblance to Dayle and Ryan. She had the same hair color, same face shape, her mother's eyes. Maddening warmth filled Elizabeth's face. She felt ridiculous for not seeing it before. Ryan's sister, the pain in the rear.

"Well, small town." Nora gestured out the window. "Have you enjoyed your stay?"

Elizabeth nodded, swallowing. "They've made me feel . . . very welcome. The inn is . . . well, it's beautiful." She looked down at her food, her heart beating rapidly.

"Thank you. You know, David and Ryan built it."

"David?"

"My husband."

Elizabeth remembered the business card Nora had given her. David Dalton. Woodworks. She remembered Lily's words. *I thought you were Dave.*

Her head started to spin. Could it be possible? Nora had family across town, in the other . . . *ward*. The prayers, the porcelain figures, the . . . the light. Yes, the light that drew her in like a moth, at the same time threatening to expose every weakness she had.

Nora was watching Elizabeth curiously. One of the other women drew the attention away.

"Nora, how are you feeling?"

Nora looked down at her swelling belly. "Oh, fine. A little tired. Some morning sickness." She made a face. "It's hard when Dave is gone on these long jobs."

"When does he get back?"

"Late Saturday. Mom's birthday is Sunday, and we're all getting together at Ryan's."

This was one of the oddest sensations Elizabeth had ever experienced. She found herself watching Nora closely, hanging on her every word.

Nora continued, looking at her watch. "I left Levi with Mom. I better get going pretty soon." She sighed. "I promised the kids I'd make them cookies today before they got home from school." She leaned on her hand and looked at Elizabeth. "Heaven knows I could use a few cookies." She smiled gently.

Elizabeth had no idea what to say.

A cell phone rang. Elizabeth jumped, realizing it was hers. She excused herself and looked at the caller ID. "I should take this." She turned away from the table, facing the window. Raindrops had begun to splat against the walk outside. Her hand trembled as she held the phone to her ear.

"Hello?"

"Hi, Liz. It's me again." Alisen's voice sounded rough. "I know you're coming home tomorrow, but something's happened, and I think you should get here sooner than that if you can."

"What's happened?" What would need her there twenty hours sooner? She felt a sudden heaviness, a dread. She was already dizzy.

"It's Dad."

* * *

Ryan came in the side door from running errands for the inn, and his dad was waiting for him there in the kitchen.

"Son, I'm sorry, but Elizabeth had to leave. She left this for you." He handed Ryan an envelope, the inn's stationery.

Ryan furrowed his brow as he took the note. "Had to leave?"

"She got a call from home. It seems her dad is really sick . . . I didn't get the details. But she said she's sorry, and she'll call you."

"Why didn't she call my cell?"

"She was in a hurry . . . She had to make a flight that could fit her in last minute . . . I assume she made it, but it must have been barely. I offered to call you, but she asked me not to."

Ryan swallowed. He looked at the note. *It takes time to write a note.*

"Son . . . she was kind of a mess, crying. Poor thing. The Franks stopped her on her way out. I was bringing their baggage down, and she clung to Celia like . . ." He shrugged. "I know things were just getting started with you two, but is everything all right?"

Ryan felt remorse for his previous thoughts. "I don't know, Dad." He looked up to the calm of his father's eyes. "I don't know."

His dad put his hand on his shoulder and patted down hard twice.

Ryan took the note and leaned against the butcher-block island as his dad left for the front desk. Ryan opened the envelope and removed the paper, unfolding it as his head tried to convince his heart that a note was good.

Ryan,

I have to go. I'm sorry this is rushed. My dad needs me. I don't know when I'll be back. I didn't want to leave it this way. Maybe this is better though.

Please, let me work this out. I'll try to keep my promise.

You've turned everything upside down, you've endangered me, and I still can't imagine being without you.

That's how I know I love you.

I just have to figure out how that could possibly be enough.

Elle

Ryan read it several more times as his heart tried to convince his head that a note was still good. It was a feeble attempt.

He couldn't help but focus on three words.

You've endangered me.

* * *

Elizabeth spotted Alisen searching above the incoming passengers, standing on her toes. She saw Elizabeth and waved her hand in the air. Elizabeth was certain she'd never been so grateful to see her sister. Between the worry about her father and uncertainty about Ryan, the fatigue was hitting hard, and Alisen—well, she was Alisen.

As Elizabeth stepped forward, she set her carry-on down, then slowly opened her arms to her sister, who, after a split second of making sure it was what Elizabeth wanted, stepped in to give her a hug. Elizabeth held her longer than the usual quick greeting.

"I'm so sorry," Elizabeth whispered with a catch in her voice.

Alisen pulled away to look up at her. "It's all right, Liz." Elizabeth read the questions in her eyes. "Let's get your bag." She picked up Elizabeth's carry-on and took her sister's arm. "We can talk on the way to the hospital."

"It's going to take a lot longer than that. Let's save it for later."

Alisen nodded. "Okay. Later, then."

On the phone, Elizabeth had only touched on how things were going in Jackson and how a man named Ryan Brennan had tilted the earth a bit. It was only a matter of time before Alisen would make her spill everything. But it would wait.

In the car, Elizabeth asked, "Where's Derick?"

"He'll be home in two days. He's in Bolivia again. They're setting up new offices there. I was going to go, but I had a cold, and Derick insisted I stay. When I called him about Dad, he said he'd be home as soon as he could."

"Good." Elizabeth smiled ruefully. "I have a feeling I'm going to need his feeble attempts at humor in the next few days." She sighed and looked up, shaking her head. "He is just going to *love* this." Alisen gave her a confused look. Of all the people Elizabeth dreaded going to about anything of a spiritual nature, it was Derick. They might throw insults and bicker back and forth, but she knew he would give her straight answers. She changed the subject. "How has Dad been since I talked to you?"

Alisen shrugged, morose. "I've never seen him look so bad. He hadn't woken up yet when I left to get you. The doctors said it was close . . . they said they hadn't seen anything quite like it."

Elizabeth swallowed. "And it was just a gall bladder infection?"

Alisen nodded. "A gall bladder infection that had spread to his liver and kidney. It was so far gone when they operated that they couldn't tell at first what was what."

Elizabeth dropped her head into her hands. "And what do they say about recovery?"

"They've pumped him full of antibiotics and fluids. It's a waiting game."

"How is Sheryl?" Elizabeth asked through her hands.

"Terrified at first. Dad was fine, then running a low fever, then just collapsed, white as a sheet. She's calmed down though. She, uh, let Greg and Stephen Michaels give Dad a blessing. Don't tell him." She threw Elizabeth a smile, but it faded. "It helped her a lot, I think, to hear that prayer." Alisen kept her eyes ahead. "Of course, we've all been praying."

Elizabeth was quiet. Her brother-in-law, Greg Stewart, shared a dental practice with Stephen Michaels, a friend of Alisen's. These men also believed as Ryan did. They prayed too. She heard herself whisper, "What is it about prayer?"

She sensed Alisen's hesitation to answer. Talking about church with Elizabeth was a known taboo. It never made her mad, just uncomfortable and dismissive.

But after a few moments, Alisen answered anyway. "Sometimes prayer is just a plea for peace." She glanced sideways at Elizabeth. "And sometimes we're granted that."

Elizabeth leaned back against the seat. "But how do you know it will work, that it *has* worked . . . that it isn't just some coincidence?"

She watched Alisen proceed with caution. "Well," she cleared her throat, "if you flip a light switch, expecting the light to turn on, and it does, why would you doubt the connection?"

"But what if it doesn't work? What if the light *doesn't* come on?"

The intensity in her question surprised her. It probably surprised Alisen too.

"Then . . . I guess you would have to check the connection, make sure you have what is needed, maybe get a new bulb. And sometimes . . . we're trying to turn on the wrong lamp." She paused. "But you know the power source is there. It just needs to be tapped into."

Elizabeth made no reply. Alisen, to her credit, didn't push. But something had changed. Elizabeth had always kept her defenses, her safeguards against these exact kinds of discussions or anything with an undercurrent of emotion or humility. "But when you *know* the power source is there . . . Ryan talked about somebody switching on a light"—Elizabeth breathed—"That is faith, right? Praying to somebody, God, believing you'll get help?"

Alisen glanced at her sister, not hiding the curiosity in her expression. "Yes."

She made the turn into the hospital and found a parking spot. She turned off the ignition and sat back, turning her keys over in her hands. Elizabeth hadn't moved to leave yet either.

Elizabeth stared out the window and plowed on. "*How* do you know the power source is there?"

Alisen reached over and rested her hand on her sister's arm. Elizabeth turned to her.

Alisen shrugged her shoulders. "You test it."

Elizabeth considered that.

Alisen took a deep breath. "Elizabeth, what—"

"Later." Her eyes tightened. "Let's go see Dad."

Alisen forced a smile, and they both got out of the car.

* * *

"Why is he so yellow?" Elizabeth asked worriedly. She looked over her father's ashen face, the undertone making him look waxy.

"It's the infection."

She accepted the simple answer and touched her father's hand. He looked so frail. She'd never seen him like this. He was always so strong, so . . . intensely alive. He was dependable that way. "Why is his stomach bloated?"

"A side effect from the operation. It's air."

Elizabeth looked over at Sheryl, sitting opposite her in a chair next to the head of the bed. She looked worn-out but calm.

Sheryl smiled sadly. "You look exhausted, Elizabeth. Have a seat. Have you had anything to eat?"

Elizabeth looked back to her father, nodded her head, and continued to run her finger down the back of his hand. Alisen pushed a chair over to her, and she sat down where she was. Alisen sat on the end of the bed.

They stayed like that, waiting. The nurse came in every so often, checking his vitals and IVs, and she offered beverages, urging them to eat or drink, then she'd leave again. The hospital sounds became echoes in Elizabeth's ears, and the only two things she allowed her thoughts to linger on were her father and Ryan.

Elizabeth ignored a sound at the door, thinking it was the nurse again.

"Well, this is a solemn picture."

Elizabeth turned at the soft voice. She smiled. "Amanda."

"Hi, Elizabeth." Her youngest sister came forward and put her arm around Elizabeth's shoulder, giving her a small squeeze. "You made it."

Elizabeth nodded. She eyed Amanda. "Are you bigger?"

Amanda broke into a grin and nodded. She placed her hand on her belly and turned a little for a curtsy. "You can really see him now, huh?"

Elizabeth muffled a laugh at her sister. Irrepressible. That's what Amanda was. Unsinkable. She used to be such a pouty little thing.

Amanda crossed over to give Sheryl a hug. "Any change?"

Sheryl shook her head. "No, but not worse."

"Well, that's good, then." Amanda stepped forward and smoothed her dad's hair. "You're looking a little peaked, Dad." She leaned down. "You gonna wake up soon so we can tell you how awful you look? Or are you going to be stubborn about that blessing Greg gave you?"

Elizabeth watched as her father's eyes opened, then blinked slowly at Amanda. Amanda smiled and whispered gently, "Hi, Dad. Welcome back."

They all took in a breath.

A corner of his mouth came up as Sheryl and Alisen moved forward, gathering around the head of the bed.

Elizabeth sat unmoving as her eyes became wet with emotion. His hand moved under hers, and she looked down, wrapping her hand around his. It felt so fragile.

"Elizabeth."

His voice was weak and scratchy, but as she looked up and saw his eyes looking at her, she was filled with relief. She took a deep breath and nodded. "Dad." The tears fell, and she leaned forward, resting her other hand on his shoulder.

"How am I?" he weakly asked them.

"Dad," Amanda said, "you look great."

Elizabeth watched his other hand slowly reach up for Sheryl. Sheryl quickly took it in both of hers and bent down to kiss it.

"Marry me, Sheryl."

They all brought their heads up.

Sheryl let out a laugh of bewilderment and nodded her head. "Okay, love." She smiled through tears. "I'll marry you."

"*Dad.*" Alisen stared wide-eyed at her father, smiling incredulously.

His eyes turned to her. "What?" he said weakly.

"Why . . . what made you ask . . . ?"

"I love her," he answered simply, quietly. "Life's too short."

Elizabeth watched Alisen's face as she let out a laughing gasp, bringing her hands up to her mouth, and then Elizabeth watched Sheryl's reaction. A slow smile spread across Sheryl's face. Then she bent forward, kissed Elizabeth's father on the cheek, and whispered, "I love you, Keith Embry."

"Now, *that's* more like it," Amanda said, tears streaming down her smiling face.

* * *

Elizabeth lay on the sofa, and Alisen leaned against it on the floor, her head next to Elizabeth's, her chocolate curls pressed to Elizabeth's golden mane. They were at their father's condominium in Kalispell, an hour north of Alisen's home on Flathead Lake. Amanda's husband, Greg, had brought them all dinner at the hospital, and after they ate, everyone agreed that Alisen should take Elizabeth home to rest. Elizabeth had argued ineffectively.

Elizabeth had told Alisen everything about her time in Jackson: the inn, the waterfall, the truck, the hike, the school bus, Seven Pines, Travis, the card game, everything. The dream. Ryan. The past.

The tissue box sat empty. The windows had grown dark. Only the faint hiss of the gas fireplace could be heard.

Alisen slowly got up and walked down the hall. She returned with blankets and pillows. She placed a pillow under Elizabeth's head and threw a blanket over her, pulling it up to her chin. She made a bed for herself on the floor, went to turn off the lights, and knelt down. Her lips moved softly in the firelight, and Elizabeth watched and listened to the faint whisperings. Alisen finished, placed her hand on Elizabeth's cheek, and then lay down.

Gradually, both women fell asleep.

Chapter 23

CHLOE CAME INTO THE HOUSE, dropped her bag, unwound her scarf, and pulled off her jacket. She hung up her things in the closet and dragged her bag behind her as she headed to her room.

"Chloe."

She turned. "Yeah, Dad?"

"Could I talk to you for a minute?"

She set her bag down again. "Sure."

Ryan pulled out a chair next to him at the dining table. He watched a wrinkle appear between her eyebrows as she took the chair and looked at him, waiting. He searched for a trace of the surly toddler he remembered, blowing raspberries and patting his cheeks. He pushed a letter on the table in her direction.

She looked at him questioningly.

"Read it," he said.

She took it and read. He watched her face flush.

"Dad, I . . ."

"Turn it over."

She brought her eyes up to his and turned the letter over. She looked down again.

P.S. Tell Chloe I want to believe her.

He watched her read it again, looking perplexed. Suddenly, her eyes drew up to the hutch. She looked back down at the words on the paper, and her face softened. She swallowed.

Ryan was quiet. "Can you please tell me what that means?"

"I think so." She looked at the hutch, her eyes going to the top shelf. "She wants to believe we'll both see our mothers again." Chloe looked at her dad. "I told her we'd see them again. She wants to believe it's true."

Ryan followed her gaze to the hutch. He stared at its contents.

"Dad?" She read over the letter. "I think there's something else."

He took a deep breath. "What?"

"I'm pretty sure she thinks Mom was a kind of . . . perfect saint. Or something."

He frowned, and he looked back at the hutch. He stood up and saw it through Elizabeth's eyes.

"Dad?"

"Hmm?"

"I think you were right. I think Elizabeth is just trying to do what's right. Like the rest of us."

He turned to Chloe and blew out a breath. "Thank you."

Her eyes searched his. "Dad? Do you . . . love her?"

He looked past her. He began to nod. "Yeah, Chloe, I do."

She nodded.

Chloe pushed the letter back toward him. "Maybe she's just figuring out what she really wants. Who *wouldn't* be scared of us?"

Ryan looked at his daughter. Was he really having this conversation with a fifteen-year-old?

She tapped the table. "So you didn't get a chance to tell her about the Church?"

Ryan shook his head. "I started to, but," he rubbed his eyes with his hand, "it didn't happen." *Because I scared her. I scared her and endangered her and made her think she had to be some perfect echo of what I lost.*

"Well, you need to make it happen."

"Listen, Chloe, it's difficult to be seduced by somebody when they're miles away, okay? I told you to trust me with that." Why was she so insistent?

Chloe blushed again and shook her head. "No, Dad. That's not what I mean. You need to tell her because it's fair to her, to know what you believe, so she can decide what it means to her . . . and because I liked watching you with her."

His head snapped up. "Really?"

She gave him a small smile. Then she rolled her eyes.

He narrowed his. "How old *are* you anyway?"

* * *

Elizabeth emerged from her room. She flopped her arms at her sides. "How's this?" She'd tried on four outfits. Alisen looked over her copper-colored sweater, slim black skirt to her knees, and black dress boots. "You look wonderful. Are you ready?"

Elizabeth shook her head.

Alisen grinned. "Great. Let's go."

They drove to the hospital and found Sheryl moving their dad's tray out of the way when they walked in.

"Good morning. Hey, is that breakfast?" Alisen said.

"No, you can't call it that," Keith said.

Sheryl gave them a knowing glance.

"You look better every day, Dad." Alisen went over and kissed his cheek.

"Thanks. I wish I could say the same thing about the food here."

"You just started eating again, Keith. You have to go slowly," Sheryl said.

He grunted.

Elizabeth smiled. "Well, you have your humor back."

He glanced at her, then looked again, noticing her dressy appearance. "Where are you two going?"

Elizabeth looked at Alisen, then looked at the floor, pursing her lips.

Alisen took over. "Oh, we just stopped in for a minute, but we'll be back this afternoon." She took a deep breath and faced their father. "We're going to church with Amanda and Greg in Bigfork."

Keith's look of surprise went back and forth between his daughters, then rested on Elizabeth. Sheryl reached over to hold Keith's hand, squeezing it softly.

"Hmm." He rested his head back against the pillow. "Well, I'll see you in several hours, then."

Elizabeth raised an eyebrow, waiting for more, but he just gazed steadily at her.

"All right, then. Be good," Alisen said. She turned and gave Elizabeth a little push toward the door.

* * *

Amanda stood to introduce her older sisters to the Sunday School class. "You know my sister Alisen. And this is my sister Elizabeth Embry. She's in the process of moving from Kalispell to Jackson to run a boutique, so we'll miss her. She'll be back up in December, though, when Greg and I are sealed in the temple. Oh, and when the baby comes, right?"

Elizabeth nodded, and the class murmured nice things.

Amanda and Elizabeth sat down and Elizabeth whispered to Alisen, "She forgot to give them my phone and Social Security numbers."

"She already gave those to the bishop in Jackson," she whispered back.

Elizabeth froze, and Alisen giggled.

"I'm *kidding*."

"Welcome," the teacher said. "We're glad you're here." He turned back to the board and finished writing, and then somebody said a prayer, and he began the lesson.

Elizabeth stared at the words on the chalkboard.

Faith Dispels Doubt and Fear

She looked at the teacher, then back at the words. She even looked around a little, trying to shake the feeling that someone had set this up. She looked at Alisen, but she was opening her books.

The lesson was filled with references to things she did not know about, names she did not recognize. She'd been reading along with Alisen but was becoming silently frustrated. How was this helping?

The teacher continued. "Christ is here among the Nephites, teaching them, and it is time to go. They are tired, He has given them a lot to think about, but He is filled with compassion. Someone read verses two, three, and five."

A woman read: "I perceive that ye are weak, that ye cannot understand all my words which I am commanded of the Father to speak unto you at this time. Therefore, go ye unto your homes, and ponder upon the things which I have said, and ask of the Father, in my name, that ye may understand, and prepare your minds for the morrow, and I come unto you again."

Elizabeth sat up, pulling in a breath. She understood that perfectly.

"And it came to pass that when Jesus had thus spoken, he cast his eyes round about again on the multitude, and beheld they were in tears, and did look steadfastly upon him as if they would ask him to tarry a little longer with them."

Elizabeth wondered how He could be such a man, to evoke that response from His listeners. From what she'd gathered, He was really just . . . kind.

"Then," the teacher said, "what does He do? He is filled with compassion, His bowels are filled with mercy, and He heals them. Not just as a whole but individually. Brothers and sisters, do we have individual afflictions?"

Nodding and sounds of agreement went around the room.

"And what does He say? '*Your faith is sufficient that I should heal you.*'" He gestured to the chalkboard. "Faith dispels doubt and fear."

So there it was. *Faith*. But she knew so little. This was all new to her. She felt so . . . undeserving, small. She bowed her head in thought, looking at her empty hands. *Did you think I would judge you?* She winced at the memory of Ryan's words. Would he?

Alisen was turning her pages to another part of her book. Elizabeth listened with her head down as the teacher read quietly. "Therefore, fear not, little flock; do good; let earth and hell combine against you, for if ye are built upon my rock, they cannot prevail. Behold, I do not condemn you; go your ways and sin no more."

Elizabeth's head came up slowly.

"Look unto me in every thought; doubt not, fear not."

Silence settled on the room, and Elizabeth felt her heart pounding. She felt very self-conscious and very . . . curious.

She half listened and half turned things over in her mind, feeling an anxiousness to have more questions answered.

She didn't know how much time had passed, but suddenly, the teacher was closing. She blinked and let go of the breath she'd been holding.

She was surprised. She didn't want the lesson to end.

* * *

Elizabeth sat reading on the couch when Alisen's husband, Derick, opened the front door and let himself in, dropping his bags. "Alisen? I'm home!" He smiled as Alisen came around the corner from the kitchen, broke into a run, and threw herself into his arms. His hands came to her hair as they kissed. Elizabeth looked away, reminding herself they were barely off their honeymoon.

"I missed you," Derick said. "How is your dad?"

Alisen's arms remained wrapped tightly around her husband. "Better. His color is better. He's cranky."

Derick smiled. "That's good news."

"He asked Sheryl to marry him."

"What?"

"I know. I'm still wondering if it was the drugs, but Sheryl is so happy."

Derick laughed. Elizabeth found herself watching this exchange with a new perspective. Before, Alisen and Derick's open affection for each other had made her uncomfortable. But now she couldn't help but consider it and what it might be like to have someone to hold for however long, whenever you needed to hold someone.

"I expected to come home to someone a little more distraught," Derick said. "I'm glad you don't have a reason to be."

"Me too." Alisen pulled into him again. "Thank you for coming home."

"No problem." He nuzzled into her hair.

The man had dropped everything in *Bolivia* to be here for his wife *in case* her father hadn't made it through.

They walked into the living room, arms around each other.

Alisen smiled. "And look who's here." She gestured to Elizabeth on the couch.

Derick drew back half a step in surprise. "Elizabeth, I didn't . . . even . . ." He stopped, staring, his mouth open crookedly.

Alison stretched up on her toes and kissed Derick's cheek. "I left something on the stove. I'll be right back." She left him frozen to his spot.

Elizabeth looked up at him expectantly. "Hello, Derick. Have a good flight?"

He swallowed. "Sure. Yeah."

Elizabeth enjoyed his baffled expression. "What?"

"Um, nothing." He put his hands on his hips. "I just, uh . . ." He trailed off again. He furrowed his eyebrows.

"Surprised to see me?"

He nodded. "Yeah." He scratched his head and turned to the kitchen. "Alisen?" he called and made a few quick strides in that direction.

Elizabeth shook her head, smiling after him, guessing at the hushed conversation that would take place in the kitchen. She looked back down at the thick set of scriptures resting open on her lap and the list of verses Alisen had made her about faith. Her smile sobered as she read, and then she turned the page, settling farther back into the sofa.

"But she hates it when we say 'Bless you' after a sneeze."

"I can hear you," she called.

Chapter 24

Ryan opened the door and smiled. "Hey, sis, come on in." He nodded. "Dave. Glad to see you made it home all right."

David took his wife's coat and his own and handed them both to Ryan as three young boys ran past him, each carrying a pumpkin.

"Hi, Ryan," they called as they dropped their pumpkins off at the dining table with the others, then trampled downstairs.

Ryan looked at the small pile of coats and shoes they'd left behind. He shoved them out of the way with his foot and hung the adults' coats up in the closet. As he turned around, Nora reached up and pecked him on the cheek.

"It's good to see you."

He looked her over and smiled. "I haven't seen you for a couple of weeks. You look good." He took the casserole dish from her.

"Thanks. I feel a lot better now that David is home."

David came up behind her and rubbed her shoulders. "It's hard to build a lodge in a blizzard anyway." He pulled his wife gently. "C'mon, you're tired. Let's sit down."

"Mom and Dad aren't here yet?" Nora set a gift bag on the dining table with the other packages and the pumpkins.

After a quick knock on the door, their parents entered, stomping their feet.

"Hey, we were just talking about you." Ryan looked behind them out the door. "Did you walk?"

"Yup," Jeff answered. "It's good to walk."

"And we know someone who will drive us home later," Dayle added.

Ryan chuckled. "Well, come in. The fire is going, and dinner is just about ready." He looked at the dish he held and headed to the kitchen.

He returned and went to his mother, who was seated on the sofa. "Happy birthday, Mom." He leaned down to give her a hug.

"Thank you, my Ryan." She pulled back and rubbed his hair, then held his face. "How are you?"

He'd kept a low profile the last couple of days, what with the kids' weekend schedules and trying to avoid too many questions. But the way his mom looked at him, he knew what she was asking.

"Fine," he said softly. "I'm fine."

"Where are all the kids?" his dad asked, looking around.

"They'll be up soon, I'm sure. I think Chloe and Sam started a foosball tournament down there." He sat down in the chair and put his feet up on the ottoman.

Nora dropped her head back on the sofa. "Let's just enjoy the quiet for a minute."

"Rough day?" her mother asked, smiling as if she'd been there and was glad she wasn't anymore.

"Oh, I guess, if you want to count the mad dash before church. Jacob couldn't find his belt—again—and he seems to be wearing all of his church socks in one week because there was not one pair in his drawer. Levi decided to flush one of his action figures down the toilet—"

"What?" Apparently, David hadn't heard that one. His hand went up to his face.

"And a few Legos, just for kicks. You'll have to fix that for me. I don't do plumbing. And Jared was running and smacked right into the corner of the piano right before we left, so that was a few more minutes of taking care of that owie, which, of course, made us late because I haven't learned yet to plan for those things." She sighed. "But church was really nice, and it wasn't until afterward that the nursery leader came to tell me Levi is kissing all the girls and we need to get him to stop because it is causing some tears."

David leaned forward and groaned.

Nora put her hand on her husband's back and rubbed. "I blame that one on you, dear."

He nodded his head in his hands.

Ryan smiled but was staring off into the fire.

"Ryan . . . I, uh, wanted to ask you something," he heard his sister carefully say.

David sat up and looked at her. "Now?"

She shrugged. "Why not?"

"Because then he wouldn't be mad at you for the rest of the evening . . . or *me* either."

She smiled and turned to Ryan. "You promise you won't be mad?"

Ryan let out a small laugh. "All right."

"Yeah, sure," David grumbled.

Ryan waited, slightly amused.

"Well, I met someone last week, and I just have this feeling about her, and I had this idea . . ."

"Oh *no*." Ryan brought his hand up to his jaw and rubbed it back and forth, looking into the fire. "Uh-uh, *no*." That was all he needed.

"But she's great, beautiful, smart, *single* . . ."

"Hon, he's getting mad," David murmured.

"And I got to know her a little, and she—"

Dayle patted her leg. "Nora, he's just—"

"But I can totally see the two of you hitting it off."

"Didn't we try this before? That was a total disaster," David said.

Nora turned to David. "But that was *your* idea. I *know* Ryan. I know—"

"Nora, this isn't a good time, honey," Jeff said.

"But I just think if you met her—"

Ryan stood abruptly. "Nora, I know what you're trying to do, but . . ."

"Her name is Elizabeth Embry, and—"

"What?" Three heads turned to her.

Her eyes got big and a little fearful. But she persevered. "Her name . . . is Elizabeth Embry, and she works at Wildberries, that boutique in town. She just moved here." She looked at all of them. "She's been staying at the inn."

Ryan stood there, staring at his sister. "What?"

Nora proceeded with caution. "I went into the store to look for something for mom, and she was there, working, and we got to talking and just sort of hit it off. And . . . I thought of you."

"When was that?"

"Umm, Thursday before last."

He furrowed his brow, thinking. That was the day he'd hit her with the truck.

"And then we had lunch last week, twice, so I've really—"

"What?" Again, three heads turned to her.

"Would you please tell me what's going on here? Why am I starting to feel guilty about this? *I* like her, even if Ryan wouldn't." She huffed. "But I still think he would."

"Oh, he'd like her all right," Jeff mumbled. Dayle elbowed him in the ribs. "Oww."

"You had lunch with her?" Ryan was trying to get his head around this. "Was it Wednesday?"

"Yes."

He closed his eyes. *You are kidding me.*

"And on Friday."

He looked at her again. "This *last* Friday?"

Nora narrowed her eyes. "Yes . . . I invited her to join my friends and me. I thought it would be good for her to get to know the girls."

"The girls?"

"Yes. My girlfriends. From the *ward*."

"And she went with you?"

"Well, I met her there, but yes, she came. We had a good time. But then she got an emergency call from her sister, and . . . wait, why am I telling you all this? What is going on here?"

Ryan ignored her question. "So you were there when her sister called about her father?"

Nora nodded. "Yes, which was really quite interesting because . . . *wait.* I didn't tell you about her father."

Ryan brushed that aside. "Did she know that . . . you're my sister?"

"Umm, yes, it came up at lunch when she said she was staying at the inn."

He vaguely noticed the others were watching them like a tennis match. "And what did she say?"

"Oh, she seemed to be surprised, and I told her it was a small town. Which is why it was interesting about her sister because—"

"And she didn't tell you she knew me?" His voice had quieted. "That we were . . . seeing each other?" He felt the heat climbing up his neck.

Nora looked away, then looked back, shaking her head. "No . . . wait, *what*?"

Ryan looked into the fire again. Why wouldn't she have said something? Was Elizabeth just surprised by the coincidence, or was she trying to avoid any more complications . . . because . . .

"Ryan, tell me what is going on *right now*."

He pulled his gaze away from the fire. "I've been seeing Elizabeth. Not for long, but . . ." he dropped his head down, "long enough."

"No way."

He nodded. "Way."

"That's amazing. Isn't that amazing?"

Everyone nodded.

"And I tried to get you together last Saturday."

He looked at her, scowling. "You did?"

"Yes, remember? I invited you all over, and *you* were being so stubborn about not coming. I couldn't understand it. But then Elizabeth had a date—" Her eyes widened. "Ooohhh."

Ryan rubbed his face with his hand. He sighed, exasperated.

She took that in. "So, then, you already know."

He looked at her. "What?"

"About it being a small world . . . that even though she isn't a member of the Church, her sisters are."

Ryan stared at her, trying to understand what she'd just said. "I . . . I didn't know that."

"Really? Both of her sisters have joined the Church just in the last few years. I would have thought she would have told you when she found out you were LDS too. People usually like to find connections like that."

He scowled at himself. "She doesn't know I'm a member."

Nora was silent for a minute. Finally, she said, "I'm pretty sure she does."

His head came up. "Why?"

"Because she knows I am, and now that I think about it, I think she did figure it out."

He turned sharply to look at the hutch. He sat down hard and covered his face in his hands. "I'm such an idiot."

"No, you're not," Dayle interjected. "You were just dealing with the . . . other things."

"What other things?" Nora asked.

Ryan rolled his eyes at his sister. "Sorry, Mom."

"For what?" Dayle asked.

"For making *your* birthday all about me."

"I *told* you not to mention it," David muttered.

Nora pursed her lips and rubbed the side of her belly. "Well, *I* didn't know," she glowered back at him.

"Yes, you did. You said you had a *feeling*."

Nora stared at the fire. "I did say that, didn't I?"

They all nodded slowly.

* * *

Ryan sat on the edge of his bed, holding his phone in one hand and her note in the other. He had so many questions, and there was so much he wanted to say, but he kept remembering her words. He was supposed to let her work it out. He glanced down at the note again.

I'll try to keep my promise.

She'd asked him to do something too.

He set the phone and letter down and turned around to kneel. It took him a minute to focus, but once he began to pray, the words flowed, and after asking for forgiveness for being impatient, he looked outside himself and prayed for *her* happiness.

* * *

Alisen knocked on the open door, then peeked in. "You all right?"

Elizabeth looked up. She sat on the edge of the bed, looking at her phone. She nodded.

Alisen stepped in. "Has he called?"

Elizabeth shook her head. "That was Nancy. She called for an update. I told her I had to work some things out at Saks and Dad was better and I still wasn't sure when I'd be going back. She was totally supportive, of course." She looked up. "I don't think he'll call. I sort of asked him to give me time."

"Well, why don't you call *him*, then?"

Elizabeth sighed. "Because part of me is mad at him."

"Why?"

She looked back down at the phone, rubbing her thumb over the keys. "Because he didn't tell me. Because," she rolled her eyes at herself, "I had to find out from his sister, who I didn't even *know* was his sister." She shook her head. "Not that we've had time to really talk about that . . . We always seemed to be addressing something else . . . and I know he did try to talk to me about . . . spiritual things a couple of times, but I . . ." She trailed off. Her eyes came up to Alisen's. "I guess I should have known. I should have seen it." She sighed. "It's so obvious now."

"How?"

"Well, he's just . . . he's just so . . ." Elizabeth looked at her window. Her voice softened. "I wouldn't change anything about him. Even his kids."

Alisen's eyes widened. "Well, if you wouldn't change anything about him, then what's the problem?"

Elizabeth laughed softly and shook her head. She brought a finger up and pointed it at her chest. Her eyes misted over. "How am I supposed to keep up with that? How am I supposed to . . . ? When his wife was . . . ? When I've done things . . . ?" She shook away the tears.

Alisen sat down next to Elizabeth and put an arm around her.

Elizabeth tried to control her emotions. "Why didn't he tell me?"

"Would it have made a difference?"

Elizabeth thought. "I might have been more wary, more cautious, but . . . no. I still would have fallen for him. There was no stopping that."

"Well then . . ."

"But I would have kept him from falling in love with *me*."

"Oh, Liz, you couldn't have—"

"Yes, I could have. I can really turn the witch on when I want to." She laughed a little, and Alisen joined her. Elizabeth sobered. "I just . . . didn't want to." She sniffled. "If he had pressed the Church stuff though?" She shook her head. "No way. I would have backed out fast; I would have left that inn, and . . ." The thought of what else brought the tears again.

"So is he pressing the Church stuff now?" Alisen reached for a tissue and handed it to her.

Elizabeth shook her head. "Not really. But he's definitely making me think."

"That's not so bad, is it?"

Elizabeth blew her nose. "It's fantastic," she dead-panned.

Alisen smiled. "You know, you're selling yourself short. You're more than you think you are."

Elizabeth threw her arms out as she sat up. "Why does everyone keep telling me that? How can I be more than I think I am? I *know* who I am. I *know* what I've done. That's it. There is no more."

A minute passed.

Alisen reached up a hand and smoothed Elizabeth's hair. "Liz." She slid off the bed to kneel in front of her sister, looking up into her down-turned eyes. "There *is* more. There is *so much more*." She paused. "You just have to *hope* and *believe*."

Elizabeth nodded and rolled her eyes, dabbing the tissue. "I know. Faith, right?"

Alisen nodded. "Doubt not, fear not."

Elizabeth put her hands down on the bed and straightened her shoulders. She flipped her hair back and looked up, blinking. "This is going to be difficult."

Alisen smiled gently. "It doesn't have to be."

Elizabeth looked down at her sister. "I think for me, it *has* to be." She sighed. She fingered the phone.

"Call him."

Elizabeth shook her head. "Not yet."

Chapter 25

ELIZABETH LOOKED AT DERICK. "THE missionaries?"

He smiled at her patiently. "Why not? You've read the Book of Mormon and half of the New Testament."

Alisen folded her arms. "I wouldn't be surprised if she's memorized the Articles of Faith."

Elizabeth ignored them. "Why can't I just keep talking to *you*?" She wasn't ready to bring strangers into this.

"Because I think we've come to a point where you need to talk to the elders. It's what they've been called to do."

Elizabeth groaned. "I don't know."

Derick looked her in the eyes. "Do you know it's true?"

Elizabeth looked down and shrugged.

"Have you prayed about it?"

She looked up at him through her eyelashes and bit her lip.

"She hasn't yet," Alisen said.

"Why not?"

Elizabeth looked away. He looked at Alisen, but she just raised her eyebrows at him.

"Elizabeth, why haven't you prayed?" he asked gently.

"I've tried." She brought her eyes back to him. "I just . . . can't start. I just . . ." She shook her head. "I can't bring myself to *talk* to God."

He placed his hand on her arm. "He's your Father. He wants you to talk to Him."

"But isn't He all-knowing? He knows already, right?"

Derick nodded and remained patient. "Yes. He knows."

She placed her hand over her eyes. "Then why . . . ?"

"He wants to hear your voice calling Him. He misses you, Elizabeth."

She kept her hand over her eyes. "I don't know why," she croaked.

"Pray," he told her.

She felt like such a hypocrite, remembering her request of Ryan. She nodded. "Okay," she whispered. She breathed out, frowning. "You're going to be rubbing this in for the rest of your life, aren't you?"

A smile crept over Derick's face. "Would I do that?"

* * *

"Daddy, I want to be a black cat for Halloween."

He looked up from his paper. "I thought you wanted to be Supergirl?"

Lily was coloring a picture of a jack-o-lantern she'd brought home from school.

She made a thoughtful face. "Well, Kaitlyn and Amber are going to be black cats, and I want to be one too so we can be three black cats."

He grunted. "What are we supposed to do with your Supergirl costume? We already bought it, remember? It's hanging in your closet."

She looked up, thinking. "Oh yeaaaah." She shrugged. "Well, I guess I can be Supergirl." She went back to coloring.

He laughed. Why couldn't everything be that easy? The phone rang, and he got up to answer it.

"Hello."

"Hello, is this Ryan Brennan?"

"Yes, it is."

"Hi, um, this is Alisen Whitney . . . Elizabeth's sister."

He paused, his heartbeat picking up its pace. "Oh. Hi."

"Hi." He could hear her smile. "I wanted to call you . . . Actually, Elizabeth doesn't know I'm calling, but I felt like you should . . . I don't know, hear from *somebody* instead of nobody."

Ryan sat down and swallowed. "Thank you. I've been . . . wondering." *Every minute of every hour.*

They were both silent, then they both spoke at the same time. "I wanted to—"

"How is your—"

They both stopped, then he said, "You go."

"No, you, please."

"I was just going to ask how your father was. I don't even know what happened . . . I didn't get to see Elizabeth before she left."

"Oh, Dad is doing well. It was a gall bladder infection that went a little out of control, and we weren't sure he would even make it through the operation, so . . . But he did, and he's recovering steadily now."

He breathed. "Well, that's good, then. I'm glad. I got the impression Elizabeth and her father are close."

"Yes, they are."

There was another pause.

"I just wanted you to know that Elizabeth is . . . thinking of you and trying to . . . sort through things," Alisen said.

He didn't answer.

"Ryan?"

"Yes?"

"Elizabeth is . . . Well, just keep her in your prayers, okay? Don't give up on her."

"I won't give up on her."

"Oh?" Alisen sounded surprised at his simple answer.

He swallowed again and said, "I love her." The pain in his chest roiled as he said the words. He watched Lily smile as she colored.

He heard relief in Alisen's voice. "Thank you, Ryan."

"Alisen?"

"Yes?"

"She's been through a lot, hasn't she?"

Alisen grew quiet for a moment. "Yes. But I think she's working around it. She's doing it for you."

He tapped the table with his fingers. "She needs to do it for herself."

"I know, Ryan. I think she knows that too."

They were silent another moment. He said, "Thanks for calling. It's good to hear . . . something. If you get a chance, tell her I miss her." His voice caught. "And when she's ready, to come home."

"All right. Good-bye."

"Good-bye."

He hung up the phone and stared out the window at the melting snow dripping off the eaves.

"Daddy?"

"Yes, sugar?"

"I love Elizabeth too."

He looked at Lily and sighed. "You do?"

Her smile widened. "Yes."

He smiled and winked at her.

She happily went back to coloring.

He looked up.

Help her. Help her realize she is Thy daughter, and there is power to erase our mistakes. He breathed. *And help her know I'm sorry for my stupid ones.*

* * *

"Hey, Dad." Elizabeth leaned over to give him a rare kiss.

He looked at her curiously. "Hello, pumpkin."

Derick chuckled.

Keith looked at him sternly. "What have you been feeding my daughter?"

Derick raised his eyebrows. "Nothing, sir. She was already helping herself when I got to the kitchen." He gave him a crooked smile.

Keith turned back to Elizabeth. "Are you going to become one of these Mormons too?"

Elizabeth gazed at him. "I don't know, Dad."

He looked her over. "Well, just be sure before you do anything."

"Of course, Dad."

Alisen threw her hands up. "Oh, *sure. That* answer would have been nice to hear."

Keith smiled sheepishly at his other daughter, and she returned it. Derick laughed and hugged his wife as Elizabeth felt a pang of compassion for her sister. Alisen had grappled with all of these feelings and choices without the support of—and quite a bit of animosity from—her family. How had she done it?

"Dad?"

He looked back to Elizabeth. "Hmm?"

"What did we do with the piano?"

He looked at her, confused. "What piano?"

"Mom's piano."

His expression changed to one of mild surprise. "It's at John Shepherd's. When you stopped playing, I offered it to him to hang on to until . . . if you ever wanted it back. His daughter played, remember?" He frowned. "Why do you ask?"

Elizabeth took a deep breath. "I think I want it back."

Keith stared at her. "Are you . . . are you *playing again?*" he whispered.

She watched his face as she nodded.

"What made you . . . now . . . after all these years?"

She looked down. She hadn't realized he'd missed it. "Someone reminded me how much I loved to play."

"Alisen."

"Yes, Dad?"

"Find out if there is a piano in this blasted place. We're going to hear Elizabeth play."

Alisen grinned. "Yes, Dad." She was gone before Elizabeth's protest could reach her ears, not that it would have mattered.

* * *

"How long will you be gone?" Alisen asked as she watched Elizabeth pack.

"A few days, maybe more. They want me to help with interviews and give a bit of training." She pulled a couple pairs of pants off their hangers and folded them neatly into the suitcase. "Then, if I decide, I'll come here and oversee the movers and then leave for Jackson . . . I think."

"You *think*?"

Elizabeth looked at her sister. "I just . . . I'm not sure I'll be ready."

"Ready for what?"

Elizabeth looked at Alisen like she was crazy. "Ready to make that decision. Ready to face Ryan . . . to face . . . *everything* again." She resumed packing, covering her torn emotions with indifference. "Besides, Dad will just be coming home from the hospital. He'll need me here."

"He'll have Sheryl. He's doing great."

Elizabeth shrugged. "We'll see."

"Elizabeth, *he misses you.*"

Elizabeth glanced at her. "How do you know?" She turned away and muttered, "He's probably realizing how much easier life is without me."

"He wants you *home*," Alisen said firmly.

Elizabeth stopped. "How do you know that?"

Alisen looked at her steadily. "I talked to him."

"What? He called here?"

Alisen pursed her lips and didn't answer.

Anger flashed through Elizabeth's thoughts, but it immediately softened. She swallowed. "What did he say?"

"He said he loves you."

Elizabeth stood there for a minute, breathing. She sat down on the bed. Her heart filled with emotion, something she still wasn't used to. "I miss him so much," she whispered. "More than I ever thought I'd miss any man."

Alisen reached over and rubbed her back. "*Call* him."

Elizabeth wiped the tears away. She shook her head. "No. Not yet."

Alisen sighed. "You know, if this is real, if this is bowl-you-over-like-nothing-else love, you've got to ask yourself how you're going to feel four years from now if you let him go. Because if it's regret, that never goes away. And time? It doesn't care one bit that you're unsure or frightened or hurt. It just keeps flying by."

* * *

"Dad?" Chloe walked into the game room. She found her father throwing darts.

"Yeah?" *Thunk.*

"I think we should talk."

"About what?" *Thunk.*

"About you going to get Elizabeth and bringing her back here."

Clunk. The dart bounced off the electronic score board and fell to the floor.

He turned to her. "No. She said she needs to—"

"I know, I know, figure this out on her own. I know what you're doing, Dad, and chivalry is great and all. You're a dying breed, believe me, but it's time to go get her."

"Says who? You?" *Thunk.*

"Yes."

He looked at her like it would take more than that.

"And Grandma."

He paused.

"And Grandpa."

He shook his head.

"And Sam and Lily."

He dropped his head and leaned against the edge of the ping-pong table. He rubbed his eyes. "Chloe, I'm not sure she . . ."

"We want you back, Dad. And that means we want her back too." She folded her arms and stood straight, watching him steadily. "You need her."

"But she—"

"*Tell* her that."

Chapter 26

ELIZABETH KNELT DOWN, EXHAUSTED AFTER wrapping things up at work. She would be flying back to Kalispell in the morning. It all seemed very far away, as if she was halfway around the world. Between Jackson and New York, she may as well be.

But she'd made herself a promise.

The small impersonal lamp by the very standard hotel bed gave the only light in the room. Her apartment in the city had gone fast, as well as most of the furnishings. She'd already shipped what was left to her father's condo. She'd sort through everything there. Everything.

Her mind swam with all that she had read, the things she had heard, the answers she'd been given about faith, and every possible feeling she had about and for Ryan.

No fear. She bowed her head and looked at her hands folded in front of her. Her foot moved nervously, a metronome in a rapid rhythm. She took a deep breath, stopped her foot, and closed her eyes.

"Heavenly Father," she whispered. She swallowed. "Heavenly Father, I . . ." She blew out a shaky breath. "Please. I don't know . . ." She felt something she didn't recognize, but as she waited, she realized what it was. He was listening. He was patient.

He recognized her.

* * *

Elizabeth watched a small child, a little girl, sitting on the story rock. She felt warm, though there was snow around the edges of the beach, in mounds over the river. The little girl hummed a song, familiar. Elizabeth tilted her head up to feel the sunlight on her face.

Rustling in the bushes drew her attention away, and she braced herself. Her arm rose protectively to the little girl, who stopped singing. But then Elizabeth relaxed, and the girl giggled.

A man walked through the woods to them, smiling. He was dressed simply in a light tunic over linen pants, and his eyes were kind, gentle. The little girl seemed to be expecting him, though he was a surprise to Elizabeth. The light filtering through the trees moved with him, the leaves wavering as He passed. He looked familiar as he held his hands out to the little girl.

"Elizabeth."

She looked up sharply. His eyes remained on the little girl.

She watched as the child held her arms out to him and he took her up on his hip. He looked into her eyes and touched her blonde hair. The girl started to hum the song, and he joined her, the music so lovely Elizabeth was moved to tears. The bond between them was simple and true. Elizabeth found herself longing for that bond. When it ended, he set the girl, the little Elizabeth, down to play. Then he approached the rock, sat down, and brought his warm, penetrating eyes to her. She was drawn to sit next to him.

In his gaze, she felt he could see everything she wished for, and she wanted him to see, to share those hopes with him. Then abruptly, she realized he could see the other things too. She tried to look away, to protect him, to make him understand he didn't want to see those things. But she couldn't look away. His eyes held hers like a vise, still gentle, still kind, only now tears rolled down his face. She hated doing this to him. She hated that he had been so filled with love and joy and now she had ruined it.

He placed his hand on hers, and she blinked. He smiled tenderly. She couldn't smile back.

She heard the rustling sound again and tore her eyes away to see the bear come at them. She searched and realized with a wrench in her stomach that the little girl was unprotected on the ground. The bear reared up, giant in its size and strength, terrifying in its fury, and then threw itself down to roar at the little girl, who huddled in front of it, inches away.

Elizabeth felt the man's hand on hers tighten and tremble, but the little girl stayed still. The bear paused, baring its teeth, its breathing labored in aggression. Elizabeth looked at the man next to her, confused. He shivered with torment, watching the bear, his jaw tight, breathing his fear silently. She looked back at the little girl, feeling the terror for her, feeling her helplessness . . . and she realized. It was her. This little Elizabeth was her. The knowledge coursed through her with painful clarity. She shuddered a silent sob. With a deep breath and sudden strength, the man pushed himself forward and stood, his hand stretched out. The bear whined, then backed away, grunting with frustration, swinging his head back and forth. He disappeared into the woods.

The little girl stood, and her shoulders rose and fell with a sigh. She turned to run into the man's waiting arms, though Elizabeth could see he was exhausted. The little girl brought her hands to his face.

"Thank you," she said in a light voice, musical in its tone.

He pressed his forehead against hers. "You're welcome, little one." He turned his head enough to look into Elizabeth's eyes. "I'll take your pain, Elizabeth."

* * *

Elizabeth sat up in bed, feeling something tight around her chest and her heart pulling for room to beat. She gasped for air and then let out a soft cry. The band loosened, and she felt herself breathe again. She wiped her eyes and flipped the light on, searching the hotel room. She was alone. She replayed the dream in her mind, hearing her name again, his voice filled with love and compassion. She calmed down and lay back on her side. He knew everything. He knew her name. She had loved him as a child loves. But she had caused him such grief.

She rolled her face into the pillow with shame. She brought her arms around her head and cried softly until she fell back to sleep.

* * *

Elizabeth sat on the rock again. But it was the rock on the trail. Ryan's trail. And she was alone.

But she wasn't. She could hear the whispering in the trees. Men's voices, sometimes laughing, sometimes teasing, sometimes tempting.

"Liz."

She would look in one direction, then hear something that turned her head in another. They were coming closer, and she caught glimpses of them, their smiles, their sultry looks, their hands pulling around tree trunks.

"Ryan," she whispered, needing to say his name. Someone laughed in mockery. They were getting closer, but there was no one to call. She was too ashamed to invite anyone to help. Her terror rose.

Then she remembered the man from the story rock. He knew. He knew everything. But she didn't know his name. How could she not know his name?

One of the men jumped out from the trees, walking toward her with a lustful smile.

"No," she whispered. She scooted back on the rock, but he laughed. She felt at her side for a weapon, but there was nothing.

Another man came out of the woods, speaking her name, shaking his head condescendingly. When the third emerged, closer, her blood chilled. His vile grin had her gasping for breath as he neared.

"No. No, *please.*" She looked behind her for some way out. A cry escaped her as the dusty silt beneath her fingers fell away behind the rock, crumbling straight down a plunging cliff. Vertigo threatened to pull her over as someone roughly grabbed her wrist.

She twisted as the man pulled her, her strength muted with his touch. "*No!*" she screamed. She squeezed her eyes shut as the man laughed icily. More laughter joined in, and she felt hands at her legs, her arms. Desperation filled her. "Help. Help me, Heavenly Father. I need Him," she cried. "I need Him."

The grip on her wrist let go. Silence blanketed everything but a soft breeze.

She opened her eyes. He was there, sitting next to her on the rock. He leaned on his hands, shaking with exhaustion, perspiring, looking at her with pleading in his eyes, the same eyes that had seen everything she was, everything she wanted to be.

"Elizabeth." He held out his hand to her, and she took it. She saw the scars on his hand and wrist. "They're gone."

She looked. The woods were no longer threatening. She could hear birdsong and the water. Her waterfall. She looked back to him. He tilted his head up to the sun, closing his eyes, renewed.

She suddenly knew. "Jesus."

He looked at her. "Elizabeth."

She nodded. She opened her mouth to speak and cringed at the doubt escaping her tongue. "Why? Why would you do this?" She waited, quivering at her own audacity. But she had to know.

"Elizabeth," He sighed and took her hands now. "You are more *to me* than you think you are."

His smile filled her with peace, blanketed her in warmth and sudden hope. She found herself smiling back because she knew He loved her, despite everything . . . and somehow, He understood. It was belonging, full and unfaltering. He had come when she needed Him. Even when He knew everything. And He took it away.

* * *

Elizabeth opened her eyes and looked at the clock. The alarm had been going off, but she hadn't heard it. She switched it off and sat up, wrapping her arms around her knees, still feeling His peace. She took a deep, soft breath, left the bed, and knelt down.

Her voice shook, but it was with wonder. "Heavenly Father . . . thank you for sending Him."

She knew what she had to do.

But first she had a plane to catch.

Chapter 27

ELIZABETH GLANCED AT HER WATCH as she drove into Jackson, Wyoming, fresh off her flight. A new layer of snow covered everything, but the roads were clear and wet. The clouds had broken up, and pale blue peeked through the early afternoon sky. She parked in front of the store and went in, the sound of tires on wet pavement behind her.

"Miss Embry, hello."

"Hello, Andrew. I want to buy a painting."

"We have some." He smiled.

"I want to buy that one." She pointed.

He looked. "Perfect."

She carried the wrapped package out of the gallery and walked to the boutique, pausing in front of the window display. The Halloween scene was gone, replaced by an interior display of a dinner party, the mannequins dressed more formally, holding empty plates, posed in conversation with one another. A large window frame hung in the background, suspended, and snow glistened through the panes and collected at the corners and on a branch of pine. An electric fireplace, complete with a decorated mantel, sat in a corner. A chandelier hung over a small, elegantly set table, and underneath hid a turkey, wearing a beautiful scarf over his head.

Elizabeth chuckled and shook her head. *Wildberries.* She looked below at the lettering on the window.

Nancy Colette ~ Elizabeth Embry

She took a deep breath and smiled.

The door opened to the familiar jingle of the bell, and Christmas music played softly. Marisol was humming, hanging up a new line of bathrobes, but looked over. Her radiant smile lit up, and she came rushing forward to throw her arms around Elizabeth's shoulders. Three customers turned to watch, then went back to their browsing.

"You're here. Oh, welcome back! Is everything good? How is your father? When I heard, I just felt awful. I want you to know I was praying for him. Did you see the new display? Is it too corny? I wanted to do something fun . . . lighten the mood a little. Nancy loves it, of course." She gave Elizabeth another little hug. "Oh, I'm so glad you're back. Does Nancy know you're back? She didn't say anything. She'll be in pretty soon . . . She went out to lunch with Hank. All their windows are in, and he finished drywalling the guest room and tiling the new bathroom. I think she said the flooring and cupboards were up in the kitchen too. We'll have to go take a peek. It's amazing what can happen in a few weeks."

"Excuse me." A woman holding some items stood at the counter.

"Oh." Marisol turned to the customer. "I'm sorry. Are you ready?" She went behind the counter and began to chat pleasantly with the lady.

Elizabeth looked around her, walking slowly. She reached out and touched a velvety white plush bathrobe, found one her size, and took it off the rack, holding it up. She laid it over her arm and made her way back to the office.

They had placed a new desk against the free wall, and she knew it was waiting for her. She was touched by Nancy's confidence. She set the painting and robe down on the desk and pulled out the rolling chair. She sat, thinking. The back door opened, and she got up, moving to the doorway of the office.

Hank came in, holding the door for his wife. His eyes found Elizabeth. "Well, hello there, beautiful stranger."

At his words, Nancy's head came up, and her eyes widened. She clapped her hands together. "Oh, darling, you're here, oh!" She pulled Elizabeth in for an embrace and a peck on the cheek. "How is your father?"

Elizabeth smiled gratefully. "He's good, getting better every day."

"Oh, that's wonderful." Nancy searched Elizabeth's eyes. "We've missed you . . . *all* of us."

Elizabeth raised an eyebrow.

Nancy pursed her lips. "Have you seen him yet?"

Elizabeth shook her head. "I came here first."

"Well, he is just about beside himself."

Elizabeth looked at Nancy, confused. "How . . . ?"

"Oh, he's been in here a few times . . . stopped by while he was running his errands just to ask if we'd heard anything. So quiet and sweet. When I told him you hadn't committed yet, I thought I'd crushed him. Of course, I reminded myself that was *you*, not me." She smiled slyly and took Elizabeth's shoulders. Her voice softened. "Darling, don't let this one get away."

Elizabeth's heart began to swell, and she didn't want to wait any longer. "Do you have the papers?"

Nancy's eyes widened, and she flew to her desk, opening a folder. She grabbed the phone and called her notary.

After the notary arrived, Nancy selected a pen and shoved it at Elizabeth, who took it, smiling. Elizabeth leaned over the desk and pressed the pen to paper, sure.

Nancy breathed a sigh of relief and signed as well. At the sound of the notary's stamp, she embraced Elizabeth. Elizabeth returned it, welcoming the touch and familiar scent of her friend.

Nancy let go and brushed a tear aside. "I can't take scares like that." She flopped back in her desk chair. "Stick to the plan. Yes, I like the sound of that." Hank chuckled, clapping his hands slowly. Then Nancy pushed herself up and threw her arms around Elizabeth once again. "I know this charming place in the woods you need to see. I happen to know the owner is incredibly handsome . . . and single. His name is Brennan. Such a lovely, strong name. I've already bought the vinyl sticker for the front window, in case a name change happens to come up."

Elizabeth's jaw dropped.

"Well, I can't help it. I like to be prepared."

Elizabeth muffled a laugh through her emotion and squeezed Nancy hard.

She made her way to the front of the store with her bag and the painting, waving to Marisol behind a customer and promising she would see her tomorrow. The door opened, and a male figure paused, then stepped aside to allow her to pass.

"James." She stopped and smiled as he nodded his hat to her. She took a step back, and he came into the store, removing his hat.

"Miss Embry."

"I just"—she held the package out—"I just bought your painting."

"Andrew told me. Thank you."

"Well, I love it. It's . . . perfect."

He smiled, and his clear-blue eyes gleamed. "I'm glad you like it." His eyes held hers for a moment, then they moved to find Marisol. He looked back at Elizabeth. "Well, excuse me."

She nodded, and he walked toward the counter, where Marisol was all but jumping up and down waiting for him.

The trees flew past as Elizabeth drove to the inn. The Lantern came into view, giving her the sensation of coming home. She half expected the suite to be ready for her, but, of course, it wouldn't be. She walked up the front porch, pulled open the door, and stepped inside. Her gaze went to the table in front of the windows and the piano in the corner. She turned to the long, gleaming wood counter. She was being watched.

She stepped forward and set the painting down against the base of the counter. "Hi," she said.

"Aren't you supposed to be in Montana?" The corner of Nora's mouth lifted, and she walked around the end of the counter.

Elizabeth shook her head. "No."

Nora beamed, then suddenly closed the distance between the two of them.

Elizabeth allowed the embrace. "What are you doing here?"

Nora pulled back and laughed. "I could ask you the same thing." She looked behind Elizabeth and down at the painting. She shook her head with a sigh. "I was needed to cover for my brother's absence."

Elizabeth looked around. "Where is he?" Her heart skipped, picturing Ryan walking in any second.

Nora leaned against the counter. "Well, he's in Montana . . . surprising you."

Elizabeth's jaw dropped. "What?"

"He flew out a few hours ago." Nora suppressed a smile, which Elizabeth appreciated.

"You mean, he just . . . he just dropped everything and . . ."

"Left to rescue you, yes."

"But that's what I was doing."

"Hmm, you both have great ideas. You should consider getting together."

Elizabeth smiled, then groaned, folding her arms on the counter and dropping her head into them. "I hate surprises."

* * *

Ryan glanced around for something recognizable and found it. A younger man held a sign up high. *Brennan.* The young woman next to him bounced up and down when he made eye contact, and as he stepped to them, they came forward. But it wasn't only them. An older man turned at the action, a woman on his elbow. Ryan stopped and swallowed.

Elizabeth's father.

The group approached carefully, the young woman grinning. "Ryan?"

He extended his hand and nodded, glancing again at Elizabeth's father, feeling the scrutiny. He hadn't expected a family reunion. "Alisen, right?"

"Yes, and this is my husband, Derick. My father, Keith, and his fiancée, Sheryl."

He shook hands firmly with the men, and Sheryl smiled encouragingly. He swallowed and looked around, hoping his nerves were hidden behind a calm exterior.

"She isn't here."

Ryan's head came back around. He nodded and felt the rock in his stomach. "Does she know I'm coming?" Had she found out? Did she refuse to come? Is that why they were all here? To console him?

Alisen shook her head, and Derick reached out, firmly patting Ryan's arm. "Let's talk and walk." He picked up Ryan's bag and led him toward the other wing of the airport.

But Ryan stopped. "Listen, I only came because . . . because I needed her to know she was important enough to me to . . ." He held his breath and looked around. "To come after her. But I know she needs her own space, her own time, and you can tell her—"

"Ryan, she's not here. *Here*."

He blinked at Alisen.

"She flew to Jackson." Alisen's grin returned.

"But . . . but—"

Derick pulled Ryan's arm, and Ryan's feet moved to follow. "No buts. My eccentric sister-in-law caught a flight from New York to Jackson about three hours ago."

"We couldn't reach you, so Derick found you a return flight. It leaves in just over an hour, so that will give us a few minutes to get to know you," Alisen said.

Ryan stopped again, firmly, pulling Derick back half a step. "Wait." He glanced at Keith Embry, who, though thin and a bit pale, had been pressing a stare into Ryan so intensely he could feel it through the back of his head. "Let me get this straight. Elizabeth was here. Then she went to New York. And she was going to come back here and take care of you," he gestured to Keith, who raised his eyebrow so much like Elizabeth that Ryan had to shake his head, "for who knows how long because she wasn't sure she could face . . . me again." Alisen winced. "But now that I've convinced myself to come here . . . now that I've realized I *needed* to come here to see her, to tell her everything, how I feel . . ." He took a deep breath and swallowed the mixture of emotions boiling inside him. "Now you tell me she's not here, she's flying to Jackson . . . and she couldn't tell me? This whole time . . . she couldn't *tell* me?" He breathed and looked around the airport again. Derick let go of his arm.

"Ryan?"

He looked into the very blue eyes of Elizabeth's sister.

"She's going because she loves you."

"I'm really tired of communicating that sentiment through other people."

Derick slapped his shoulder. "That's why we got you the return ticket."

Ryan blinked again, then he caught Keith's expression. The man stood straight, his arms folded across his chest, his eyes narrowed. And he was chuckling silently. He took a step forward, shaking his head and lifting a finger, pointing it at Ryan's chest.

"You've got my girl going in all directions, looking for that one place to settle down. I'm not sure you understand how significant that is, and I don't blame you . . . Elizabeth is as closed a book as I ever was. But let me tell you something, Ryan. Any man who can change that girl's world around, bring out that heart she hides so well . . . I'd like to see how that turns out."

Ryan swallowed.

Keith placed his hand on Ryan's shoulders. "And I hear I owe you my thanks."

"For what?"

"If you don't mind, I'd like Elizabeth to keep playing the piano. I was told she has someone to play for again."

* * *

The phone rang.

"Hello, you've reached the Lantern. How may I help you?" Nora's eyes widened. She tapped Elizabeth's arm.

Elizabeth's heart thumped in her throat.

"Really? You're kidding. Weird. No, no, I haven't seen her. Okay. Yes, okay. See you soon. Bye."

Nora hung up the phone. She had a shrewd look on her face. "I might have just done something really mean."

Elizabeth stared at her incredulously.

"But it might be really good."

"Elizabeth?"

They both looked down the hall.

Dayle walked quickly up to Elizabeth. "Honey, you're back. He didn't know. He went to get you." She gave Elizabeth a hug, and Elizabeth closed her eyes, amazed at how good it felt to be back here.

"I know. Nora told me. It's my fault . . . It was a last-minute decision."

Dayle pulled back to look at her. "Well, you both had the same idea, and in my mind, that's a good thing, right?"

Elizabeth smiled. "Sure. Both of us are absolutely brilliant. And still apart."

Nora spoke up. "Mom, Ryan just called, and I sort of didn't tell him Elizabeth is here. I was thinking it's not too late to make this work."

Dayle looked at Nora conspiratorially. "What did you have in mind?"

Elizabeth set her hand on the counter. "Wait. I know what to do."

* * *

Ryan opened the front door and stomped his feet.

"Hey, Ryan. Welcome home. You okay?" Nora was annoyingly cheerful.

He grunted a reply as he removed his gloves.

Nora drummed her fingertips on the wood. "Any word on Elizabeth?"

"No. What's this?" He nodded to the large package leaning against the counter.

"Oh, that was delivered while you were flying off on your wild goose chase. They said it was for you."

His sister seemed to have forgotten *she* had encouraged him to go on the wild goose chase. He set his gloves on the counter. "You helping out?" He hefted what felt like a frame through the padded paper.

"Yup. Dad's running a few errands, and Mom wanted to get the deep cleaning done now that the rooms have cleared. Season picks up again this weekend."

As if he didn't know. He frowned as he tore off the front of the wrapping. "Who dropped this off?"

"Oh, this came with it." Nora held out a folded piece of paper. He took it, setting down the painting but looking at the forest scene, ablaze with light and shadow, a trail leading into its depths.

"I better go see what Levi's up to and switch the linens to the dryer." She put her hand on his arm. "I'm sorry about the mix-up with Elizabeth."

Ryan nodded, but she was already down the hall. He unfolded the note and read.

His hand went to his head, and he spun to face the doors. He spun back, looking at the painting. Movement in the hallway caught his eye. His mother peeked out from the kitchen.

"Mom?" He held out the note.

She smiled. "Why don't you go for a walk?"

He opened his mouth to argue, but in another moment, he grabbed his gloves and pushed through the front door. He paused on the steps and watched his dad come whistling from around the side of the inn.

"Son!" he exclaimed, his hands in his pockets. "You've returned." His breath made puffs in the cold air, and he looked up at the blue sky. "Great day for a walk. I always said a walk does a soul good." He patted Ryan on the shoulder as he climbed the steps.

Ryan stared after his dad, willing his thoughts to settle. If only a walk would be enough.

Just before the door closed, his dad turned. "Son, you best get on with it. It's not getting any warmer."

Ryan turned and glanced at the note once more. He shoved it in his pocket, turned up the collar on his coat, and walked east, toward town.

The chill seemed to ease the heat of his skin. With the steady rhythm of his gait, he lost himself in his thoughts.

"Excuse me—"

He halted at the voice and at the figure up ahead.

"Do you know if this road is safe? I'm looking for a place to run."

Chapter 28

She held her breath.

"Elizabeth," he said.

The wind messed with his hair, and his complexion was flushed from the walk, but his eyes . . . His eyes were distant. She shivered and took a short breath. "Hi."

He held up the wrinkled note in his hand. "What's this?"

She couldn't read him. "I heard we missed each other." She glanced around, attempting a smile. "I thought—"

"You thought you'd stay away for weeks, no call, no nothing, and that you'd surprise me?"

She straightened and tried to breathe. She nodded, but fear clamored through her body. "Surprise." It came in a whisper.

She didn't break away from his piercing gaze, hoping if she searched him long enough she could sense what he was thinking, see what he was feeling.

He broke the stare and took a step, and her whole being felt its tie to his. He looked down the road. "Why here?"

Didn't he know? "Because," her voice strengthened, "this is where I first knew I would be staying in Jackson." He had to remember. "Where I first . . . fell." She blew out a quick breath and rolled her eyes, keeping the tears at bay. It had sounded so much better in her head.

She peeked at his profile. His hands were set at his hips, and his breath formed long, thin clouds, disappearing almost as soon as they were made. This couldn't be wrong. She opened her mouth to speak again, but he beat her to it.

"I didn't *want* this. I wasn't looking for it." He swallowed, his brow furrowed. "How could I? I couldn't . . . I couldn't *forget*. I swore I would never forget."

Her heart leapt for something to make his pain go away. "You don't have to forget." His frown frustrated her. "No one would ask that of you."

"I was fine." He shook his head. "But everything kept putting you next to me, in my arms, and I couldn't *fight* it. And you had every reason to fight it too, but . . . you *didn't*." He finally looked at her again.

She stared, unsure of what to say next. He was so close and so cold. She hugged herself against it, shivering, and took a step toward him, but he stepped away.

His expression softened, and he looked down. "C'mon," he said, heading back toward the inn.

"But—"

He ignored her hesitation to leave. "You're cold."

She took three long steps to him. "So are *you*." She flinched at the hurt in her voice.

He whirled and looked at her. "Elle, I—" His words stuck.

She could read him now. She could see his fear, his worry. His . . . *loss*.

"Ryan, I'm *sorry*." The pent up emotion of the last few weeks threatened as her apology surfaced. She felt the weight of it, hating it, wanting it if it meant less pain for him. "I should have called you . . . I should have let you know. I shouldn't have left you like I'd . . ." The tears spilled over. "Like she . . ."

In a sudden move, he stepped to her, gripping her arms, bringing her close. "No." His voice was deep, intense. "No, Elle, I won't let you compare . . . I can't . . ."

She relaxed in his arms, unable to fight the hope his touch promised. "Ryan."

He pulled back, creating space between them. Her hope wavered, but she whispered, "I was frightened out of my mind."

He nodded, his eyes softer. "I know." He looked down.

"I thought . . . I thought I had to be . . . better." She shook her head, looking for the right word. "That I had to have all the answers before I came back. I was wrong. Forgive me. *Please*." She took a quick breath and whispered, "I'm back. I'm home."

Elizabeth watched his pain fade and felt a measure of relief. They both shivered. Hesitantly, his fingers shifted on her arms, and she could feel the pull, his eyes searching hers. She leaned forward, but he pulled back, and she blinked.

He took her hand and continued down the road.

"Where are we going?"

"I know where there's a warm fire. We need to talk."

She let him think as her own mind raced, but she clung to hope and the fact that he held her hand firmly in his. They made the turn in the road, past the inn, and headed to his place.

He finally spoke. "I'm sorry." He gazed toward the trees. "I—"

She stopped him. "You don't have to apologize."

"I do." He shook his head, his brow furrowed. "You were shivering pretty hard back there. I was worried about your core temperature."

She suppressed a pathetic laugh at how that sentence thrilled her. "I think I'm good now."

He nodded, rubbing her hand with his thumb. Their feet crunched on the roadside. He looked ahead of them and blew out a breath. "You brought that painting?"

"Yes. It reminded me of us."

"It's good."

"A friend of a friend painted it." She wished she could lose the quiver in her voice. "He did one of a grizzly that I'm considering, for old times' sake."

She thought she saw the corner of his mouth twitch upward. She breathed.

His brow furrowed again. "What have you been up to?" It was a loaded question, and she suspected he knew it when he asked.

She took a moment, then answered. "Figuring out if there was more."

"More?"

"More to me than I thought."

He pursed his mouth, considering. "Can I ask you something?"

She nodded.

He was quiet, then said, "Here you have this natural gift of music. You see beauty in everything around you. You are graceful, intelligent, funny, you're strong . . . and you have a capacity to love . . ." She stopped, and he stopped with her. He shook his head. "You offered me a chance to . . . find myself again. My question is: What was it that *kept* you from thinking you were good enough? Was it the Church?"

She faced him, gathering all the determination she could find. "No, it wasn't the Church . . . maybe that was a small part of it, later, but no, it wasn't that." She tilted her head to the side. "By the way . . ."

He shook his head, looking off. "I know. Nora. And I didn't want to push you with the Church. You seemed so hesitant. But I should have said something. I'm sorry."

"I'm not."

He looked at her.

"Ask anyone who knows me. If you would have pushed, I would have pushed away. I would have found another room in a hotel. A plain old room with a card key and a television and a continental—"

"Hey."

She bit her lip and thought she saw a glint of humor in his eyes. She felt stronger. He looked out at the woods. "Then if it wasn't the Church . . . was it . . . Brooke?"

She watched him steadily. *Breathe.* He turned to her, and she said, "I'd be lying if I said no."

He nodded his head and looked down.

"But that pales in comparison to the real truth," she whispered.

He lifted his eyes questioningly.

She swallowed the pain in her throat. "Do you remember when we were walking back after the bear, and I was telling you about growing up and school and my career?"

He nodded. "You couldn't tell me any more. You were terrified."

She paused, feeling like she was standing on the edge of a chasm.

He stepped to her, taking a careful hold of her arms. His gaze met hers. "Have I *ever* given you any reason not to trust me?"

His intensity drew her in, nudged her to continue. She shook her head. "I'm not afraid to tell you anymore." She turned, holding her hand open, and he took it. They began to walk again. Walking was good.

She breathed softly, speaking quietly. "I met the kind of people who use you. People who take advantage of you."

His grip firmed around hers.

"I was asking for it." She dropped her eyes to the ground. "I knew how to dress, how to act. They would figure out how to get me just a little drunk." She bit her lip, and her resolve wavered as he slowed his step. She kept moving one foot in front of the other. "I'd wake up somewhere, not knowing where I was. Nancy tried to warn me . . ."

He looked up at the sky.

"One night . . ." Elizabeth took a quivering breath and blew it out. "Somebody wanted more from me than I could give, I guess," She wiped the tear away as she let out a weak chuckle. "It was pretty bad. See, I fought back." She brought her shaking fingers up to her lips. "I wasn't drunk enough for what he wanted. He beat me senseless and left." She gulped in a breath and shrugged, letting her vision blur with tears now. "When I woke up, I could hardly get to the phone. That's when Nancy pulled me out. She found me a good therapist, a job within the company where I was home more, could work from home. I remembered . . . that my family was far from perfect, but they would never . . ." She wiped her eyes with her hand. She had stopped walking again.

He looked at the woods as if searching for something, his voice gruff with emotion. "You could have been . . . You could have gotten . . ."

"I know. I was lucky." She looked up at him, and he nodded, his jaw tight. Fear teased at the edges of her newfound strength, but she was trusting him. Faith.

"Did they get the guy?"

She gave a quick shake of her head and a hint of a shrug. "I was in a foreign country . . ." She sucked in a quivering breath and whispered shamefully, "I didn't even know his name . . . his car . . . *anything.*" The confession stripped her of everything, leaving her vulnerable before him. Another hot tear left its path down her cheek.

It was forever, his step to her, his arms enfolding her. His lips touched her forehead, leaving warmth. She breathed him in with the fresh air, drank in his embrace like water after a hard run.

Her voice had grown hushed with emotion. "I recovered. Nancy was right there. My dad doesn't even know. And I still traveled, but I kept my guard up. I became this cold ice queen, running away from relationships like the plague." She shook her head. "I don't know which was better."

He raised her chin and gave her a questioning look.

She rolled her eyes, swallowing her tears. "Well, I *do* know. But when your younger sisters get married . . . and start having babies . . . you begin to wonder how you got where you are and why you're still . . ."

"Still what?"

She could feel him work to steady his breathing. She searched his eyes, looking for trust, or strength, or forgiveness. "Alone," she whispered, her heart thudding.

His gaze was no longer distant.

"Then," she continued, feeling the beginnings of a smile, "you came along and hit me with your truck. With your reserve and your soft gray eyes and warm hands and your compassionate heart." She dropped her eyes. "Your amazing children. It was more than I deserved. More than I could accept."

He leaned his head down to hers and brought her chin up again. "Nobody deserves to be treated the way you were. *Nobody.*" He slowly shook his head back and forth, and she brought her nose up to touch his.

"I realize that now. You helped me realize that." Her smile grew. "Your whole *family* helped me realize that."

He broke into a quiet laugh but only for a moment. He sobered, pulling her closer.

How did this happen? His arms around her, this feeling of belonging. She brushed a finger over his ear, and as he tilted his head, she whispered, "I can list a thousand choices that brought me to you."

He smoothed her hair and stroked her cheek. "I can list a thousand more to keep you here. I love you, Elle," he whispered back.

She pulled in a trembling breath as her eyes closed, and he brushed her lips with his, then crushed her, kissing her deeply.

Everything. All of it. Worth it.

A sigh escaped her, and she mingled the words with his kiss, "Ryan"— dazed, amazed, and passionate with relief—"I love you more . . ."

She felt his smile as everything around them faded away.

A long minute later, the ground shook, and a flurry of exhaust blew past them. They both turned to watch the back of the school bus continue down the road.

"Oh no," Elizabeth said, breathless. "Not again."

"You know what?" Ryan asked, breathing heavily himself. "I don't think it's going to be a problem."

"Why not?"

He nodded toward the bus and they watched as it pulled over. The doors opened, and they could hear shouts and cheers. Sam and Lily tumbled out, punching their fists up in the air.

"Woo-hoo! Hooray!" They jumped and pirouetted in the air.

Sam stopped briefly to look at Ryan and Elizabeth. He made a fist and brought his elbow down to his hip. "*Yesss*! I am *so* glad we hit her with the truck."

Chapter 29

ONE MONTH LATER, ELIZABETH FOLLOWED the freshly dug path. Three feet of snow lined each side as she carefully approached the gazebo. She slowed, looking around her. The tree house looked like it was made of gingerbread . . . the snow frosting hanging over the slanted roof and the windowsills. Frosting layered every branch, every clinging berry. This trail in the snow was the only mark in the yard, though the front of the house had been stomped and rolled over and was now guarded by a stout snowman wearing an old fishing hat and a designer scarf and holding a pair of hiking poles.

They had spent the morning at the elk feeding station on a sleigh ride over the bright snow. She and Ryan had been dating for several weeks now, and the kids had been more excited for Elizabeth's first ride out than for their own experience. Sam and Lily had pointed and shared everything they knew about elk, and Chloe had worn a smile almost the entire time. As the kids made a fuss about her being there, she realized she no longer felt inadequate, just . . . loved. Their open smiles and knowing looks had won. She had taken picture after picture.

She stopped and looked ahead at the gazebo. Two heads leaned close together, Ryan's arm around Chloe's shoulders. They were talking low, and Elizabeth didn't want to interrupt, but she'd been sent on a mission. They laughed quietly, and she continued forward, making a little noise now to warn them of her coming.

Ryan's head came around, and he broke into a smile, making her heart melt into a sloshy puddle. *No more ice queen*, she thought.

She smiled back as Chloe peeked around her father. Ryan got up and walked to her, his hands held out to take hers.

"Hey, Elle." He kissed her cheek. "Ooh, you're warm."

Elizabeth laughed quietly as he tried to press his face against hers. "You're not. You two need to warm up."

He nodded and came at her again. "Man, you smell good."

Elizabeth smiled and pulled away. She gave him a warning look and flickered her eyes toward Chloe. "Lily is done with her marshmallow snowmen and would like you to see."

He looked up at the house. "How did they turn out?"

"Very . . . interesting." She smiled. "They're a work of art."

"Okay." He pulled her close to brush her nose with his. "Are you coming in?"

She shook her head and gestured to their surroundings. "Not yet. I want to stay out here for a little bit."

He nodded and turned to the gazebo. "See you inside, Chloe."

"Okay, Dad."

As he turned back, Elizabeth said, "I'll be in soon. I don't want to turn into a Popsicle."

He grinned and attempted to warm his face next to hers again. She shivered as she let him.

He gave her hands a squeeze and whispered faintly, "I love you," and headed up the path to the house, not waiting for her response.

She watched him go, her heart doing a little rhythmic skip. *Yes, I would do this again. Whatever may come.* Then she slowly turned to the gazebo.

Chloe watched her pause. "You can sit down," she offered.

Elizabeth gave her an appreciative smile. "Thanks." She stepped in and looked around.

Chloe patted the space Ryan had occupied next to her on a folded quilt. Elizabeth tried to hide her look of hesitancy and took the seat. Her relationship with Chloe was still sensitive. They were happy with one another but careful too.

She took a deep breath as she looked out over the river. "This is beautiful. No wonder you're out here so much."

Chloe nodded. "I know. I think my dad worries about me a little bit." She leaned forward, resting her chin on her mittened hand.

Elizabeth smiled to herself, knowing that was true.

They were silent for a minute, listening to the water. A winter bird landed on a branch and lumps of snow fell silently into the white below.

Elizabeth looked at Chloe. "I have something I want to show you." She reached into her pocket and drew out the photo.

Chloe leaned over and looked, then took it when Elizabeth offered it to her. "Is this . . . is this your mother?"

Elizabeth nodded, looking at the picture. "That's me . . . I was three. She was holding me so I wouldn't run out of the boat."

Chloe looked at her with her eyebrows raised.

Elizabeth smiled. "I was very independent."

Chloe laughed a little, then concentrated on the photo. "She's really pretty. She's . . . expecting, isn't she?"

"Yes. My sister Alisen."

Chloe nodded. She tilted her head at the picture, then looked at Elizabeth. Elizabeth read her look. "I know. We don't look much alike, do we?"

Chloe shook her head. "Maybe in the way you smile."

Elizabeth leaned over. "Maybe. Alisen is the one who looks like Mom. It's crazy." Elizabeth shook her head. "I was always a little jealous of that."

Chloe's head came up, and she nodded understandingly. "Sometimes I look at Lily and I think that. But . . . mostly, I'm just glad she reminds me of her. There were times I was afraid I would forget . . ."

Elizabeth watched Chloe. She could see the little girl who, somewhere along the way, chose to be the woman the family had lost. Again, she wondered how Chloe felt about the possible role Elizabeth might play in her family.

"I want to thank you, Chloe."

Chloe looked at her. "For what?"

"For saying what you did that night I met you, about seeing our mothers again."

Chloe dropped her eyes. "I was sorry I said it . . . I saw how uncomfortable it made you, and I didn't mean to do that. Everything was so awkward that night, and I just forgot . . . I mean, it's such a part of me . . . of what we believe . . ."

"I know. I could see that. Don't be sorry. It made me think because . . . it was something I really wanted to believe. I think it was something I already knew was true."

Chloe looked away to the woods. "Sometimes . . . when I'm out here, I feel like she's near me."

Elizabeth looked out too and felt a shiver run through her. It was a strange thing, to be loved in the place of another. No, that wasn't it. It wasn't *in the place* of another. It was *next to the memory* of another. She took a breath. "I'm glad," she said. "I don't know if your dad told you, but he was the one who got me to play the piano again."

Chloe shook her head.

"When I play," Elizabeth turned her gaze to Chloe, "*that's* when I feel her."

Chloe nodded in understanding.

"Thank you, Chloe. You and your dad, you gave me that." Elizabeth took Chloe's hand without thinking. Her eyes were becoming wet. "You know how much that means. Thank you."

Chloe watched her with those translucent eyes, then she suddenly leaned in, her arms going around Elizabeth's waist. "I'm glad too," she whispered, and Elizabeth drew her arms around her and rested her cheek on her head.

"We want them with us forever, don't we?"

Chloe nodded. They understood each other perfectly.

"Elizabeth?"

"Yes?"

"Will you watch me dance?" There was a catch in her voice.

Elizabeth smiled, looking out over the river, and the tears were hot on her cold cheeks. "I would love to watch you dance, Chloe." And she rocked a little, back and forth, to the music of the water.

* * *

"So what do you think?" Lily cocked her head sideways and watched her dad.

"I, uh, think it's great, Lily." He looked at the little snow family constructed from marshmallows and toothpicks, cloves pressed in for buttons and eyes and smiles, red hot candies and gumdrops glued on with frosting for noses and hats, boots, and wherever else Lily had wanted more color. A dad, a mom, two sisters, one tall and one short, and a brother. The girls each had different colored yarn for hair: yellow, orange, and brown. He lifted a finger and pointed. "What's this?"

"That's the baby." She smiled at him gloriously.

He swallowed and nodded. "That's what I thought." He nodded again, then looked at Lily. "And Elizabeth helped you?"

"Uh-huh, but the baby was my idea."

"I'm not surprised."

"But she made it."

His head snapped up. Lily giggled.

* * *

"Yes, Dad, I'm sure." Elizabeth smiled into the phone. She would become "one of those Mormons."

"That's all of you, then."

"Yes, we'll have you surrounded. It'll be miserable for you."

Her father chuckled. "Well, I'll talk to Sheryl. I have to admit I'm curious. I missed the other girls' baptisms."

"Fortunately for you, they seem to be very forgiving creatures. Oh, I forgot to tell Amanda we're leaving for Montana right after the girls' *Nutcracker* performance. Try to convince her we'll all be there in time for the sealing."

He sighed. "I'll do that."

"Give my love to Sheryl."

"I will. I'm proud of you, Elizabeth. Tell Ryan . . . he's a good man."

"I will. Thanks, Dad."

"Good night, Elizabeth." She could hear his smile.

She hung up and settled back into the sofa.

"Sounds like that went well." Ryan took her phone, turned it off, and tossed it on the ottoman.

She nodded. "I think he'll come."

"And the other thing?"

She broke into a grin, wiggling her finger, watching the light play and dance off the diamond ring there. "He'll get over it."

He chuckled, and she leaned into him.

She felt his gaze on her, the tether between the two of them she never wanted broken.

She looked at the tree, the lights twinkling, the star glowing at the top. They'd spent the evening decorating it with the kids. It was late now, the kids long gone to bed, and quiet, the fire glowing low. "It's beautiful."

"Mm-hmm." He still watched her.

She sighed. "I already know the perfect honeymoon spot."

"Where's that?"

"A small cabin . . . out somewhere in the woods. Snowed in, a fire . . . quilts . . . and you."

"Sounds perfect."

She smiled as he kissed her behind her ear.

"But," he sat up, "the snow?"

She wrinkled her brow. "What about the snow?"

"Well, it only sticks around here a *very* short time."

She looked at him, seeing the teasing behind his concerned expression.

"I see," she said as he returned to kissing her softly. "Well, I guess we'll just have to move things along, then, won't we?"

"I don't mean to rush you." He pulled away, his concern sincere.

She looked into his eyes, remembering to breathe. "Bring it on."

He smiled. "I have something for you."

"Something *else?*" His proposal, the ring, the day . . . it was enough.

"It's a wedding present. Since we're moving things along."

She smiled and bit her lip. She'd been smiling so much lately that she'd become one of those people who made her sick. She could hardly live with herself. Hardly.

Ryan got up and went to the office, then returned holding a thin rectangle wrapped in brown paper.

She narrowed her eyes.

Grinning, he handed it to her and sat back down, anticipation lighting his eyes. "Surprise," he said quietly.

She pulled the paper back and caught her breath. "Is this . . . ? Did James do this? How—" She breathed. "I love it. I love it."

He smiled, watching her. "I took James out there, asked if it was inspiring enough."

She shook her head.

"Good surprise?"

She nodded and whispered, "Good surprise."

She read the title. *Elizabeth's Waterfall.*

He took it from her and set it against the ottoman.

She leaned closer to him and whispered, "I'm still not sure what I ever did to deserve you."

"Don't you know?"

She shook her head.

He leaned in and kissed her, lingering long enough to take her breath away. Then he whispered, "You found me when I was lost."

He pulled away, and they looked at each other, their hands wound together. Finally, he put his arm around her, she settled her head on his shoulder, and they looked at the painting.

"I'll make you breakfast," he said.

She lifted her head. "What?"

"In that little cabin in the woods. I'll make you breakfast every morning of our honeymoon."

She laughed. "I'll grate the cheese."

"Oh," he grinned, "you'll do much more than that."

She shook her head at him, and he nodded back, his eyebrows raised.

From the back rooms, Lily shouted, "I think she said *yes*."

The other kids giggled.

"Go to sleep," Ryan called.

Elizabeth grinned.

She'd said yes.

About the Author

NEARLY EVERY ONE OF KRISTA Lynne Jensen's elementary school teachers made a note on her report card pointing out that she was a "daydreamer." It was not a compliment. But Krista forged ahead, and when she grew up, she put those daydreams down on paper for others to enjoy. When she's not writing, she enjoys reading, hiking, her family, and sunshine. But not laundry. She never daydreams about laundry.

Krista is a native of Washington State and for many years lived in the northern Rocky Mountains of Wyoming before returning home. She finds herself bewildered about being a published author.

Falling for You is the second book in a series about the Embry family. After finishing book number one, *The Orchard* (2012 Whitney Award Finalist), Krista just had to give Elizabeth a story and a place to call home.